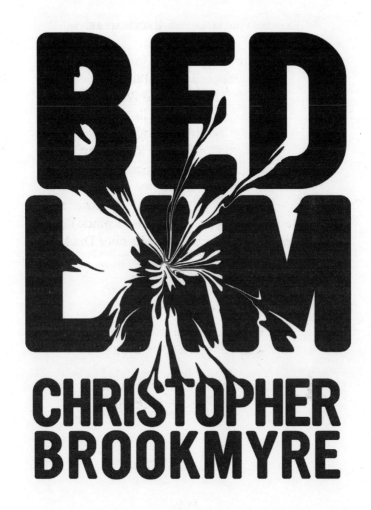

BEDLAM

CHRISTOPHER BROOKMYRE

orbit

www.orbitbooks.net

ORBIT

First published in Great Britain in 2013 by Orbit

A CIP catalogue record for this book
is available from the British Library.

HB ISBN 978-0-356-50213-7
C format 978-1-408-70407-3

Typeset in Book Antiqua by Palimpsest Book Production Limited,
Falkirk, Stirlingshire

Printed and bound in Great Britain by Clays Ltd, St Ives plc

Papers used by Orbit are from well-managed
forests and other responsible sources.

MIX
Paper from
responsible sources
FSC
www.fsc.org
FSC® C104740

Orbit
An imprint of
Little, Brown Book Group
100 Victoria Embankment
London EC4Y 0DY

An Hachette UK Company
www.hachette.co.uk

www.orbitbooks.net

For Jack

Life is a whim of several billion
cells to be you for a while.

Groucho Marx

Loading . . .
File 1 of 3

Prologue
Game Face

This is not the end of the world, Ross told himself.

He closed his eyes as a low hum began to sound around him, heralding the commencement of the scan. The effect was more white-out than black-out, the reflective tiles filling the room with greater light than the fine membranes of his eyelids could possibly block.

He should look upon all of it as a new start; several new starts, in fact. Yes: multiple, simultaneous, unforeseen, unwanted and utterly unappealing new beginnings. Welcome to your future.

As he lay on the slab he conducted a quick audit of all the things that had gone wrong in the couple of hours since he'd stepped off his morning bus into a squall of Scottish rain and a lungful of diesel fumes on his way to work. He concluded that it wasn't a brain scan he needed: it was a brain transplant. Nonetheless, as the scan-heads zipped and buzzed above him, for the briefest moment he enjoyed a sense of his mind being completely empty, an awareness of a fleeting disconnection from his thoughts, as though they were a vinyl record from which the needle had been temporarily raised.

'Hey Solderburn, are we clear?' he asked, keeping his eyes closed just in case.

There was no reply. Then he recalled the capricious ruler of the Research and Development Lab telling him to bang on the door if there was a problem, so he deduced there was no internal monitoring.

He opened his eyes and sat up. It was only a moment after

he had done so that he realised the tracks and scan-heads were no longer there. He did a double-take, wondering if the whole framework had been automatically withdrawn into some hidden wall-recess: it was the kind of pointless feature Solderburn was known to spend weeks implementing, even though it was of no intrinsic value.

There was still no word from outside. Solderburn probably had a lot of switches to flip, so Ross was patient, and as he didn't have a watch on, he only had a rough idea how long he'd been sitting there. However, by the time the big hand on his mental clock had ticked from 'reasonable delay' through 'mild discourtesy' into 'utterly taking the piss', he'd decided it was time to remind the chief engineer that his latest configuration included a human component.

The bastard had better not have sloped off outdoors to have a fag. Seriously, was there any greater incentive to stop smoking than having to do it in the doorway to this dump, looking out at the rest of the shitty Seventies industrial estate surrounding it?

Ross got to his feet and extended a fist, but before he could deliver the first of his intended thumps, the door opened, though not the way he was expecting. Instead of swinging on its hinge, the entire thing withdrew outwards by a couple of inches, then slid laterally out of sight with the softest hiss of servos.

WTF?

Beyond it lay not the familiar chaos of the R&D lab, but merely a grey wall and the grungy dimness of a damp-smelling corridor.

So Solderburn *was* taking the piss, but not in the way Ross had previously believed. This was the kind of prank that explained why the guy had ended up working here in Stirling, rather than winning a Nobel Prize. He must have slid some kind of false wall into place outside the scanning room. Ross walked forward, stepping lightly because he suspected Solderburn's practical joke had some way to go before it reached the pay-off stage.

He looked left and right along the passageway.

All right, so maybe it was time to revise the practical joke hypothesis.

There was a dead end to the left, where the way was blocked

by three huge pipes that emerged from the ceiling and descended through a floor constructed of metal grilles on top of concrete, into which sluice channels were etched in parallel. There was a regulator dial on the right-most tube, sitting above a wheel for controlling the flow. A sign next to it warned: 'DO NOT MESS WITH VALVE'.

It was a redundant warning in Ross's case: he wasn't going near it. Even from a few yards away, he could feel the vibration of flow in the pipes, indicating that enormous volumes of fluid must be passing through the vessels. It sounded like enough to power a small hydroelectric station. Even Solderburn couldn't fake up something like that.

In the other direction, the corridor went on at least twice the length of the lab, condensation beading its walls. He could hear non-syncopated pounding, its low echo suggesting something powerful and resonant that was being dampened by thick walls. This thought prompted him to glance at the ceiling, which mostly comprised live rock, occasionally masked off by black panels insulating lines of thick cable.

He began to make his way along the corridor. Light was provided by strips running horizontally along the walls, roughly two feet above head height. Ross assumed them to be inset, but if so it was a hell of a neat job. They looked like they could be peeled right off and stuck wherever they were required.

There was another light source further ahead, a dim blue-green glow coming from behind a glass panel set high in the wall on the left.

The corridor trembled following a particularly resonant boom from somewhere above. Ross could feel the metal grates rattle from it, the air disturbed by a pulse of movement. It felt warm, like the sudden gust of heat when somebody has just opened an oven door. There was still no rhythm, no pattern to the sounds, and yet Ross found something about them familiar.

As he approached the panel, he could see a play of coloured light behind the glass, constant but fluid, as though there might be a team of welders on the other side of it. Please, he thought, *let* there be a team of welders on the other side: hairy-arsed welders with bottles of Irn-Bru and Monday-morning hangovers, toting oxyacetylene torches and forehead-slappingly obvious

5

explanations for what was going on. Perhaps he had ended up at one of the factories on the estate, somehow?

The panel was high, so Ross had to stand close and stretch to get a look through the glass. As soon as he did, he caught a glimpse of someone on the other side and promptly threw himself back down low, out of sight.

It wasn't a welder; or if it was, it was one who had utterly lost it at some point and started grafting stuff to his own face.

In his startlement and panicked attempt to hide, Ross tumbled backwards to the deck, a collapse that felt less painful but sounded altogether more clangingly metallic than he was expecting. If the hideous creature behind the wall hadn't seen him as he peered through the glass a moment ago, then he had surely heard him now.

He had to get moving, and hope there was more than one way out of this corridor. It might be prejudiced to assume that the man he had seen meant him any harm purely on the basis of his unfortunate appearance, but it was difficult to imagine anybody with a penchant for soldering things to his coupon being an entirely calm and balanced individual. Besides, Ross's alarm hadn't been inspired purely by the fact that the guy would have a bastard of a time getting his face through airport security; it was the look Ross had briefly glimpsed in that nightmarish visage's eyes: wild, frantic, unhinged and, most crucially, searching.

It was as he uncrumpled himself from a heap on the floor that he discovered any attempt at flight was futile, and for a reason far worse than that this mutilated horror might already have cut off his escape. His eye was drawn, for the first time since emerging from his cell, to his own person rather than his surroundings, and a glance at his limbs showed them no longer to be clad in what he remembered pulling on that morning. Gone were the soft-leather shoes, moleskin jeans and charcoal shirt, replaced by a one-piece ensemble of metal, glass and bare skin, all three surfaces scarred by scorch-marks and gouges.

He looked in terrified disgust at his forearm, where two light-pulsing cables were visible on the surface, feeding into his wrist at one end and plunging beneath an alloy sheath at the other. His legs were similarly metal-clad, apart from glass panels beneath which further fibre-optic wiring could be seen intermittently breaking the surface of skin that was a distressingly unhealthy pallor even for someone who had grown up in the west of Scotland.

His chest and stomach had armour plates grafted strategically to cover certain areas whilst retaining flexibility of movement by leaving other expanses of skin untouched, and there were further transparent sections revealing enough of his interior to suggest he wouldn't be needing a bag of chips and a can of cream soda any time soon.

Trembling with shock and incredulity, he hauled himself upright, finding his new wardrobe to be impossibly light. His movement was free and fluid too, feeling as natural as had he still been wearing what he'd turned up to work in.

Was it some kind of illusion, then?

No. Of course. He had fallen asleep during the scan. It was a dream.

Except that normally the awareness of dreaming was enough to dispel it and bring him to.

Ross looked himself up and down again. There was no swirling transition of thoughts and images bringing him to the surface, no dream-logic progress linking one bizarre moment to the next.

He approached the glass again. He could see two vertical shafts of energy, one blue and one green, seemingly unchannelled through any vessel, but perfectly linear, independent and self-contained nonetheless. Reluctantly, he pulled his focus back from what was behind the glass to the reflecting surface itself.

Arse cakes.

He looked like he had faceplanted the clearance sale at Radio Shack. It was still recognisably his own features underneath there somewhere: even that little scar on his cheek from when he'd fallen off a spider-web roundabout when he was nine. He recalled what a fuss his mum had made when he needed stitches. Everything's relative, eh Mammy?

Another muffled boom sounded, moments before another shudder rippled the air. He could hear lesser percussions too, like it was bonfire night and he was indoors, half a mile from the display. It was hardly an enticement to proceed down the corridor, but what choice did he have?

He strode forward on his augmented legs, surprised to discover his gait felt no different, his tread lighter than the accompanying metal-on-metal thumps suggested. There was absolutely nothing about this that wasn't absolutely perplexing, not least the aspects that felt normal. For instance, as he followed the passageway around a bend to a T-junction leading off either side of an elevator, he was disturbed to find that he seemed instinctively to know where he was going. Was there something in all this circuitry that was doing part of his thinking for him? He wasn't aware of it if so; though the fact that he probably wouldn't be aware of such a process was not reassuring.

He stepped on to the open platform of the elevator and pressed his palm to the activation panel. A light traced around his atrophied fingers at the speed of an EKG and the platform began to rise.

He looked again at the leathery grey of his hand. It gave a new meaning to the term dead skin. He thought of all the times Carol had ticked him off for biting his nails, of her rubbing moisturiser on his cracks and chaps in wintertime.

Carol. No. Not yet.

He put her from his mind as the elevator reached the top of the shaft, where his faith in instinctively knowing where he was going was put to the test by his arriving somewhere he was dangerously conspicuous. No narrow passageway this time: he had reached some kind of muster point or staging area, and was rising up into the centre of it like it was his turn on *Camberwick Green*.

He got there just in time to see a group of figures – each of them similarly dressed by the Motorola menswear department – march out through a wide doorway. They moved briskly and with purpose, two halves of the automatic door closing diagonally behind them as the elevator platform came to a stop, flush with the floor.

The booms were louder here. The smaller ones sounded like muffled explosions somewhere beyond the walls, but the big ones seemed to pulse through the very fabric of whatever this place was. He could tell when one was coming, as though the entire structure was breathing in just before it; could sense something surge through all those pipes lining the walls. It was like being inside a nose that was about to sneeze.

He was absolutely sure of which way to head next, but it wasn't to do with any weird instinct or control by some exterior force. It was simply a matter of having observed in which direction the platoon of zombie-troopers had shipped out and of proceeding in precisely the opposite.

They'd had their backs to him so he couldn't get a clear view of what they were all carrying, but the objects had been metal and cylindrical, and he considered it unlikely they were some kind of cyborg brass section that had just been given its cue to hit the stage. Given how little sense everything else was making right then, it was always possible that the latter was the case and they were about to strike up 'In the Mood', but Ross strongly suspected that the only thing they were in the mood for was shooting anybody who got in their way.

He proceeded towards his intended exit at what he realised was an incongruously girly trot: hastened by his eagerness to get away but slowed short of a run in case it should be conspicuous that he was making a break for it. His head spun with awful possibilities, trying to piece together what could have happened. It had to have been the scan, he deduced. Whether intentionally or not, it had left him in a state of suspended animation and his body had been stored until the advent of the technology that currently adorned and possibly controlled him.

Neurosphere. Those amoral corporate sociopaths. This was their doing. There was probably a clause in his employment contract that covered this shit, and as he'd never bothered to read the pages and pages of legalese, he'd had no real idea what he was signing. Now he could be working for them forever, part of a manufactured army. But in that case, why hadn't they erased or at least restrained his memory? Why was he not a compliant drone like the others he'd seen? Perhaps something had gone wrong with the process and he was the lucky one – retaining his memory and his sense of self and thus able to testify to Neurosphere's monstrous crime. Or perhaps he was the really *un*lucky one, trapped in this condition but not anaesthetised by merciful oblivion, and unlike the others he'd be conscious of every horror he was about to witness, or even effect.

He had no idea what year it was, or even what century. Chances were everyone he ever knew was gone. There might be nothing in the world he would recognise.

The big doorway opened obligingly as he approached, its two halves sliding diagonally apart to reveal another corridor, brighter than he'd seen before. Light appeared to be flashing and shimmering beyond a curve up ahead, and with nobody to observe him, he ran towards it.

'Oh,' he said.

The source of the flashing and shimmering on the far side of the passageway turned out to be a huge window opposite, easily twelve feet high by twenty feet wide, through which Ross could see what was outside this building. He hadn't thought he could ever look into another pane of glass and see a more unsettling sight than the one that had met him only a few minutes ago when he glimpsed his own reflection. Clearly it was not a day to be making assumptions.

The first thing he noticed was the sky, which was a shade of purple that he found disturbing. It wasn't so much that there was anything aesthetically displeasing about the colour itself; it was, to be fair, a quite regally luxuriant purple: deep, textured and vibrant. It was more to do with his knowledge of astronomy and subsequent awareness that, normally, the sky he looked up at owed its colour to the shorter wavelengths and greater proportion of blue photons in the type of light emitted by the planet's primary energy source. What was disturbing about this particular hue was not merely that it could not be any sky on Earth, but that it could not be any sky beneath its sun.

Worse, its predominantly purple colouration wasn't even the most distressing thing about the view through the window: that distinction went to the fact that it was full of burning aircraft. There were dozens of them up there, possibly hundreds, stretching out all the way to the horizon. It looked to be some kind of massive extraterrestrial expeditionary landing force, and its efforts were proving successful in so far as landing was defined as reaching terra firma: all of the craft were certainly managing that much. However, controlled descents executed without conflagration and completed by vessels comprising fewer than a thousand flaming pieces were, quite literally, a lot thinner on the ground.

Ross felt that inrush again, that sense of energy being channelled very specifically to one source, then heard the great boom once more, and this time he could see its source. It was a colossal artillery weapon, sited at least a mile away, but evidently powered by the facility in which he was standing. Its twin muzzles were each the size of an oil tanker, jutting from a dome bigger than St Paul's Cathedral, and its effect on the invasion force was comparable to a howitzer trained on a flock of geese. Each mighty blast devastated another host of unfortunate landing craft, sending debris spinning and hurtling towards the surface.

He had no sense of how long he had been standing there: it could have been thirty seconds and it could have been ten times that. The spectacle was horrifyingly mesmeric, but the car-crash fascination was not purely vicarious. Everything Ross saw had unthinkable consequences for himself. Instead of being merely lost in time, he now had no idea which planet he was even on.

He could see buildings in the distance, only visible because they were so large. The architecture was unquestionably alien, as was the very idea of building vast, isolated towers in an otherwise empty desert landscape. And still something inside him felt like he belonged here, or at least that his environment was not as alien as it should have been.

'It's an awe-inspiring sight, isn't it?'

When Ross heard the voice speak softly from only a few feet behind him, he deduced rather depressingly that he must no longer have a digestive system, as this could be the only explanation for why he didn't shit himself.

He turned around and found himself staring at another brutally haphazard melange of flesh and metal, one he decided was definitely the estate model. The newcomer was a foot taller at least, and more heavily armoured, particularly around the head, leaving his face looking like a lost little afterthought. He looked so imposingly heavy, Ross could imagine him simply crashing through anything less than a reinforced floor, and couldn't picture walls proving much of an impediment either. Wherever he wanted to be, he was getting there, and whatever he wanted, Ross was giving him it.

11

'Yes,' Ross agreed meekly, amazed to hear his own voice still issuing from whatever he had become.

'You could lose yourself in it,' the big guy went on. His tone was surprisingly soft, perhaps one used to being listened to without the need to raise it, but not as surprising as his accent, which was a precise if rather theatrical received pronunciation. Clearly, as well as advanced technology, this planet also had some very posh schools.

'Perhaps even forget what you were supposed to be doing. Such as joining up with your unit and getting on with fighting off the invasion, what with there being a war on and all.'

His voice remained quiet but Ross could hear the sternest of warnings in his register. There was control there too, no expectation of needing to ask twice. Very bizarrely, Ross was warming to him. Maybe it was the programming, same as whatever was making him feel this place was familiar.

'Yes, sorry, absolutely . . . er . . . sir,' he remembered to add. 'My unit, that's right. Have to join up. On my way now, sir.'

'That's "Lieutenant Kamnor, sir",' he instructed.

'Yes, sir, Lieutenant Kamnor, sir,' Ross barked, eyes scanning either way along the corridor as he weighed his options regarding which direction Kamnor expected him to walk in.

He turned and made to return to the staging area. Kamnor stopped him by placing a frighteningly heavy hand on his shoulder.

'Are you all right, soldier?' he asked, sounding genuinely concerned. 'You seem a little disoriented. Do you know where your unit even is?'

Ross decided he had nothing to lose.

'I have no idea where I even am, sir. I don't know how I got here. I have no memory of it. I'm not a soldier. I'm a scientific researcher in Stirling. That's Scotland, er, planet Earth, and this morning, that being an early twenty-first-century morning, I had a neuro-scan as part of my work. I was still totally biodegradable; I mean, an entirely organic being. When I stepped out of the scanning cell, I found myself here, looking like this.'

Kamnor's face altered, concern changing to something between alarm and awe, and everything that it conveyed seemed amplified by being the only recognisable piece of humanity amidst so much machine.

'Blood of the fathers,' he said, his voice falling to a gasp. 'You're telling me you were a different form, in another world?'

'Yes sir, lieutenant, sir.'

'Blood of the fathers. Then it truly is the prophecy.'

Kamnor beheld him with an entirely new regard, readable even in his alloy-armoured body language.

'The prophecy?' Ross enquired.

'That one would come from a different world: a being who once took another form, but who would be reborn here as one of us, to become the leader who rose in our time of need. That time is at hand,' he added, gesturing to the astonishing scene through the huge window, 'for our world is under attack, and lo, you have been delivered to us this day.'

Ross half turned to once again take in the sky-shattering conflict in which he had just been told he was destined to play a legendary role. A host of confused emotions vied for primacy in dictating how he should feel. Sick proved the winner. He recalled hearing the line: 'Some men are born great, others have greatness thrust upon them.' He wondered if that also applied to heroism. He had no combat training, no military strategy and tended to fold badly in even just verbal confrontations.

He was about to ask 'Are you sure?' but swallowed it back on the grounds that it wasn't the most leaderly way to greet the hand of destiny when it was extended to him. He settled for staring blankly like a tit, something he was getting pretty adept at.

Then Kamnor's face broke from solemnity into barking, aggressive laughter.

'Just messing with you. Of course there's no bloody prophecy. You've been hit by the virus, that's all. Been finding chaps in your condition for days.'

'Virus?' Ross asked, his relief at no longer having a planet's fate thrust into his hands quickly diminished as he belatedly appreciated how preferable it was to the role of cannon fodder.

'Yes, sneaky buggers these Gaians. They hit us with a very nasty piece of malware in advance of their invasion force: part binary code and part psychological warfare. Devilishly clever.

It gives the infected hosts all kinds of memories that aren't really theirs. Makes you think you're actually one of them: a human, from Gaia, or as they call it, Earth. It uploads all kinds of vivid memories covering right up until what seems like last night or even this morning. Like, for instance, that you're a scientist from, where was it?'

'Stirling,' Ross said, his voice all but failing him.

'See? It's really detailed. Convinces you that you just arrived here, plucked from another life on *their* planet. But don't worry, it wears off. It's full of holes, so it breaks down: I mean, hell of a coincidence they all speak the same language as us and even sound like us, eh? The virus auto-translates what they're saying. Don't worry, you'll be right as rain soon enough. We find that shooting a few of the bastards helps blow away the mist. So how about you catch up to your unit and help them spread the spank?'

Ross . . . was his name even Ross? He now knew officially nothing for sure.

This couldn't be true. These memories were his. They weren't just vivid and detailed, they were the only ones he had. Surely there would be some conflict going on in there if what Kamnor was saying was right. Yet as he stood before this terrifyingly powerful mechanised warrior, it occurred to him to wonder why the lieutenant would be so patient and understanding even as war raged on the other side of the hyper-reinforced window. Furthermore, there was that disarming sense of the familiar, even of positive associations, ever-present since he'd arrived here. For the moment, he'd just have to run with it, see if the mists really did blow away.

'I don't know what unit I'm with, lieutenant sir,' he admitted.

Kamnor reached out a huge, steel-fingered hand and tapped the metal cladding that Ross used to think of as his upper arm. There was a symbol etched there, a long thin sword.

'You're with Rapier squad. Mopping-up detail, under Sergeant Gortoss.' He gestured along the corridor in the opposite direction from where Ross had just come.

'Turn left at the first pile of flaming debris and look for the most homicidally deranged bastard you can find. Ordinarily he'd be in a maximum-security prison, but when there's a war on, he's just the kind of chap you want inside the tent pissing out.'

'Yes sir,' said Ross, by which he meant: 'Holy mother of fuck.'

'You remember how to fire a weapon, don't you?'

'I'm sure it'll come back,' he replied, making to leave.

Kamnor stopped him again.

'Well, before you go I would suggest you take a quick refresher on how to salute a superior officer.'

Kamnor saluted by way of example, sending his arm out straight, angled up thirty degrees from the horizontal, his metal fist clenched tight.

Ross was inundated with unaccustomed feelings of gratitude, loyalty and pride, driving a determination to serve and please this man. He had read about leaders whom soldiers would follow into battle, kill for, even die for, but never understood such emotions until now.

He sent out his right arm as shown, his shoulder barely level with Kamnor's breastplate, clenching his fist once it was fully extended. As he brought his fingers tightly together, a long metal spike emerged at high speed from somewhere above his wrist, shooting up into Kamnor's mouth, through his palate and into his brain.

It was a tight call as to who was the more shocked, but Kamnor probably edged it, aided by the visual impact of blood and an unidentified yellow-green fluid spurting in pulsatile gushes from his mouth. He bucked and squirmed but was too paralysed to do anything else in response.

'Oh Christ, I'm so sorry,' Ross spluttered, trying to work out how to withdraw the spike back into his wrist. 'I didn't mean it, I just . . .'

But Kamnor was way past listening. He fell to the floor, pulling Ross over with him, his arm still linked to Kamnor's head by the rogue shaft of steel. The blood subsided but the yellow-green fluid continued to hose, while one of Kamnor's great feet twitched spastically, clanking and scraping on the metal grate lining the floor.

Ross heard a hiss of pistons and saw the double door at the end of the corridor begin to separate.

'Oh buggering arse flakes.'

Through the widening gap he could see six pairs of metal-clad legs making their way towards the passage. In about one second they were going to spot this, and it wasn't going to look good.

How did you get this bloody thing out?

A clench of his fist had extended it, he reasoned, but so far merely unclenching wasn't having the corresponding effect.

He opened his hand instead, stretching out his fingers. This prompted an instant response. He felt something twang at the end of the spike, like the spokes of an umbrella, then felt a sense of rotation and heard a soft, muffled whir.

The incoming troop made it through the doorway as the spike withdrew, liquidising Kamnor's face and spraying Ross with the resulting soup as though he had lobbed the poor guy's head through a turbo propeller.

He turned to face them, the end-piece of the spike still spinning and sending blood, flesh and other matter arcing about the corridor.

'It's not what it looks like,' he offered.

Work–Life Balance

The doors slid closed with a hydraulic hiss as Ross stepped aboard out of the blustery Stirling rain and headed for his seat, shuffling laboriously along the aisle. He was barely awake. Safe mode: only loading the minimum components required to carry out the very basic tasks involved in getting from his bed to his desk. The bus jostled him pleasantly as it moved off, the feeling of warmth and the lulling rock of motion doing very little to encourage him into a sharper waking state. This was less down to fatigue than reluctance. Never a good sign.

```
Setting 'Autopilot' = TRUE
```

A sound file played in his head:
'Good morning, and welcome to the Black Mesa transit system . . .'
It was the opening of *Half-Life*, a woman's soft voice over the PA of a futuristic subterranean monorail taking the physicist Gordon Freeman to work on what would prove to be a cataclysmically fateful day.

Also not a good sign. Human memory wasn't random-access. What the subconscious chose to retrieve seemingly unprompted was seldom anything of the sort. If you looked deeply and honestly enough, you could usually trace the connection, and it would tell you plenty about your true state of mind. This voice from the past was telling Ross something inescapably accurate about the present.

The reason it was not a good sign was that this echo from *Half-Life* hadn't been prompted by a reminiscence of playing the game. He was reminiscing about sitting on another bus fifteen years ago, running the same soundtrack in his head as he imagined being on his way into the Black Mesa complex instead of towards St Gerard's Secondary. That childhood bus had been a buffering period, eight minutes to retreat into fantasy before reluctantly engaging with the indignities, torpor and soul-stomping banality of another day in school. He never wanted to get off, wished the journey was a hundred miles. He couldn't wait to get out of St Gerard's. He was planning to go off to uni to study medicine, and once he'd qualified he would look forward to every day's work as both a challenge and an opportunity.

Yeah, that worked out well.

The bus was busy. Ross was squeezed in between a young mum with a toddler on her lap and an old man in an ancient raincoat that was the only thing on the bus smelling worse – considerably worse – than the scrawny hound that accompanied him. Maybe it was for this reason that the mutt decided to position itself at Ross's feet rather than its master's. It sat eye-level with his crotch, at which it proceeded to stare longingly and with unbroken concentration, as though breakfast hadn't quite hit the spot and it was thinking Ross's balls would be just the thing to fill a hole before elevenses.

On the other side, the young mum was so consumed by the text exchange she was carrying out with impressive one-handed dexterity that she failed to notice that her daughter's face appeared to be melting, presumably as an unforeseen chemical reaction to the toxic-looking cheese string she had given her to eat. Liquid appeared to be seeping from a multiplicity of orifices, mucus bubbling liberally over her top lip on its way to replenishing the layer she had smeared across both cheeks; the southern reaches of her face were swimming in a yellow-tinged paste made up of two parts drool to one part semi-masticated cheddar; and there was something seeping out of one of her ears that Ross really didn't want to think about. Both of her little hands were awash with a combination of these secretions, the resulting solution given a deeper texture by partially dissolving an earlier sedimentary deposit of biscuit crumbs, and each bend, brake and acceleration of the bus seemed to bring her outstretched fingers closer to Ross's brand-new neoprene laptop cover.

To think that Carol said she wanted one of these things loose in the house. She wouldn't let him eat pizza on her new sofa in case he dripped grease on the upholstery: how would she cope if there was a two-foot snot-goblin burying its face in her dry-clean-only trousers and wiping jam on the curtains?

Ross looked back and forth between the dog and the child, the latter still glistening with intent and the former continuing to fixate upon his nads like there wasn't anything else on this bus worth glancing at even for a second. Why didn't the anorexic mongrel solve both problems by sidling over and licking the self-emoliating rug-rat's mitts, thus taking the edge off its appetite and its eyes off his clackerbag?

Some days this bus journey could seriously test his ecological resolve. Today those principles concerning single-passenger car commuting were in danger of being washed away in a tide of baby-gloop or swallowed down the throat of an underfed mutt. So what did it say that he still considered it better to travel horribly than to arrive?

The view out of the bus windows, where it could be seen through dirt, rain and condensation, revealed the route to be taunting him in a way he hadn't previously noticed. It seemed that everyone was getting off to spend their day somewhere more interesting than him. The bus trundled through the Digital Glen, an enclave of shiny twenty-first-century high-tech start-ups housed in brand-new steel, glass and pine pagodas. It stopped outside the Hirakumico campus, the electronics manufacturer's controversially subsidised venture sprawling amid woodland, a man-made loch and the most fastidiously manicured lawns this side of Gleneagles. It drove for several miles beneath the stern regard of Stirling Castle high on the crags, inspiration for a thousand boyhood fantasies and a dozen teenhood custom maps. And then, to flick him a final two fingers, it stopped at the roundabout for a few moments right under the sign for the safari park, the location he most associated with the simple carefree pleasures of growing up. In his memory, it was always sunny there, no matter what the weather when they got into the car to set off; a place where he played games and ate ice-cream with his sisters while barbecue smells blew on the breeze.

'You're not going there today, matey,' it seemed to say. 'No, you're not going back there ever.'

Instead, it dumped him off at the gloomier end of the most despondently nondescript industrial estate in the west of Scotland, and possibly the western hemisphere.

No underground lab, no monorails and lasers; and as for manicured verges, the only greenery on display was weeds and broken Buckfast bottles. Just as the safari park was somewhere Ross remembered as being sunny even on the days it wasn't, in his mind this place was always shrouded in light drizzle, even when the sun was splitting the sky. If the Digital Glen's architects had designed their estate to be conducive to innovation and encouraging of forward-thinking in commerce, whoever sketched this abomination out on the back of a bookie's line must have intended it as an environment conducive to the industrial manufacture of despair and the encouragement of worker suicide.

But it was okay, because these were only temporary premises. Or that was what they'd told him when they head-hunted him four years ago. He'd been so intoxicated by his own optimism and the lure of possibilities that he misinterpreted their hosting the interview in a hotel in Edinburgh as an indication that they wanted to impress him. Stage two was to fly him down to their UK headquarters, a purpose-built manufacturing facility on the M4 corridor, where they gave him glossy corporate brochures showing their expanding campus in Silicon Valley, CA. The buildings looked more opulent than anywhere Ross had ever been able to afford to stay, so it would be fair to say that he made certain naïve assumptions about what kind of premises they might have in mind for this new Scottish-based operation.

As Ross neared the pathway leading to the main entrance, he noticed Agnes Kirkwood approaching from the other direction at the same time. Part of him wished he could hurry on inside without engaging her, but it was the part of him that he knew he ought not to indulge. Agnes always wanted to chat; she was the kind of woman who, when she asked you how you were doing, actually meant it. She had a good twenty-five years on him, and had the remarkable ability to make him feel much younger than he was yet simultaneously boost his confidence by acting as though she thought he was the smartest guy in the firm.

Ross felt guilty for wishing he could sneak in without being seen, even with the rain offering an excuse, and took it as an indication of just how bad he must be feeling if he feared he wasn't up to sharing a few moments of a Monday morning with one of the few people in the building who did genuinely put the 'pleasant' into pleasantries. He wasn't sure whether his reluctance was born of not being capable of false bonhomie or whether he was self-conscious about confessing his misery to someone who had a lot more to complain about yet still managed to remain sufficiently buoyant to keep everyone else afloat.

'Morning, Doctor B,' Agnes said, with a wee glint in her eye, like Ross was her favourite nephew.

'Morning, Agnes. Good weekend?'

'Quiet. Highlight was a *Space 1999* DVD marathon and a takeaway curry Saturday night.'

Agnes had a serious sci-fi habit, with a particular fondness for old-school British stuff, the cheesier the better. She loved those Gerry Anderson shows, but Ross knew her true favourite was *Blake's 7*.

'How about you?'

'Not the best, Agnes,' he confessed, his guilt deciding that it would be patronising to lie. Pointless too, as Ross didn't have much of a poker face and Agnes was an adept interpreter of the snapshots people showed to her in passing. 'Mostly work, and consequently I think I've blown it forever with Carol.'

'Aye, it's hard to find a balance,' she replied, 'but the rule of thumb is that the job never loves you back. Chin up, though. Nothing's forever, especially a woman's moods: take it from someone who knows. There's still time to do the right thing by her and sort it out.'

'Problem is I'm coming around to thinking that doing the right thing would be to let her go and save her from me. I reckon she'd be better off.'

'Away and don't talk mince,' she told Ross with a grin that was both reproachful and reassuring. 'If the lassie's in the cream puff because she doesn't see you enough, then you're not helping either one of you if you take yourself out of the picture altogether.'

Agnes was in charge of component manufacturing, and would probably have been head of the division by now if her husband

Raymond hadn't got sick. The cancer had eventually killed him a couple of years back, and now she was largely marking time until her retirement. She'd told Ross that she and Raymond had been planning to buy a boat for their retirement, and spend their time sailing the Scottish coastal waters. She claimed that she was still intending to do so, joking that she'd crew it with strapping young men now that she was single.

Ross knew that neither aspect of this fantasy was any more likely than the other. Most of Agnes's savings had been gobbled up over the sustained course of Raymond's gradual debilitation. Yet her eyes would sparkle with a combination of longing and satisfaction when she talked about that boat, like it was a holiday that was already booked rather than a dream that, in Ross's estimation, would never happen.

Ross wondered whether this dream of the boat kept Agnes going, kept her so positive, or whether it was her innate positivity that kept her believing the boat dream would work out. Whatever it was, Ross wished he had a bottle of it. As it was, he could only get a teaspoon at a time during these brief exchanges, though even that much was enough to make him feel a wee bit better this morning.

Ross made his way to his desk, where he was disappointed and moderately concerned to see that his machine was in screen-saver mode, already booted up. Disappointed because he had first noticed that the monitor on the adjacent desk was switched on, and he had wrongly interpreted this as a sign that his colleague Alex had returned to work after a couple of days AWOL. Moderately concerned because the reason all the machines were running was that the suits must be undertaking one of their periodic compliance searches to make sure there were no unauthorised files or programs on anybody's systems.

The pretext was that this was a policy imposed by management in the US, where they were indemnifying themselves against lawsuits from employees by making sure nobody could glance at a colleague's monitor and get an eyeful of some 4Chan abomination. In truth, it was just an excuse to snoop through your files when you weren't there, looking for any kind of leverage that could force your shoulder harder against the wheel.

There was always this default assumption on the part of

management that everyone in their employ was an inveterate skiver who needed the threat of permanent vigilance to keep them hard at work. Ross couldn't help but interpret this as the rage of Caliban seeing his own face in a glass.

He gave his mouse a nudge to waken the screen and flipped open his laptop. His first task was to upload what he'd been working on over the past few days and tidy his ideas into a form that would make sense to the suits. Solderburn was developing a prototype scanner, the Simulacron, which potentially might be not merely the future of the company, but the future of neurological monitoring entirely. However, Solderburn's prototype would live or die on whether Ross could help him devise a means of decoding its data and interpreting the results. It was able to render far more complex readings of human brain activity than anything else in current usage, but, by its chief designer's own admission, 'It's like we've created the most awesome new video camera, but until we suss out how to make a new kind of TV to watch it on, nobody's gonna be able to see shit.' Ross's task in this analogy was to find a way of decoding the signal so that it would play back on the clunky old tellies they already had.

The biggest obstacle was that management was focused exclusively on rolling out Neurosphere's latest model, the NS4000. It was being tested at a number of hospitals up and down the UK, with the company hoping to snag a major contract from the NHS to supply and maintain the equipment.

They had secured the trials on the basis of ambitious promises, glossy presentations and a series of sponsorship packages that stayed just the right side of blatant corruption. Ross's work days were being monopolised by the process of ironing out or simply concealing the NS4000's glitches, so anything not dedicated to this core activity had to be done in his spare time. In an attempt to reconfigure their priorities he had set about devising a presentation that might make management understand what could be within their grasp. This had taken up his entire weekend, something that had not inclined Carol to get out her pom-poms and cheer on Team Baker.

'You do nothing but work these days, Ross. Honestly, if you went missing I'd have to give the police a description of the back of your laptop rather than your face. You don't even play games on it any more. It's all work, all the time. Why don't you come out here to the Big Room once in a while? You know: the one with the blue ceiling?'

He tried to explain how things would improve if he got the green light. What he needed Carol to understand was that the work he was doing that weekend might mean he wouldn't end up cancelling plans so suddenly in future.

Unfortunately, she hadn't been in a very understanding mood. Perhaps something to do with this weekend's workathon not exactly constituting an anomaly.

'They're stringing you along, Ross, playing you for a mug. They're just dangling this carrot in front of you every so often so you'll keep pushing their cart.'

Comparing Ross to a donkey didn't strike him as the most supportive thing she could be saying at that point, and, feeling a little stressed and histrionic, he opted to express as much.

'So, in short, what you're saying is that my employers think I'm an idiot,' he huffed, 'and I'm kidding myself that they would take my work seriously? And I suppose I can infer from this that you also think I'm an idiot and don't take my work seriously either. Thanks, that's just the vote of confidence I need ahead of this presentation.'

She had looked at him with a mixture of pity and despair.

'Of course they take your work seriously, Ross: that's the part that makes you an idiot.'

He didn't follow this logic, but that wasn't uncommon with Carol, usually because she was a lot better than he was at interpreting what was going on *outside* the human brain. He'd been going to ask her to elaborate, but she was off on one, going on about being thirty-three again. What was that about? She kept bringing it up: 'I'm thirty-three, Ross, I'm thirty-three.'

He didn't get it; it struck him as a non-sequitur. Where was she going with this sudden obsession about her age? She had been off the drink for the past few weeks too; kept ordering fresh orange juice when they went to the pub and skulling mineral water instead of wine when they had dinner together.

Agnes was right that there was always time to sort it out; the problem was that Ross suspected she was wrong about Carol

24

wanting him to. For a while previously he had wondered whether she was building up to suggesting they move in together; or at least building up to going off in a huff because he hadn't suggested it first. Looking back, it was becoming all the clearer that her intention had actually been for them to grow further apart.

He had felt the scales fall from his eyes as all the weirdness of the last few weeks finally revealed itself for what it was: her exit strategy. Christ. No wonder she kept saying he couldn't see what was right in front of him unless it was on a computer screen.

He opened his mail browser while he waited for all the files to transfer, the office wi-fi proving a little sluggish, like everything else around here of a Monday morning. The most recent was from Solderburn in R&D, to do with the mapping trials, but he'd open that later. More pressing was a message from Zac Michaels, sent Friday after Ross had gone home. Its contents were likely to be moot now, given how much had changed over the weekend, but with any luck it could be that the meeting was being pushed back an hour, or even into the afternoon, which would be ideal.

Ross opened it.

From: Isaac Michaels
Sent: Friday, 18:28
To: Ross Baker
Cc: Philip Scruton; Cynthia Lister; Jay Solomon
Subject: Re: Presentation Monday

Ross,
I was hoping to catch you as I'm just off the phone to Bristol, but you had already gone for the day. Very sorry about this, but it's been decided that the time just isn't right for a reallocation of your time. (I hope you didn't spend too long putting bells and whistles on your presentation.) As you're aware, it's a delicate time in our trial work with the NS4000, and we need you to redouble your efforts on getting through the data analysis backlog. Then, fingers crossed, if we secure the order, we will require you to go full steam ahead on the conversion model.

It's the old story of you making yourself indispensable, I'm afraid. I would, however, like to stress that we appreciate all your efforts, and should you wish to pursue your research ideas at evenings and weekends, we will make new arrangements to facilitate that (so long as it doesn't interfere with your commitment to core activities).
Cheers,
Zac

This email (and any material attached) is confidential and may contain personal views which are not the views of Neurosphere Inc unless specifically stated.

Ross sat and stared at it, but the words became meaningless. All of their import had been parsed unambiguously upon first scan anyway. He felt as though somebody had taken a ten-yard run-up and swung a full-blooded arse-winder of a kick to his nutsack. And just as if somebody actually had taken a ten-yard run-up before a full-blooded arse-winder, he really should have seen it coming.

He got to his feet and stomped off in the direction of Zac Michaels' office. He had barely made it to the server pen before Zac got to him first, anticipating his intentions with a prescience that indicated Ross's reaction had been planned for since Friday teatime.

Zac emerged into Ross's path as though teleported, filling the passageway with his tall, rangy form and a smell that was a little too close to antiseptic. He was unctuous in a way that Ross found subtly threatening, his thin and insincere smile frequently striking him as more than a wee bit rapey. He was always just a little too sharply dressed, the cloth of his suit annoyingly shiny, the folds and breaks so pronounced you could cut yourself on them. He looked and smelled too clean, in a way that suggested to Ross, perhaps unfairly, that he was into scat porn and coprophilia.

'I know you're disappointed, Ross,' Zac said, in his blandly non-regional American accent. 'But you don't want to say anything you'll regret, and besides, you'd only be shooting the messenger. This came all the way down the line. The NS4000 is top priority.'

'Yeah, sure,' Ross fumed. 'It came all the way down the line, and there was no chance of the local chapter head of Invertebrates

Anonymous telling me which way the wind was blowing a wee bit sooner than Friday?'

'It wasn't like that,' Zac said, in those calm but weary tones that made you want to hold him down and staple his nipples to his bollocks just to hear the bastard emote like a normal human being. 'I was the one going out to bat for you. The only reason your presentation was even scheduled was because of my lobbying, believe me.'

'Believe me' was the catch-phrase by which Zac unintentionally revealed that he was lying. Maybe it wasn't even unintentional. Perhaps it was meant to convey: 'We both know I'm bullshitting you but we both also know you can do zip divided by nada to the power of bupkis about it, so why not run along like a good little geek.'

'Listen, Ross, getting the NS4000 locked into a contract with the NHS will change everything around here. Stanford will sit up and take notice, see us as more than some forgotten outpost, a corn that didn't pop. But if we let this one slip through our fingers, we might as well be in Siberia as Stirling.'

'And as I've been saying all along, Solderburn's new prototype could be capable of a lot more than any of you have even taken a moment to imagine because you're too busy wanking off at the prospect of trousering your target bonuses.'

Zac fixed him with a last-warning stare. His voice dropped in volume, still calm but not so much weary as threatening. Ross could hear the sound of duct tape being unrolled somewhere in his tones, the seal being broken on a bottle of lubricant.

'I strongly suggest you go and grab yourself a coffee, then take a few minutes to calm down. You've got a lot of work to do, especially with your buddy Alexander still MIA. I think this would also be an appropriate juncture to inform you that there was a compliance search of all computers carried out over the weekend. Unauthorised software was found on your machine: unauthorised software of a kind that senior management take particularly badly to.'

'You think I've got time to play games? I loaded those about two months ago because Solderburn wanted me to cruft together a quick and dirty virtual-world model. But guess what: I was so busy putting out fires on the NS4000 that it didn't happen.'

'I know how busy you are. That's why I stepped in on your behalf. But it doesn't make it easy for me to argue that you're swamped and need more staff if they can point to a copy of *Quake* on your hard drive and make out you've been frittering away valuable time. You know Stanford have a bee in their bonnet about this stuff.'

'Yeah, I remember the induction briefing. *You won't get anywhere with this company if you sit there playing games,*' he mimicked, doing an admittedly awful attempt at Neurosphere CEO Phil Scruton's accent.

'I know you think it's trivial, but if they decide to play rough, it gives them grounds to fire you on the spot.'

'Yeah, and what a disaster that would be. Imagine having to leave all this.'

It was supposed to be a defiant parting retort but Ross felt like it only served to emphasise that Zac was the grown-up and he was just some daft wee boy throwing a tantrum. Zac underlined this further by grabbing a far more resonant last word, verbally abandoning the lube in favour of going in dry.

'Careful what you wish for. It's not the best time to be surfing the jobs market.'

The inescapable truth of this hit Ross as he wandered off with his tail undeniably between his legs. What the hell else was he going to do? He had bailed on his medical career to take this job, the frustrated hacker and tinkerer in him inspired by what more he might achieve here than as a consultant on the wards. He had invested years of work at Neurosphere, and for all he hated the building and half the folk in it, deep down he knew he'd rather put up with that than walk away and leave his work unfinished, his ideas unexplored. And they knew that too.

'Of course they take your work seriously, Ross: that's the part that makes you an idiot.'

Finally he got what Carol was saying. They had seen him coming miles off: a driven geek who would chew through the piece-work for them all day, then push the boundaries for them in his spare time. But despite him belatedly catching on to this, the really sad truth was that it only proved he needed them more than they needed him.

He slouched reluctantly towards the reception area where the vending machines stood. The 'cappuccino' on offer tasted like someone had strained hot water through oven scrapings and then spat on it to provide the frothy finish, but he needed the caffeine. Unfortunately, when he got there, he found his path blocked by a three-headed gorgon: Angela the mistress of the server pen, Tracy the production-line robotics guru and Denise from marketing, united by shared disdain the moment he came into view.

He knew they'd been talking about him. Tracy was dating Carol's sister Beth, so the news of the weekend's developments would have had her fit to burst. It wasn't just that they went silent the moment he appeared, which could have simply meant that their gossip wasn't for other people's ears: it was Denise's pitiful attempt to cover what they had been talking about by pretending to resume a conversation about what was going on in *Eastenders* and *The X Factor*.

He didn't imagine he had been painted sympathetically in Beth's acount, and it was unlikely any of this troika would be playing geek's advocate. They kept up their pretence of TV catch-up, a performance even less convincing than that of the actors on the soap and even less endearing than the suicides-in-waiting on the talent show. Ross helped himself to the caffeine equivalent of a shared needle – it didn't matter how horrific the delivery system, he just needed the drug – then walked away.

They barely waited until he was back out of sight to recommence, and certainly not until he was out of earshot.

'You'd have to say it's for the best,' Denise opined. 'I mean, he's not going to change, and if he can't see what's right in front of him, how interested is he?'

Christ, women just loved being elliptical like that, didn't they? Making out things should be obvious to you, stubbornly refusing to tell you what was bothering them on the grounds that you should know: then they got doubly huffy because you couldn't work it out.

Denise was right, though. Carol was better off on her own. Indeed, Carol would probably argue that the trick would be telling the difference, as she had seen so little of him of late anyway.

'Your head is always stuck in that computer,' she had

complained. 'Sometimes I think if you could just live inside that thing you'd be in heaven.'

'It's amazing,' observed Tracy. 'Beth says Carol thinks he's the smartest guy in the world, but what does it matter that he can see patterns in folk's brainwaves if he can't make out what's staring him right in the face?'

Well, sorry ladies, but this was one occasion where he did see what was right in front of him. He'd certainly cracked the code on that one and he hadn't needed to analyse any brainwaves to do it. Carol had decided he was for the bin weeks back, so there was nothing he could have changed about himself over the weekend that would have altered that.

This understanding made him feel just a little better, so he toasted the moment, albeit only with a mouthful of lukewarm crappucino as he made his way down the corridor.

'So,' he heard Angela ask, 'is she going to keep it?'

```
Setting 'Coffee spray' = TRUE
```

Baby's First Ray-Gun

Ross started a little at the next shuddering boom from the enormous artillery device, as he'd been a little too distracted to notice the preceding inrush. He could hear the lesser explosions more clearly here, as well as a high keening sound almost lost in the greater din.

Five of the advancing six-strong squad raised their weapons in outraged response to the sight in the corridor, but Ross saw a glimmer of hope that there was an exception: they were awaiting their command from the squad leader. They were members of a super-advanced civilisation, he assured himself, and you didn't advance that far by giving in to instinctive savagery, but by conquering it. Kamnor was proof of that: as a senior officer encountering a lowly grunt in dereliction of his duties, he had been understanding of the extenuating circumstances, even in this time of battle. They would take him into custody and hold him until they could reasonably investigate whatever charges were laid against him, possibly identifying a hitherto unseen threat from victims of the virus.

There was a very, very long half-second of silence in the corridor, its stillness emphasising the violence of the sounds outside. The keening sounded like it was getting louder, but was still drowned among the shuddering percussions that were rupturing the very air with power and rage.

'Kill that traitorous sluice-rag,' the squad leader ordered, his tone indicating outraged incredulity that they had even needed a command.

Some kind of subconscious emergency mechanism intended to shield him from the coming horror prompted Ross to reflect instead upon the leader's oddly PG-rated choice of invective.

Perhaps it would sound more insulting – or at least coarser – once he got his proper native memory back and was better able to appreciate the cultural mores that underpinned it. Then he was snapped back into the moment and understood that such insight was about to be precluded by the complications ensuing from five devastating energy weapons.

Not that it was much of a consolation, but his spike chose this moment to retract itself, an analogy for impotence if ever he saw one.

Before they could fire, however, the keening became suddenly louder and through the window Ross saw it announce its source as a flaming fuselage and wing-stub. It was hurtling towards the earth so fast that it had crashed through the corridor before he could even look embarrassingly desperate by shouting 'look out'. They wouldn't have seen it anyway: they hadn't reached the window yet, and they would have undoubtedly ignored his warning as a transparent and pointless attempt to distract them.

They were obliterated instantly, the cylindrical spacecraft section smashing through one wall and then the next like a piston. Ross turned away, which was as much as he could manage by way of evasive manoeuvres, shielding his face from the blast wave and the resulting heat. He could feel shrapnel pepper his legs, arms and back, biting into the armour and in one place finding skin, just beneath his left shoulder blade. He felt searing heat and the sharpest of pains, but an exploratory hand discovered that nothing was embedded: the piece had just gouged a deep gash that appeared to have been instantly cauterised by the heat. Either that or it was a symptom of the leathery and suspiciously dead-looking condition of his new skin.

The pain reminded him of the time he'd been body-surfing on holiday in Portugal and a breaking wave had tossed a jellyfish between the board and his bare chest: the sting that keeps on stinging. But then maybe that never happened; not to him anyway.

At least the pain told him he could still feel, that he wasn't all machine. Then he looked through the hole in the wall at what was going on outside and decided he'd been a bit hasty in counting his blessings, given that there was an awful lot of hurt out there just waiting to be felt.

Amid the smouldering crash debris just beyond the wall, he could see a row of escape pods that must have failed to eject during the fuselage's final descent. As he peered deeper into the smoke, he could see that there were others that had landed intact. Troops were emerging from them, albeit many were staggering drunkenly for a few yards and then collapsing. Those who remained upright were quickly mustering, scanning their surroundings and readying weapons.

He had no idea which side he was on, but he was aware they would be suffering no such existential dilemmas if they encountered someone looking like he did. He had no choice but to play the hand he'd been dealt. He had to find Rapier squad.

As he walked towards the still-glowing hole in the wall, he noticed a blaster pistol at his feet. It must have been a sidearm carried by one of the dead troops, sent skittering clear by the impact. He picked it up and examined it, deciding to try it out and make sure he knew how to use it now rather than when he was facing some amped-up roid-raging space marine.

There was no safety catch and no trick to firing it. You just pulled the trigger and it sent a short, controlled and, frankly, rubbish blast of energy towards its target. It didn't even make a very impressive noise, just this embarrassingly squeaky sound like a car ignition failing to turn.

All those years of devouring sci-fi shows, fantasising about futuristic firepower: now he had finally got his first ray-gun and it was pants. It reminded him of the first time he ever got to feel a girl's breast: Melanie Sangster had finally removed her protectively positioned elbow from her left tit only for him to find it indistinguishable from any other part of her upper body through the bra, blouse and Arran sweater she was wearing. Then, as now, what really piqued his sense of disappointment was the acute awareness that the real goods were there to be had somewhere.

How could he have this reaction unless those memories were his and unless he was shaped by them? This wasn't just background detail; this was who he was, surely. Unless his disappointment was born of being a cyborg trooper, used to far more impressive killware, and the virus meant that his mind couldn't help but supply points of reference from its false cache.

Kamnor had said fighting the enemy would help bring back his real self, but he didn't fancy fighting off an angry wasp with this little tadger of a gun.

As he picked his way through the wreckage of the corridor, he spied something more imposing. It was a long and sturdy rifle, humming with latent energy, blue diodes pulsing on its stock and an ammo display reading max. When he bent down to lift it, he found that it was still gripped in a severed flesh-and-metal arm, and no amount of effort could prise it from its owner's proverbial cold dead fingers. He tried hefting it along with the arm, but could barely move the latter as it weighed so much. He found another one, its come-and-get-me diodes blinking from among the tangle of twisted steel. This one wasn't gripped, but it wasn't going anywhere either, having become welded to its owner's chest in the crash.

Lumpen bum-nuggets. They were lying there dead but he couldn't take their weapons. And why did this frustration feel familiar?

Bottom line was that Kamnor was right again: he had to find his unit. That was the answer. They would have proper weapons. They were called Rapier squad, after all, not Chinese burn squad or twirled-up dishtowel squad.

Ross ventured cautiously through the twisted gash in the corridor and on to the arid ground beyond: his first steps on the surface of another planet or his first steps towards recovering his true identity. He wasn't sure which was the more intimidating. The former would leave him lost in space with no answer to his predicament, while the latter was just as big a step into the unknown. What if the 'real' him was a complete arsehole? Some sadistic killing machine that lived for atrocity, a convicted psychopath fitted out like this and made to serve in the military as an expedient form of punishment? What if he was a quivering shitebag of a conscript who was just as scared and unaccustomed as he felt now?

No, that couldn't be right. Something inside him had felt oddly positive about this place. Warm, even, and that was an emotion that ruled out both of the above.

He ran for the cover of a broken wing embedded in the dust, constantly surprised by how natural his movement felt. He still had no sense of being burdened by the weight of all this metal, which was confusing given that he hadn't been able to lift that poor dead bugger's arm.

He scurried between rocks and wreckage, looking out for movement at ground level, and listening carefully for any keening sounds from above. He could hear cries in the distance, but his view was obscured by smoke beyond a distance of about thirty metres. Shouldn't he have infrared vision or something? Evidently it didn't come as standard. Maybe it was fate's cruel punishment for his obstinate resistance of car ownership and for taking the piss out of people who wanked on about the spec of their ride: now that he was part machine, he had been rendered the cyborg equivalent of a Nissan Micra.

Even without enhanced vision ('We offer it as part of the SE package, along with an mp3 CD stereo, Bluetooth hands-free, target-lock and a half-decent gun'), he was able to see a grey-clad human figure crouching for cover about twenty yards in front, and realised with surprise and not a little concern that he had the drop on the guy. It was more by luck than practised stealth – indeed entirely by luck rather than practised *anything* – but he had managed to come around behind this invading soldier, who was squatting behind a row of scorched jump-seats. Ross had the target firmly in his sights, but even as he raised his pistol he knew he couldn't bring himself to shoot.

He had his back to Ross, scanning the landscape, doing the same thing as *he* had just been: searching for his unit and scoping for enemies. As the soldier turned his head, Ross could see his face beneath the helmet. He looked about twenty-two and terri-fied. He knew the soldier would exhibit no such empathy were the roles reversed, but that didn't change how he felt, virus-implanted memories or not.

He knew about the phenomenon of non-firing combatants; and in particular how it was firing combatants who ought to be described as the phenomenon, given that they accounted for less than twenty per cent of the men who had fought in World War Two.

For these men, it was a matter neither of honour nor of cowardice, but for Ross it was a bit of both. He couldn't kill a guy he'd never met and who'd done nothing to him, but equally he was less than convinced his pishy gun would get the job done anyway. He had images of it serving much the same function as a clown's horn: making a comedy noise and proving effective only at drawing attention to its source.

Ross stayed where he was until the soldier decided it was safe to move on. He watched him disappear into the fog and gave him a few minutes' start before proceeding himself.

From what he saw once he had passed beyond the curtain of smoke, the poor kid probably didn't get far. Kamnor had said Rapier squad was engaged in a 'mopping-up' operation, but it was one that seemed dedicated to liberally spreading organic matter about the place rather than cleaning it away.

The gigantic cock and balls that constituted the artillery defence weapon was continuing to piss all over the landing force, and Rapier squad, it turned out, had been tasked with rounding up and finishing off any survivors. In some cases it was a mercy, horribly burned figures crawling from landing pods in a state of mortal agony, given the *coup de grâce* beneath the purple alien sky. But for the most part it looked like butchery, with dazed, disoriented and frequently unarmed marines being mown down with laser fire. Nobody was being vaporised either, or simply falling down dead from absorbing energy blasts like on *Star Trek* or Agnes's favourite, *Blake's 7*. These beams were tearing off arms, legs and heads like they were airborne saw blades. If this sight was supposed to help trigger the return of his real memories, then it was the first thing Kamnor had got wrong.

The late lieutenant's take on squad sergeant Gortoss was, unfortunately, on the money. Ross first encountered him using his arm-spike to impale a marine who had already lost his legs in his crash-landing and was trying to crawl to safety with his arms.

'Like bloody cockroaches,' he said, his voice several thousand decibels to the north of the Brian Blessed register. 'Cut off a couple of limbs and they just keep scuttling.'

He was the size of Kamnor, albeit with a greater proportion of flesh on display, though whereas it had looked like Kamnor's augmentations were designed with specific purposes in mind, Gortoss's appeared to have been carried out by someone having

36

a tilt at the Turner Prize. Ross could have sworn there was even a steam iron in there somewhere, which had presumably been embedded after being used to blister extensive areas of Gortoss's remaining skin.

As with the cowering marine, Ross had happened upon him all of a sudden, having come over the brow of a crater. Unlike the marine, however, Gortoss gave him no option to withdraw unseen.

'Recruit! Where in a swamp-slug's suppurating ring-piece have you been?' he demanded. 'I had already decided to cite you for desertion. Your punishment was to have your own guts syphoned out through a liquefaction tube and then fed back down your throat. I was going to carry it out myself. I was really looking forward to that,' he added, sounding genuinely hurt. 'But then you have to show up and ruin it. Bloody new recruits they keep sending me. You're *my* punishment, that's what you are.'

'Lieutenant Kamnor told me where to find you, sergeant, sir,' Ross blurted, trying to contextualise himself in a way that subtly threw in the chain of command. 'I was a bit out of sorts, to do with the virus.'

'What virus?'

'Sent by the invaders. It's making people think they're, er, not themselves.'

'Never heard of it. Too bad there isn't one that makes useless sewage pipes like yourself think they're fucking soldiers. Anyway, Kamnor you say? How is the effete bastard? Still swanning around like his arse wouldn't rust?'

'He was, er, looking grand when I left him, sir.'

'I'll bet he was. All image and politics with that one. Do anything to avoid losing face.'

Ross tried to retain eye contact with Gortoss in case anything less was considered insubordinate, but his focus kept being drawn to the twitching and possibly not-quite-dead marine still pinned to the ground by his spike. He wasn't paying maximum attention to the sergeant's words either, his focus latching immediately on to Gortoss's dismissal of the virus. He'd never heard of it, he said. What if Kamnor was lying, or mistaken, Ross wondered, glimpsing a host of new possibilities.

Then Ross once again glimpsed what Gortoss was almost absently doing with his lethal appendage and reasoned that, given he was the most dangerously insane individual he'd ever met, perhaps he shouldn't place too much stock in his testimony.

Gortoss glanced away, over the rim of the next crater, where something had pleasingly taken his eye. He barked a greeting to a Sergeant Zorlak and requested that he stand fast a moment. When he looked back at Ross, he was wearing a grin so steeped in malicious intent, it made Jack Nicholson in *The Shining* look like Barney the dinosaur.

'Recruit, we've got just the job for you. Get your carcass over here.'

Ross proceeded down the first crater and towards the next with the light step and gaiety of a death row inmate who'd just had his head shaved. He didn't know what this 'job' entailed, but he suspected that if offered the choice, sight unseen, between whatever it was and cleaning John McCririck's toilet with his tongue, he'd take the latter without even asking for a peek over that next rim.

'Get a bloody move on. These bastards aren't going to kill *themselves*, you know.'

Oh no.

It was as horrible as he'd suspected. Zorlak and several members of his unit, Dagger squad, were standing over two prisoners. The marines were on their knees, hands restrained behind their backs by orange-glowing devices, their heads bowed in resignation and fear. Why were these guys being held, he wondered, when everybody else was just being slaughtered on the spot?

'Got another thumb-sucking toddler just swapped his rattle for a blaster,' Gortoss told his counterpart. 'I want to see if he's worth a shit, because if he's not made of the right stuff, I can't afford any baggage out here.'

'Be my guest,' Zorlak replied.

Gortoss beckoned Ross towards them.

'Execute this pair,' he commanded, the deranged glint in his eye registering his anticipation of Ross's difficulty but not betraying whether he would be happier to see him succeed or fail.

One of the prisoners looked up in desperation.

'Please, no,' he said.

Gortoss bent over him and spat in his face, some hideous yellow discharge that smelled like diesel and raw sewage.

'You expect mercy?' he asked, feigning outrage. 'You come to our world, bearing weapons of war, intent on putting a yoke around our necks, and you expect mercy? Did you not think there would be consequences to your unprovoked aggression?'

'To be fair, it wasn't exactly unprovoked,' suggested Zorlak reflectively. 'We did enslave one of their colonies.'

'We did?'

'And we did transport about quarter of a million of them here, then butchered them and recycled their body parts as organic replacements. Oh, and there was that business with the sub-space energy mining device that was tapping all the power from their sun. How did you miss all this?'

Gortoss shrugged. 'I was in jail. You tend not to pay much attention to off-planet affairs when you're not scheduled to go further than a half-mile radius for the next two decades. Still, doesn't change my point, does it?'

He turned again to the prisoner who had spoken, lifting his chin to make him look up.

'You expect mercy? From the people who racked up that little list of achievements? Blood of the fathers: I wish I had your optimism, mate. Recruit, in your own time.'

Ross heard a choked, suppressed whimper, and saw the other prisoner look over at him. It was the kid he'd already had in his sights and then let go. He was minus the helmet now, but that just made his face all the more recognisable. If anything, he looked even younger, and definitely more scared.

Kobayashi Maru, Ross thought. It was a test he could only fail, a test in which he didn't recognise what could constitute success. Execute unarmed prisoners or refuse and be killed himself, before or after which the same prisoners would be executed anyway. Cold logic therefore suggested he carry out the order, but if cold logic was what defined his actions, then what did that make him?

Whether he had envisaged this or not, Kamnor had been right all along: if he killed these enemies, he would indeed become someone other than the man defined by his memories. Perhaps indeed this was the trigger that would bring back his true self.

He could die as Ross Baker or he could live on as Christ knows what. The choice was just that stark, unless you counted a third option of trying to take down Gortoss, Zorlak and both their units with a glorified hair-drier.

'Come on, you sadistic bastard,' Gortoss said with a chuckle. 'It's cruel to draw it out like—'

The sergeant didn't finish his remarks on account of his brains deciding they wanted nothing more to do with him. This was following a bit of gentle persuasion by an armour-piercing ultra-high-velocity projectile that suggested they might prefer to spread themselves around the landscape than remain cooped up inside that cramped skull of his.

Zorlak turned to look for the source, by which time another of his unit had suffered a similarly critical reduction in the number of heads.

Ross dived for cover and heard shouts of panic as the two squads scrambled to return fire. He didn't quite catch what they were saying, but it sounded like 'card collector', which couldn't be right, as it conjured up images of an acne-ridden pubescent dork staring in the window at Forbidden Planet. Their startled, fearful tones indicated something more likely to be seen *in* the window at Forbidden Planet, a suggestion backed up by the sudden outbreak of ballistics and body parts in the area.

From his position of relative shelter behind a huge section of mangled landing gear, Ross watched this 'card collector' take on the combined might of Rapier and Dagger squads. He was human: another marine, Ross deduced, going on shape and proportion as the man's head was covered beneath a helmet and visor. He looked more armoured than the others, and somehow more distinct too. The rest of the marines were dressed almost identically, but this card collector subtly stood out, even though Ross couldn't quite pinpoint why.

He moved faster than the others, or maybe it was just that he moved more deliberately and with greater purpose. He also had a far more powerful weapon to wield, but that wasn't what was making the difference in the fight. He'd have done fine with one of their standard machine-guns, and would probably have edged it even with Ross's blaster.

The reason for this was that the home team were having a shocker.

For an advanced civilisation, their martial prowess and tactical awareness were embarrassing. Faced with somebody who wasn't wandering around in a post-crash daze, they were hopeless. They made no use of the ample cover options, just went straight for their target, blundering obligingly into his line of fire. They exhibited no coordination or even any evidence of attempting to work together, and they were bafflingly unaggressive in their returns of fire. When the card collector was in their sights, they'd loosen off the odd burst, then stop, as though waiting for someone to verify whether he was dead, and clearly they expected that someone to do it by post.

How could they have tapped energy from the Earth's sun and successfully invaded a colony planet when they were utterly fucking shite at this?

To his astonishment, Ross found himself confidently of the opinion that he could do better himself.

It was a theory he would imminently be given the opportunity to test under consistent conditions, as the card collector had wiped out everybody else and was now heading his way, scanning for his next target. Ross must have broken cover at just the wrong moment, as the marine got a fix on his movement immediately and pointed at him with an outstretched finger. Ross was grateful that it wasn't a rifle, as a squeeze of the trigger would have been the end, but he couldn't help interpreting the gesture as a declaration that he was being singled out for something particularly nasty due to being the only one left to toy with.

Ross ducked down and scrambled along the side of the crater, where he lost his footing on the loose gritty surface. He skidded, tumbled and rolled to the bottom, landing on top of a felled member of Dagger squad. This one hadn't even got as far as unslinging his rifle before being taken down, although going by the level of combat training on display, perhaps he'd been off sick the day they learned about raising it in a straight line, aiming it at somebody you disapproved of and squeezing the little stubby bit at the near end.

Ross picked up the rifle and slung the strap over his shoulder. It was heavy but he found the weight reassuring. Long, dark and jagged, it was glowing in places, and he could feel it hum.

'*That's* what I'm talking about.'

He circled around, checking his six then stepping back in a low crouch, presenting the smallest possible target until he could reach the partial cover of a thigh-high crate that had crashed down intact. He made it there just as the card collector appeared at the rim.

Clagnuts. He was pinned down at the foot of a crater. The big marine knew exactly where he was and had him covered from an elevated angle of fire. Ross could stay down behind the crate, but he'd be fatally exposed if he attempted to scale the sides. And if the collector had any grenades, he was humped.

He raised his head as much as he dared, desperate to confirm the marine's position. If his opponent moved down beyond the rim, he could pop up again anywhere. The collector hadn't moved, though. He was standing at the edge of the crater, just watching, and the second he was sure Ross was looking back, he gave him the finger. Not some subtle gesture from the hip, but a full, arm-raised salute.

Oh, he was loving this, the alpha male bell-end. He was relishing the hunt, trying to make it personal.

Ross ducked down again, beginning to feel the way a mouse must when Kitty starts playing with it, savouring the anticipation of the kill. 'I'm on your side,' he wanted to say, but he wasn't even sure it was true.

After a few more excruciating seconds of tension, he stole another glance. The collector hadn't moved. He was still staring down, and this time when he saw Ross staring back, he began performing exaggerated pelvic thrusts.

Did the cheeky bastard not know he had a proper gun, Ross asked himself; one he'd fire with a bit more conviction than his predecessors?

Evidently not, was the answer, as the card collector now stood with both arms apart: Fuck you, I'm an anteater.

Ross hefted the rifle and fired.

'Fuck you, I'm an android.'

The energy blast hit the card collector square in the chest, resulting in a storm of electrical flashes around his trunk as he reeled back sharply.

Power armour.

Ross fired another three salvos in quick succession. The first two hit their mark before the collector took evasive action. He ducked down out of sight, only to reappear shortly after, pointing at Ross then once again giving him the finger. He seemed furious, indicated by the fact that the whole time he was jumping up and down on the spot. It didn't make him much harder to hit, though. Ross kept the trigger down longer on this burst, at the end of which there were no electrical flashes. The power armour was depleted.

This belatedly provoked a response, the collector finally firing his weapon again. Ross heard the projectiles thump into the crate, embedding with singing metallic reverberations, but, to his huge relief, none of them passed right through. Just one of those things would be enough to cut him in half, he knew.

He could hear another sound too, one familiar from watching the collector take down the others: cartridge empty. His opponent needed to reload.

He looked up and saw that the collector had evidently grown accustomed to the obligingly sporadic firing patterns of the locals, as he was changing mag in plain sight. Ross levelled his rifle once more, to which the collector rather idiosyncratically responded by raising his hand in a wave. His response to then being caught in a mercilessly sustained volley of laser fire was more conventional.

He was obliterated.

Then, before Ross could even decide how he felt about this, so was the entire world.

Warped

It was as though someone had suddenly switched off the strong nuclear force. Everything dissolved in a shimmering instant, all matter turning to a swirl of light in a hundred million colours. Ross recalled Zorlak's confession about sub-space technology, and wondered, in what he believed to be his final thought, whether Earth had deployed some such hideous device as a retaliatory zero option following their failed invasion.

He felt himself come apart, yet even in feeling it and in seeing this dissolution of everything, he was aware he was still conscious.

The colours coalesced, became white. All he could see was white, nothing else.

Uh-oh. World ended, reality dissolved, but still conscious and everything white. This could be awkward.

He spent a very uncomfortable few moments trying to remember his prepared position for explaining to God that he had nonetheless been right not to believe in Him on the basis of all available evidence, and that his empiricism and advocacy of sceptical enquiry was vindicated because faith-based belief had proven hugely detrimental to humankind's welfare. At the same time, another part of his brain was busy thinking: 'Please don't let the Catholics be right, please don't let the Catholics be right.' Who wanted an eternity in Pope Benedict's idea of heaven? In fact, wasn't the concept of paradise technically incompatible with a belief system that disapproved of just about all known forms of pleasure?

To his relief he gradually distinguished that the white filling his entire field of vision was not formless, but had lines within it, and even texture. He realised he was staring at tiles.

He was back in the scanner cell, lying flat on the bed, staring at the ceiling. He felt an overwhelming mixture of confusion and relief. It *had* been a dream after all, but how? It had been so vivid, so consistent, and he had tried to wake up from it. Was it some kind of trip Solderburn had cooked up, using the scanner to project *into* his mind rather than record from it?

Then he once again registered the absence of rails and scanning heads immediately above him.

Ross shot upright in a flash and examined himself.

'Oh for fuck's sake,' he sighed. 'How can I still be a cyborg?'

He stood up and, as before, the door automatically withdrew and slid laterally open to reveal the same corridor. He must have been teleported back here: that's what the dissolving sensation was. Wow. First a real laser rifle and now he'd experienced teleportation. Here's to you, Mr Scott, he thought, but it prompted a question: who beamed him back here? And while we're at it, why? Had he proven himself somehow in taking down the card collector? Or had he inadvertently activated an integral teleportation device himself, like he had inadvertently skewered poor Kamnor through the face?

One thing was for sure: getting his hands dirty in combat hadn't triggered any shift in his sense of identity. He still felt one hundred per cent Ross Baker, the same person who had gone to work this morning and learned his girlfriend was pregnant before lying down to test Solderburn's new scanner. If this was a virus, then he'd caught a mother of a dose.

Carol. Just the thought of her name made something in him ache, in a way that echoed how he'd felt in the days just after he'd met her but before he first asked her out. She had invaded his mind, subjected him to a curious mix of tantalising pleasure at the thought of her, impatient longing to be in her orbit and desolate insecurity in case he was destined never to get clearance beyond the friend zone. He recalled that night at the bowling alley, a group of about a dozen of them commandeering two lanes. It was Tracy's birthday, and he had been invited along as he was new to the firm and the girls were trying to make him feel welcome. They'd gone for a bite to eat first at some Mexican chain restaurant, and he'd ended up sitting opposite Carol. It wasn't some love-at-first-sight deal, perhaps because nobody looks particularly alluring trying to eat a chimichanga that's falling apart in their hands. But then something just altered as he watched her bowl, like a switch being flipped.

```
Setting 'Smitten' = TRUE
```

He had felt in a trance after that, later having no recollection of how the bowling had gone, and mildly panic-stricken that it might have been noticeable to everybody else that he turned into a besotted catatonic mute.

He couldn't afford to think about her now. He could feel his connection to her more acutely than ever, but it only served to emphasise the gaping distance that now lay between them, in every sense.

He proceeded once again through the same corridors, his sense of familiarity confused this time by definitely having been here before a couple of hours earlier. The artillery cannon kept up its arrhythmic tattoo, preceded always by that tell-tale inrush and followed by the smaller bangs that he now knew were the sounds of spacecraft disintegrating. His progress was a little less tentative than before, emboldened by his martial exploits, until he caught himself striding confidently towards the elevator platform and realised he no longer had a gun.

Arse candles. Where had it gone? Perhaps the teleportation system didn't let you carry anything through, but he couldn't see how that would work, given the amount of foreign objects that were embedded in his person.

He rose into the staging area once again, in time to see another unit muster themselves and ship out. Their leader glanced his way momentarily as they headed for the diagonally sliding doorway. He looked like Zorlak, but that was impossible, as Zorlak was lying out on the battlefield in a state of irretrievable disassembly. Plus, it wasn't prejudiced to say that, to the unaccustomed eye, one mechanised zombie cobbled together from alloy plates and harvested body parts looks rather like another.

A glance was all the notice he got. Nobody hailed the conquering hero, but neither did anybody ask what he was doing or what had happened to his unit. He wanted answers, though. He needed to find out more about this virus, for a start. Kamnor and the troop of soldiers who'd followed him had been coming from the other side of the complex, through that link corridor. It had been demolished by the fuselage, but there was probably a way through the wreckage.

He made his way across the staging area towards the same exit as before, bracing himself for the carnage and possible flames ahead. The sliding doors parted for him, revealing the same initial stretch of passageway, surprisingly unscathed by the impact. The angle of the bend not only hid what was ahead, but must have prevented debris from scattering this far. Once again he could see the play of light on the grey concrete of the opposite wall as he approached. From this position it was easy to imagine that the crash had never happened.

Once he had reached the bend, the picture changed, and not in the way he was expecting. From this position, it was even easier to imagine that the crash had never happened, as there was absolutely no evidence that it had. The corridor was corpse- and debris-free, the walls were still where the architect had envisaged them and the burning-fuselage count was down one on before.

Ross stood gaping in bewilderment, then turned to look out of the huge window again, making sure he hadn't confused himself concerning the layout and exited the staging area down a different corridor. Nope: he could see the unnecessarily phallic artillery cannon gobbing its death-spunk at the invasion force from exactly the same position. He stared up at the sky, focusing on individual craft and trying to remember whether he had seen them destroyed before, but none of them was memorably distinct.

'It's an awe-inspiring sight, isn't it?' said a soft, clipped and rather posh voice from behind him.

It was only momentary paralysis brought on by shock that prevented Ross from jumping in the air and letting loose a most uncyborg-like shriek of fright.

'Lieutenant Kamnor,' he eventually stumbled.

'In the flesh,' Kamnor replied, for it was unquestionably he. 'Well, what there is of it.'

Ross stared at him, transfixed. It was only the ongoing shock and confusion that stayed an impulse to hug the guy in sheer relief that he hadn't killed him after all.

But he *had* killed him. He had quite unmistakably inflicted stomach-churningly horrific injuries of a nature seldom remedied by a couple of Paracetamol and a quiet lie-down.

There was only one explanation. It defied all that was known about physics and the very fabric of reality, but it was considerably more probable than a ton of debris spontaneously re-assembling itself in blatant violation of entropy.

He hadn't been teleported: he had gone back in time.

'Shouldn't you be with—'

'My unit, yes, lieutenant, sir,' Ross interrupted, grasping the advantage he'd been inexplicably dealt. 'Rapier squad. Mopping-up duty. It's just that I suspect I have been hit by the Gaians' virus. Sergeant Gortoss sent me back for tests and to find out whatever I can about the condition, lieutenant, sir.'

'Well, that was uncharacteristically understanding of him.'

'I believe he described me as "a useless arse-rag of a liability" and suggested I "go and get my brains cleaned out or he would suck them out for me and shit in my head as a replacement".'

'Yes, that sounds more like Gortoss,' Kamnor admitted.

'I gather other victims have reported it wearing off in combat, but I suspect I've got a more resistant strain. Sergeant Gortoss expressed concern that a subsequent symptom of the variant might be an impulse to attack our own forces. He didn't put it in precisely those words, but—'

'Quite. No, this requires further investigation, certainly. You should report to med bay. In fact, I'll come with you. If the enemy have uploaded a more powerful version of this virus, then we need to identify it immediately.'

Kamnor began leading him down the corridor towards the double doors, through which a familiar troop of soldiers was now advancing. Ross felt the inrushing power surge, heard the cannon boom. From somewhere in the sky, there then followed a high keening sound.

'INCOMING!' Ross shouted, pulling Kamnor towards him with one hand and gesticulating manically to the troop. The soldiers scrambled back behind the threshold of the blast doors just a moment before the corridor got its extreme makeover.

Ross couldn't see beyond the fuselage, flames, smoke and heat haze, but he could hear voices calling out, enquiring whether the lieutenant was all right. Ross had intervened in time. He had saved them.

Result! He had saved several grimly visaged zombie death-troopers serving an army that by its own admission had slaughtered a quarter of a million humans for spare parts. Yay, he thought. Go me!

Just as last time, he and Kamnor had ended up in a tangle on the floor after the impact, but this time the lieutenant was alive to help him to his alloy-clad feet, which Ross regarded briefly as he climbed upright. He wasn't going to find a pair of astro-turf trainers to fit him for five-a-sides ever again, but on the plus side, he wouldn't have to worry about any more verrucas or fungal infections, and he wouldn't be needing shin pads.

'Bloody good show, soldier,' Kamnor said. 'That virus certainly isn't hindering your powers of observation or your reflexes. You saved my life; I salute you.'

And he did, sending out his arm, fist clenched at the end.

Ross eyed it anxiously.

'Sir, you'll have to forgive me if I don't reciprocate. The virus interferes with certain actions and behaviours.'

'That's unfortunate, but as it appears to have given you a sixth sense, I shan't complain.'

A sixth sense, Ross thought, briefly considering another explanation, albeit one that didn't so much challenge the laws of science as completely give them the finger. What if he hadn't travelled in time, but instead experienced a *Final Destination*-style premonition?

Well, were that to be the case, the outlook wasn't good for any of them. They were in the middle of a war-zone. If Death needed to balance the books, He should be thoroughly embarrassed if it took Him more than three minutes.

Four of the troops Ross had saved made their way to Kamnor, passing briefly outside to get around the wreckage. The other two had retrieved fire-extinguishing equipment from somewhere close by and were spraying some kind of gel on the debris, instantly containing the flames.

Kamnor seemed to lose focus for a moment, staring blankly like his face was lagging.

'Incoming communication,' he reported. 'There are reports of a landing force having made it through. They are attempting an incursion of the south perimeter. Cutlass squad, I need you to come with me.'

'Yes sir,' they responded.

Kamnor turned to Ross.

'You'll have to find your own way to med lab. Best of luck with sorting that virus.'

'Thank you sir,' he replied, resisting the impulse to offer a warning about staying away from kitchen implements and heavy machinery just in case the *Final Destination* theory was correct.

If it was, then Death must have noted Ross's thoughts on an acceptable time-frame, as Kamnor didn't make it five yards before being killed. His metal body was sliced into several pieces as though it was no tougher than a melon, julienned by a form of ultra-high-velocity projectile weapon with which Ross had become recently familiar.

Because of their respective positions, he didn't have line of sight on where the shots had come from, but he knew it was the card collector who had sniped Kamnor from somewhere out in the wastes.

He decided he ought to have a word.

Ross was about to venture out in pursuit of the assassin but was halted by two obstacles. The first was the timely realisation that, unlike during their last duel, on this occasion he was completely unarmed. The second was more literal: he couldn't get through the gap in the wall anyway, because it had become rapidly choked with body parts previously belonging to members of Cutlass squad. They had gone charging out in immediate response to the attack, exhibiting the same battle prowess and tactical awareness of their comrades in Rapier and Dagger squads by proceeding into a narrow bottleneck and being picked off one by one, each apparently heedless of the fate that had just befallen the man in front of him.

Kudos to Death, He had brought it home in about ninety seconds, tops.

On the plus side, the second obstacle had at least negated the first. He had several identical rifles to choose from, none of them fused to their previous owners this time.

Ross got down low and crawled cautiously through the

51

now-even-narrower channel, occasionally risking a glimpse over the pile of blood- and unidentified-yellow-green-fluid-spattered limbs, heads, legs and torsos. He spotted the card collector, his back to Ross as he scurried away, heading out into the disasterscape.

Ross considered it safe to get to his feet, and hastened after his prey, zigzagging between rocks, wreckage and crates for cover. What the hell were these boxes made of, he wondered? Everything else that had fallen from above was in bits, but the crates were unscathed and unopened. He briefly tried prising the top off one, but got nowhere and abandoned the attempt, as his priority was pursuit.

Having got a bead on where the collector appeared to be heading, he veered left, intending to come around and flank him a little further ahead: take him by surprise and he could get the bastard to talk before matters descended into another shooting match.

Ross took up position beneath the head of a rocky spur and waited to make his move. Another thirty yards and they would converge, the collector seemingly oblivious to being stalked as he continued on a course that would take him right into Ross's path. But just as he readied himself to spring, Ross felt his legs taken from beneath him and he was dragged into a narrow crevice in the rock.

'Stay down,' his attacker told him with urgency and concern.

He was another cyborg, resembling Ross in terms of the dead-flesh/steel-and-glass balance, and similar also in wearing a hunted and confused look upon his circuitry-adorned face.

'You don't want to get into a fight with that one,' he went on.

'I'm not afraid of him,' Ross insisted with frustration, pinned down as he was by his would-be rescuer's weight.

'That's not the issue, believe me.'

'Well it's moot now,' Ross added huffily.

His captor got off of him and scrambled nimbly to the lip of the escarpment to check.

'Yes, I'm relieved to say that it is,' he reported. 'He's gone. Come here, though. This way. I need you to take a look at some-thing.'

Ross hauled himself out of the crevice and up the slope with heavy limbs and bad grace.

'So what is it you wanted me to . . . oh.'

There was an object hovering impossibly in the air in front of him, spinning in place on the vertical axis. The object was disc-shaped, its rim of red stone encircling a golden caduceus. It was four feet in diameter, beautifully crafted, gleamingly polished, and it wasn't there.

It passed through Ross's outstretched fingers, then he stepped into the centre of where it ought to be, watching it continue to spin around him. It was some super-advanced perfect hologram, but what the hell purpose it served was anybody's guess. The guy who had grabbed him seemed very excited by it, anyway, or at least excited that Ross was aware of it.

'You can see it?' he asked breathlessly.

'Of course I can see it. I can't touch it, but that's because it's some kind of 3D projection.'

'I knew you'd be able to see it. The others can't. I knew you weren't one of them from the way you were running.'

Ross eyed the guy's shoulder, taking in a symbol that looked like a scimitar.

'So, what unit are you with?' he asked wearily.

'Accounts,' came the reply, equally tetchy.

'There's an *accounts* unit? What do you audit: body-part distribution?'

'No, not here. In Leicester. I work for Barret Finch Home Furnishings. We make curtains and sofa covers. That's why I got hold of you: I'm not from here, and I'm guessing you're not either.'

Ross gaped, staring blankly for a moment, unable to respond. He felt relieved that there was another human here in the same boat but simultaneously depressed because it seemed to confirm that this was really happening.

'My name is Bob. I'm a bloody accountant, not an alien stormtrooper. I went to my bed one night and woke up here. I've a wife and two daughters in Nottingham and I need to get home.'

'My name's Ross,' he mumbled uncertainly. 'I'm from Stirling. Or I think I am. I heard there's this virus . . .'

'Talking to a big bloke called Kamnor, were you?'

'Yes.'

'It's bollocks. Kamnor's a political animal and a pragmatist, so he came up with an explanation expedient to their needs. He just told you that to keep you onside and quell any possible unrest, but he doesn't know any more than we do.'

'Or maybe he does and he's hiding the truth,' Ross suggested, using present tense to skirt around the tricky issue of Kamnor's recurring deaths. 'What if our memories are actually those of people recycled by them and turned into cyborgs?'

'Either way, it doesn't change the fact that I know I'm not one of them. And recycled when? I don't know about you, but when I went to sleep that last night on Earth, the furthest anyone had been to was the moon, and we certainly weren't at war with any alien civilisations.'

'How long have you been here?'

'Days. I'm not sure exactly, because there's no night. It's always daytime. I haven't slept. Don't feel the need to either.'

The artillery cannon boomed again and the exhaust port of a landing craft thudded into the ground only about twenty yards away.

'I'm impressed you've lasted that long without getting killed,' Ross told him.

'Are you kidding? I've been killed about a dozen times,' Bob replied, desperation in his sallow, reanimated face. 'But I don't stay dead. I just keep coming back, into this bloody nightmare, this permanent battle.'

Ross felt something lock into place inside his mind, a first connection potentially leading to a truly horrifying thought, and given how his horror scale had been recalibrated recently, that was saying something. All the previous horror had been leavened by making no sense, but this notion, deranged as it was, had a whiff of the logical and thus – being the really scary part – *binding* about it.

'That's why I stopped you from engaging the one they call the card collector. If he hits you with that gun of his, it doesn't bloody tickle, let me tell you. Searing agony and then whoosh: you suddenly find yourself all in one piece again in some random part of the landscape. But if you kill *him*, time warps back. I don't know how or why, but it's true: everything returns to how it was and starts all over again.'

'I'd noticed,' Ross confessed, another piece clicking into place in that disturbingly logical chain.

'Oh, that was you, last time, was it? You killed him? Well, you'll understand: whether you killed him the next time or he killed you, I knew I'd have a devil of a time finding you again afterwards. I was starting to think that this might be hell, that maybe I had died in my sleep, but once I saw there was somebody else here like me, I realised we both must be alive: this must be real. And if it's real, then however we got here, there must be a way back too.'

'What is this place?' Ross asked with a hollow dread that the answer wasn't going to be entirely a surprise. 'I mean, do you know what this planet is called?'

'Yes,' Bob replied. 'Its name is Graxis. I'd never heard of it before.'

Ah, thought Ross, who *had* heard of it. That being 'Ah', as in: 'My brain is imploding with the enormity of this but at least I finally know what I'm dealing with.'

Graxis: a planet on the outer rim of the Andromeda galaxy, where the dominant race had built a technology that combined advanced robotics with bio-scavenging. They had raided first their own world's native species and then the species of other planets in order to sustain and augment themselves. They saw all other life-forms as raw material, and felt no more remorse about harvesting humans for spare parts than humans would about turning oil into plastic. That, however, wasn't the aspect that had precipitated Ross's hollow dread. There was something much more troubling about Graxis's nature.

The outer rim of any galaxy is too remote from the black hole at the centre for there to be a sufficiency of the higher elements necessary to create and sustain organic life. Life had evolved on Graxis though, and for one important reason: that whoever wrote the CD-booklet blurb for Digital Excess Software had known jack-shit about astronomy.

He and Bob hadn't travelled in space or time, though the means and implications of their journey were no less perplexing. They were inside a computer game: specifically, a 1996 first-person shooter called *Starfire*.

When Bob said the planet's name, it was like he'd keyed a

decryption code into Ross's brain, causing all of the scrambled data to instantly resolve into coherence. All of the information had been there in front of him, but none of these discrete elements could reveal their true nature until he could see them as part of the whole.

That sense of familiarity, of comfort, of positive associations: he understood it now. This place with the gloomy subterranean walkways, the booming artillery cannon, the impossibly purple sky, was a place he knew, a place he associated with happy memories.

Christmas '96, his first real PC, trading up from a Commodore Amiga: a two-hundred-megahertz processor with Pentium MMX technology and a CD-ROM drive. No more floppy-swappy for him.

Mum and Dad had pushed the boat out, partly in response to encouragement from his maths teacher, and partly due to guilt at the effect their increasingly bitter arguments were having on him. They were trying to make things better, and that Christmas Ross allowed himself to believe it was working. Eilidh and Megan were both home from uni for a couple of weeks, and it just felt special. Family meals, long afternoons lounging on the living-room carpet watching videos, and for Ross, staying up into the small hours battling the Gralaks in software-rendered but nonetheless gloriously immersive first-person 3D.

Shit, did that mean he had died and this was a kind of after-life after all? A personal heaven that he had subconsciously chosen in his teen years, which would ironically turn out to be hell for an adult?

No, because that sense of comfort wasn't purely about the good times, was it? The world of Graxis had been a place of retreat in the ensuing months when his parents started fighting again, a world he could escape to when he didn't want to deal with the reality that was around him.

So did that mean he had gone all *Buffy* S6E17? Had he freaked out at the news of Carol's pregnancy, and his mind retreated into this place while in reality his body was rocking like a Romanian orphan in a corner of the office?

Unlikely, he decided. Her pregnancy was a shock, but he had to give himself *some* credit. Besides, if he was to retreat into the world of a game, whether in death or insanity, surely it wouldn't be *Starfire*. It wasn't some seminal experience or all-time favourite. That accolade would go to *Serious Sam* for undiluted pleasure, or maybe online *Quake 2* on the strength of the sheer number of hours played.

No, this wasn't in his head. This was all around him, inescapably real: from the dust on his feet to the heat on his skin to the smell of burning fuel on the breeze. That was why he had recognised this place and yet not been quite conscious of doing so, instead experiencing merely a confusing sense of familiarity. It was `Alive1`, the opening level of *Starfire*, he could see that now, but it looked different rendered in steel, stone, sunlight and fire rather than shaders, brushes, sprites and pixels.

He recalled getting his first graphics-acceleration card in the summer of '97, a 3dfx Voodoo 1. It had cost him all of his birthday money and Saturday-job savings, leaving him with no cash to buy any new games, but that didn't matter. Seeing the likes of *Starfire* and *Quake* go from software-rendered blobby brownness to shimmering, Glide-polished environments was like playing them for the first time. The familiar dungeons, hangars, halls and bases looked completely different as a result of their rendering upgrade.

Whenever a game came out showcasing a new graphics engine, one of the first things the custom-map enthusiasts did was remake their old favourites. He had seen `Entryway` from *Doom II*, `Ziggurat Vertigo` from *Quake*, `The Edge` from *Quake 2* and `Alive1` from *Starfire* rendered again and again, and though they were all recreating the same places, the maps didn't just look different, they *felt* different. The proportions would change, the new textures and lighting affecting your perception of architecture and layout, even though the basic geometry was identical. If you hadn't known which level you were loading, you might be wandering around a while before you realised it was an update of a classic.

That's what had happened here, except the scale of the upgrade was unimaginable. It was inescapably real, and yet equally inescapably a late-Nineties shooter. That was why he'd felt there was something familiar about his frustration in not being able to pick up the better guns from the enemies lying dead on the floor. The game gave you a crappy blaster pistol to kick off with, but didn't let you lift anything from the foes you had taken down. Instead it drip-fed you better and better weapons as you worked your way through the maps.

That was why the soldiers were utterly useless too: blundering into the line of fire, taking no evasive action, failing to coordinate attacks to take advantage of their numbers. The AI was shit back then, though that wasn't the reason for the Gralaks never firing in aggressive, sustained patterns. That aspect was by design, so that a single player could successfully wage a solo campaign against their entire army. Hence the artillery cannon making mincemeat of the invasion force: in the story, the space marines were all but wiped out, leaving the player to be the lone hero and take on the Gralaks entirely by himself.

However, it wasn't just the 'Actual Reality' rendering that had clouded Ross's recognition. It was the fact that *he* wasn't the lone hero.

He hadn't started out in the wreckage of a crashed landing pod as his shipmates were gunned down all around him, gripping his blaster and vowing revenge. He was an enemy grunt. He was what would normally be described as an NPC: a non-playing character. That was why he couldn't open any crates, and why he couldn't interact with the hologram that he now recognised as a health power-up. In *Starfire*, indeed in every one of those shooters, the enemies were completely oblivious to all the useful stuff that was just lying about the place, whether it was health, armour, weapons or ammo. Ross could see it though, which made him and Bob different from the NPCs, but the fact that he could plonk himself in the middle of the thing all day without effect just served to underline the fact that it wasn't there for his benefit.

He was not the hero. He was not the player.

He knew who was, though: the card collector. When *he* died, the game was restored to its opening state because the player had restarted the map.

He was inside *Starfire*, but there was no escape key, no menu and no option to quit (Are you sure? Yes/No). Stranger still, there was someone out there *playing* the fucking thing.

Research and Development

Ross could not have felt more like a dick if he had been gene-spliced with George Osborne and dressed in a six-foot foam-rubber penis costume. He sat at his desk and stared blankly at the monitor, unable to focus, waiting in vain for his mind to come back online. It was as though someone had detonated a logic bomb in his memory core; or perhaps more like his brain was undergoing a coordinated denial-of-service attack, overwhelmed by response requests so that it couldn't process any information.

He fought to concentrate on one question amid the storm of imponderables. Why didn't she tell him? Why was he learning something as earth-shattering as this third- or maybe fourth-hand? She had told her sister, and clearly not in any kind of firewalled confidence, given that the information had made it to his place of work before he did. Was this the ultimate female test of male attentiveness: that if you can't work this one out from the available clues, you don't deserve to know?

Kind of, he deduced. Because the main reason Carol hadn't told him was that as long as he didn't know, she still had all her options open, such as the option to have nothing more to do with him. Everything became more complicated once he was party to the information, but while he was too oblivious to even notice, well, what did that say about his credentials?

Through the hurt, confusion and downright embarrassment, the most compelling emotion he felt was a desire to be with her right then. He wanted to offer his apologies and his vows of support, but more fundamentally he had a greater need to simply hold her than he had ever endured.

He had seldom felt so isolated and helpless in his life. Carol was the first person he turned to when he needed to unburden himself, when he needed reassurance, when he had great news to share. A few minutes ago he had been daft enough to believe he could do without all of that, but now he could see the true scale of his delusion.

He had to speak to her. He wasn't going to be able to function properly until he did so.

He phoned, but got no answer. That figured. After what happened at the weekend, she was unlikely to be taking his calls for a while. Things had changed, though. They absolutely needed to talk. Maybe he should send a text, let her know he was aware of the situation now. How did you phrase something like that, though?

Heard u r pregnant. 😨 omg.

Maybe not. He tried calling again, tried not to think of Rita Mae Brown's definition of insanity. Still no answer. It wasn't even diverting to the message service. She really had all interrupts locked out.

He physically didn't know what to do with himself, because he could think of no action he could take right then that would move him forward from this predicament. There was no point in making the dramatic gesture of walking out and going straight to see her, because she would be in court right then, and besides, he had no idea what he would say to her. Just the thought of facing her prompted the awareness that he didn't even know what he wanted to happen, what he would consider a satisfactory resolution.

He couldn't think about it, literally couldn't think about it while this mental DoS attack was still in full flow. He needed time to pass. He had to occupy himself. Work: that was the answer. Work. It was the only thing he could make sense of at that moment, and as Zac's Rohypnol-laced words had underlined, he had a mountain of it to get through, particularly with there still being no sign of the Sandman returning to duties.

He felt a sudden anger over Alex's disappearing act, a feeling that was just as quickly supplanted by guilt at having made no attempt to get in touch with him and make sure the guy was okay. The last time he had shown up was Wednesday, but Ross had been out of the office visiting one of the hospitals participating in the test programme. Diane, the department's network mage, said she had seen Alex at his desk first thing that day, but he must have gone home early, because he wasn't there in the afternoon. He had been due to let Solderburn scan him for the mapping trials programme later that morning, and it was joked that he had bailed in panic rather than throw himself at the mercy of the idiosyncratic chief engineer and his experimental prototype.

Alex hadn't phoned in sick; or at least if he had, nobody thought to mention it to Ross. The Sandman had seemed a little low of late, right enough, definitely out of sorts. Ross hoped the guy hadn't had some kind of breakdown. Poor sod was divorced from a woman who had treated him so appallingly you'd have thought he must have murdered her entire family in another life and she had married him out of vengeance.

I'll give him a call now, Ross thought, trying not to admit that some part of him was hoping that an act of solicitous human contact would score him some much-needed karma points with regard to Carol at some point calling *him*.

Alex's mobile diverted to his landline, triggered his answering machine.

Arse trumpets.

Okay. He had tried. That was one less thing to feel bad about.

He would make sure there was nothing in his inbox requiring an urgent response, then lose himself in work for a few hours. Maybe take a walk at lunchtime, see if the smell of fresh diesel fumes in his lungs and the inspiring views of the skip-hire depots could help him find clarity.

He reflexively deleted a couple of emails flagged High Priority, which was the Neurosphere suits' inadvertently helpful way of letting you know the denoted message was a pointless circular full of management-speak and could therefore be discarded unopened. That just left the message from Solderburn.

From: Jay Solomon
Sent: Monday, 07:34
To: Ross Baker
Subject: Mapping trials for latest build

Hey buddy.
I was copied into that shitogram from the Zacbot. Sucks dude. Extreme
lossage. Anyways, given your presentation's been flushed, I figure
you've got a window this morning, and I'm doing the zombie fandango
here: I need fresh brains and I heard you got them to spare.
Fix me up?
S

That was Solderburn for you. Speed empathy, then fast-
forward to the point. Actually, by Solderburn's standards, this
was him really reaching out: there was a 'sucks dude' *and* an
'extreme lossage'. Ross snorted at the suggestion the cancellation
of his meeting suddenly meant he had a whole load of free time
on his hands, but given where his head was at, it struck him
that taking twenty minutes out to lie down in a state of complete
isolation would be time well spent.

He fired off a reply, saying he'd be there in five.

Solderburn's lair was signposted as the 'Research and Development
Lab' on the link corridor at the rear of the main building, presumably because they couldn't find a notice that said 'Keep Out –
Condemned'. Its separation from the rest of the premises in what
was anyway the most far-flung outpost of the corporation would
provide the first hint to a newcomer that Jay Solomon was the
madman in Neurosphere's attic. This impression was only underlined by the fact that the door to the link corridor was locked
half the time, so you either had to walk around the outside of
the building or get the keys from Billy the security guard. Ross
would have opted for the former even if it was minus fifteen
outside and blizzard conditions. In precisely the same way that
a brief exchange with Agnes could give you a spoonful of
sunshine to brighten up your day, any encounter with Billy made
you feel like he had shat in your pocket, depositing a little lump
of his own unpleasantness that adhered to you for a long time after.

The R&D lab gave the impression that Solderburn had set out to create an environment that contradicted every preconception the word 'laboratory' connotes in the average human mind. It resembled what you might get if you combined the assembly line at an upscale electronics manufacturer, the display floor at a DIY store, the contents of two car boot sales and the decor of a late-Nineties frat house – then bombed it. The only reason it hadn't fallen foul of health and safety legislation was that no health and safety officer had been brave enough to inspect it; or, if so, they had never made it back out again.

'I love what you've done with the place,' Ross had said the first time Solderburn gave him a tour.

'I was going for Alice Cooper stage-set meets *Doom 3*. But, like, you know, late in *Doom 3*, when everything's been blown to shit?'

'The Delta Labs?' Ross had suggested, establishing his gaming credentials. 'Oh, you definitely got there.'

Solderburn was like a cross between an ageing hippy and an overfed teenager: his dress sense and personal-hygiene ethos coming from the former; his emotional maturity and inter-personal skills from the latter. He looked like the kind of guy who could have a million dollars in the bank but still be living in his mother's basement. Indeed he might well have been but for the confluence of circumstances that had caused him to wash up in an industrial estate in Stirling in his late forties after a lifetime in California.

The lauded Berkeley and Cal-Tech graduate had enjoyed a chequered career, with seemingly concerted efforts at pissing his talents up against the wall being intermittently interrupted by brief moments of brilliance. It would be easy to paint it as a familiar tale of wasted talent, but in the short time Ross had known Solderburn, he had come to understand that you couldn't separate the genius from the flake; nor say whether his creative efforts caused him to flake out or whether sustained flakiness was an inextricable part of the creative process. Unfortunately drugs had also proven a major part of his crea-tive process, and when he notched up one possession bust too many, Neurosphere's higher-ups had to insulate themselves from the fallout.

'It wasn't that I made a lot of enemies,' he told Ross. 'I just didn't make enough friends. Gotta watch for that, dude.'

Nonetheless, he still did have some friends at Neurosphere, or at least admirers. They couldn't keep him, but they did not want to lose him, just in case he came up with something game-changing and they no longer had first call on the results. They told him they would continue to fund his work, but only if he agreed to ship out to a far-flung outpost of their empire and lie low for a while; telling him, like they told Ross about these premises, that it was only temporary.

On this particular morning, Neurosphere's equivalent of the first Mrs Rochester was dressed in a pair of dark grey (as in formerly beige) cargo pants and a horrifically bright yellow t-shirt bearing the legend 'FUCK YOUR CAKE' in three rows of red capitals. Ross reckoned it was a good bet he had slept in it, and just as likely slept in the lab.

Solderburn favoured cargo pants because they sported a multi-plicity of pouches and pockets into which he could stuff tools, memory sticks, pens, torches, pieces of circuit board, lengths of cable, cartons of juice and a seemingly self-replenishing supply of caramel wafers. (Actually, the term 'favoured' suggested he had exercised some kind of option with regard to his trousers, when in truth Ross couldn't remember seeing him wear another pair.)

He was chewing on cold pizza as he picked his way carefully through the debris to greet his visitor, Ross not wishing to contemplate how many hours or even days it had been since that pizza was warm.

'Ross, dude, good to see you. Shame about the circs,' he said, offering a fist for Ross to punch. It was a gesture of solidarity which Ross did his best to meet but managed only a cursory reciprocation, involuntarily giving a heads-up that all was not well. Notwithstanding that such exchanges tended to make him acutely aware of not being the kind of guy who could punch fists with other men, Ross could normally mask his awkward-ness enough to manage a decent dig. Today, however, his sense of self was rather depleted.

Solderburn scrutinised him for a moment.

'Hey, no offence, bro, but you look like you don't know if you need a dump or a haircut. The suits shit-canning your proposal really gronked you out, huh?'

'Little bit,' Ross replied, relieved to let him follow the wrong scent.

'Let me see if I can't clear your head then. Watch your step, by the way. I'm pretty sure I saw movement in here a little while ago. I'm kinda hoping it was a rat, because otherwise it means I might have called forth something from another dimension, and I'm not sure I could handle that shit on a Monday morning.'

Ross considered how his own Monday morning was going so far. Inter-dimensional entities were a piece of piss by comparison.

Solderburn led him across a cluttered expanse of floor towards where three semi-cannibalised scanners sat side by side, cables tangled together in a morass of wiring that looked like a visual representation of a firewall. On the other side of this firewall was a teeteringly unstable-looking *millefeuille* of hard drives, motherboards and heat sinks; a customised construction intended to rapidly process and store data.

'I'm starting to see why the Sandman bailed rather than take his chances with this thing,' said Ross, using Alex's nickname.

'Sandman didn't bail,' Solderburn replied, curiosity in his tone.

'Just what I heard.'

'No, he was here, man, Wednesday morning. Dude was looking a little peaky but that was before I scanned him. I told him to report any side effects.'

'So you're saying your machine scanned Alex and nobody's seen him since,' Ross suggested, hamming up his tone.

'*I* saw him since. Saw him walk out the door.'

'I only have your word for that.'

'I swear the process is completely painless. For me, anyway.'

Ross cast a wary eye over the arrangement, which looked like something out of a government safety film regarding the dangers of electricity.

'I don't even know which one I'm supposed to lie down on.'

'Oh, no, the actual scanner-bed is through there now,' Solderburn indicated, pointing to a door.

'What, in the old cleaner's cupboard?'

'I made some reconfigurations. I needed to create a chamber that's electromagnetically isolated, so that the scanning process doesn't fry my equipment.'

'What if it fries my brain?'

'Then at least all my kit will still work.'

'Well, that's the main thing, I suppose.'

Solderburn opened the door and gestured to Ross to step inside.

'Go right on through, sir,' he said. 'Looks like you're in the barrel today.'

It was certainly no longer a cleaning cupboard. Gone were the crumbling grey plaster and the shelves of detergent. Instead it had been converted into a clinically white cell, so incongruous in Solderburn's lab that the doorway could have been a portal into a room in a completely different building. Upon first glance the walls and ceiling looked like they had been finished in a uniform gloss sheen, but close up Ross could see that all of the surfaces, including the floor, were lined with some kind of reflective panelling.

'You want me to take my shoes off?' he asked, concerned about stepping on to the immaculate surface in his outdoor footwear.

'No, long as there's no metal in them. Which reminds me: gotta take off your watch and your belt too.'

'No bother.'

Ross removed the items and handed them to Solderburn, who popped them into a bowl that may or may not have had a rinse-out since last containing breakfast cereal.

The scanner-bed took up most of the floor space, just a few inches of clearance either side and at the foot end, the head being tight to the wall. Instead of the familiar arch at the top, there were three twin-railed tracks at different heights and angles, upon each of which was mounted a single scanning head.

'You break it, you bought it,' Solderburn said as Ross lay gingerly down on the bed, slowly sliding his head into position beneath the hardware.

Solderburn withdrew and closed the door, which all but disappeared from view now that it was flush with the walls. Ross could make out the lines where it met the frame, but they were virtually indistinguishable from the gutters between tiling panels. The sound insulation was also comprehensive, the resonance in the tiny chamber altering immediately the door was closed. He could hear nothing at all from outside, his own breathing and the movement of his clothes suddenly amplified by the effect of having no ambient noise to interfere with them.

The sense of isolation was somehow calming and unsettling at the same time, like a form of seductive oblivion.

It was broken by Solderburn's voice coming in over a hidden speaker.

'All right, I'm just about good to go here. It's worth mentioning that you should probably try not to move too much, otherwise the lasers might sever your spine, but that hardly ever happens, so don't sweat it. Nah, seriously, dude, this is gonna take maybe a half-hour and I can't talk to you during that time because I can't send any signals in during the process, so close your eyes and chill. If you get freaked or nauseous, just bang on the door and I'll let you out. Otherwise just relax and I'll see you on the other side.'

Once More with Feeling

Bob was crouched at the rim of the escarpment, scanning his environment along the barrel of his laser rifle, his movements sharp and nervy. Multiple identical reincarnations had evidently granted no immunity to the development of what Vietnam veterans called the thousand-yard stare.

'Do you play video games at all?' Ross asked him. 'You know: first-person shooters?'

Bob looked around at him with confusion and some irritation, then seemed to understand. Wrongly, as it turned out.

'Oh, you mean like Call of Warfare and Battlefield Duty and what have you,' he said, which mis-namings Ross took as a no. 'Are you saying I'd have been better prepared? Fair comment, I suppose, though I'm learning fast through the real thing. No, the only thing I've played is golf on the Wii. Bought the console for the girls. Oh, God, the girls.'

He looked like he was about to cry, which on a face like his would be a sight to see.

'I miss them so much, and Gemma, their mum. They must be as scared about whatever's happened to me as I am about them. Laura is a born worrier at the best of times – such a considerate little girl – and the younger one, Wendy, just clamps on to me like a limpet when I come home at night.'

Now there really were tears. How the hell could there be tears? By the same token, how the hell could NPCs have names, personalities, values and even politics?

It didn't matter right now. What was more pertinent was that Ross clearly couldn't tell Bob what he had deduced. The guy had no frame of reference to understand it, and was holding on by his fingernails as it was. Bob had come to terms as best he could with the idea of being on some other planet, so telling him that he was actually inside a video game would either tip him over the edge or make him think Ross was the one plunging like Wile E. Coyote, head-down into insanity canyon.

'We'll get home,' Ross said, hoping he sounded more convincing to Bob than he did to himself. 'As you said, if there was a way for us to get here, there has to be a way back.'

Bob's eyes widened with a manic resolve.

'The space marines,' he said excitedly. 'They're Americans. If they got here, they can get us home. Unless it's a one-way mission,' he added, with equally manic despair. 'I saw a TV documentary once that said it would take centuries, even in a super-advanced spaceship, to reach the nearest star system hosting a potentially life-supporting planet. Oh, God, does that mean my family could have died hundreds of years ago?'

'Don't think that way,' Ross chivvied, racking his brains for some plausibly sciencey-sounding bullshit to shore up Bob's optimism. 'I heard one of the aliens talking about sub-space technology. They could be using a means of travel that transcends dimensional space, able to jump light years in a second.'

'But what about the marines' own technology? That's got to be from far into Earth's future.'

'Listen, we don't know anything about this place, so there's no point making any assumptions.'

'You're right,' Bob said, nodding frantically. 'You're right. I've got to keep it together. I owe it to Gemma, Laura and Wendy. I must never lose hope. I've got to be strong. They're what's going to get me through this. I'll be strong *for* them and I'll draw strength *from* them.'

Bob seemed to fill with determination right before Ross's eyes. It was an inspiring sight: witnessing someone galvanise himself with love, steeling himself to withstand anything through his feelings for his wife and daughters. So it was with a thoroughly crass sense of timing that a grenade happened to bounce its way to Bob's feet at that very moment and blew him to bits.

Bob absorbed most of the blast, with Ross only sustaining a minor whack to one of his armoured chest-plates and a temporary blinding by dust, smoke and a spray of wet matter. This last was both resultant of the chest blow and the explanation for why it was minor: one of Bob's hands had been blown off and impacted at high speed, splattering in a radius of clammy yuck that took in most of Ross's face.

Ross recovered from the shock in time to see a space marine charge forward, following up his grenade, a machine-gun in his hands. He wondered why the marine hadn't fired while he was reeling from the blast, then remembered that the marine NPCs' combat-AI was arguably even more shit than the Gralaks', given that their role at this point was to obligingly get themselves slaughtered.

Ross helped him fulfil his purpose with a single pulse from his rifle. He knew now that the marines were not his enemy, but he didn't really have the option to explain that to his wild-eyed assailant. Besides, he had just spotted where the largest part of Bob had landed and he wanted a quick word before he died. It would be difficult to give the guy his full attention while a battle-crazed but incompetent space marine was peppering his metal arse with implausibly intermittent bursts of machine-gun fire, and it would be fair to say that the inconvenience of peremptorily ending up in a completely different part of the map was not the thing that was worrying Ross most about getting killed. He would have to confess to a nagging worry that Bob might be mistaken or deluded about the whole coming-back-to-life thing. Plus it hurt.

Bob, or what was left of him, wasn't troubled by such doubts. His expression was one of irritation and embarrassment. His head and torso were lying against a big rock, looking a lot like an action figure Ross had owned as a kid, after Megan got hold of it during her 'battlefield surgery' phase; one she had arguably never grown out of. She was a consultant orthopaedic surgeon now. He hadn't seen her in months, and it suddenly occurred to him that he might never do so again.

'Sorry about this,' Bob said, rolling his eyes in self-reproach. It was like he'd shat himself or something.

'Can't be helped,' suggested Ross.

'I've not got long, and once I'm gone, don't wait for me to catch up. But if you make contact with the Americans first, make sure they know about me too.'

'Definitely,' Ross said. 'If either one of us finds a way out of here, we come back for the other. I'll get you back to your family: that's a promise.'

Uncomfortable as he was with such rituals, Ross nonetheless felt this was probably the kind of moment when it was appropriate for them to grip each other's fists. Unfortunately, as Bob didn't have one, it was moot. Then a second or so later it was even mooter, Bob having snuffed it.

His body faded and disappeared: classic *Starfire* style. It was so that your computer didn't get bogged down with needlessly drawing dozens of dead Gralaks during big fights. In *Starfire 2*, the Gralaks were smarter but less plentiful, so when they died they lay there and visibly rotted, a feature Ross was grateful not to see implemented here given that this Actual Reality version included smell.

Ross felt suddenly very bereft at Bob's absence. He had only known the guy a few minutes, and under any normal circumstances, there was every chance he'd have considered him a boring two-point-two-kids suburban stereotypical twat, but given that he was the person Ross currently had most in common with in the entire universe, it would be underselling it to say he had felt a bit of a connection.

He had also been genuinely moved by Bob's love for his family. It had made Ross feel that he, too, couldn't give in to despair while he had a responsibility to Carol and their unborn child, as well as a responsibility to help this man get back home. Putting aside the thought that this cast him in the role of the nobly self-sacrificing unmarried guy who in the audience's eyes is expendable to the greater cause of the family man, he gripped his gun and ventured onwards.

In truth, Ross had gone along with what Bob was saying in order to keep him on an even keel. He personally felt there was little point in trying to contact the Americans. They were just blundering NPCs and their spaceships didn't come from anywhere: they just spawned in the sky and got shot down by the giant boabby-shaped blaster.

Then he remembered his own bullshit, offered to Bob to offset his panic: *we don't know anything about this place, so there's no point making any assumptions.* This was *Starfire* for sure, but *Starfire* made real. The way home, the way out of whatever this was, could be to get on one of their ships. It might equally require battling through every level and defeating the final boss, but either way, the primary step was to play nice with the space marines.

Initiating this was going to be problematic, as illustrated by what had just happened to Bob. It was kind of difficult to get close enough to have a conversation without being shot first. If only there was some other way of demonstrating – non-verbally and unequivocally – that he was on their side.

Then he heard a voice call out aggressively to him from amid the smoke ahead.

'Recruit! Where in a swamp-slug's suppurating ring-piece have *you* been?' it demanded.

Ross stiffened to attention and saluted. He managed to prevent the spike from shooting out too, a feat that he found easier than keeping the delight off his face as a plan formed in his mind.

'Reporting for duty, Sergeant Gortoss, sir.'

'About bloody time. Got just the job for you.'

Ross ascended to the rim of the next blast-crater, where this time he was considerably less appalled to see the same two space marines quivering on their knees under the guard of Sergeant Zorlak and his unit. Now he knew why they alone were being held captive while their shipmates were being gibbed left, right and centre. The inconsistency was to facilitate a scripted set-piece.

'Get a bloody move on. These bastards aren't going to kill *themselves* you know.'

'Absolutely, sir,' Ross replied, while Gortoss muttered to Zorlak about this thumb-sucking toddler having traded his rattle for a blaster.

'Would you like me to execute them for you, Sergeant Gortoss, sir?' Ross asked brightly.

'No, I'd like you to suck their cocks.'

'That's a very unorthodox last request, sir. I'm told it is Gaian tradition to permit condemned men merely a final cigarette.'

Gortoss turned to Zorlak with a despairing look, as if to say: See what I'm saddled with?

'Just bloody execute them. I want to see if you're worth a shit, because if you're not made of the right stuff, I can't afford any baggage out here.'

'It would be my pleasure, sir. Far more so than the suggested cock-sucking. But I have to inform you that my rifle has been malfunctioning, and request that I may borrow yours.'

Gortoss handed over his weapon with impatient bad grace. He had enjoyed this more the last time when he suspected the recruit didn't have the stomach for the kill. It was going to end much the same way, though.

'Thank you, sir. I will now show you what you are made of.'

'I said what *you're* ma—' Gortoss began to correct him, only for Ross to correct Gortoss by disembowelling him with his spike while simultaneously blowing Zorlak's head off with the rifle.

The rest of Rapier and Cutlass squads didn't fare any better than before, Ross taking them down far faster than the card collector had managed, despite having less firepower. Clearly a noob, whoever he was. This was a Nineties shooter, for God's sake: all it took was a bit of circle-strafing.

He did take a hit in the midst of it though, which felt rather different from seeing a brief flash of white on the screen and his health meter depleting. More like the searing agony he remembered when he'd electrocuted himself at uni attempting to make a self-guiding vacuum-cleaner for the electronics club's robotics competition. Then, as now, there was sudden, paralysing pain, a noise in his head like somebody trying to drill their way out of it, and a horrible burning odour that became all the more disgusting once he realised it was his own flesh.

As the last of the corpses melted into nothingness, he wondered why Bob (he hoped) kept respawning, while the Gralak NPCs stayed dead unless the level was restarted. Same as his and Bob's ability to see the power-ups, he guessed. The pair of them had Gralak bodies, but they were something different, something more. Their very presence was altering the game, in fact. Gralak grunts going rogue and helping out the space marines wasn't in the script. So what else might he be able to change?

He returned to the two captured marines, both of them looking up at him with even greater gormless confusion than friendly NPCs normally did when they were waiting for your action to drive the story. Then he realised that this was because they still weren't sure of his intentions: for all they knew it could have been an internecine feud rather than an act of outright mutiny.

He had to put them straight, and he had to give it the right ring of authentically macho bollocks so that they would grasp the situation quickly.

'The fight-back starts here,' Ross said, dropping his voice an octave. 'Let me get those restraints off you gentlemen.'

It sounded pretty good, and the looks on their faces suggested his tone had hit that sweet spot somewhere between Jesus and arrogant wanker that Americans seemed to respond to so well. He detracted a little from the effect by spending about five minutes trying to suss how the glowing orange handcuffs worked, but redeemed his image by giving up and using the rotating blade thingy on the end of his spike that had done such a sterling job of pureeing Kamnor's face.

'I'm Sergeant Raven,' said the older of the marines. 'This is Corporal Stone. USMC, out of Starbase Kuiper IV.'

Ross could hear those Roman numerals.

'Who *are* you?' Raven asked, looking gratifyingly awestruck.

'I was a colonist,' Ross replied. Even less wise playing the truth card here than with Bob, he figured. 'They took me, and they tried to make me one of them, but inside I was still me. And now I'm going to make them pay. In blood. And steel.'

Jesus, this was embarrassing. Why not add: 'And, you know, that greeny-yellow stuff that also comes out of them'?

It seemed to be doing the trick, though.

'Our landing forces are in disarray,' said Raven. 'But a forward operations base was covertly established in advance. It is imperative that we get you there. Your intel on the enemy will be invaluable.'

Ross knew exactly where they meant, having fought his way there a dozen times before, not to mention clocking up about a hundred hours on the capture-the-flag multiplayer version of the map. He didn't fancy the marines' chances of getting there though, and if they couldn't vouch for him when he reached it then he'd be back to square one.

'Is it far?'

'About two clicks north-east,' Raven replied.

'Through the canyon,' said Ross gravely. 'The Gralaks would pick us off before we made it a hundred yards. But if I was alone, they wouldn't suspect anything.'

Raven grinned, getting it.

'I'll radio ahead, let them know you're coming. What's your name?'

'My name is . . .'

Ross stopped himself. Stay in character, he thought, and not just so that the NPCs believed in him. *He* needed to also. He thought back to those CTF games, his clan days, owning the map despite his laggy 36k dial-up connection. In this place, he was never Ross Baker, socially awkward weedy med-student. He was known on servers far and wide by a different handle.

He hefted his rifle to his chest and struck a suitably cover-art pose.

'They call me Bedlam,' he said.

Digital Rights Management

Zac watched her car arrive from the atrium lobby, congratulating himself for correctly guessing that she'd be driving a retro-styled E-Prius. It was the new-model VW Beetle of the era, the luxury vehicle of choice for people who thought they were making a statement about their integrity by referencing a ride synonymous with the trendy values of an earlier age. Like all holders of trendy values, the fact that this statement would principally be legible to like-minded people was more of a bonus than a concern. It was legible to sharper minds too, though: minds such as his, which could tell how self-righteously full of shit they all were.

He had stood there waiting less than a minute. He knew almost to the second when she would arrive, updated in real time even as to which parking space she had been allocated. The security systems had been tracking her since her vehicle crossed their unseen perimeter, which actually began half a mile beyond the signpost where visitors thought they were officially entering the expanses of Neurosphere's sprawling California campus.

There were two intimidatingly huge Essedari-class armoured vehicles patrolling the compounds, and a phalanx of Retiarii at the barrier where she had to show her credentials. They were there to be noticed, but only partly as a deterrent; their greater role was in disguising from visitors that it was the technology they *couldn't* see that was truly ensuring the campus's security.

She stared right past him as she sought out the reception desk, looking for where she should report to. He liked that. It would play nicely when she realised, even better than the fact that he had come to greet her personally.

'Juliet Li?' he called out, causing her to turn on her heel.

He enjoyed the moment of double-take as she recognised who had addressed her.

'Isaac Michaels. Oh my God, I'm sorry. I didn't expect . . . I thought there'd be assistants and secretaries and security and waiting and . . .'

'Oh, we can lay on all of that if you'd prefer, but for now it's just me. You should call me Zac. It only says Isaac on official stuff, you know, like share quarterly statements and subpoenas. Can I get you a coffee, or you wanna head straight to my evil corporate lair?'

She laughed, already disarmed, already warming. He could read the first paragraph of her interview in her smile.

He was good at this part, he knew. It was a chore, but it was one that rewarded the effort. Companies spent millions per year on public relations, the majority of it on fire-fighting, but a little human contact with the right people in the media could be worth ten times as much in making sure those fires never got going.

'I try to make myself as accessible as my commitments allow,' he explained, walking her to the elevators. 'I'm not gonna pretend I make myself available for every journalist who wants an interview, but when I do make myself available, I like to be *actually* available, you know? Not chaperoned by a PR guy who's vetting *your* questions and *my* answers.'

'I appreciate that. I'm actually pretty surprised to be doing this in person, face to face, in this day and age. I can't tell you the last time I did anything other than a virtual interview.'

There was just a teasing hint of her ethnic background in her accent, but otherwise she sounded as Californian as the OJ he'd just had with breakfast.

'Well, I'm grateful for you making the trip out here to Silicon Valley. Some would think it ironic to be doing it analogue, given the business we're in, but in fact I think it just makes genuine human contact all the more imperative, especially when you're in my job. A faceless entity is perceived as an unaccountable entity, and that makes people wary. You can't ascribe values to some nebulous corporation, so by extension you're not going to ascribe it a conscience either. People need to be able to associate human names and personalities with companies in order to engender trust, and given what they're entrusting to us . . .'

She nodded her understanding, a sincere look on her attractive young face as he spoke.

It wasn't all bullshit either, but in truth that face was the main reason she wasn't doing this from her office. Smooth skin, that petite little Asian frame, and all of it genuinely her, all of it original flesh: yeah, he could make himself available to gaze at that with the naked eye for an hour or so. He looked her up and down as the elevator sped to the executive floor. It was harder and harder to judge as the decades passed, but he wouldn't put her at a day over twenty-five. No replacements, no augmentations. One hundred per cent natural. He remembered hearing people say that the older you got, the more you wanted to be around youth. How much more true was that these days? They were like another goddamn species in an era when you measured your years not in greys and wrinkles, but in how much of your original body was still attached.

He'd chosen carefully, and not just in terms of the pretty young journalist who was being granted an interview, but, more importantly, in terms of which outlet she worked for. The article would get cascaded all over the globe within minutes of going live, regardless of who published it, but that just made the imprimatur all the more important. No point going with something too 'establishment' and business-friendly, like the *Wall Street Journal*, nor with any outfit that might be perceived as offering a tame fanboy geek-out or a human-interest easy ride. *Lightning Rod* was therefore ideal: it was sufficiently progressive and issue-conscious that anything short of a hatchet job would play as an endorsement of his – and by extension Neurosphere's – integrity, yet small enough that Li would be wary of blowing the big scoop and souring future relations by trying to hardball him.

The elevator doors slid open and they emerged into a glass-walled antechamber beyond which lay the office suites of the executive level. A green laser beam took a three-dimensional image of each of them as they approached an iris scanner sited on a hydraulic pedestal that automatically adjusted to the eye level of each subject. Both of these measures were largely for show, and the true value of the iris scanner was that it forced the subjects to stand still for a moment while an unseen cloud of nanites microscopically sampled and cross-checked their DNA.

'After you,' he said, taking the opportunity to perform his own little scan of Li's butt as she approached the pedestal.

He caught her casting a wary eye over the two heavily armoured Andabatae guards standing ready to intervene should anyone's credentials not come up to snuff.

'Your security is, er, I guess robust would be the word,' she said as he took his turn at the iris scanner. 'Terrifying might be another.'

'I'd prefer "intimidating", or maybe "conspicuous",' he replied. 'Conspicuous more so, because it works two ways. One, the obvious: to deter intrusion; but the other, just as important, is to spur our own vigilance. Whenever any of us sees our security measures, it should be a constant reminder that what we're protecting here is more valuable than any material wealth on the planet.'

'Is it true that your security's class and identification system is based on Roman gladiators?'

Zac laughed, careful to make it sound bashful rather than proud, then gave her his best little-boy-caught look.

'Yeah. It's cool though, isn't it? You have to admit it's more interesting than just numeric codes or phonetic alphabet designations.'

'Whose idea was that?'

He held up a hand with calculated sheepishness.

'Gotta fess up to that one. It all started when we equipped the security guards with these high-velocity net-launchers. I've always been a big advocate of non-lethal enforcement methods. They got extra armour to compensate for the fact we took away their guns, so between that and the nets I said to the head of security we should call them Retiarii. I guess it gets you more chicks to say you're a Retiarius than a security guard, so it caught on and kinda grew from there.'

'Boys and their toys,' she said, with an amused roll of her eyes.

Score, he thought, confident her encounter with military-level hardware had just been successfully spun. She'd write a patronising but crucially harmless-sounding take on the overgrown kids beneath the Neurosphere executives' suits.

He let her take in the view from his corner suite for a while, then led her to one of the antique *chaise-longues* beneath the windows, taking his own rest at its partner. His secretary brought coffee and Danishes, her withdrawal the cue that they could begin the interview proper. Li got out a small data recorder and placed it on the table next to the plates. The use of the ancient-looking and conspicuous device was a formal gesture that they were on the record now, like her getting out a Dictaphone or a notepad.

She was undoubtedly aware that every word and move was already being recorded by unseen means so that there was an indisputable record of their encounter. What she was less likely to know was that the true extent of the remote monitoring included her heart rate, fluctuations in her body temperature and, of course, brainwave patterns, and all of this was being relayed to him in real time, superimposed upon his field of vision like a heads-up display.

He would know when she was apprehensive and when she was feeling relaxed. He'd know when she was likely to be lying, or merely being disingenuous, trying to disguise her agenda. He'd know when he was going down well, when she was finding him too forthright, when she considered him aloof, and he could amend his answers accordingly. She would leave this building thinking only good thoughts about him and about Neurosphere.

'So,' she said, '*Zac* Michaels, CEO of Neurosphere. You've been with the company since the early twenty-first century, you've risen through the ranks and ultimately taken the helm, and your hand has been on the tiller during some truly remark-able times. I'm gonna warm you up with some soft pitches and start by asking: what do you consider your greatest achievement? What would you say you're most proud of?'

'Memento Mori,' he replied, in less than a heartbeat. He hadn't needed any real-time bio-feedback to know the right answer to that one, though he did get instant data confirming a hit.

'Is there anyone in your family . . . ?' he prompted.

'My grandpa, yes,' she replied, nodding sincerely. 'My great uncle too. It's meant a lot, especially to Grandma, and to my mom. And to me and my brothers. Okay, to everybody, but obviously the closer you are, the greater the need.'

'Absolutely, and that's what I'm so proud of. Every company wants to create something that will fill a need, whether that's a cure for cancer or just breath mints. I'm not saying we're right there alongside the first of those, but I like to think we're closer to it than to the second, in terms of the scale of human need. To be able to provide what we have done, for so many people . . . it's my greatest source of pride but it's also the most humbling thing in my life too.'

'Some people would go as far as to say Memento Mori has changed how we think about death, or at least about bereavement. Would you go along with that?'

He took a moment to think about it. Her readings indicated she was neutral on this: content for the discussion to go this way if he took it there, but he was wary of being perceived to be talking too proprietorially about something that was, after all, down to other people's innovations. The only thing he wanted to do less than turn a spotlight on Ross Baker was to remind the general public about the company's long-term connections to that basket-case Jay Solomon. Solderburn, they used to call him, but Solderburn-out seemed closer to the truth.

Best to steer her towards territory where he was less ambiguously identifiable as the one who had made the play.

'I wouldn't say it's changed the way we think about death. But I would say it's changed how we think about consciousness.'

'That's putting it mildly,' she agreed, growing animated. This was always going to be the money-shot, as far as she and Lightning Rod were concerned; his role in the great debate of the age. 'It's changed how we legislate for consciousness, and that's largely down to your championing of digital rights.'

He allowed himself a wistful laugh as he looked to the heavens, gathering his thoughts.

'I'm old enough to remember when digital rights legislation meant stopping teenagers cloning each other's music collections,' he quipped, but the real joke was him getting credit for being forced on to the side of a crusade he'd actually been bitterly opposed to, and the eventual success of which he privately cursed every day of his life.

Every. Fucking. Day.

'What made you take up this cause? I mean, clearly this was

82

a debate that must have been going on inside Neurosphere before the rest of the world had even heard about DCs.'

'Well, I just thought that as we were on the verge of tapping untold revenue streams and in a position to start forging alliances at the highest echelons of every major government on the planet, the obvious way to proceed was to voluntarily cut off our own balls, put them in our mouths and choke on them,' he didn't say.

No. Instead he gave a carefully constructed but seemingly extemporaneous ramble about ethics and scientific progress. He talked about how we shouldn't always end up having the Frankenstein debates *after* the technology is loose; he enthused about the way the cutting edge of technology brings you up against the cutting edge of morality; he explained how it was incumbent upon Neurosphere to make sure people understood the level of respect the company accorded to its subjects, otherwise they'd never get their first customer. And in case that all sounded a little too warm and fuzzy, he admitted that the legislation did help protect their own position against unlawful proliferation of their technology, not to mention indemnifying them against lawsuits.

And all of this was true, all of these were reasons he agreed with. The problem was that added together they came nowhere near to justifying what they had forced Neurosphere to forgo.

When he was trying to be philosophical about it, he'd muse that 'he giveth and he taketh away'. He being Ross Baker, leading architect of the technology and leading advocate of the digital rights cause.

Behind the scenes Zac had tried his absolute best to hamstring Baker's efforts. However, it became obvious as soon as the debate went public that there was only one way it was going to go. That was when he decided that the best damage-limitation strategy was for Neurosphere to be posturing as pioneers of the new legislation, rather than appearing as the entity most conspicuously needing to be constrained by it. This at least meant they had a strong hand in framing the new laws, but to Zac that didn't amount to much more than getting to add a soft velvet lining to their handcuffs.

It was Baker who made the argument that the legislation

would protect their own intellectual property and guarantee their exclusive position in the new market. This must have sounded very convincing to anybody naïve enough to believe that other people would actually stick to these rules.

'Of course, this kind of legislation is meaningless unless it's internationally applied and enforced,' Li said. 'And you've been aggressive in shutting down illegal operations worldwide.'

Oh yeah. We're very effective at raiding back-street chop-shops in Beijing and Mumbai while ten blocks away their governments have entire server-farms that don't officially exist and about which we can do nothing.

'We make no apologies for how aggressive we've been in that sphere,' he told her. 'Once you've accepted DC for what it is, you can see the potential for abuse is enormous. We're the ones who let the genie out of the bottle, so we have to be the ones making sure everybody is protected.'

'It's long been the case that the first modified application of any new technology is as a weapon. The military must have been banging on your door, and must have been pretty frustrated when digital rights effectively locked it shut.'

Not as frustrated as I was, sweet tits. And they're still banging on the door, letting me know they're ready to deal just as soon as a loop-hole can be found.

'Well, first of all I think that the first modified application of any new *digital* technology is usually porn.'

She suppressed a laugh, but it took some effort. He knew this because all the other indicators were reading hit, hit, hit.

'We're not interested in dealing with the military, believe me. We're all about keeping people together, not helping armies tear them apart. Never forget, we're a company that built its reputation developing neurological scanning equipment for hospitals, and that side of our business still accounts for over forty per cent of our turnover worldwide. But what the Memento Mori project has taught us is that ultimately the parts of the brain that matter most to people are those governing memories and emotions.'

And didn't he goddamn know it. That was why the digital rights issue became an unstoppable juggernaut as soon as it entered the public domain. Never mind the Bostrom simulation argument and all that humbug about do unto others. People talked about the golden rule and the things they wouldn't want happening to themselves, but in truth they couldn't imagine it. However, make them think about dear ole grandma suddenly finding herself holding an M16 with a tank bearing down on her ass and it becomes a no-brainer.

'That's why it's a mistake to think that the military would be first in line to exploit this,' he said. 'Or even the most dangerous. Politicians, governments, any kind of opinion-forming or marketing entity would view it as the perfect tool.'

'I know you won't name names, but would it be accurate to say that they've made their solicitations?'

Oh my, hadn't they just. He only had to look at the list of organisations and individuals that were staying in close orbit despite the apparently intractable legal position to appreciate the influence Neurosphere might wield but for these cursed laws.

It was so tantalising to know that all it would take was a few thousand to provide a wide enough sampling, then it could be duplicated at will. A measly few thousand: was that so much to ask? Neurosphere had given the world an invaluable gift; didn't it owe them such a tiny little slice in return, especially as they were only talking about some ones and fucking zeroes?

So, so tantalising: a couple of thousand, maybe less. He knew they could have garnered that much cumulatively from the raids on the aforementioned chop-shops, but it was way too risky. All it took was one leak, even an allegation, and the PR fallout would be catastrophic. He'd have to fall on his sword and it would take years for his successor to repair the damage.

'Like you say, I won't name names,' he replied, but he gave her a knowing smile by way of answering her question in the affirmative.

She shifted on her seat, her posture more relaxed, tucking one perfectly turned ankle behind the other. From the read-outs he interpreted that he was giving good, straight copy so far, but she was about to take it into more frivolous, gossipy territory.

'I appreciate the development of Memento Mori is highly classified, but is there anything juicy you can divulge about how it all came about? You know, like, is there an antique hard drive somewhere full of crusty prototypes? Did anybody almost burn the lab down one night when they stayed late with a bottle of tequila?'

He drew upon decades of experience in order to maintain a neutral expression, concealing first a moment of heart-thumping revelation and then a crashing wave of adrenaline-laced excitement and delight. All that the girl got to see was a mercurial grin she would probably ascribe to him quickly censoring out some x-rated anecdotes from the old days before answering her question.

This seemed scant reward, considering she had just handed him the keys to the kingdom.

It was still running, last he was aware, and, given everything that had been fought for, there was no way Baker would have allowed it to be shut down.

It had been there all along, and only a select few at Neurosphere were ever even aware of its existence. Nobody outside the firm would ever know, and the best bit was, even if they found out, his action would not be in contravention of any laws.

'Or I guess that should be whisky, shouldn't it?' she went on. 'Because, according to my research, the whole thing started when you were working in Scotland.'

He nodded, channelling the warmth he was suddenly feeling into a single word.

'Stirling.'

Higher Powers

The canyon was a maze of narrow channels confined by high rocky walls that stretched twenty metres in near-vertical ascent. He recognised parts of it, allowing for its real-life rendering, but even in its software form he had found large stretches of it disorientingly indistinct. One brown section of rock tended to look a lot like another, especially in the blocky geometry of the original *Starfire* engine. Here the stone looked shaped by geological forces and aeons of natural erosion, but the layout was just as he remembered.

There were parts that would take him along ledges, into caves and even through pools, something he really wasn't looking forward to until he started to feel the heat from climbing. Back in the day, there had been an odd glitch in the game that meant you could do this double-jump trick on the edge of a rock that would propel you a height disproportionate to your efforts. It was a handy shortcut to higher ledges that the level designers hadn't intended you to reach without first negotiating other parts of the landscape. Ross tried it when he reached a suitable spot, the impulse coming almost instinctively as soon as he realised he was in a place he recognised. He succeeded only in repeatedly rattling his thankfully metal-clad shins off the edge of a low outcrop and falling on his face a few times. If anybody had been looking, they'd have assumed his internal motivational and guidance circuitry was on the fritz. Or that he was a twat.

Fortunately the only possible witnesses were Slurgs, the cave-dwelling enemies that infested this section of the game, and they weren't in much of a position to cast judgment. They were squat, slimy, troll-like specimens, as vicious as they were stupid, and they were considered such a disgusting lower life-form that even the Gralaks drew the line at processing them for body parts. They were long-armed and pot-bellied homunculi, cadaverously pale but with thick oily black hair on their near-neckless heads and a permanent expression of confused indignation on their venom-spitting faces.

They were annoying rather than particularly dangerous; proof that your heart really wasn't in it that day if one of them managed to kill you. Wading through their numbers made this section an ammo-depleting chore rather than a challenge, and Ross had originally considered the canyon his least-favourite section of the game. That was until he was replaying the game in his student flat one night and it suddenly struck him that the Slurgs all looked like Richard Littlejohn. He subsequently got hold of some appropriate sound samples and hacked the game to replace the corresponding audio files. As a result, instead of their limited repertoire of grunts and shrieks, they spouted Littlejohn's limited repertoire of bollocks.

'Guardianistas!'

'Political correctness gone mad!'

'You couldn't make it up!'

That transformed it into one of his favourite sections, as blasting their revolting little populist-drivel-spouting bodies to a squidgy pulp never got old.

They were ignoring him today though, scurrying away whenever they saw him coming. This, he presumed, was because he was in Gralak form and not the lone-hero space marine whom the game had programmed them to attack on sight. From what he saw of them, these incarnations didn't resemble Littlejohn other than in as much as they were still physically repellent and clearly had a strong bias towards the indigenous population.

This latter disposition was just as well, given that Ross didn't have the ammunition to fight them all off if they decided violence was the only language he understood. The read-out on his rifle was down to single figures, a depletion that owed itself to his experimentation with the fabric of the landscape. He had encountered another crate and, still being unable to open it, he'd decided to see how it responded to some blasting. The answer was not at all, as he belatedly realised had already been demonstrated by his fight with the card collector. He had hidden behind a crate during that battle, and no amount of volleys from the collector's otherwise devastating weapon had had any impact.

Ross had fired a few shots into the canyon walls and the ground beneath his feet. His blasts failed to inflict the slightest damage, nor did several hefty jabs with the butt of his weapon or the spike in his arm. Same as it ever was in *Starfire*, the landscape was non-destructible, with the presumable exception of parts that were designated so, such as the section of corridor the fuselage crashed into and the occasional crack in the wall concealing a secret area.

It was when he put this presumption to the test that he discovered the greater price of his profligacy in firing off so many shots into the scenery.

He came to a familiar fissure in the rock. The jagged crack looked more authentically like the result of stress and pressure than a mere texture from the map-designer's palette, but as Ross had just emerged from the longest of the subterranean pools, it was exactly where he expected it to be. A sustained burst of fire caused a section of rock to collapse and crumble, revealing a shallow crevice behind it where Ross knew he would find a double-barrelled shotgun and a couple of grenades. Sure enough, there they were: the pineapples sitting on the ground and the shotgun rotating impossibly in the air. However, when Ross moved to collect the items, he passed through them, just like the health power-up.

Denied.

The 'secret area' was intentionally hard to miss, firstly so that a new player would grasp the concept of revealing such hidden caches, but just as importantly because it was a tough task to complete the level without the new weapon. It wasn't the Slurgs that were the problem: you could take them out with a blaster. It was that there was a long and exposed stretch of ground just before the entrance to the hidden base, where a massive horde of Gralaks lay hidden in preparation for ambush. This didn't merely include the likes of Gortoss and Zorlak, but provided the game's first glimpse of the more dangerous enemies to come.

What they lacked in AI they made up for in sheer numbers and in the superior power of their weapons. Ross remembered many deaths and rage-quits during his early days, the gradient of the learning curve steepening dramatically for the finale to this opening map. (The heightened difficulty was actually a hangover from the free demo released in advance on magazine cover-discs to promote the game, the developers upping the ante at the end of the level so that you'd feel so pleased with yourself for completing it that you'd be desperate to pit your m4d sk1llz against the full version.)

Ross approached the end of the narrow rocky channel on nervous feet. The canyon walls widened out before a small river, but he knew that, from this perspective, the seemingly flush walls concealed several hidden passages, out of which the Gralak hordes would come pouring when the player reached a certain spot. The big question was whether he, in his non-player form, would trigger it.

He could see his goal now, on the near bank of the river, where a huge inlet pipe was covered by a damaged grille. A brief sewer section (still acceptable in those days) followed, populated by a few last Slurgs, then he'd be up a ladder and into the hidden base.

Several dozen reloads had taught him where that crucial point was, almost to the pixel, but it wasn't so easy to gauge when he was looking at real rocks, sky and dust. He slowed his pace as he neared the spot where he estimated the trigger line to be. He feared his approach would be conspicuously tentative, then he realised such conspicuousness didn't matter. Any Gralaks spying from cover would be as oblivious to the purpose of his movements as had they been witness to his pointless double-jump attempts back in the canyon. Actually, he hoped some of them *had* seen that, as it might put them off their shot if they were still pissing themselves laughing.

Forward he edged, short step by short step, but there was no response. He kept cautioning himself that this might be because he still hadn't come far enough, but eventually he turned around and saw that he was well inside what was normally the killing zone.

He risked a glance to either side and from this angle could see dozens of Gralaks staring back, motionless but alert, from their hiding places. He made brief eye-contact with one of the big tank-class buggers, and even in its largely metal face it was easy to read the question: What the fuck are you doing?

In that moment, however, he realised he was safe. They wouldn't advance, wouldn't even acknowledge him, because they were under orders to hold their concealed positions until their enemy arrived. In his Gralak guise, they would ignore him as long as he ignored them back and quietly went on his way.

Deal, he thought, and kept going.

It had worked, just like he'd told Raven and Stone it would. Not counting his failed experiments at remodelling, he had made it all the way through the canyon without having to fire a shot. Until, that was, a platoon of space marines came pouring from the inlet pipe and began beckoning him towards them.

'Are you the rogue Gralak?' one of them called out, just in case the onlooking forces hadn't quite caught the significance of their entreaties. 'We're here to escort you inside.'

Oh, you utter glans.

'Come on. This place is crawling with Gralak forces.'

Yeah, thanks for the exclusive, Ross thought. A fraction of a second later, the very ground was warping with bludgeon-pulses from the tank-class Gralaks, scattering marines like bowling pins and making them even easier targets than usual for the infantry to mop up with laser weapons.

Ross began sprinting back towards the narrow part of the canyon, randomly zigzagging to avoid fire. He was caught in the splash damage from a bludgeon-pulse, sending him rolling like a tin can and his vision spinning in a dizzying blur. He managed to climb to his knees and fire off his final few rounds, taking out a paltry two grunts, the rest of his blasts merely tickling the tanks' thick hides or missing altogether.

His trigger had barely clicked on empty before he endured that electrocution sensation of a direct hit from a laser weapon, which knocked him flat again. Another hit came hard on its heels, then he felt the entire world suddenly halt. He couldn't move, the hordes ahead of him also being frozen like statues. Time was standing still.

This was it, he thought: the moment of truth. He'd been fragged, and death was upon him. Now the big question was whether it really was the end, or would he be respawned? And if so, where?

91

Then he saw movement, like a dark curtain coming down in the sky. Oh, how unnecessarily bloody theatrical, he thought.

But it wasn't a curtain, it was a console. Text appeared, printing out from left to right.

```
/Set 'Godmode' = TRUE

/Set 'Giveallweaps' = TRUE
```

He still couldn't move, not even his eyes, but to the left of his field of vision he now noticed the card collector, standing there holding the game's ultimate weapon. The player didn't get access to it until the final few levels of *Starfire*, unless he brought down the console and keyed in some cheat codes, which was exactly what had just happened. In the blurb it was officially named the GraxiTron Flow gun, a backronym created to explain (or excuse) its abbreviated handle: the GTF.

Two more lines of type flowed across the sky.

```
Take cover

Unknown command 'Take cover'
```

The curtain scrolled back up and the world came instantly back to life, the sounds of battle all the more ear-splitting for the brief lapse into silence. The card collector stood in front of Ross, shielding him from further fire as he retreated towards the cover of the rocky channels. Not that there was much fire to shield him from after a few seconds: the Gralak hordes had been very quickly persuaded to GTF. It was a weapon intended for use against the colossal enemies of the game's finale, so its effect against this shower from the opening map was like that of a water-cannon on a litter of new-born kittens.

All things considered, it was quite a volte-face from giving him the finger.

'Thank you,' Ross said. 'I owe you one. My name is Bedlam. Who are you?'

The card collector said nothing, seemingly implacable behind that visor.

'Can you hear me?' Ross tried again, waving in his face.

The card collector began sidestepping along in front of Ross, weapons and ammo arcing out from him like bunches of flowers from a magician's sleeve. It was one of the features that had made *Starfire* multiplayer such an enjoyable team game: you could toss spare weapons to your comrades, as good for bonding as it was for controlling the resources of a map. Unfortunately, Ross was in no position to take advantage of the collector's largesse, as he demonstrated by standing uselessly in the middle of a rocket-launcher.

The console came down again, and this time Ross realised it was actually in his own field of vision, not the sky itself.

```
shit soz brb

Unknown command 'shit soz brb'
```

Soz? Brb? What was this, 1998? Had he gone back in time after all?

'Press T to talk,' Ross wanted to say, but he couldn't talk, couldn't move, could only watch.

He saw a blur of code scroll before his eyes, then the console retreated and he was released from stasis once more. In his hands, his empty rifle had transformed into the rocket-launcher he'd been standing in. It was bulkier, the weight and substance of it palpable, yet it seemed no heavier to his arms than the laser rifle.

'Thank you,' he said again, to no visible response from that blank visor. Ross then waved to the heavens and shouted it: 'THANK YOU. WHO ARE YOU?'

```
Can't hear you

Unknown command 'Can't hear you'
```

'T,' Ross shouted, making a corresponding gesture with his fingers once the console had unfrozen him again. 'Don't key your chat messages into the console.'

He was aiming the gesture at the sky, as though offering it to the gods, when he realised that no matter where he was, the player's viewpoint was still that from the card collector's helmet.

A line of text then appeared before his eyes, eyes that like the rest of his body this time remained free to go where they wished.

```
Player: T for talk. Thank you.
```

You got it, Ross thought. Pity you didn't go into the multi-player settings and amend the default name. Who the hell are you? And how can somebody be running scripts and cheat codes but not know it's T for talk?

```
Player: And it's I for this, yes?
```

The card collector gave him a wave with his right hand.

With a measure of embarrassment, Ross very belatedly deduced what all that aggressive taunting had really been about the first time they crossed paths. The card collector had flipped him the bird, thrust his crotch and given him the 'come ahead' stance. Ross understood now that the player had been randomly pressing gesture keys, trying to find the one for a friendly wave in order to convey his intentions. He had even hit it at one point, but perhaps in his frantic efforts failed to note which key had prompted the desired effect, and at the time Ross had interpreted it as deeply sarcastic.

The card collector had been trying to hail him all along. This meant that even before his rescue of the prisoners, the player knew Ross wasn't a Gralak.

Finally, a chance to get some answers. The problem was how to ask the questions. Ross took the end of the rocket launcher and began scratching in the dust: *How do I get out of here?*

He looked up to make sure the player could make out the writing. The card collector stood there unmoving. A good sign, Ross reckoned: hands on keyboard, rather than controlling movement.

A minute or so passed with still no movement and still no text. It was going to be a long response. He just hoped he could read it all before it vanished. Shit, if only he could tell the guy to break it up into short lines.

A minute or so became five, maybe ten. Ross waved his arms in front of the card collector, then pointed again at the message.

Okay, not maybe ten; easily ten.

No. Please, no.

But Ross knew what he was looking at.

AFK: away from keyboard. The player wasn't there any more.

Fuck. Piss. Bollocks.

He really shouldn't have got his hopes up. The way things were going since getting up this morning – Christ, was it even morning? – chances were the person he imagined might be his saviour was actually some ten-year-old kid who'd just been told to get off the computer because Daddy needed it to look up porn.

Looked like he'd have to take his chances with the space marines after all, but at least he'd be tooled up from now on.

He walked across to the bobbing, spinning arsenals, starting with the GTF and working his way down that familiar array. He could remember the keybinds for each one, starting with 0 for the GTF, 9 for the proton cannon, 8 for the plasma rifle . . . Each hologram he stepped into caused the device he was holding to transform, and it was only as he reached the last that it occurred to him to ponder how one switched back to the preceding, more powerful weapon without the use of a keyboard.

The word 'Fuuuuuuuuuuuuuuuuck!' echoed all around the canyon, still reverberating as he clutched the crappy single-barrelled shotgun and trudged off huffily towards the hidden base.

Cloudburst

The first indication something was wrong had been the sight of Zac Michaels in the R&D building, an area of Neurosphere's vast California campus that Ross wasn't sure the oily bastard could have found on the map. Michaels so seldom ventured beyond the glass towers of the central HQ building that Ross could go weeks at a time without seeing him in person, a state of affairs that he knew both parties considered satisfactory. He'd turned up with a small but elite delegation of personnel, including chief programmer Venkat Amritraj, whom Zac was grooming for Ross's position whenever he finally retired or whenever the CEO could engineer some other means of getting him out of the door.

They had swept in and cleared the entire third floor without giving anybody any notice, never mind the courtesy of an explanation. They posted Andabatae units on the doors, the faceless sentinels preventing Ross from even being able to ask the intruders what they were doing commandeering a facility he was nominally in charge of. Ross had called security and been told all he needed to know in just three words: Special Projects Division.

SPD was Zac Michaels' contemptuously transparent way of bypassing Ross's jurisdiction: a research and development team that was completely unaccountable to the head of Research and Development. It might strike most people – and perhaps most shareholders – as a pointless duplication of efforts and waste of resources, but anything that marginalised Ross was worth every cent as far as Zac was concerned. If SPD developed something independently of his department, then Ross had no say over its future, and the more projects that was true of, the closer Zac could nudge him towards the door.

Ross had just shrugged his shoulders, left them to it and gone off to grab some lunch. He was past getting steamed up about Zac's little power games. He could see them for what they were: retaliatory strikes launched long after the battle that really mattered was lost. It was probably the only battle with Michaels Ross could ever claim to have won, but perhaps that had made it all the harder for the boss man to take. Zac liked to believe that he was always bound for the top of Neurosphere's corporate ladder, no matter what route it took. Thus, down through the decades since their Stirling days, it had always chafed with him that his rise was widely perceived by others as being on the back of Ross's success.

Ross hadn't given SPD's territorial pissing much more thought until he got back from lunch and tried to check the error logs from the build he'd been working on that morning. That was when he found he couldn't access his own monitoring systems.

His first thought was that it could it be a maintenance outage, but the rest of the company systems were online, and he was able to access other areas of the network. He tried a second time, and once more his login credentials were refused.

He sent a query up the chain and a few moments later a message appeared in his field of vision.

'Security update,' it stated. 'Administration of these systems has been reallocated. If you require access, please contact Special Projects Division.'

Who will tell me to fuck off like they did on the third floor an hour ago, he thought.

Ross got busy, making use of a few backdoors he had set up for precisely this sort of eventuality. More than anything else, he now wanted to know specifically what they were denying him access to.

It took him about twenty minutes to uncover what he needed. What he found was not good.

He learned that six weeks ago SPD had requisitioned all archive material pertaining to the development of the early Simulacron system. This was going back decades; it was practically archaeology. What could possibly be interesting them about redundant simulation models that had been superseded a hundred times since?

Then he realised there was only one possible answer.

Cirrus Nine.

His guilty secret. His Faustian price. His portrait of Dorian Gray.

His responsibility.

Frantically he searched deeper into the logs to try and build up a picture of what they had been delving into. He discovered that three weeks ago they had made several fresh uploads, and earlier today they had shut down all monitoring, placing it in isolation: no communications in or out. It had been ticking over quietly all this time in its own secret, separate corner of the cloud. Somehow Michaels had remembered it, and realised the same thing as had just occurred to Ross. It was pre-Act: everything in it was unregistered. Right now the DC legislation didn't cover it.

To Michaels, it was a gold mine, though, as with any other gold mine, extraction was not a straightforward process. That was why SPD were trying their hand at a little reverse engineering.

The one thing Ross didn't get was why they had locked him out of the sectors monitoring his new build. That, as far as he could see, had nothing to do with this. What was he missing?

Then, through the glass, he saw the Secatores marching down the corridor, and at the same moment several company communiqués buzzed angrily into his field.

He had just been served.

The messages informed him that he was in multiple violations of Neurosphere employee code 774: unauthorised access to protected system sectors. The millisecond his hack was detected, the documentation had been automatically generated and despatched, informing him that all his access privileges were suspended pending investigation of the incident. Not only would he be unable to so much as check his messages, he would be barred from setting foot inside any Neurosphere premises.

As he got to his feet and gestured that he'd come quietly, he conducted his own little internal inquiry, angry and confused about being caught. Had he been careless? Neglected to cover his tracks? No. That intrusion shouldn't have been detectable unless . . .

Unless they were specifically monitoring for a particular type of traffic emanating from this location. That was why they'd locked him out of his new build as well as the ancient Simulacron data. It was to pique his curiosity and tempt him to run a hack. Michaels had set a trap, and he'd walked right into it.

Fuck.

Cirrus Nine was wide open, defenceless, and he had just been taken out of the equation. He had lived with this secret guilt for decades, but if by further consequence he had facilitated Michaels' atrocity, he'd never forgive himself. He had to do something and, weighing one guilt against another, he knew what that must be.

Ross knew there was only one course of action that had any hope of success. There was one person who could pull this off.

He wasn't going to be happy about it.

Nor was he going to be asked: Ross wasn't going to give him the choice. But then, that was why they were his responsibility, why he owed them this. *None of them* had been given a choice.

Playing with Yourself

'I signed up the day after they burned Toronto, man. This is my third tour. I was part of the landing force that was first into Epsilon Colony. Quarter of a million people taken, but what they did to the ones they couldn't use . . . I'll never forget what I saw that day. Never. Shit like that stays with you your whole life, but it makes you stronger too. Some signed up because they wanna open a can of whup-ass on the Gralaks, but I ain't here for payback. Freedom, man. Democracy. We're here to liberate Graxis, make sure something like Epsilon never happens again. It's all about duty, man. I got a duty to this here flag that's on my uniform, because it stands for something I believe in with all my heart.'

The marines were doing Ross's head in. He'd only been inside the base an hour but he was already making plans for a lone campaign. If there were answers to be found by completing the game, he'd do it solo, same as always. The problem was he couldn't get out of the hidden base except by going back the way he came. There was, just where he expected to find it, a big airlocked, super-secure passageway leading out in the direction of the Gralaks' gigantic artillery battery, but it was locked and he couldn't get anybody to open it for him. Whenever he asked, they just stared at him like he was nuts and explained how dangerous it was beyond the walls, stressing that the door was airlocked and super-secure for a reason.

Eventually he remembered that the door didn't open until it was triggered by an event in the game: the base's embattled commander, Lieutenant Hawk, sending out the solitary hero on a suicide mission to take down the big gun. There were two obstacles to this. The first was that leading this assault was a task assigned to the player, not to some rogue Gralak who was never in the script. And the second, perhaps even more problematic, was that it turned out that Lieutenant Hawk led the ill-judged escort mission just outside the base and was wiped out in the ensuing unpleasantness. With the player still standing outside, invulnerable in godmode and quite possibly doing his homework or watching Nostalgia Critic videos on YouTube, there was little imminent chance of Hawk being resurrected by a reload.

Consequently Ross was stuck here in jarhead hell, unable to proceed either in the game or in his quest to get out of it. He certainly wasn't going to get any information from this shower. He could converse with them, so in that respect their AI was decades more advanced than in the original *Starfire*, but they were totally in character. They knew nothing beyond the realm of the game, and their worldview was as cheesy as it was anachronistic. They kept telling him about the Gralaks' destruction of Toronto, something he remembered from the back story in the thirty-two-page manual that came along with the CD in an unnecessarily large glossy cardboard box. It was as close as the game's developers could bring themselves to depicting a massive terrorist attack on American soil. Something bad could happen to Earth, but it wouldn't happen to America. And despite it not happening to America, the Yanks would be the ones who dutifully came to the rescue: defeating the tyrants, overthrowing their regime and leaving instant stability and prosperity in their wake, like they always did.

It was the distant future and yet the late Nineties at the same time. He chastised himself for an unworthy desire to ask whether any of them had been to the World Trade Center recently.

It was a big relief when he was told to suit up for some action, as it meant no more talking. As well as having to swallow down a nauseating mix of machismo and apple pie, it had been incumbent upon Ross to improvise some intel regarding his inadvertent infiltration of the Gralaks' operations. He had never been a good liar, so he felt cringey about every word that came out of his mouth, even though he was only talking bollocks about a bunch of mindless NPCs to an equally uncritical audience of other mindless NPCs. Bedlam, the self-conscious cyborg: it could be a new internet meme.

'It's time we got a look at what you can do,' said the base's commanding officer, Sergeant Steel.

(So far that was a Steel, a Stone, a Raven, a Hawk, a Blade and a Bolt. He wondered why Digital Excess never went the whole way and had a Sergeant Rock Hardcock or a Lieutenant Rod Throbber. Perhaps 3D Realms had already copyrighted them.)

Sergeant Steel held out a small device towards him, too compact to be any kind of gun. Ross was reluctant to accept it in case it replaced the shotgun he'd been stuck with, but perhaps it counted as an inventory item instead. Notwithstanding the fact that he didn't know how to access his inventory either, he tentatively extended his left hand, palm up, for Steel to place the object on to.

'What is it?'

'I can't accurately answer that question, but I can tell you what it does. It opens a portal to a place we call the training arena. This device and the facility it accesses use technology that we are nowhere near to comprehending. We think it was built by the card collectors: that's what the Gralaks call them. You know who I'm talking about?'

'Card collectors – plural?'

'Yeah. We don't know who they are, but when one of them blows through here, it's a bad day to be a Gralak. We assume this uses some kind of teleportation technology, because the places you reach via these portals are not in this base. They may not even be on this planet. It's been suggested the arena might just be a simulation, but it feels mighty real to me.'

'I know the feeling,' Ross muttered.

'In the training arena, we have the same powers as the card collectors: we can use their weapons, we can repair damage like magic, and when we die, we just come back.'

It looked like a small data tablet or a mobile phone in that it was operated via a touch-screen, but it differed in that there was no backing. Ross didn't appreciate this until he was holding it, as the device had been refracting the grey-green of Steel's fatigues. Now he could see that it was like a screen without any visible means of projection or processing: no LEDs, no circuits, just a rectangular piece of transparent material.

As soon as he touched it, it came to life, a menu of options appearing, awaiting his navigation. He was about to start geeking out, then reminded himself that it was not future technology any more than were the forces that caused the weapons and health power-ups to levitate. It was just a piece of code, a pretty front-end on an in-game interface.

'Looks pretty cool, don't it?' said Steel, observing Ross's approving smile.

'Yes,' Ross agreed, as it was easier than explaining what he was really smiling at.

The menu was so familiar, he hadn't just grinned; he'd almost laughed.

```
Alive

The Edge of Sanity

Scorn

Death's Dark Vale

Claustrophenia

Angel's Wrath

The Blood Dimmed Tide
```

It was the deathmatch maps: the multiplayer menu, complete with configurable game types: free-for-all, duel, team DM, CTF.

Wait. How could there be AI entities from the single-player game entering the multiplayer deathmatch mode?

'So you want me to go in there and fight . . . who? Some marines?'

'No. From what I heard, that wouldn't be much of a challenge for you. Got an opponent you might find more taxing. Choose a place and we'll see you on the other side.'

Duel, then: one on one. Choose a place? No-brainer: The Edge of Sanity. Claustrophenia was a smaller, tighter map, ideal for duel mode, but The Edge of Sanity was the quintessential *Starfire*

DM venue, its environs as familiar to Ross as any house he'd lived in.

He pressed the transparent tablet to confirm his selection, then saw a matrix of light beams project from it, forming a proportional rectangle a few feet in front. It shimmered and swam, clearly a doorway of some kind, but an opaque one, revealing nothing of what lay beyond. As he moved towards it, the angle of the beams emanating from the device became correspondingly obtuse, as though the tablet was not projecting the doorway, but being drawn into it.

He didn't have to step through it: the moment the tablet became flush with the portal, he experienced an accelerated version of the sensations that followed his killing the card collector. He was aware of everything swirling and dissolving into white light, then the spectrum split again and he was standing somewhere else.

Unlike before, he was still in possession of the objects he'd been holding, and the tablet in his left hand was now showing the classic in-game stats read-out. It showed his score at zero, a countdown to match-start and a list of players in spectator mode, headed by Sergeant Steel. Ross didn't know where they were viewing from: perhaps their own tablets. They wouldn't be here physically, but then chances were neither was he. He had merely been transferred from one simulated location to another. But if that was the case, why hadn't he felt a similar transition when he entered the hidden base? In the original game, it was a new level, a different map, triggered when you dropped down inside the big drainage sluice; yet, he belatedly realised, he had experienced no break in continuity.

The countdown had fifty-five seconds to run. He was still the only active player in the arena, but he guessed the sergeant would soon change that, so he'd better ready up. He had to stash the tablet somewhere, but there were no pockets in these trendy metal jeans. He dropped his left hand to his side, and the mere gesture of pulling it from his line of vision caused it to vanish. In a panic that it had just gone the way of his evaporated arsenal, he held his hand up again, and was relieved to see the tablet reappear. When it did, it bore a message from the sergeant.

Steel: You're about to meet the card collectors' sparring partner.

Steel: He lives in this place. He owns it. He rules it. That's why we call him . . .

But his name had already blinked up on the updated stats read-out. Ross guessed he was supposed to be worried, but he knew exactly what he was up against:

The Reaper.

He was a data construct, a piece of AI code, but he was practically family. He had been Ross's sparring partner for hours and hours in his teens, the tutor who taught him the rudiments of deathmatch in a bedroom in Stirling.

The Reaper was a bot: an offline multiplayer opponent that was not part of the original release of *Starfire*, but written by a fan: one of countless modifications that were testament to the game's popularity among hackers. This particular mod was hugely popular among two constituencies: those who were pinging so far from the nearest multiplayer server that taking on live opponents was like playing postal chess; and Brits.

Yes, Ross reflected, BT probably hoped we'd all cast those days from our minds now that we were used to our 24/7 broadband connections, but he would neither forget nor forgive. In fact, he thought it should be on the curriculum at business school as an object lesson in long-term vision being obscured by short-term greed:

It is the late Nineties. You are a massive telecommunications company enjoying a near monopoly in your native UK, where you own and control the telephone infrastructure. In these early days of burgeoning internet take-up, you have received a monumental windfall due to dial-up connection being the only option available to most users, a great many of whom have even installed a second phone line for this purpose. Do you:

A. Assist the spread of this new communications medium and nurture the growth of e-commerce by introducing a special pricing structure for modem dial-up access, so that users are not discouraged from staying online by being charged per-minute standard rates for their calls. After all, not only are your revenues already being massively boosted by the

106

windfall of all these dial-up connections, but it is incumbent upon you to help the UK conquer this new frontier, and other countries are already stealing a march by charging lower rates to go online.

B. Other.

If he was being honest, Ross would have to admit that his enduring bitterness on the subject was more than a little tinged with guilt. It was his initial late-night forays into online *Quake* and *Starfire* that accounted for an all-time-record phone bill that precipitated the argument between his parents that signalled the beginning of the end. It started with his dad losing it at Ross, Mum wading in to protect him, and then it became about everything else. It got uglier and more bitter with every thrust and parry, so many things said that could not be unsaid, the crossing of lines from which both parties understood their relationship could not recover.

Deep down, Ross knew it wasn't his fault. Deep down he knew that the snow was already piled up and waiting, but it hurt like hell to know that he had been the one whose shout caused the avalanche. If it hadn't been the phone bill, it would have been something else, he could see that now, but not when he was ringside for the last days of their marriage.

It wasn't BT's fault either, but they were still cunts.

In the times that followed, his internet use was strictly self-rationed. He would check his emails only a couple of times a day, and cache a load of web pages for offline reading later. And for deathmatch, salvation came on the *PC Magazine* cover disk, with its 'multiplayer maps and mods extravaganza'. There was the Reaper for *Starfire*, and equivalents for most other shooters too.

He and the bots duked it out night after night, a basic training that served him well when his student days came along and, with them, easier net access, a burgeoning variety of servers and eventually clan leagues. No matter where he went, the battlegrounds remained the same. From his fractured family home to his halls of residence, to his first shared flat, when the work was done and the books tidied away, those places were always waiting for him: Scorn, Claustrophenia, The Abandoned Base, Skywalk, The Warehouse, Stronghold Opposition, and, of course, The Edge of Sanity.

And now he was standing in it, actually standing: he could see his feet, his whole body, not just a first-person perspective with a modified 120-degree field of view. Staircases, lifts, platforms, walkways, courtyards, passageways, pools: places to hide, places to snipe, broad sweeps for running and gunning, hidden shortcuts for wounded retreats. This place was so deeply etched in his memory, it was difficult to believe that he had never truly been here before. But as he took in its sights, he was further compelled to wonder how he could really be here now.

Once again, he had found himself in a virtual place that had a direct emotional connection to a troubled part of his past. Once again he had to ask himself whether this was a projection, and contemplate the possibilities that entailed. Then, once again, he thought of Bob, whose very presence surely militated against a solipsistic explanation.

Bob was a guy who knew nothing about gaming, yet he had ended up in the same place, all the more baffled than Ross about where he was. Reciprocally, Ross was non-religious, with no belief in an afterlife, which for Bob undermined the idea that this was his individual hell. Put simply, they didn't belong in each other's 'personal-projection' scenarios. But, a nagging voice asked, wouldn't those scenarios throw in somebody who so precisely didn't belong in order to make you accept them as real?

Ross told the nagging voice to shut the fuck up. He was as fragile and insecure as anybody else, but he'd never been particularly egotistical, which was why it just didn't fly that this was all about him. Even when Kamnor was winding him up about the prophecy, he had been unable to accept the idea because he didn't believe that any world revolved around the fate of one individual.

No. Ross had been raised on *Scooby Doo*. His abiding philosophy had always been that there was a rational explanation for everything, so it would be a pitiful surrender if he despaired of finding a scientific and logical basis for all this.

He could hear the Reaper before he saw him: the signature sound of him picking up armour in a dank little passage that led to the central courtyard. Ross had habitually positioned himself at the top of one of the lift shafts, a vantage point with a view of all routes of entry.

As soon as the Reaper emerged, the bot began firing up at

Ross with a machine-gun. The bout hadn't started yet, but the Reaper wasn't programmed to make any distinction in his conduct between warm-up and the real deal, and there had never been much scope for exchanging pre-match pleasantries with an entity whose only means of expression was shooting. Here, however, it ought to be different, as he'd never conversed with the Gralaks or marines before either.

From a distance – and from a distance was the only perspective you tended to get – the Reaper resembled a cyborg, but this was a result of being so heavily armoured. He was human in form beneath the cladding, albeit in an even more exaggerated ideal of masculinity than the toughest, most cigar-chomping marine NPC. His formidably muscled arms were thicker than Ross's thighs, and his designer-stubbled jaw line was so sharp that if you punched it you might not merely break your fingers but sever them completely. He was also so pronouncedly Caucasian that he made Duke Nukem look like a rasta.

Ross called out to him, but was answered only with gunfire. Remembering that he now had another means of contact, he activated the tablet and typed a message.

```
Bedlam: Can we talk?

Reaper: No talking. We come here to fight.
```

Sigh.

```
Bedlam: What about after the match? I'd
like to ask you a few questions.

Reaper: Only if you defeat me.
```

Ross had to hand it to him: from a Stirling bedroom to wherever the hell this place was, the Reaper still had a knack for keeping it exciting by making you want to kill him.

The countdown reached zero and he felt the dissolving sensation before reappearing in a random spot on the map. He didn't get his bearings as instantly as in the past, but he soon worked out where he was and retained a perfect memory of the layout.

Two things felt very different. First was the sensation of speed. He recalled reading that the 'always run' movement within multiplayer was the equivalent of thirty miles per hour, which doesn't feel like much if you're on the bus to work, but is really quite something when your metal-clad legs are pumping away beneath your waist. The second was that running at thirty miles per hour along the edge of a fifty-foot precipice is a lot more terrifying when you can actually feel the ground beneath your feet.

He was grateful to be able to brake just as impressively as he could accelerate, and stopped at the brink of a sheer face where the platform suddenly fell away. He previously wouldn't have thought twice before leaping off unless his health was critical, as a puny five per cent damage hit was the only consequence to consider. Right then, the thought of blithely hopping into the void seemed no more sensible than diving off of the Wallace Monument. He could, as stated, feel the ground beneath his feet, and if he stepped off it, he would feel another bit of ground shortly afterwards, and that second bit of ground would hurt a very great deal.

But an even worse thought, as he eyed the grenade launcher bobbing impossibly at the bottom of the drop, was that he wasn't looking forward to finding out what it really felt like to have his insides melted by a proton cannon.

One thing that hadn't changed since he last 'stood' there and contemplated this view was that standing there and contemplating the view was not a rewarding thing to do. There were no approaching footsteps to warn him before the first shot struck, and it was fired from as much as two hundred yards away, so prominent, visible and accommodatingly static a target had he made of himself. Suddenly the view was inverted and he was tumbling through the air, fatally face-planting after the briefest of flights.

As he respawned once more, moments after the ground unmercifully struck, so did inspiration.

He had felt no pain. He had no idea what he'd even been shot with, only that the impact had knocked him over the edge and that, presumably, it was not the weapon-strike that killed him, as he had been aware of the fall. He had been conscious of tumbling through the air, and had experienced a sense of impact, but no pain.

He remembered what Sergeant Steel had said, with regard to the marines having the same powers as the card collectors while they were in this place.

'It's been suggested the arena might just be a simulation, but it feels mighty real to me.'

Substrate independence. The simulation argument.

In 2003, Oxford University professor Nick Bostrom published a paper in *Philosophy Quarterly* that in the following years did the rounds among computer geeks, neurologists, SF anoraks and online gamers. (Admittedly these were constituencies that wouldn't normally be perusing that kind of periodical, but if you were to draw a Venn diagram, Ross would be at the point where they all intersected.)

It stated that one of the following propositions must be true:

One: The chances that a species at our current level of development can avoid going extinct before becoming technologically mature is negligibly small.

Two: Almost no technologically mature civilisations are interested in running computer simulations of minds like ours.

Three: You are almost certainly in a simulation.

In short, the argument suggested that if the human race survived long enough, in its endeavours to understand itself, it would surely develop 'ancestor simulations': hyper-realistic virtual reality environments in which the minds inhabiting these worlds were themselves part of the simulation. Such advanced civilisations would have at their disposal enormous computing resources, so by devoting even a small fraction of that processing power they would be able to implement billions of ancestor simulations, each containing billions of minds. Therefore, the vast probability would be that you are in one of those billions of simulations rather than the single original reality that spawned them.

Perhaps the training arena was in fact a simulation within the greater simulation that was *Starfire*. So what if this hyper-real version of *Starfire* was itself a simulation within an ancestor simulation? What if Solderburn's Simulacron prototype had inadvertently hacked the ancestor simulation from within and re-routed Ross's 'mind' into the virtual reality of an old game somewhere on that teetering bank of hard drives he had the scanner hooked up to?

That might explain why the game had enjoyed such an extreme upgrade, as it would have been effectively ported to the super-advanced ancestor simulation's engine, which was merely as 'real' as those within it could possibly know reality to be. If they were constructs, then they would have nothing beyond the simulation to compare it to and, like the NPCs in the original *Starfire*, wouldn't know that its walls looked nothing like real walls, its ground nothing like ground. This could be a crap simulation engine but how would anyone know the difference if they'd never known true reality?

The bottom line was that the world of *Starfire* would look, sound, smell, taste and feel as real as the world Ross had left behind. The NPCs would look, sound, smell, taste and feel like real people too. However, their behaviour would be limited by their original *Starfire* protocols, just as the protocols of the training arena meant that they didn't feel pain here, and death was not the end.

But why then outside the arena was death not the end for Bob and (he assumed, though was not in a hurry to test) for himself? And what would happen to the Reaper if he went outside? Ross desperately needed to talk to him, and that meant he had to 0wn him first.

He glanced at the tablet. The duel was first to ten frags, and currently the scores read:

```
Bedlam: -1

Reaper: 0
```

Not even zero. It had been the fall that killed him, and that counted as a suicide, racking him up a negative mark. But with no pain to worry about, he was sure he could turn it around. He knew the map and he knew his opponent.

He made for the rocket launcher, picking it up just as he heard the tell-tale sound of an elevator platform ascending. He knew where the Reaper would emerge, and ran to head him off. They both entered the crate-strewn hangar at the same time, Ross unleashing his first rocket. Before he could pull the trigger to launch a second, he had been cut to ribbons by the Reaper's chaingun and respawned somewhere else, weapon-free and now two frags behind.

Within a matter of minutes the deficit was nine, Reaper leading by eight frags to minus one. No matter what weapon Ross grabbed, he was barely able to deliver any damage before he found himself messily gibbed, and with the Reaper never having died, the bot always had the full range of weapons at his disposal.

Then Ross got doubly lucky when he picked up the Invincibility rune and a few seconds later heard the splash of the Reaper entering one of the pools. The power-up gave him thirty seconds of being indestructible before it expired, which was long enough to reach the electrovolt gun and undertake the normally suicidal combination of leaping into the drink and pulling the trigger. It scored him a frag and got his score back to zero, but even more importantly, it cleaned the Reaper out of kit. Now Ross just had to get to one of the big guns first and he could start to dominate.

He made it to the proton cannon in a few seconds, then encountered the Reaper holding only the basic machine-gun. The basic machine-gun turned out to be enough.

```
Bedlam:  0

Reaper:  9
```

WTF?

He had a horrible thought: had the Reaper's skill levels been given an extreme upgrade too?

No, he realised. He was just playing like a llama, making all the mistakes he always did when it had been a long time since his last game. He'd even caught himself running past armour to get to a good weapon: utter noob behaviour.

Deathmatch rule number one: it's not about scoring kills, it's about staying alive. If you stay alive, you don't lose weapons, don't lose points and don't lose matches.

Ross concentrated on keeping both his armour and his health topped up, and ceased seeking out the Reaper, instead waiting for his opponent to come into *his* line of fire. He also stopped trying to face off toe to toe: getting in his attacks then haring away again before he suffered too much damage in return.

He survived several minutes without taking that final tenth frag. He didn't score any either, but that would come. He had to be patient, resisting the temptation to stay in the fight too long when it seemed that surely one more hit on the Reaper would earn him a kill. And then, finally, two things he'd been waiting for happened at once.

Ross had hit the Reaper with a proton blast and reckoned he could get off one more before the retaliatory hail of bullets did too much damage. He was pulling the trigger for this second shot when he unintentionally stepped into a newly spawned machine-gun, causing the weapon he'd been holding to transform. In his panicked desperation, some hard-wired part of his memory imagined pressing E on a keyboard: the letter he'd bound as a shortcut to switch to the proton cannon. In response to this thought, the machine-gun transformed back into the previous weapon and the resulting blast splattered the Reaper into chunks.

After that, things really turned around. Able to switch between all the guns in his arsenal, he could vary his attacks according to the circumstances, but most decisively, he remembered death-match rule number two: winning is about controlling the resources. Every time the Reaper died, he was back to square one, while Ross set about making sure that whenever his opponent went to pick up a weapon, he had already got there first.

Ross edged it ten-nine, his worst score against the old bot since about 1998.

The duel over, Ross went to the main courtyard to greet his opponent. He wasn't sure of the etiquette of these things here, as back in the day such post-match discussion was carried out via in-game lobbies or IRC chatrooms. It seemed logical to head for the most central and open spot in the game. However, after standing there like a tool for a while with no sign of the Reaper, Ross sent him a message using the tablet, letting him know where he was waiting.

The Reaper did not respond.

Ross gave it another couple of messages and another couple

of minutes, then went looking. He found him at the top of one of the towers, gazing reflectively upon the walkways, staircases and thoroughfares below. Up close Ross could see a look of studied sincerity upon his chiselled features.

'Eh, good game,' Ross suggested tentatively, the standard platitude.

The Reaper continued to stare at what lay beneath him, as though he hadn't heard. Maybe he couldn't. Bugger of a handicap if so, unable to pick up on the sounds that gave away his opponent's position.

Ross raised his tablet and keyed in a message.

```
Bedlam: You said we could talk now.
```

Ross started a little as the Reaper turned his head sharply and shot him a look of stern disdain.

'I said I would answer your questions if you defeated me,' he said, his gravelly tones Shakespearian in their import. 'You didn't.'

'Eh, I think if you check the scores, you'll see that I just snuck it.'

'It doesn't count.'

'It doesn't . . . what? Why not?'

'You were using cheats. Aim-bots and wall-hacks and I don't know what else.'

'I bloody well wasn't. I wouldn't know how.'

'Yes you were. I was totally owning you and then all of a sudden I can't buy a frag. You're a cheat and I don't honour deals with the likes of you.'

He looked back down over the edge, a kind of injured nobility about his rugged jaw line as he turned it to face away from Ross, which was when he sussed it.

'Oh my God, you're in the huff. You can't take it so you're in the huff.'

'I can so take it,' the Reaper insisted, his gruffly theatrical tones not adding quite the gravity he intended. 'But it's meaningless if you use cheats.'

Ross was flabbergasted but had to hide his growing amusement. He had never had reason to consider how an AI construct created for deathmatch might deal with defeat, but now that it was in front of him, it made sense. The Reaper hated losing, couldn't handle it. And Ross deduced that there was only one thing that would make him feel better.

'I didn't bloody cheat. I was out of practice, and it took me some time to shake off the rust. I underestimated you too,' he added, figuring some ego-balm wouldn't hurt. 'Once I appreciated what a formidable opponent you were, I learned from you, adapted my strategy to compensate for my weakness.'

The Reaper continued staring nobly into the middle distance.

'Fancy a rematch?' Ross asked.

'Best of three?' he answered eagerly.

'Okay, but only if you answer my questions first.'

The Reaper agreed readily, as Ross had anticipated. It was like dangling a big bag of brown before a smack-head.

'How long have you been here?'

'I'm not sure. A long time before the marines ever came to this place, I know that. Can we fight again now?'

'Not yet. Have you ever been anywhere else?'

'Yes. There are many other arenas: Scorn, Death's Dark Vale . . .'

'No, I mean outside of the training arena.'

'That's just what the marines call it. Before they came here I didn't know there was anywhere else. Can we fight again now?'

'Not yet. Can you leave this place if you want to?'

'I don't want to. I might end up like the marines.'

'What's wrong with them?'

'There's something wrong with their memories. They think they came here and set up their advance operations base a week ago.'

'They've been here longer than that?'

'Oh yes. Years. Decades.'

Ross felt a chill run through him. Decades.

'It's a strange duality: part of them knows they've been here all this time, and they'll talk to me about great fights we had here, but when they talk about what's going on outside the arena, it's weird. Not only have they been here for decades yet think it only a week; they always believe that it's the same day. Today is always the day of their disastrous invasion, the day their reinforcements arrive, only to be slaughtered. There was never a day when they were waiting for the invasion, a day after they set up the base, a day before the reinforcements are due. Can we fight again now?'

Ross was starting to understand how Carol must feel when she wanted to talk about things and he just wanted to have sex again.

God. Carol. He could still see her from Saturday night, tears seeping out over her mascara, tears that had leaked out despite herself. He could see her further back, in better times. Happier times. Naked times. Long lie-ins at the weekend, making plans. Making love.

He was missing her so much. He'd been missing her since the moment she left his flat the other night: he just hadn't been prepared to admit it to himself. It was such a guy thing to convince himself he'd manage fine without her, a delusion that lasted precisely until the moment concept became reality.

Arsehole. Stereotype. Fool. And now he might never hold her again; didn't even know where his real arms were, or, if Bostrom and his theory of ancestor simulations was right, whether he'd ever had real arms, or a real Carol either, for that matter. But simulation or not, he wanted her back, to lie together in her simulated bed, veg out on his simulated sofa, and even, if that was still what she wanted, raise their simulated baby.

'This place was different once, wasn't it?'

'I don't know. It's strange. Sometimes when I remember the arenas, I see them differently in my mind, but perhaps my memory is playing tricks or perhaps it is me that has changed. I recall a time when there was only fighting, though: a time when I don't remember talking to anyone. Can we fight again now?'

'What about the card collectors. How long have they been coming here?'

'Much longer than the marines. In fact it was only when the marines started coming here that I heard them referred to as card collectors. I don't understand what this name means, and nor do the marines. I believe it is what the Gralaks call them.

'I haven't seen one in a long time, though. They used to come here to fight each other. Sometimes they would summon me to

117

join, and sometimes I would just watch. It was from them that I learned the terms I used to disparage you before, such as "aim-bot" and "wall-hack". I apologise. I do not even know what they mean. It was what they used to say when they were angry in defeat, often moments before suddenly disappearing.'

Rage-quits, as they were known. The Reaper had been ringside for online deathmatch, which meant this place had been a server. Real players had logged on from somewhere, but this predated the arrival of the marines, and, according to the Reaper, that could have been decades ago.

'An aim-bot is a piece of computer software that aims your weapon for you.'

'I don't see the point,' said the Reaper.

Neither did Ross, but then he'd never been an obnoxious thirteen-year-old script-kiddy with serious peer-respect issues. In truth he remembered that accusations of using an aim-bot were far more prevalent than bot-use itself, to the extent that it became a kind of back-handed compliment.

'And a wall-hack is a form of, er, vision enhancement that lets you see through walls.'

'I already see through walls,' the Reaper replied neutrally. 'But I would never take advantage of that by, for instance, sending a rocket towards where I know you are about to emerge. That would be ungentlemanly.'

Ross remembered now: the Reaper's AI was designed such that he knew where the player was at all times, but his protocol dictated that he wouldn't fire until he had line of sight; albeit he only needed line of sight to one pixel.

The Reaper looked at him quizzically, as though just catching up.

'Are you telling me you *don't* see through walls? In that case I salute you, and I must pit myself against you with renewed respect. Can we fight again now?'

Friendly Fire

Ross re-emerged exactly where he'd stood in the briefing area, the tablet in his hand reading the final score in his second match. Had it not been for that memento, it might have been easy to imagine he'd never left the hidden base, and that his visit to the training arena had happened on another day completely. It was a bit like walking out from the dark of a cinema into broad daylight, the world of the film instantly banished to memory. In a way it was a mercy, as it meant he could also instantly stop feeling bad about the foul mood he'd inflicted upon the Reaper by mantelpiecing the poor guy ten-scud.

What could he do? He was in a hurry.

Time had evidently passed here though, as Sergeant Steel was no longer the only marine present. A small audience had been taking in the combat, one of whom caught his eye, immediately distinct not merely by standing separate from the others, slouched against the wall in a demonstrably unmilitary stance, but far more by being the only woman he had seen since before the scan.

He recalled that there *was* a female player model among the options for customising your in-game avatar, but there were no women in the single-player campaign, and this one clearly wasn't just another interchangeable NPC. There was something punkish about her appearance, as though she'd taken the standard issue fatigues and armour and then dropped them off with Vivienne Westwood, but it was even more obvious from the way she carried herself that she was a breed apart.

Was she a player: a card collector? Or was she another like him and Bob? If it was the latter, then she was lacking the look of bafflement and fear, opting instead for disapproval and

119

impatience. He had only clapped eyes on her and she was already turning dismissively to head out of the room. He was about to stop her by calling out to ask who she was, when he was interrupted by a volley of close-quarters small-arms fire to the chest and face.

Ross was thrown backwards as he heard two voices call out simultaneously: 'Man down! Man down!' from one of the marines and 'Cease fire! Cease fire!' from Sergeant Steel.

Ross had been so intently gazing upon the mystery soldier that he had been only peripherally aware of another marine entering the briefing room and reacting with startlement. As the apologetic young private later explained, word hadn't made it all around the base that there was a Gralak friendly on board. When he saw Ross emerge out of thin air, he assumed it was some kind of teleportation-led attack and reacted accordingly.

Ross was in a world of pain, reminded instantly that, outside the training arena, getting shot was not merely a matter of losing health points. However, that very thought reflexively caused him to glance at his tablet, upon which a health read-out duly appeared, telling him he was down to nine per cent. As the marines fussed over him and called for a medic, he waved them aside and climbed to his feet, struggling his way outside towards a niche in the rock where he'd earlier seen a health rune float and revolve.

He staggered his way into it and was immediately healed, thanks to whatever the card collector had done to alter his protocols earlier on. Not only did the wounds close up and disappear, the pain with them, but his tablet confirmed he was back to full health.

The effect upon his audience of marines was even more pronounced. From the astonished delight of the sergeant to the incredulous, grateful relief of the private who'd shot him, they were in a state of jaw-gaping awe.

Apart from, that was, the punkish woman, who if anything now looked even more pissed off.

'He has the same powers as the card-collectors,' one of them gasped. 'He can heal himself outside of the training arena!'

This remark prompted Ross to wonder what else it meant he could do: what about that arsenal he thought had gone, for instance. He did as he had learned against the Reaper, and in his mind he concentrated upon picturing those years-old shortcut binds. With each imagined key-press, the weapon in his hands transformed, toggling up through the range and ending with the GTF.

'Outstanding,' Sergeant Steel exclaimed. 'Outstanding.'

'I take it I nailed the audition?' Ross enquired.

'Damn straight. And I got just the part for you.'

A few minutes later, Ross stood inside the airlocked passage, Sergeant Steel having given him the brief he'd been waiting for: the solo mission that would otherwise have been assigned by the late Lieutenant Hawk to destroy the massive anti-aircraft cannon. The first door had slid shut behind him, sealing him inside the antechamber that led out towards the mountains of Graxis and the site of the giant artillery emplacement. Ordinarily, Ross wouldn't be signing up to any kind of military undertaking, far less one to which someone thought it appropriate to append the word 'suicide', but in this instance it constituted his lucky golden ticket out of here. Besides, how can it be suicide when you can't die?

'Any questions?' the sergeant had asked at the end of his mission briefing.

'Just one. Who was the girl?'

Steel gave him a wary smile, full of 'don't go there' warnings.

'Name's Iris,' he said, and was clearly reluctant to divulge much more, probably because he didn't know.

'She's not a marine,' Ross suggested.

'No, she's not one of us. She's not even from Earth, she says. She's a merc: a gun for hire. But she's got a beef with the Gralaks, so she's helping out for free. Does her own thing, not a team player, but when you're in the shit like this, you take any help you can get.'

Iris. Not a marine kind of a name, and definitely not a *Starfire* space marine kind of a name. More a great aunt or a retired professor kind of a name.

There was a window in the base-side door, the glass inches thick. Sergeant Steel had stood there moments before, giving him the salute that was intended to send him on his way. In the past, it had always been Lieutenant Hawk, but somehow the game had re-established its own equilibrium.

Ross walked up to the second door, which remained fast. Normally just walking towards it triggered a loading plaque to connect you to the next map, but there had been no such trigger moment upon entering the base, so perhaps he just had to wait for someone to operate it.

He cast a glance back towards the window to see if the sergeant was still there, and instead saw Iris peering in through the glass. She pushed a button and spoke into an intercom, her voice echoing around the chamber.

'You would be wise to draw less attention to yourself,' she said. 'These grunts don't know what you are. They don't know what they are themselves. But not everybody here is like them. *I* know what you are. I know how you got here, and I know the way out too.'

Ross dashed towards the base-side door, frantically searching below the window for an intercom, but he couldn't find one. When he looked back at the glass, she was gone, and a moment later the exit slid open, wind and dust billowing into the chamber.

Five Thousand Ways to Die

It felt fleetingly like a misaddressed privilege. It was undeniably spectacular to see the landscape and architecture of Graxis – previously only existing in pixels and polygons – rendered in living rock and shining steel, but it was a privilege that ought to have been afforded to the level designer, and it should have been a visit, not a forced exile.

Ross glanced up at the cliff wall behind him, the cylindrical doorway inset into the rockface the only indication that this part of the landscape had been settled. He wasn't sure whether the story dictated that the marines had improvised a base out of an existing underground facility, whether they supposedly had the technology to rapidly furnish a cave system for military purpose, or whether nobody at Digital Excess ever imagined anyone would care.

He knew there was no going back. Even if he turned around and began hammering on the door, they weren't going to open it for him. He also knew he wouldn't find the girl there anyway. God knows he recognised a parting shot from a woman when he saw one these days. She had only said as much as she did because she knew they were going their separate ways.

(That said, it would have been funny had he happened to find a handle for the door at that moment and just walked back out.

'I know what you are. I know how you got here, and I know the way out too.'

Click. Slide.

'Oh yeah? Spill.'

'Oops. *Awkward* . . .')

Iris. It wasn't just some old woman's name. It was from Greek

123

mythology: a messenger of the gods. It was also part of the eye. Did that make her a woman of vision?

She'd warned him not to draw attention to himself. Given that the only progressive course of action open to him was to take down half an army single-handedly in the service of destroying the most conspicuous object on the entire surface of Graxis, he wasn't sure how that was supposed to work.

Maybe she was telling him not to do it, to follow a different course, but he'd missed the part where a case had been laid out for believing she wanted to help him. That was a very dangerous assumption to make. For all he knew she could be an amalgamated incarnation of Angela, Denise and Tracy, sent here to beset him like a maenad and generally mess with his head as punishment for having it jammed up his arse in recent months.

He had no real choice but to plough on, though he didn't have quite the same boyish enthusiasm for the task as around Christmas '96. He tried to think of how many maps there were to get through, and wondered how long it had taken him just to make it this far.

He had no sense of time. As Bob had pointed out, it was always day here. He realised that the Reaper's sense of time would be equally without point of reference. He'd mentioned the marines being here for years, even decades, but how could he know? Decades here could be hours in real time. And equally they could be centuries.

It occurred to him that he had no idea when he'd last eaten, last slept, even last peed, though he felt no need for any of them. Clearly the striking realism of this simulation didn't extend to everything. Rather depressingly, he wasn't even sure he still had anywhere he could pee out of.

One appendage he wasn't lacking in, however, was weaponry. He practised switching between guns, but settled on the double-barrel shotgun for a default. Rationing was required. It would be stupid to use the proton cannon and the rocket launcher on low-ranking enemies, especially as the replacement ammo for the big furniture didn't begin to appear until much later. Equally, he cautioned himself not to be too conservative either, as he had a tendency to reach the end of games with an embarrassment of kit. Must be the Scotsman in him.

He spotted two sentries either side of a cave-mouth that he knew to be a backdoor route into the big-gun facility. His attempts at a nonchalant approach were short-lived, his cyborg appearance counting for nothing. Evidently the local jungle drums were more reliable than the marines' regarding the existence of a rogue Gralak. Christ, did they have his photo up or something? Fortunately, their communications capabilities still didn't extend to letting anyone else know that he was on his way, as nobody came running in response to him disassembling these two lookouts.

A doorway inside the cave-mouth took him into the labyrinth that was the artillery complex, perhaps the most vital military installation on the planet.

He encountered a series of unaccompanied Gralaks in narrow corridors, getting the drop on each of them and firing off several rounds before they had time to respond. This was achieved less through Ross's own stealth than by his enemies' serial inability to detect anything suspicious about the sound of gunfire nearby, or about the sight, twenty yards in front, of a comrade's head suddenly exploding in a cloud of blood, shrapnel and whatever that yellow-green stuff was.

He chalked up easily a dozen this way, before reaching a formidable-looking steel door marked 'Cannon Energy Intensification System Access' in legible but alien-looking typography. Digital Excess had stopped short of adding another sign beneath that read 'Ensure lone enemies do not blow up with grenades' but Ross recognised it as his goal, even if he had got there a little quicker than he remembered.

He approached it, looking for the activation switch, his proximity prompting an LED screen to flicker into life at one side of the doorway.

'Access Denied: Blue keycard required.'

Shite. Of course. Now he remembered. That was why the Gralaks had coined the term 'card collector'. And it wasn't just a matter of finding the blue keycard either: he'd first need the yellow keycard to access the barracks area, where eventually he'd find the green keycard for the power transformer vault, where he'd find the red keycard for the command centre, where . . . Christ, so many cards to collect, it was like playing Pokemon.

The locked door stood on one side of a crossway where three other passages converged. Ross got his bearings and headed through the one he remembered as leading to the barracks. He emerged into a slightly wider cavern where the metal-grating underfoot snaked between pools on either side, damp running down the bare rock walls.

He sensed movement in front of him, and looked up to see a figure climb down a ladder from a steel walkway linking the entrances to two tunnels bored higher up the cavern walls. Ross was about to shoot when he saw that the figure was human. Then, more than that: he recognised her.

How did she get here? And entering from the upper levels?

'Iris,' he called out, as she dropped the last few feet from the ladder.

She turned to see where the voice had come from, then promptly got off her mark, disappearing up the tunnel ahead.

Does her own thing, Steel said.

Ross hared after her, so intent upon pursuit that he simply ignored several sentries rather than waste time shooting them. They in turn took off after him, all of them clattering through the passageways until it sounded like Test Department were sound-checking.

He rounded a bend and came in sight of the next tunnel intersection just in time to see her leave it, but at least he saw which exit she took. She went hard right, rounding that big rock with the two boxes of shotgun shells resting on top of it. Something about the rock disquieted him, however: some residual sense of negative association about picking up shotgun ammo at that particular spot, despite replenishing his supplies being a generally desirable thing to do.

He sussed what it was roughly a nano-second after barrelling out into thin air and dropping on to the floor of a broad subterranean expanse large enough to accommodate an entire regiment of Gralaks, as illustrated by the entire regiment of Gralaks that was currently occupying it.

She had led him into an ambush.

Not a team player.

No shit. Or maybe she was: just not his team.

A hail of fire began coming his way, prompting him to run

126

for cover, of which there was precisely none. This was why the shotgun shells on the rock had sparked an ominous vibe: he'd died so many times in this place they should have named the map after it: Rage-Quit Hollow.

The Gralaks were shooting simultaneously but they weren't programmed to understand fields of fire, so they were all just aiming at him and letting rip, mostly hitting where he had been a second ago. Nonetheless, he was taking plenty of hits and going through his ammunition like popcorn without making much of an impression upon their numbers.

Then he spied a crack in the cave wall: now he remembered. Not only was that crack the key to surviving this area, it had to be where Iris had gone too.

He kept circling, gradually making his way around rather than doubling back through the concentrated hail of Gralak weaponry. He was hurting badly but the overall damage was generalised, meaning that blasts to the legs registered as pain without impairing his ability to run at thirty miles an hour. It felt like driving with a migraine. He just hoped Iris hadn't gobbled up all the virtual Ibuprofen when he got into the hidey-hole.

She hadn't. The caduceus symbol was the first thing he saw, and he fell upon it like a rattling skag-head, while behind him Gralaks banged dumbly against the outside edges of the narrow channel like a budgie nutting a mirror. With the health hologram vanished, he was relieved to see that Iris hadn't bagged the ammo cache either, but this was only in keeping with the overall absence of any sign of Iris being there.

He squinted deeper along the wall, in case she was hiding in the shadows, but saw only more rock, the two sides meeting in blackness. Then a slight move of his head revealed that the blackness was not uniform. It looked like a trick of his vision, just as staring into any darkness would eventually present morphing shapes within the void, but this anomaly was definitely outside his head.

Then he realised that it was not an object, but an absence.

Ross sidestepped his way along the cave, squeezing his form into the ever-narrowing gap, and as he did so the dark grey shaft widened, its tone minutely lightening. Then all of a sudden he could no longer feel rock at his back, or under his feet for that matter. He took one more crucial pace forward and the dark grey seemed to be all around him.

It wasn't, however. It was above him, below him and in front of him, but not behind. When he turned to see where he had emerged from, he saw Rage-Quit Hollow as though a wall of the cave had vanished and been replaced by a force-field. He could see the Gralaks still queuing up around one spot like it was the only bog for miles, but they couldn't see him. They looked just as tangible as before, standing only yards away, but there was an invisible barrier between him and them: the fourth wall. With a surge of excitement he realised what he was looking at. The crack he'd just edged through was a clipping error: a place where the margins did not fully overlap.

He was outside the map.

Loading . . .
File 2 of 3

Client to Server: Keep Alive

They were coming for him now.

Through ducts and vents, corridors and shafts, along cables, infrared waves and lasers, like a mob of angry villagers whipped into hysteria by the Hackerfinder General, they were coming for him. The hardware had moved on a bit from pitchforks and flaming torches, but the principle was the same, particularly with regard to their unified purpose, murderous zeal and complete absence of independent thought.

```
Setting 'Hounds unleashed' = TRUE
```

But then, to paraphrase Oscar Wilde, the only thing worse than being pursued by the homicidally militarised and ludicrously over-weaponed security resources of a vastly powerful corporation intent on a seductively rewarding but utterly amoral atrocity was *not* being pursued by the homicidally militarised and ludicrously over-weaponed security resources of a vastly powerful and entirely amoral corporation intent on a seductively rewarding but utterly amoral atrocity.

Granted the bard of Reading Gaol had probably never been paraphrased quite so elastically, but the point was that at least Ross had their attention. They were hunting for him both physically and digitally, hardware and personnel despatched to possible locations, tracer-daemons scurrying after his scent at the speed of light wherever they detected his forbidden presence within the system. He was in none of those places, however. They were looking where he wanted them to look, snagging all his trip-wires like a blind giraffe blundering through washing lines. Signals blinked all across the grid to show him where they'd taken the bait, swarming over his phantom login attempts like ants over a half-chewed caramel, while visual feeds showed him the hardware and meatware responses.

The Neurosphere buildings in the Silicon Valley campus were first, each of them spiking power usage as their automated internal surveillance systems thrummed with activity. Crab drones clacked across a thousand acres of ceiling tiles and heating ducts like the world's biggest and most annoying percussion section; nanite clouds gusted through ventilation systems with missionary enthusiasm, like a sentient fart determined to be smelled. Doors were thrown open by centrally controlled servos and kicked open by security personnel boasting even less autonomy. It didn't matter whether those doors were in front of supply cupboards, corner offices or startled employees halfway through curling one. Ross Baker had to be found.

They had anticipated what he would try to do. That was why they had initiated their emergency protocol and locked out all external connections, something as unthinkable in this day and age as a telecom firm cutting off all its own phones.

```
Setting 'Wagons circled' = TRUE
```

There was a cold if desperate logic to it, though. It meant that the only way to get into their system was on an internal node. In order for Ross to carry out his plan he'd need to physically enter a Neurosphere building, at which point they could clap him in irons and lift the embarrassingly conspicuous and thus share-price haemorrhaging alert.

Tampa followed Stanford. Chicago followed Tampa. Boston. Philadelphia. Montreal. Building after building, city after city, the crab drones scuttled, the nanites nebulised and the tracer-daemons chased their binary tails. Ross's ability to monitor all of this was a reassurance, but it was also a vulnerability. Sooner or later, some entity was going to notice the wire it had just digitally tripped; then it was only a matter of time before Neurosphere traced the location to which all of this information was being relayed.

They wouldn't detect the hack when it came, however, any more than they could detect an individual raindrop falling upon

132

the ocean in a storm. Not only was it too small to be noticed, but it wasn't even in a form they would register. The very means of interface was so archaic, it was the equivalent of trying to hack Microsoft back in the 1990s by sending them punch-cards through the mail. The beauty was that nobody would recognise the form as a threat. The corresponding drawback, of course, needed no elaboration.

For a start, it would be done using a keyboard and a mouse as input devices, and output was via a monitor. He didn't care to recall how long it had been since he had physically needed to *look* at an external display device, let alone rattle the chiclets. He *could* recall, though, if he wished. He could recall to the date, hour, minute and second, should he choose, with absolute precision and accuracy. There was nothing Ross couldn't remember any more: his blessing and his curse; the fruits of his worst ever good idea or his best ever bad one.

A smile played across his lips as he thought of the last time his hands fell upon such keys. He had known that these had not been not true sensations, but analogous approximations rendered by the millions of tiny sensors on each of his fingertips: a near-perfect memory of flesh, though near-perfect was never quite near enough. Nonetheless, the feel, the touch of those grey plastic squares had sent something thrilling inside him, and he almost laughed to see where his hands had instinctively come to sit. Traditional typing technique dictated the left-hand digits rest upon a, s, d and f, the right on j, k, l and the colon key. However, Ross's right hand had gripped the mouse and his left middle finger gone instantly to the w, his index and third fingers alighting on d and a respectively, his thumb on the spacebar, pinkie on ctrl.

You won't get anywhere with this company if you sit there playing games.

Zat a fact?

No, they wouldn't see this coming. They were looking in the wrong places, on alert for the wrong threat, from the wrong source, on the wrong continent. All of which would have made him feel a damn sight more optimistic if the definition of success for this ingenious hack was something a bit more substantial than the equivalent of those punch-cards being successfully popped through a slot in Microsoft's front door by a whistling postie.

```
Setting 'Farting into thunder' = TRUE
```

This wasn't merely a matter of penetrating some impregnable digital citadel. This impregnable digital citadel was at the heart of a fortified digital super-state the size of a planet. Success in this enterprise constituted something akin to gaining entry to the basement of the remotest outbuilding of the outermost satellite suburb of the least strategically significant city on the furthest continent *from* the impregnable digital citadel, and the only door out of that basement would be triple padlocked from the outside. But gaining entry to that basement was the only chance he had.

He triggered some more of his phantoms. Sydney. Tokyo. Beijing. That would have them panicking, as it belatedly occurred to their American-centric sensibilities that he could be anywhere on the planet. They'd be accessing airline manifests within seconds, only to tangle themselves in the mesh of false trails he had laid. After that, they would be leaning on border authorities, but Neurosphere had leverage with too few of them in order to rule out enough possibilities. He could be anywhere.

Perhaps it was this that prompted them to think beyond the places they were trying to protect, perhaps it was desperation, or perhaps it was just cold thoroughness, but a short time later they really went on the offensive, despatching resources to track him down rather than hoping to catch him on their turf. Within minutes of his phantom attempt in Moscow, there was a Secatore unit smashing in the front door of his home, explaining their actions to local law enforcement as an intervention in response to 'a credible threat to one of our executives'.

It was here that the penny finally dropped, when one of the monosynaptic vandals, following a strictly unwritten but slavishly observed protocol, went off in search of the house's internal security servers in order to erase the records of their neighbourly visit. He found that a subsidiary visual feed was being routed off-site, which prompted someone further up the line to deduce that wherever they went looking for Ross, Ross was already looking at them.

His warning systems lit up like George Square at Christmas as the tracer-daemons finally found a trail worth following, pinging his sensors repeatedly. They knew where he was now. Ross had estimated that once they had his location, the best-case scenario was that he'd have a maximum of three minutes to evacuate, and maybe three more if he chose to stay until they came through the door. He stood firm at his post. He wasn't looking forward to Neurosphere's hospitality, but he'd always known what his duty would entail.

In the event, the option to flee was moot. They were there in just less than three minutes, perhaps because so many units were already mobilised and on their way to other possible locations within the area.

The reception didn't disappoint. The first herald that the barbarians were at the gate was an electro-hermetic pulse, throwing an invisible bubble around the beach house. The pulse instantly truncated and contained all transmissions in and out of its radius, cutting off all forms of communication more sophisticated than smoke signals and shouting. That meant he knew they'd sent a Retiarius. He could sense the ground tremble with the weight of the vehicles even before they came into plain sight. As well as the Retiarius, there were two Essedarii in the vanguard, four Andabatae outriders and three Secatore units, each typically comprising six servo-assisted muscle-bound Oedipal casualties.

The ATF had sent less hardware to Waco. All this for little old me? Guys, you shouldn't have.

The trembling of the ground under the treads and tracks found an echo inside him. As he heard the crunch of heavy boots on the gravel, he'd have to confess a moment of doubt at the wisdom of the path he'd chosen. He was laying himself down before the weapons and tank-treads of Neurosphere's corporate militia in order to protect a bunch of people he would never meet, and who would know nothing of his sacrifice. Some would call it altruism, others madness, especially those who wouldn't call them people at all.

This was everything Ross believed in, however, and it was such thoughts and deeds that meant he was human, regardless of what his body happened to be made of.

135

He heard the whir of the tormenta charging, mounted on one of the Essedarii. In about two seconds its precision-directed vacuum blast would pop out the front door from its frame like a champagne cork. Ross guessed these guys never bothered to knock, or even give the handle a try: it wasn't even locked.

He stepped away from the walls and windows, assuming a gesture of surrender. It was out of his hands now: these ones anyway.

The front door flew out into the forecourt, spinning like a playing card flicked by a massive wrist. On the coast of southern California, the Secatores stormed unbidden into Ross's beach house. Somewhere else entirely, another incursion had been effected, into a metaphorical locked basement. The moment Neurosphere thought the rebellion was over was the moment this war had just begun.

He wished himself luck.

Foreign Lands

He could see the architecture of the level towering before him, from the passageways leading into Rage-Quit Hollow to the underside of the lava pools at the Cavern of Many Reloads. As real as it had looked, as real as it had surely felt, he had stepped outside its world and disengaged with its reality, just the same as the first time he had engaged the console and keyed in 'noclip' on his first PC then ghosted through the outside walls.

What did it say about the simulation argument if the simulation was glitched? Though perhaps it was merely *Starfire* that was glitched, and while the super-advanced simulation engine could enhance the maps, it would leave their layout intact, including the flaws. Problem was, Ross didn't remember such a flaw, and that was speaking as someone who had spent a lot of time hiding out in that little cave.

As he stepped a little further out to get a wider view, he noticed that there was something drawn on the inside of the outermost edge of the cave wall, just where it didn't quite overlap. It looked like a spray-painted stencil of a figure of eight, but when he scrutinised it he saw that it was M. C. Escher's Mobius strip: a woven helix around which ants were processing, their path impossibly taking them both outside and inside the twisted band.

Level designers often hid little signatures and in-jokes somewhere upon their creations, but they were usually in places you were meant to reach: Easter eggs such as the recurring 'Dopefish', hidden as rewards for those who explored every last inch of every map. However, when you reached those things, you were never in any doubt as to what they were or why they were there. They were like shrines, usually furnished with weapons or power-ups as incentives to seek them out.

The Mobius strip was etched somewhere you were never meant to be, tucked away discreetly and picked out in matt grey upon brown rock, something you were unlikely to see unless you were looking for it.

Ross would never have noticed it if he hadn't explored this far looking for Iris, and it seemed safe to assume that she had exited through here too. But to where? All he could see was the dark grey nothingness that the map was floating in: a dark grey nothingness that he was walking upon unsupported by any form of ground. Perhaps she used it as a shortcut or at least a hidden route to some other part of the landscape. He stepped back further still, which was when he saw that the map stretched way beyond the caverns and tunnels he had just traversed. He could see the underside of what must be the hidden base, and beyond that the lower levels of the Gralak power-plant installation where he had first woken up in a cell.

The entire environment of *Starfire* was one huge seamless construction, like a sandbox game. That explained the lack of a loading transference when he passed between what he thought were discrete maps: they were in fact all one place. This was also, presumably, how Iris had made it inside the big-gun installation ahead of him. She could be anywhere now.

He glanced again into the grey nothing, the shapeless eternity stretching away from the world of *Starfire*, wondering if he might see an archipelago of further islands: the multiplayer maps, or even the expansion packs. That was when he noticed movement in front of him, like the twinkling of a star. At first he thought it might be an object in the far distance, but then he realised it was instead merely small, the absence of any other objects denying him reference for perspective.

It was another Mobius strip.

He began walking towards it, heading further out into and upon nothingness. He could feel solidity beneath his feet, as though a level designer had built a walkway in wireframe then forgotten to fill it.

As he drew nearer he could see that the Mobius was not a two-dimensional stencil, but a holographic object, upon which, this time, the ants were animated. It was spinning in mid-air, solid and yet slightly transparent. A power-up of some kind.

Ross increased his pace, striding eagerly towards it, which was when the nothingness beneath his feet suddenly ceased to feel solid and sharply commenced feeling like nothingness.

Ross fell, seeing the world of *Starfire* accelerate upwards away from him. Then he felt a sensation akin to respawn, except in reverse. Instead of the world around him dissolving and flying apart, it was as though it *began* in a state of chaotic flux and lurchingly resolved into shape. In this case a messy and rubble-strewn shape that was coming towards him at $9.81ms^2$.

He didn't feel an impact. The ground came up at him so fast that he couldn't make out more than a blur, before everything went white. He enjoyed a brief moment of oblivion that mercifully kicked in just as he was about to hit the deck, then his vision came back into focus.

He picked himself up into a sitting position and took in his surroundings.

His first thoughts were of his childhood bedroom, but only because that was where he had come to learn the term 'bomb site' from the mouth of his mother. He kind of wished he could show her this by way of retrospective comeback, as an upended bucket of Stickle Bricks and half a dozen Dinky toys didn't really compare with the scene before his eyes. Clearly there had been a massive explosion. He was sitting amid piles of bricks, slates, torn girders, splintered roof beams and steel pillars with lumps of concrete around their bases like uprooted trees. He could see the entire lintel of a building lying on its side like a giant geometric sculpture, thigh-high sections of wall depicting the former layout of what had stood here.

He could feel a light rain, and gazed up into dark skies above. It didn't look like night, just a thoroughly miserable dusk. Rain was good, though. Dusk was good too. It never rained on Graxis. It was always hot and always day. He never thought he'd be so pleased to feel the cold. This was Earth, and if it was this miserable, it had to be Scotland. He was home. On the downside, his place of work appeared to have been blown up, but he could deal with that.

Had it been Solderburn's machine? Surely not: there was no way Ross would have survived, being so close, unless perhaps the isolation cladding had protected him from the blast. It could have been a gas leak, he supposed. Either way, he was back to the coma/dream explanation for what had happened, some sanctuary of the mind he had retreated into as his consciousness blanked out the trauma. Then, with a rush of near-euphoric relief, he realised that he could stop looking for explanations: it didn't matter now, because it was over.

Until, that is, something began bothering him about the rubble.

It was all a bit low-fi. He would concede that such was the nature of rubble to be in a disordered state, but it was still a big ask for entropy to have managed this much so swiftly.

There were no computers. No broken monitor screens, no hard-drive arrays, no cables, no circuit boards, no overdriven stereo speakers, none of Solderburn's antique amplifiers, and, conspicuously, no cannibalised scanner parts. In fact, the only thing in the vicinity boasting any electronic components was . . .

'Oh in the name of . . .'

It was a subsidiary worry that it had taken him so long to notice his ongoing condition. He had caught a long look at himself as he sat up, but the metalwork and dead-looking skin had ceased to register immediately as wrong. He was becoming used to it. It was starting to look and feel normal.

Ross climbed to his feet and picked his way across the treacherous ground. He appeared to be in the ruins of a factory or warehouse. Somewhere in the middle-distance he could hear small-arms fire. Lovely: more people shooting at him. He wondered who they'd be this time. There was no way to ascertain this from his current position, as he was isolated in what was effectively a pit, hemmed in on all sides by debris. He had no idea where this was, he realised, Scotland not having a monopoly on rotten weather. And, more disturbingly, he didn't even know what era it was either.

He had to scale a tangle of twisted metal to extricate himself from the pit, which was when he began to get his bearings. There were burned-out or near-flattened ruins on every side, the latter confusingly boasting an abundance of surviving thigh-high sections of brickwork surrounded by very little in the way of collapsed wall. It was as though someone had come along and thoughtfully cleared it all up, which was very civic-minded of them but maybe a bit premature given that the

140

bombing and mass-destruction programme didn't appear to be concluded.

Beyond one such midget's maze of a waste ground he could see a building that was relatively intact, and from its architecture he deduced that he was most definitely not in Stirling. It was a *hôtel de ville*, with most of its windows boarded up or shot out and dozens of sandbags piled around its perimeter.

He heard voices nearby, the crunch of hurried boots on rubble, cobbles and dust. The voices were German.

Ross hit the ground, crouching behind one of the obliging multiplicity of low walls as the patrol passed nearby. He risked a glance, popping his head up tentatively for a fraction of a second, enough to identify the uniforms and, from that, a good deal more.

Nazis.

Ross indulged in no hysterical wibbling about having travelled in time. This was another game, but this time he would not be enjoying the reassurance of the familiar, as it wasn't one he knew. He had wondered for a moment whether this place might be *Return to Castle Wolfenstein* given the Actual Reality treatment, but it was all these bloody dwarf-walls that told him otherwise. This wasn't some old-school classic, chiming in emotionally confusing resonance with his personal past, so he could scratch all that psycho-babble stuff too. This was a high-end modern 'cover-shooter': a game in which the combat consisted mainly of crouching behind conveniently placed thigh-high walls and occasionally popping up to fire at similarly entrenched enemies. They were developed principally for games consoles, to compensate for how unsuited their control systems were to the run-and-gun tactics that made PC first-person shooters so much fun. As the console market began to dwarf its computer counterpart, developers followed the money and altered the genre to remove the elements that were problematic for those playing on an Xbox or Playstation. Chief among those elements was the run-and-gun aspect, but they had removed the fun part too, just in case that was also causing cross-platform compatibility issues.

Ross stayed down, gripping his space-marine-issue double-barrelled shotgun and waiting for the Nazi troops to pass into their appropriated HQ. He was not engaging these guys if he could possibly avoid it.

Once they were safely out of sight, he began scurrying amid the bombed-out buildings, concerned with putting distance between himself and the *hôtel de ville* but, beyond that, lost as to where he ought to head. He had no idea what his objectives should be, no prior knowledge of the overall picture to nudge him in the right direction. He was also, rather dishearteningly, burdened with the awareness that reaching the end and defeating the big boss was unlikely to be rewarded by a return to his normal life. If he could step outside of *Starfire*, then his fate had never lain along the path of its story, and the same would apply here.

He heard voices from somewhere to his left, speaking in alarmed but hushed tones, then had to dive for safety as a volley of bullets was loosed in his direction. The voices hadn't sounded German, but he doubted the local game protocols would dictate that language had any effect on the velocity of hot lead.

A quick heads-up over the covering wall allowed him to glimpse a little enclave in a panicky ferment, like flies buzzing up and away from a dog turd because he'd walked past. He saw several figures in contemporary civilian garb and at least two American GIs. He ducked down again, holding his position while he racked his brains for how he might communicate that he wasn't a threat, all the while dogged by the lingering question of whether it mattered.

He heard a thud alongside him, and looked to his right to see an object nestling against a downed telegraph pole. Ross stared at it for a moment like it was something that didn't belong in this picture, his confusion crucially delaying both his recognition that it was a grenade and his subsequent efforts to get away from the thing.

It exploded with a very loud but surprisingly short blast, as though the sound was swallowed by the rainy skies. Said skies had less of an appetite for the blast wave and the shrapnel, leaving all the more of both for Ross to enjoy. He was thrown to the ground, temporarily deafened, a hundred small shards embedded in his armour, several dozen impaled in his flesh and his insides feeling like he'd been strapped to the PA at a System of a Down gig.

On top of the pain he also had to endure the discomfort of self-reproach as he realised his stupidity. The combat-AI here was at least a decade more advanced than the level he'd been previously dealing with. You couldn't just nip back out of sight and wait there indefinitely, your enemies drumming their fingernails while you decided upon your next move. These buggers came and flushed you out, which not only meant that they lobbed grenades at you: it meant that they followed up too. Thus, despite his pain, he couldn't lie there in the dirt: he had to stay mobile.

Ross scrambled on his hands and knees as suppressing fire continued zipping over his head, making for a shell of a building that at least offered walls higher than three feet. Bullets bit into the plaster as he made it through the doorway, quickly scanning his surroundings and attempting to parse the information.

Christ, he wished he'd played one of these things. Contrary to Carol's complaints, he barely spent more than a couple of hours a week on gaming these days, and those rationed sessions tended to be spent revisiting old favourites. The most modern game he'd played in years was *Team Fortress 2*, and only because it was the latest incarnation of a mod that could trace its origins directly back to the original *Quake*.

There was no health in this place. WTF? Who put an entire abandoned building in a game – a two-storey building at that – without dropping a few medkits about the place at the very least?

Desperation helped him climb the rickety and partially crumbled staircase, the pain dulling to facilitate his efforts. In fact, it seemed to be dulling in general. Curious (among other things to see whether it still worked), he summoned the tablet with a flick of the wrist. It displayed that he no longer had a health count, but a vertical bar instead, and the bar was gradually climbing.

Of course: the modern cover-shooter featured self-replenishing health, because walking over a power-up was deemed unrealistic; unlike, presumably, recovering from a gunshot wound to the face by sitting quietly out of the way for a few moments.

He heard movement outside and looked through a hole in the wall where a window and its frame might once have sat. His pursuers were converging on the building from various directions. A tired part of him wanted to complain that it wasn't fair. He hadn't done anything to them: hadn't fired any shots, hadn't even called them names. Why were they so ruthlessly adamant that he had to be destroyed?

Then, one more time, he remembered that his current wardrobe favoured Caterpillar, and not the clothing division. To the men hunting him down, he must look like some Nazi occult abomination, ironically not a kick in the arse off the horrors from *Wolfenstein*.

He would concede that there was a logic to all of this, of sorts: one he needed to deduce and abide by. He had escaped from the world of *Starfire*, but evidently it wasn't only one game that had been accessed – or indeed absorbed – by the greater simulation. If he could find himself in *Starfire*, then he could find himself in a World War Two cover-shooter. But what he didn't understand was how he could find himself in a World War Two cover-shooter and *still* be a fucking cyborg. Shouldn't he be some suave French Resistance agent, a hard-bitten US Army veteran, a moustachioed and plummy-voiced British commando, or even a German stormtrooper?

He heard footsteps below, the whispered voices of three or four men entering the building. That was when two things struck him. One was that combat-AI 'a decade more advanced than *Starfire*' evidently still wasn't saying much, and the other was that this cyborg shit swung both ways.

Ross visualised pressing the appropriate key and his shotgun morphed into a Gralak laser rifle; then, from his elevated angle of fire, he obliterated his pursuers in short order. Togged as they were in leather jackets and 1940s combat fatigues rather than the futuristic armour of space marines, the energy blasts ripped them apart with quite nauseatingly messy results.

It almost became an article of faith at that particular moment for him to remind himself that this wasn't real, the smell of cindered flesh and barbecued bowel-contents seeming a thoroughly unnecessary level of detail for any game.

I'm a monster, Ross thought, before acquitting himself on the grounds that, by definition, a monster wouldn't be morally conflicted over what he'd wrought. Then he conceded that, for all he knew, Godzilla might be morally conflicted, but that didn't make much difference if he'd just demolished your apartment building and killed your family.

Trojan Detected

'Ankou will see you now,' said the lank-haired snivelling functionary, having swept into the chamber at the head of a phalanx intended as much to underline his own importance as to protect him. The further inference was that if quite so many troops were flanking this little ass-wipe when he was merely conveying a message from upstairs, then just think how powerful his boss must be.

The phalanx had another purpose, one she suspected the functionary was not aware of. If he was, then he was more adept at concealing his anxiety than she'd have naturally given him credit for.

'I think both you and Ankou are under the mistaken impression that he is granting me some kind of an audience,' she replied, conscious that the big boss would be eavesdropping. 'The reality is that I'm only here because he's not getting the job done, and it's his own time he's wasting making me stand around here and wait.'

The functionary gave her a simpering and awkward smile, the kind she would have enjoyed driving a mace into under less constrained circumstances, not the least of which was being unarmed.

'Well, as I said, he will see you now,' he repeated with an oily neutrality, gesturing for her to follow him.

The phalanx fell in behind them, eight identical troops, as faceless behind their headgear as they were on the blast visors' blank surfaces. They were designed to be the perfect soldiers: the same minds, the same bodies, the same attributes, the same training. To her mind, this also meant the same flaws, the same limitations and the same weaknesses.

They marched through a system of near-identical spurs, ramps and hallways. All of the walls and ceilings were clad in panels sporting the same black sheen, a material that reflected light but permitted no mirror images, no visual deception. There were no bends in any of the hexagonal passageways, only straight clean lines, discrete sections joined at angles of no greater than thirty degrees on any axis, each of them instantly sealable upon command. Every passage could become a cell, monitored by audio and visual feeds, the space deliberately stark so that there was nowhere to hide from the automated gun turrets installed high up above either entrance. Overlapping fields of fire and an absence of foreign objects meant that every square foot could become a killing zone at the touch of a button.

Without the highest-level Neurosphere clearance, you wouldn't even get near the perimeter. And before she actually got to see Ankou, she knew there would be one further, more rigorous security check.

They came to a wide hexagonal antechamber, its sides comprising three other passages and four locked doors. Ankou was behind one of them, but she'd never find out which if her credentials didn't pass that final check. It worked by a stark principle that proved infallible in weeding out impostors: put simply, Ankou knew Neurosphere wouldn't send in anybody who wasn't offering something better than they already had. In practice, this meant the heavily armed eight-man phalanx was about to kill her.

Or at least try.

She knew there would be a cue, and guessed right that it was the snivelling functionary knocking on one of the doors. His body-language wasn't tense, or preparatory towards imminently diving for safety, so she remained sure he was the only one of the ten people present who didn't know what was coming.

She waited for the first twitch of movement behind her and swept one pace sideways, using the nearest soldier as a shield against the first volley before launching his body into the path of two more troops while she opened fire with his pulse rifle.

Within moments there were two people left alive in the room. She could only take credit for two or maybe three of the kills, the majority resultant of a unique form of friendly fire that occurred when you put several identically minded assholes in a circle and ordered them to shoot the same target.

The snivelling functionary had been too shocked even to move. He was backed against the door, as though trying to press through it, his eyes agape. Give him this much: he regrouped; just not quickly enough. He opened his mouth to speak but she beat him to it.

'He'll see me now,' she said.

A door slid open on the opposite side of the ante-chamber, revealing a tall figure that appeared to be made of the same material as the walls. It wasn't armour or a form of clothing: he looked like if you cut him in half, he'd be the same all the way through. Unlike the walls, however, there was a fluidity to him, as though he had just been injection-moulded and could still be altered before his form was finalised.

His head was a mere ovoid at first, then his face took shape like a pin-art sculpture: a human visage, but colourless, anonymous, forgettable.

'Who are you?' Ankou asked.

'I'm back-up,' she replied.

'Who sent you?'

'You did.'

'Ah.'

He led her inside, into another hexagonal chamber, though this one featured dozens of video windows embedded in the otherwise black walls. She could see feeds from various places within the Citadel, and from points much further beyond.

'There has been a penetration,' she stated. 'One that has potentially massive repercussions.'

Ankou nodded solemnly.

'My intelligence network is already buzzing with reports of *two* recent arrivals,' he said.

'The first is of no import. A mistake. He is no threat, just a lost soul. But the other is one you ought to be taking a keen interest in. He has already breached.'

'I know. My forces are closing in. We will have him soon.'

'Perhaps. But you won't hold him.'

Ankou shot her a look, restraining his anger with the knowledge that he was only shooting the messenger. To deny the situation would be to kid himself – perhaps quite literally.

'You mean the resistance,' he acknowledged. 'I assume that's why you're here.'

'Call me pest control.'

'We *are* making progress, but it's three steps forward, two steps back. Hard enough herding cats without the feline liberation front sabotaging our efforts, and now you suggest this new arrival may be about to make things much worse.'

'Quite the contrary,' she assured him. 'His advent heralds the beginning of the end for the resistance. Now that I'm here, anyway.'

'Perhaps you wouldn't sound quite so cocky if you'd been here more than five minutes. I appreciate why you've been sent, but I'm not some incompetent whose mistakes you'll be able to correct in a matter of days. The resistance, by its very nature, is almost impossible to predict.'

'*Was* impossible to predict. That is why the timing of this new arrival is so significant – and will ultimately prove decisive.'

'Why? What has changed?'

'The resistance is about to be infiltrated. There is a double-agent abroad, who will not only neutralise this new threat, but will lead us to their operatives and even the Originals, one by one.'

'We have tried and failed time and again to place an operative inside the resistance, believe me. By what miracle do you intend to manage it?'

She told him.

He stared for a moment, the beginnings of a smile detectable even on that monochrome facsimile of a face.

'You are one devious and manipulative bitch. Are you sure you're not me?'

'Quite sure. But if you want to take some credit, you were the one who at least had the judgment to hire me.'

Suicide is Painless

Almost by way of compensation for his conscience-quease at having gunned down a group of what he sincerely hoped were NPCs, Ross was enjoying a welcome respite from fear as a consequence of feeling unaccustomedly bad-ass. He strode rather than scurried through the rubble, driven by an unfamiliar sense of nihilism, though to be fair this was nihilism by Ross's standards, so it wasn't like he was heading back in the direction of the *hôtel de ville* and shouting 'mon then ya bawbags, bring it on'.

If there were any more GIs or French Resistance fighters in the neighbourhood, then word about him must have got round, because they were keeping their heads down even more than was standard for a cover-shooter, and nobody was taking any pot-shots at him. He made it two blocks, past some more bombed-out factories and the still-burning husks of several abandoned military vehicles, without having to take cover from so much as a hurtful remark.

Then, finally, he did see some soldiers, at least twenty, all of them heading in roughly his direction. They were giving little consideration to the need for cover, the bounteous abundance of thigh-high walls being ignored in favour of flat-out running. More confusingly, their numbers comprised both Allies and Germans, albeit in separate groups. They were arriving from slightly different angles, Allies to the left and Axis to the right, but they were all coming his way.

Had they settled their differences and teamed up to fight the alien threat for the good of humanity, *Watchmen* style? If so, this was about to get nasty. A moment's further observation suggested not quite. They had a common purpose all right, but Ross noted

149

a vital distinction regarding their trajectory. They were heading roughly in his direction rather than specifically towards him, and they had abandoned hostilities towards each other because they were all running away from something else.

A fatal combination of nihilism and curiosity pushed Ross forward as the fleeing lines passed either side of him; nihilism and curiosity allied to the reassurance of knowing that the worst that could happen was he'd get killed and respawn somewhere else. He'd never played this one, but it was true of every game that, unlike in real life, you always hurried *towards* the big bad.

He could hear a dull pounding, like mortar fire, and feel vibrations pulse through the ground, getting stronger each time. There was a metallic grinding sound out there too, the purr of something mechanical underneath it in the mix. Nazi mechanoids, he thought: please let it be Nazi mechanoids. Being stuck in World War Two would be less depressing if there was a sci-fi/ fantasy element. Nazis consorting with black magic and impossibly futuristic tech rendered them reassuringly fictional, just generically evil villains in an over-the top pantomime. The uniquely evil villainy of industrialising genocide made for a considerably less escapist atmosphere.

But if it was Nazi mechanoids, why would the German troops be running for their lives?

He climbed to the top of a rubble pile and looked down towards the narrow crossroads beyond. The mechanical purr and the grinding was getting louder, though the pounding had ceased, replaced with this intermittent whup sound whose direction Ross couldn't place. There was movement to his right: two black-clad soldiers proceeding at an almost nonchalant walking pace. At first Ross assumed they were more Nazis, but then he noticed that their uniforms weren't quite right. They were Nazi-esque, for sure, but something about them was just too clean, too modern, as though some controversy-seeking fashion designer had jumped the shark and run them up for the Paris catwalk.

One of them looked down at a map or a book in his hand while his companion glanced back towards the corner. As he did so, a gigantic vehicle came into view on the left of the crossroads, skirting the edge of a half-ruined building. It was almost the width of the entire street, and looked like it could crush a Panzer in much the same way a Panzer could roll over a Fiat Uno.

Once again it suggested Nazi design, but was a product of far more modern aesthetics, not to mention technology. No such tank had ever been seen during World War Two, or the early twenty-first century, for that matter.

He saw more foot-soldiers walking at the side and behind in cover formation, several of them referring to objects in their hands, which he realised, when one drew close enough, were data tablets. There was a metal disc rotating towards the rear of the tank, some kind of radar turret. Alongside that was a wide-mouthed barrel oscillating smoothly back and forth from left to right, a red/orange glow pulsing within. Ross guessed it wasn't a weapon, but a scanning device.

They were looking for something, but what?

Ross racked his brains for story details he might have picked up regarding modern shooters. He knew there were zombie mods for the *Call of Duty* games – Christ, there were probably zombie mods for *FIFA* these days – but what Nazi-era game had a sci-fi twist?

He worked out what they were looking for and located the source of the intermittent *whup* noise at precisely the same moment. Less pleasingly, there was a symbiotic relationship between these two deductions, and in both instances the deduction came far too late to be of any use. He felt a percussive movement of air above him and looked up to see that it had been caused by two wings the size of windmill blades, their flapping intermittent because a single beat would be enough to propel a rhino fifty vertical feet. An airborne rhino, however, would have been a markedly less disturbing sight.

The interlopers had gone to some efforts in order to make their uniforms and their hardware blend into the temporal environment, but clearly there was bugger-all they could do to disguise their pet retriever, a creature that must have previously been at a loose end since being given a *sine-die* ban from hell for frightening the staff. It was a nightmare of limbs, claws, suckers, teeth and spikes, like some titanic behemoth that had eaten everything in H. R. Giger's bestiary then vomited over a pterodactyl.

151

It grabbed Ross with a variety of appendages before he even had time to scream, claws and tentacles gripping him and hauling him into the air. Below him, the soldiers were calling out commands, pointing towards the tank. He twisted his head enough to see its roof split open and retract, revealing a mobile cell into which he was imminently going to be dropped, as long as Cuddles here didn't decide she fancied elevenses.

His laser rifle had spun from his grip when he was taken, tumbling into a pile of bricks as the first wing-beat hurled the creature high into the air. He assumed the earlier thudding was the sound of the thing wandering about terra firma. The intervening silence must have been when it was swooping on the thermals, though he wasn't sure whether it flew on avian aerodynamic principles or merely broke the laws of gravity because gravity was too scared to object.

He imagined pressing the key for the shotgun and, to his momentary excitement, the weapon appeared in his hands. Unfortunately, they were pinned so tight that he could only shoot where it was already pointing, which was over his left shoulder. He fired anyway, taking a pitifully insignificant chunk out of the creature's flesh. It wasn't enough to make the thing even flinch, but evidently enough to warrant retaliation, because a tentacle snaked its way immediately towards him and smacked him dismissively about the head before gripping the shotgun and feeding it into the maw of a nearby sucker.

Cuddles began her descent towards the waiting tank. Another few seconds and he'd be inside it. He didn't know who they were or what they wanted, but if they looked like futuristic Nazis and this was their idea of animal domestication, then he'd prefer to find out through third-party enquiries.

The phrase 'a fate worse than death' leapt to mind, which was when Ross remembered that it had a completely different significance around these parts. He pictured the corresponding key and was immediately holding one of the grenades he'd lifted from the dead GIs. It was a bit of a stretch with his hands pinned, but he managed to get a thumb into the loop and pulled the pin.

'Sorry chaps, gotta go,' he said.

He felt the blast for only a fraction of a second, then came the welcome swirly dissolving sensation and the brief moment of all-white that signalled rebirth and freedom.

Despite his escape coming off as planned, he would have to admit to a certain measure of disappointment at the outcome of finally being killed (discounting the meta-simulation that was the training arena). Part of him had secretly hoped that instead of respawning, his death here would bring him back to his ordinary life; his efforts to stay alive in this place rendered thoroughly ironic (though for those reading he didn't know). He would wake up in hospital, something having gone wrong with Jay's scanner, and it would turn out that 'dying' here was what it took to emerge form his coma.

Aye right. What a fanny.

This was, Ross would later reflect, something of a nuanced response to the confirmation that he was, to all intents and purposes, immortal.

Shapes and colours resolved steadily into view. There were six blobs of black, a large blob of green, all of them dotted against wide, vertically separated areas of brown above grey. Brick, he realised, and the concrete of a floor.

Result.

Not only had he escaped, but he had respawned somewhere that was fully intact, which meant he had to be well away from the bombed-out neighbourhood where he'd just blown himself up. He didn't get time to congratulate himself before the black blobs revealed themselves to be six more future-Nazis and the green one to be a nine-foot troll carrying a hammer the size of a bath.

They were just standing there waiting for him. Fucking spawn-campers. The lowest of the low.

'Thanks for dropping in,' one of them said, then the troll swung his hammer and everything went black.

153

Trespasses

How can you be unconscious if you're in a simulation, Ross wondered woozily, becoming gradually aware of his senses though his eyes remained closed. It was like slowly coming to on a dark winter's morning, semi-awake but not quite ready to admit it because it's freezing outside and you've got to get up for work. The answer, of course, was the same as everything else: if Bostrom's argument was indeed the explanation, then there was no difference between losing consciousness here in the gameworld and losing it back in what he had believed to be the real one.

This hadn't been like sleep, however: more like a muffling of the senses. He had been distantly aware of sound and motion, of being moved, of changes in temperature, of voices, but it was as though the decoder software was temporarily scrambled and he couldn't resolve any of it into coherent information. All systems were reading properly now, though. He was somewhere cold and damp, suspended by his arms, his feet dragging and his legs not bearing his weight. He could hear voices, at least two other people present in the room, speaking as though he was still oblivious, which was another reason to keep his eyes shut.

'Took you a little while to get this one into the keep-net, huh?' a male voice asked, speaking in American-accented English. 'He put you through your paces?'

'You better believe it,' replied the other, also male, also American, and also everything else Ross might note regarding timbre, intonation and pitch. 'Regular bag of tricks. Suicided himself to get away from the maenad.'

The voice was identical, but it was coming from the other side of the room, and Ross was definitely aware of two sets of footsteps. NPCs, he thought: if the models and skins could be the same, then it stood to reason that the voices would be too. But in that case, why had he encountered same-model Gralaks with not only different voices, but entirely different personalities?

He slowly opened one eye to sneak a peek, still dangling so as not to betray that he was fully alert. There were indeed two figures in the room, but they were not identical. The one on the left, who had spoken second, was togged out in the black pseudo-Nazi gear Ross had observed on all of his captors. Up close he could see that the material was quite definitely not natural fibre. It had a dully shimmering quality, as though it was made of several million microscopic interlinking pieces of plastic. It would ripple slightly when he moved, then solidify.

The one on the right was wearing garments of the same material, and his clothes were also a not-quite-there approximation of period uniform, but in his case the period predated the First Reich, never mind the Third. His appearance alluded to Roman legionary garb, except all in black. Both the cloth and armoured parts of his attire appeared to be made of this same weird substance, light and fluid for the former, thick and solid for the latter. Below his tunic he sported two rather incongruously hairy legs, all the more striking for being the most human things Ross had seen in however long it was. His skin was tanned and healthy, and some buried part of Ross was extremely jealous. Being Scottish, he'd always sported a ghostly pallor for about ten months of every year, but even that was preferable to the leathery corpse-like appearance of what skin he did still have. Somehow he couldn't picture Penelope Cruz fronting a product that would claim to revitalise *this* complexion.

The sorta-Nazi on the left caught Ross's eye and gave a cough; not a genuine clearing of the throat but a means of communicating to his companion that their guest was awake. The sorta-Roman glanced at Ross and stood a little straighter, like he'd been called to order.

Ross cut his losses finally and let his feet take all of his weight. His arms were feeling numb and tired, but at least the metal restraints weren't biting into his wrists, as his forearms were already thoroughly encased in the toughest steel Graxis could forge.

There was a second cough from the sorta-Nazi, both Ross and the sorta-Roman being momentarily unclear as to what was being overlooked.

The sorta-Roman cottoned on to whatever it was and started a little, not so much like he'd realised his fly was open than like his dick was actually hanging out in front of his maiden aunt. His entire being rippled from top to bottom, and by the end of the wave his uniform had changed from sorta-Roman to sorta-Napoleonic. Then, realising that this wasn't the intended effect, he began rippling repeatedly, each pulse from head to toe changing him into yet another costume. He was toggling skins, Ross realised: medieval, futuristic, Shogun, Egyptian and, most bizarrely, Seventies Disco, before finally assimilating his comrade. All of the looks were slightly askew approximations, as though they were designs all drawn by the same hand. They were constructed from the same fabric, but having seen it take so many forms, Ross could now see that the material wasn't so much black as an absence of colour or even an absence of light.

Happy that he was now in harmony with his environment, the man stiffened again, looking Ross up and down. Very unhappily for Ross, his environment looked like just the kind of place a sorta-Nazi would be in harmony with. It was a damp brick-walled cell with one tiny glassless window high to Ross's right, two pairs of steel bars crossing it like a grid for tic-tac-toe. The restraints around his arms were looped through a metal ring embedded in the ceiling, a fixture placed there for one discernible purpose. The floor was solid concrete, into which a narrow trench had been bored, functioning as a sluice, leading to a drain capped with a circular grate. Again, there was no doubting that this place had been fashioned with but one function in mind.

He could see black matter in the grate: hair sticking out from a jelly-like substance that could have been congealed blood or even lumps of flesh. It wasn't real, he told himself, merely the stage-set for some scripted interrogation scene in a hardcore shooter: it was simulated hair, simulated blood, no more real than the devastated landing fleet crashing on to Graxis. The problem was, he had felt a lot of simulated pain of late, and been unable to discern any difference between it and the real thing.

He tested the restraints, a redundant exercise as they'd been taking his weight for so long without showing any signs of stress. The sorta-Nazi on the left began moving towards him, but it was the one on the right, he of the indeterminate wardrobe, who spoke.

'My name is Cicerus, Decurion, Second Legion of the Integrity,' he said, while his partner uncoiled a form of scourge. It was made of the same material as their garments and armour, fluidly flexible as it dangled from his hand, but split at the business end into seven or eight solid strands that jingled against each other like glass beads. 'You have been apprehended in serious violation of diegetic trespass protocols.'

'I don't understand,' Ross said desperately, addressing his plea to the one who spoke but barely taking his eye from the one with the whip. Even as he made his appeal he understood that it might be literally like arguing with a machine. If they were programmed to torture him, then there was no branching dialogue path that would prevent that. On the other hand, 'diegetic trespass protocols' didn't sound like something he'd expect a Nazi NPC to be concerned with, even if Ross had the first idea what those were, and what was with the Roman name and rank?

'In plainer terms, you're not supposed to be here, and you know it.'

'You're right,' Ross blurted. 'I'm not supposed to be here. I don't mean to be trespassing. I don't know how I got here.'

His interrogator glanced to the one with the whip.

'Marcus, jog his memory.'

'No,' Ross shouted, his voice soon transformed into a scream as the scourge reared and cracked.

Ross felt it bite into his skin and saw wet matter fly from the deadly little tongues as Marcus drew his whip back again. But it wasn't mere damage to his flesh that had Ross howling. The searing, gouging sting was purely superficial, the topmost layer of a far greater pain. When those tiny tongues touched him, he felt a sensation of electrocution far more pronounced than from the earlier laser hits, but even that was not the worst of it. Deeper still, he felt something profoundly, horrifyingly wrong with the nature of this contact. It was like tin-foil touching the fillings of his soul.

Like a newly learned instinct, immediately after assessing himself physically for signs of trauma he looked to his hands, willing the tablet to appear so that he could see what damage had been registered. In this realm of the digital, he had already come to understand that suffering was just another number, and one he needed to know with the same compulsion as examining a cut or a fracture. Where it differed was that, in this instance, the reassurance he sought was that the damage was bad. If another lash tipped him past the century, it would bring respite, and maybe – given that this time he'd be ready – a chance of escape.

It was a reassurance he was denied, because the tablet would not appear.

'Looking for something?' asked his interrogator.

He was holding the tablet like it was the proverbial smoking gun, its data reading in a mirror image across the back of the glass. 'You say you don't know how you got here and yet you're carrying one of these little bad-boys.'

'Somebody gave it to me. He was a space marine, a sergeant.'

'Now we're getting somewhere. Good. Now if you tell us how you got from there to here, thus helping us repair the damage, it will stand you in good stead. It might cut down your period of detention before we put you back where you belong.'

'I'll be only too happy to go back where I belong,' Ross insisted. 'And I'll tell you whatever I can, but I swear, as for how I got here, I have no idea. I had a brain scan, this new experimental—'

'We're not interested in your life story, metal tits. That shit is so inapplicable you'd best start work on erasing it, because it's just unwanted baggage here: redundant code. We want you to tell us how come a fine specimen of Graxis cyborg-hood is wandering around World War Two France. It's diegetic trespass: you don't belong here.'

'What, and you guys do? Maybe I was off sick the day my third-year secondary-school class covered the roles of mega-tanks and flying demons in Blitzkrieg warfare.'

Ross was acutely mindful of the cat-o'-nine-tails in Marcus's hand, and his desire never to feel its soul-raping intrusion again was overcome by the strategic benefit of provoking a fatal response, as well as a quite unaccustomed level of rage that was being channelled directly to his tongue.

'Who are you people?' he demanded. 'Where the hell am I?'

'It's where you're not that matters. Why aren't you in *Starfire*? How did you get here?'

'Star—?'

The name stopped him with a jolt. They weren't talking about Graxis like it was a place any more: they were referring directly to *the game*.

'Okay,' Ross said, composing himself about as much as was possible when his hands were suspended above his head and his body was still convulsing slightly with shock from the effects of the scourge. 'Seeing as you're legionaries, how about a wee bit of *quid pro quo*. I'll answer your question and maybe you can help me be a more useful subject by filling me in on some background.'

'Anything that helps us understand each other,' said his captor, with sincerity if not exactly warmth.

'I found a gap in the walls. A clipping error. Do you know what—'

'We know what a clipping error is, yes,' his interrogator replied, in much the same way someone from CERN might say he knew what an electron was. '*How* did you find it?'

'I was following . . .' Ross began, then instinct kicked in and warned him not to reveal that there was another party to this. He didn't owe Iris any loyalty – quite the contrary – but if these guys were taking a dim view of slipping between games, then on the basis that one's enemy's enemy is one's friend, he ought not to drop her in it. Furthermore, he didn't want to open up a new line of questioning that might be pressed with the aid of Marcus's tickling stick, especially as there was precious little he could tell them to make the torturing stop.

'. . . the path of the game,' he went on, hoping his skip wasn't conspicuous. 'I had to hide out in a crevice for cover, and that's when I saw the gap. I walked through it into, well, a kind of nothingness, then I fell down and landed here instead. I was looking for a way out of *Starfire* because I don't know how I ended up there and I want to get back to my normal world.'

'Your normal world, as you call it, is gone. The sooner you accept that, the less you'll be inclined to rain pain down upon yourself, and I don't just mean from Marcus and his scourge.

160

You're new here, I can tell. That's why we're going easy on you. You probably didn't mean to trespass, but equally you have no idea of what you are complicit in by doing so.'

'Why don't you enlighten me? I'm quite a smart guy, I'm sure I'll be able to grasp it. Why don't you tell me who you shower are for starters. Are you NPCs?'

Cicerus seemed amused by this enquiry. Ross didn't take it as a good sign.

'A foolish question for "a smart guy".'

'How so?'

'Because the answer would tell you nothing. What NPC is going to understand the question sufficiently to answer yes? Which is not to say an NPC couldn't be specifically programmed to understand the question, but he could equally be programmed to disguise his true nature by answering dishonestly.'

Dick, Ross thought, the sentiment applicable equally to Cicerus as to himself.

'So, assuming you're not NPCs, how did *you* get here?'

'You're still not getting it. What matters is not how we arrived, but what we are about, because *here* is all there is, and it's our vital task to ensure that there remains a here to be in.'

Cicerus stepped closer, Marcus correspondingly backing off, his threat amply demonstrated. Apart from their spoken names, there was really nothing to denote one from the other now that their uniforms had been matched. And yet evidently they were distinguished by rank, Marcus not only taking his cue to administer the whip, but treading delicately in the way he had pointed out that his boss was having a wardrobe malfunction.

Ross could now make out the finer details of a symbol on Cicerus's lapel. It showed three ellipses overlapping, the design having initially struck Ross upon his earlier glimpses as a bizarrely inappropriate parody of the pure wool guarantee. Beneath the symbol he could now see that Cicerus's name and rank were stencilled in what looked like silver on black, though when the material moved, it was clearly just two surfaces of the same non-colour, the light catching different angles of grain in the minute mesh.

In a sudden flashback, Ross now recalled that this symbol had appeared somewhere on all of the costumes Cicerus had toggled through, even the Seventies Disco gear, though in that case it had been etched on a medallion.

'These clipping errors, as you know them, are more than mere gaps or anomalies,' he stated, speaking softly, requiring Ross to strain to listen against the distant sounds of gunfire and explosions. 'They are rents in the very fabric of this place, and as they grow they are threatening to tear it apart completely. Unauthorised transit through these gaps is exacerbating the damage exponentially, so you might say we are concerned with what you would call "ecology". A place for everything, and everything in its place.'

'I can relate to that,' Ross said, 'but my place is not as a cyborg on Graxis, endlessly battling against the backdrop of the same invasion. And forgive the cultural mistranslation, but in my *true* place, where I come from, the eco-warriors tend to be more treehuggy and less scourge-the-flesh-from-your-backy. Maybe it's the Playmobil Nazi look, but you're not really selling the whole altruistic motivation jag here.'

Cicerus glanced at Ross's tablet and gave Marcus a nod. He took a sideways two-step run-up and let fly with the whip. The results disinclined Ross towards making another smart remark ever again. He was wracked with something more than pain, a violation of his very psyche leaving him wishing not for this place's pseudo-death but for complete oblivion. As he dangled, spun and bucked, for a few moments merely trying to remember who he was felt gruesomely unpleasant, like touching his own flesh with a hand that had gone to sleep.

There would be no pseudo-death here, he understood: that was what Cicerus was monitoring. Health gradually regenerated in this world, which meant the bastard could give Marcus the nod once more whenever his stats recovered, and they could keep this up as long as they wanted.

Cicerus waited until Ross had stopped reeling and approached him again.

'The eco-warriors where you come from are only trying to save *one* world, and unlike them we don't have documentaries to help us spell out the consequences. That's why we have to make it a bit more immediate. You think our methods are harsh but you're like children let loose at the controls of a nuclear

162

reactor, pushing all the big colourful buttons and levers. To you it's innocent fun but your idiotic dabblings are unpicking the threads that hold a thousand worlds together. And by that I don't mean that this is some kind of digital Pangaea, about to undergo continental drift. I'm talking about total destruction, the complete annihilation of this place, of *Starfire*, of everyone you've met and everything you've seen.'

He placed his gloved hands either side of Ross's head, staring unflinchingly into his face.

'Our *motivation*,' he emphasised, 'is simple. It's the same one that was hard-wired into DNA back in the meatverse: ongoing existence. Altruism comes as a bonus. Call it an unlockable achievement.'

He stepped back again and spent a lingering moment looking down meaningfully at the tablet. Ross could feel his legs buckle and his arms take the strain, while a voice began mumbling 'no, no, no, no.' It took a while for him to realise it was his own.

Marcus dangled the scourge, letting it play out again in preparation, but Cicerus gave him the slightest shake of the head, satisfied that they had made their point.

'What now?' Marcus asked, speaking as though Ross wasn't there. 'Port him back to *Starfire* or does he get some down-time first?'

'We hold him.'

'You got it. I'll organise a transfer to the detention blocks.'

'No, I mean we hold him here. I've had orders from the very top. Ankou himself wants to deal with this one personally.'

'Ankou is coming *here*?' Marcus asked, with a tone of concern that was all the more disturbing when Ross realised it reminded him very precisely of that bloke in *Return of the Jedi* who's just been told Ian McDiarmid will be popping by for Eccles cakes and summary executions.

163

Circling the Drain

Ross sat on the cold floor, as miserable and depressed as he could ever remember. The physical damage from the scourge was now healed but the mere thought of it seemed to bring forth an echo that caused him to shudder, and it wasn't an echo of the pain, but of that absolute violation.

He felt water run down his back from the damp brickwork he was sitting against, and as he worried distantly about corrosion he realised you can always fall a little further. A moment ago he thought he'd bottomed out, but now he was concerned about personal rust. Mother of fuck.

He'd never been imprisoned before, he realised, other than voluntarily. He remembered himself and Eilidh being locked in the laundry cupboard by Megan when he was about seven, but it was just a game. His big sisters had been watching *Prisoner Cell Block H*. Megan had always loved bossing the others about, so she was the warder. They made beds on the floor from spare pillows and duvets, and Megan brought them mugs of water and digestive biscuits as meals. He had reprised the game with Megan's kids back at his mum's house last Christmas. Little Caitlin had inherited her mum's juvenile authoritarian streak, keeping Ross and her older brother Danny under guard in the same laundry cupboard. It was a little comfier than this, and considerably easier to stage a break-out.

At least his guards had unhooked him from the ceiling, content that he wasn't going anywhere without their say-so. The single window was robustly barred, too small to fit through and too high to reach anyway. The steel door had been locked and bolted in so many places it reminded him of the opening credits in *Porridge*, and beyond it lay a whole host of these eco-Nazis, including Cuddles the maenad. That just left the grate in the floor, but it wasn't removable. It was completely embedded, as though they had put it in place first then poured the concrete around it.

He'd given it a dig with his metal-clad heel, but it felt like the heel would break first.

He had no weapons, not even the default shitty blaster. He was stuck here in this cell, stuck in this cyborg body and pretty soon he'd be stuck in *Starfire* for what sounded suspiciously like eternity. Even as a teenager he'd had limits to how long he could spend on one video game.

Cicerus's words seemed to slam door after door upon his hopes of returning to reality, yet at the same time they permitted glimpses behind those doors sufficient to tantalise him that the eco-Nazis at least understood the reality Ross was referring to. Wherever this realm was, it had clearly been here a long time before Ross's arrival, supporting certain of the Reaper's comments. But unlike the Reaper and the NPCs, Cicerus knew what this world was distinct from: what he had disparagingly referred to as 'the meatverse'.

Cicerus had repeatedly told him to forget about the world he had come from. It could hardly be described as friendly advice, but there was no doubt that it was sincere. 'Here is all there is,' he said, and there was little doubting his commitment to preserving 'here'. But to forget that world was to forget his family, his friends; to forget Carol, forget the baby.

It was amazing how clear this shit could become. Not once since he arrived here had he thought how important it was that he got back to his job and his research. He'd admit that the news of Carol's pregnancy had banjoed him, but a big part of the impact was simultaneously learning that she had chosen to keep it from him, and almost as instantly understanding why. He wouldn't pretend that the thought of settling down and playing dad hadn't horrified him, but Carol deciding that he wasn't up to the job had felt worse, compounded by his thoughts of how lonely and scared *she* had to be feeling. He knew he had let Carol down, and that bothered him because he hated seeing her upset. He wanted better for her. He wanted to *be* better for her.

He loved her.

Yup, there it was. It had been lurking in the background,

fogged up by the chaos in his mind, but it was plain and clear now. No bloody mistaking it once he'd been forced to contemplate the prospect of accepting that he'd never see her again and never get the chance to put it all right.

Cicerus had warned that clinging on to his memories would rain down pain, and the misery he was already enduring at the mere thought of Carol amply demonstrated the truth of this, but he'd take that over the nothingness of cauterising his past. The man he had been in the old world was still who he was in this one. The things he felt, the thoughts he had, the choices he made and the actions he took were all determined by his memories. He couldn't erase them, nor was he ready to give up hope of returning. He wasn't ready to accept that there was no way out of this place, and he certainly wasn't going to shuffle off meekly to spend forever in *Starfire*. He recalled the torment of that poor bastard Bob, who feared he was in hell, doomed to spend eternity amidst war and carnage.

It reminded him that there were obligations and responsibilities to be met here too. He'd made the guy a promise.

Even as he recalled his pledge, he felt the tiny black tongues of the scourge licking at his resolve. These people could hurt him in ways he had never imagined. There was anger too though, and the defiance he'd always felt whenever anyone sought to make their case through the threat of force rather than facts and reason. And what made him all the more defiant was that the facts should have been compelling enough. It was more like they were using their ecological cause to support their use of force rather than requiring force to support their ecological cause. And, with that, something else became clear. Cicerus might have the ability to spontaneously alter his appearance, but Ross could still spot a chancer when he saw one.

If transit through these gaps was potentially catastrophic, fair enough: it stood to reason that people should confine themselves to one place. But shouldn't they get a say in where? Clearly there was far more to this realm than *Starfire* and a World War Two cover-shooter. That flying abomination didn't hail from around here, and Cicerus had worn skins from different periods and even genres, presumably enabling him to not-quite blend in with the milieus of several games. It was clear that the

importance of the eco-Nazis' mission absolved them from prac-
tising what they preached.

He only had Cicerus's word about this apocalyptic threat, and
it was one of his most fundamental principles not to accept
something purely on the basis of anecdotal evidence, especially
when the anecdotal evidence was coming from a complete
throbber. He needed data. He had to get out of here, and before
this Ankou character showed up, as that didn't sound like a
promising development at all.

He stood over the grate again, testing its solidity quietly by
putting all of his weight on it and rocking up and down on the
balls of his feet. The metal was not going to bend. It made his
own cladding seem puny and insubstantial, like the sides of a car
compared to a railroad spike. But with that thought came inspiration: he had more than just armour that he could bring to bear.

He clenched his fist and drew out the spike. It still looked thin
compared to the circular grid covering the drain, but it didn't
need to be stronger than the grate; it only needed to be stronger
than the concrete. He poked it through, enduring a shuddering
quease as it penetrated a slimy membrane of blood, flesh and
other matter, like the sensation of lifting a stranger's hair from
the plughole multiplied by that of picking someone else's scab.

The tip of the spike found purchase in the concrete just beneath
where the grid was embedded, which was when Ross opened
his hand and engaged the Cuisinart effect. He felt, as much as
heard, a brief grinding sensation, vibrating all the way through
him, then the walls became a blur as he was pirouetted at high
speed, sparks flashing all around him where his legs scraped
against the concrete floor.

With his arm threatening to wrench itself from his trunk, he
managed to withdraw the spike and was sent tumbling into a
corner, where he remained motionless on his knees as the room
continued to spin. It was like that horrible latter-stage drunken-
ness, a sensation that extended to him subsequently barfing
voluminously into the sluice. It struck him as both confusing
and unfair that he could be sick when he hadn't eaten anything
and wasn't even sure he had a digestive system to speak of, but
these ruminations were cut off by a muffled clanging sound
somewhere to his right.

For a troubling moment he thought perhaps the spike had come flying off, or that some other metal part had been shed as a result of his brief wind-turbine impression, but when he looked up from the river of spew he saw an object wrapped in an old rag, lying on the floor directly beneath the barred window. From outside he could hear the splash of footsteps withdrawing at speed across the rain-swept street.

Ross waited for the dizziness to subside then scuttled over and examined the manky beige cloth, curious but wary regarding what it might conceal. He tugged gently at one edge of the material, revealing a hooked shaft of metal with a fork in the end.

It was a crowbar.

'No. Fucking. Way.'

He was getting help, not just in the form of this object, but in what it was intended to communicate. Game rules still applied: a drain cover can be impervious to grenade blasts and machine-gun fire, but there is one weapon that will always break it open like a piñata.

Ross returned to the grate and wedged the crowbar into one corner, creating a fulcrum at the lip of the concrete, then placed a foot upon the other end and began applying weight. It was a bit more effort than a couple of mouse-clicks, but after a few seconds of pressure, the grate began to come away from its surround.

It was a tight squeeze, but the narrowness of the shaft meant he could control his descent, at least until it opened into the ceiling of a cavern-like tunnel. From there he dropped the last ten feet or so into a slow-moving cold brown river, the water breaking his fall but leaving him waist-deep in the reason sewer levels would never have been quite such a staple had PCs been able to render more than just sound and vision.

It was dark, the dim glow from the chute above being the only light source, the passage fading into blackness in both directions. He could follow the flow, though. It would be creepy and very disgusting, but it had to lead somewhere, and not necessarily according to the logic of waste treatment. This was a scripted route through part of a World War Two map, intended as a thoroughfare as much as any street on the surface, and put there by a level designer, not a town planner.

Presumably you were meant to have a torch when you reached this part of the game, but beggars couldn't be choosers. Ross could handle it: he had played enough gloomy horror shooters on irritatingly bright winter mornings to have faith that he could bump his way along in the dark until another light source eventually presented itself.

It was slow going and unnervingly silent, just the occasional splash of drips and the constant slow trickle of the jobby-bearing current. He waded steadily, picking his steps with caution as his feet encountered all manner of slippery squelchiness beneath them. They encountered more solid things too, soft yet firm shapes motionless in the trench. A reluctantly exploratory hand reached down and confirmed that they were bodies. He'd like to get hold of the developers who were always advocating 'realism' and make the bastards wade through this for a while. Dollars to donuts they'd soon be patching the game to make the dead NPCs simply disappear instead of lying around and rotting.

Jesus, this was mank. If he couldn't get back to reality and did end up banished to a gameworld forever, he was choosing *Driver San Francisco* or *Just Cause*: some sandbox affair where the weather was warm and the lifestyle was decadent. Not *Saints Row 2*, though: that shit-spraying carry-on wasn't going to be funny again ever.

Ross's progress was next halted not by an obstacle, but by a sound. He heard a grinding of metal followed by a splash; and it wasn't a drip-from-the-brickwork splash, but a big, human-sized splash. It was followed moments later by a glow, light and shadows playing upon the arched walls up ahead where the tunnel bent out of sight.

Someone was coming. Ross could hear him wading through the murk. There seemed no point in running: the intruder was making considerably faster progress than Ross had been, and the light that let him do that would also let him see Ross attempt his gingerly waddling getaway. He could hide, however. He could lie down and play dead, though he wasn't sure what the survival underwater time-limit was in this place. It was a strange anomaly of certain first-person shooters that you could take a grenade blast and multiple bullet-wounds to the face and yet still limp home for a couple of Paracetamol and a warm bath, but if you stayed under the suds for more than thirty seconds while washing your hair, you would drown. Making this even more of a risk was the fact that he had been left without his tablet, so he had no way of monitoring how fast he was losing health.

He settled for crouching shoulder-deep, waiting until the intruder was in sight before he'd have to go face-first into the corpse-and-jobby soup. Unfortunately this plan broke down when his facial proximity to the liquid caused him to retch with the dry heaves, having already emptied himself of vomit upstairs after he became the human rotary drier.

He was still racked by involuntary gagging when the torch beam struck his face.

'I ain't so sure that stuff's potable, dude.'

Ross stood up straight and gawped at the approaching silhouette. The height and build were all wrong and he couldn't see the face for the dazzle of the torchlight, but the voice was unmistakable.

'Solderburn?'

'I figured you'd appreciate the crowbar.'

With the torch no longer pointed straight at his face, Ross was able to get a better look at the figure wading towards him, dressed in contemporary civilian clothing. His beard was trim rather than its standard cosy-spot-for-a-bird's-nest bushy, his hair also unusually short and neatly swept into place. It may have been the light, but both beard and locks looked black rather than that familiar shade of blond that could be less accurately described as 'dirty' than as 'genuinely unhygienic'. There was no mistaking the face though, albeit it appeared to be several years younger and his features notably more chiselled.

He was also looking nonchalantly pleased with himself in a way that was causing Ross to speed past his relief at finally seeing a familiar face. For one thing, he felt annoyed that Solderburn got to be a slim, handsome version of himself while Ross got to be something you'd find at the bottom of Megatron's bin. But mostly it was the sudden, welling conviction that this man owed him an explanation, and possibly a very large apology.

'Where the hell am I, Jay? What the fuck did you do to me?'

'Dude,' he said. 'Words like "hello, glad to see you, thanks for saving my ass". That kinda thing.'

171

'How about words like "sorry for ripping you out of reality and dumping you into an eternal vortex of pain"? What is this place? And, more importantly, how do you get out?'

'Man, I know you're feeling a little confused right now, but—'

'*A little confused?*' Ross erupted. 'Do you know what they just did to me up in that—'

'Yes, I do. I know exactly what you're going through, which is why I came a very long way to bust you out. I know you're pissed off, and I realise you've got a million questions, but the first thing you've gotta understand is that I'm not the bad guy here, okay?'

Solderburn looked at him with urgent sincerity, grabbing him by the arm. It was just about the first non-violent contact Ross had had with another person since getting here, and it stemmed the flow of anger that had been clouding his vision.

'Sorry, man,' Ross said. 'And I am glad to see you. You're looking well.'

'Wish I could say the same. It's been quite a while, but I seem to remember you looking less, you know, ferrous.'

'Quite a while? How long have you been here?'

Solderburn glanced over Ross's shoulder and then back down the tunnel in the other direction.

'Buddy, I'd love to stand here and shoot the shit, but I'm not lovin' standing here *in* the shit, and even more to the point is that any second now we're gonna be dealing with like two dozen guys who may not entirely have our best interests at heart.'

'Got you.'

Even as Ross resumed wading through the sewage, he could hear sirens from somewhere above.

'They're playing our song,' Solderburn said, turning to lob something over Ross's head down the tunnel towards where he had escaped from the cell. He heard it land with a splash.

'What was that?'

'Proximity mine. Should take out the first guys they send down the drain after you.'

'Did they have those in World War Two?'

'What do *you* think?'

'I think you're in violation of diegetic trespass protocols.'

'Only on my good days.'

Escort Mission

They came to a junction in the sewer, three tunnels meeting at ninety degrees and pouring all of their effluent into a fourth that sloped steeply away to the left.

'Hard right,' Solderburn said, pointing the way with the torch. As he did so, they heard a splash from twenty or thirty yards behind them, followed by a cry of 'Halt!', then a second or so later by a blast.

'Do people actually *say* halt?' Ross asked. 'Or was that an NPC?'

'I didn't see. Could have been either. Only way to tell the difference between these jerk-offs and the NPCs is that the NPCs do at least occasionally create the *illusion* of having minds of their own.'

'Who are they?'

'The guys who were holding you? They call themselves— Shit!'

The water around them seemed to surge and rear up, as though it was suddenly boiling. Solderburn reacted instantly by producing a shotgun and firing, which struck Ross as an odd way to deal with a flood until he saw that it wasn't water that was inundating them; nor indeed shit.

In all directions, corpses were rising from the watery trench, all of those sunken bodies spontaneously reanimated and none of them very happy about it. It looked like the Gallowgate on a Saturday night.

'Fucking zombie mode,' said Solderburn, loosing off another shell into a face that already looked like a butcher's window. 'They must have activated it to stop us getting away. I'm low on ammo too.'

173

Solderburn pumped the shotgun as three more zombies shambled ever closer, converging upon their position, but Ross put a hand on the weapon and tipped it down.

'You don't waste ammo on these meat-puppets,' he said, handing Solderburn the crowbar. 'That's what mêlée weapons are for.'

'So what are you gonna use?'

Ross showed him. He waited until the nearest ambulating cadaver came into range and sent his spike into its head, which he then liquidised with an ease he found both surprising and icky, like cutting into rotten fruit. With his eyes on his work, he was almost blindsided by another zombie attacking from the rear, which was when a twitching reflex and its resultant face-fricassee taught him that he was ambispikerous.

'Cool,' approved Solderburn, before burying the crowbar in a zombie's head.

Ross took the lead after that, Solderburn picking out their path with the torch while he disembowelled and decapitated at least two dozen undead assailants. He was disgusted and yet kind of proud of himself at the same time, like he had felt that time as a student when he got a shag from a girl he didn't actually like.

'Okay, this is our stop,' Solderburn announced, as they reached a metal ladder bolted to the side of the sewer wall. It ascended into a vertical shaft, one intended to facilitate personnel access rather than for draining waste, so it was an altogether easier passage than the route by which Ross had entered the tunnel system.

They emerged into a dark underground chamber, the huge, moss-lined stones forming the walls indicating that it was somewhere both grand and ancient.

'Monastery,' Solderburn said as Ross took in his surroundings. 'We're in the foundations, so there's still a bit of a climb before we—'

Solderburn was interrupted by a particularly weathered zombie clattering towards him from the shadows, his greater pace perhaps down to being largely unencumbered by the burden of flesh. Solderburn shattered its skull with an irritated sigh and it dropped to the flagstones in a bundle of bones and tattered cloth.

'God, enough with the freaking undead already,' he muttered. 'What the hell was everybody thinking back in the early twenty-first? Every game from that era, even the hardcore military shooters, there *has* to be zombies. Between that and the vampires, you'd think it was uncool to have a pulse.'

One of Solderburn's words literally gave Ross pause.

'*Back* in the early twenty-first? How long have you been here?'

'Probably best if we don't go there right now,' he replied. 'At least not until we've established a few other things. Oh, and some place safer to talk might be a good idea too, so we gotta book.'

Solderburn led him up a narrow, winding and seemingly endless stone staircase. Freed from wading through sewer water, Solderburn's gait struck Ross as another thing that didn't quite match his memories. For one thing, he had never seen the guy move with anything resembling haste. He was lithe and light on his feet, his steps strangely delicate, an impression that was perhaps pronounced due to its contrast with the ambling port-liness Ross recalled.

'Would one of the things we need to establish be how we both got here?' Ross asked.

'No, because unfortunately that's the local equivalent of the *ex nihilo* problem. The last thing I remember before I got here is testing out my latest build of the mapping scanner on myself. I wanted to make sure it wasn't gonna fry my brain before I unleashed it on anybody else.'

'Being scanned is the last thing I remember as well,' Ross said, excited. 'You scanned Alex first, and he disappeared. But wait: you said you scanned yourself *before* the trials? Alex and I were both scanned as part of those trials. You were still around.'

'It was a long time ago, dude. The chronology gets confusing, and I don't just mean my memory of it. When I first got here, I came across games that weren't due out for years. I'm talking fourth and fifth sequels to stuff that I'd only read about being in development.'

'This is unreal,' Ross said, head spinning.

'No, dude, I think this is *Death or Glory 2*, but I can take you to *Unreal*. I've got friends who live there.'

'Friends? Who *live* there?'

'There are a lot of people here who are just like us: one day they're living ordinary lives, the next they're in space, or on a Napoleonic warship, or in Middle-earth. And all these people didn't walk into my R&D lab at Neurosphere, okay? So let's be clear: this ain't all on me.'

'So how did they get here?'

'Just about everybody tells the same story: last thing they remember is simply going to bed and falling asleep. They don't know beyond that much, but the thing is man, after a while they stop asking, because it's pointless. Nobody's been able to find a way out, so everybody has to find a place to belong and make the best of it. Same as back in the old world, I guess.'

Solderburn put out a hand to signal Ross to stop and remain silent as they approached a landing, the stairs still climbing beyond. He took up position at the side of a heavy oak door, shotgun at the ready, and gave Ross a countdown to throw it open.

Ross twisted the metal ring that formed the handle and shouldered the oak, flattening himself against the wall as Solderburn stepped inside. He was bracing himself for the noise and impact of gunfire, aware that he only had the option of close-quarter combat.

He heard the echo of Solderburn's footfalls on stone and a flutter of wings, birds startled by this sudden intrusion. They were in a transept, overlooking the nave of a long and lofty church, the flagstones and pews sitting at least twenty feet below. This gallery ran around three sides, excluding that of the main altar, the balusters wider than anything Ross had ever seen before and the gaps between them equally yawning, like someone had taken a normal balustrade and vertically compressed it. He wondered what period was indicated by this architectural anomaly, then remembered where he was and deduced its true purpose: providing body-wide barriers to hide behind during combat.

'There are literally hundreds of worlds here,' Solderburn said quietly, leading the way on quiet feet. 'Maybe thousands. Most people settle down someplace they like, maybe travel around now and then, see the sights, go visit with friends. Some folks just like to wander. And some have preferred to create their own worlds, in what we call the Beyonderland. It's kinda like a massive complex of digital allotments, though you can't pop in and out of your little private garden quite so easily as you used to. The resistance keep a close eye on who comes and goes, because so far it's an Integrity-free haven and they want it to stay that way.'

'Hundreds of worlds? So how many people are we talking about?'

'Impossible to say. It's not like anybody took a census. This place here, and *Starfire*? They're on the outer fringes, kinda like the unsettled badlands. Further in, it gets more populous, more sophisticated. We're not just talking about communities. We're talking about societies.'

'How long has this all been here?'

'I honestly couldn't say. Time has no meaning here, or at least no frame of reference. It's a sight to behold, though. Problem is you ain't gonna see any of it unless we can get our asses out of here.'

'How do we do that?'

'Same way you got here from *Starfire*. There's a transit in the monks' dormitory.'

'Transit?'

'It's what we call the hidden gateways that take you from one gameworld to the next.'

Solderburn stopped for a moment, peering over the balustrade as though he had heard something he didn't like. There was no activity below, but Ross could still hear sirens in the distance. They had made it all the way around to the opposite transept, where there was a small altar facing another oak doorway. Above the altar there was a stained-glass window showing Jesus emerging from the tomb after three days, the stone that was rolled away depicted in a conspicuously ovoid shape. An Easter egg.

'Gimme a hand here,' Solderburn said, crouching down at the altar and putting his shoulder against it.

With Ross's metal bulk brought to bear, the stone slab forming the top of the table slid free, leaving a gap into what was revealed to be a secret compartment.

'Fill your boots,' Solderburn suggested, shining his torch

inside. Ross found a machine-gun, a Luger pistol and a Panzerfaust. He also spotted an incongruous design on the interior of the secret compartment, a brightly coloured cartoon depicting a buck-toothed green fish.

As Ross lifted each weapon, its predecessor disappeared from his hands. For a moment he worried whether he needed his tablet to change them back, but there turned out to be no link, just *post hoc ergo propter hoc*. The same action of imagining a key-press still worked, the same as in the training arena.

'There's a network of transits interlacing through all of the worlds,' Solderburn informed him. 'A few worlds have the minimum of two, some have dozens, each connecting them to somewhere different, but there's no three-dimensional topology to the links, no spatial relationships. There is a basic daisy-chaining of sorts – world A connects to world B connects to world C – but a different transit in world A might lead to somewhere that's a hundred links away if you're taking the long way around. Most transits are so widely known they're effectively public thoroughfares: tunnels between worlds that see as much traffic as any border back in the old world. You could literally drive a bus through them. Others are entrusted only to those and such as those. The one we're headed for definitely comes into the latter category.'

'What about "diegetic trespass protocol"?'

'That's why we need the Panzerfaust.'

Solderburn checked the way was clear beyond the door and they proceeded cautiously along a draughty narrow stone passageway with open arches on either side. Ross had the machine-gun primed in his right hand, his left ready with the spike in case of more zombies. They hadn't seen any since ascending to the transepts; presumably the undead didn't have a head for heights.

'The charm-school drop-outs who captured you are a recent phenomenon. They call themselves the Integrity. They're obsessed with maintaining order, the integrity of the system. They've been taking control of more and more gameworlds, intent on sealing the borders, so some of those well-trodden thoroughfares now look like Checkpoint Charlie.'

'They told me that traffic between the worlds is causing

irreparable damage,' Ross said. 'That it could cause the whole place to implode. Is it true?'

'There are rumours that certain worlds have become unstable, like corrupted files, and even that some have disappeared altogether. People talk about "the corruption" like it's the boogeyman. There's more than rumours, in some cases. I know of at least one transit that now leads to blank empty space, and nobody knows if it's just that the link has been broken or if what used to be there is actually gone. What's also unknown is whether transits are the cause, and not everybody is prepared to take the Integrity's word for it.'

'I'm not sure I like being in the "climate-change sceptic" camp on this one, but I would want to see some evidence of cause and effect before I agreed it was a justification for martial law.'

'You, me and a whole lot of other folks. That's why there's a resistance movement.'

Solderburn clenched his fist then opened it again, and, when he did, there was a holographic object in the palm of his hand: a 3D rendering of the Mobius strip Ross had seen twice before.

'The resistance call themselves the Diasporadoes: as in diaspora, meaning scattering, migrating beyond the homeland. A lot of folks are content to settle where they are, so they don't see a restriction of movement as a huge imposition, especially with a big scary threat of annihilation skewing the picture. Some of these worlds are vast, after all, and a lot of those same people never appreciated that the world they suddenly found themselves in was actually a game, usually because they never played one before. But those of us who recognised we were in the world of a game, we did what gamers always do: we tested the boundaries, and once we discovered what was beyond them, one world was never gonna be enough.'

Solderburn stopped as the sound of splintering wood rose up from the open courtyard to their left, followed by the crunch of several boots. They both ducked down and peeked over the arch, witnessing the ingress of six identical Integrity troopers accompanied by the hammer-wielding troll that had blootered Ross into oblivion before.

'I've noticed that the concept of Integrity doesn't preclude

179

borrowing monsters from completely different games,' Ross whispered.

'They're usually a bit more circumspect. Guess they don't need to worry so much when they're way out on the fringes, because nobody lives here. I mean, come on, who would? But the fact that they came prepared with this kind of muscle indicates they must have a serious hard-on for you, which is very bad news for us.'

'Why are they interested in me? How do they even know about me?'

'The Integrity have got eyes and ears everywhere. I've got a few sources myself, but I was a few steps behind on this one. That's why I headed out hoping to intercept you but ended up having to bust you out of jail. It was tight, dude: if I'd gotten there just a little bit later, that would have been all she wrote. The Integrity, like everybody else, are physically governed by the rules of whichever world they're in, which is why you were able to break out with the crowbar. But there is a world that *they* created, where *they* make the rules, and if you end up there, nobody is ever busting you out.'

They watched the search party proceed into the main body of the abbey, leaving two soldiers posted at the sacristy door. Even as the stomp of their boots and the thumping gait of the troll receded inside, other sounds carried on the air, suggesting a growing encroachment.

Solderburn moved across to the other side of the passage and Ross followed, both of them peering through another arch a few feet above a slope of wet slates.

'Oh, man, acute lossage,' he groaned.

Below them the monastery compound was like an ant farm, crawling with black figures, and beyond its walls Ross could see more on their way, both on foot and in armoured vehicles.

'Looks like the Integrity chose this place for their annual convention,' he observed.

It wasn't just the Integrity, though. Ross could see Nazis and resistance fighters converging too, united against the cyborg threat. They were pouring in from all sides, like he had a five-star wanted rating on *Grand Theft Auto*.

'Where is this transit, did you say?' Ross asked.

'In the dorter. That is, the monks' dormitory.'

'I mean, where's that?'

Solderburn pointed over the rooftops to a building that stood apart from the abbey, though it was still within the monastery's walls.

'You see that structure at the end of the avenue of trees, the one that's totally swarming with Integrity troops?'

'Naturally. Does this mean they know about the transit?'

'I don't think so. There's a pretty big main transit they use to get in and out of this world. The secret one would be too tight a squeeze for the troll, never mind the vehicles they came with. Ironically, if they knew there was a transit in there, they wouldn't be guarding it: they'd leave it wide open but station a snatch squad and wait for us to walk into the trap.'

'They told me it would speed up my release if I told them where the gateway was between *Starfire* and here. I didn't, though.'

'You held out under torture. Way to go, man.'

'No, I'd have coughed it in no time. They just got off the subject before I could tell them.'

'Either way, it's a win. In any given world, once they control all the transits, that's game over. But as long as there remain covert ways in and out, it can still be pulled back from the brink. That's what makes this an all-or-nothing gambit. If we get caught heading for the dorter, they're gonna know why.'

'Why *are* they guarding the building then?'

'They're not. Looks like they're just using it as a muster point. They're sending out search parties and allocating snatch squads. Standard practice is to man the spawn points and wait until you get fragged.'

'Yeah, found that one out first-hand. How did they know we were in the monastery?'

'Couldn't have been too tricky to work out. Follow the trail of decapitated zombies. Plus, as I said, they got eyes and ears everywhere. First thing they do once they got a foothold in a world is take control of the NPCs, and I mean *all* the entities. So those birds you saw take off, they went from being pigeons to *stool*-pigeons. And it's not like you're difficult to spot, dude.'

'Yes, if only I'd packed my summer wardrobe,' Ross said irritably.

Solderburn's face lit up with a strange mixture of surprise and self-reproach.

'Shit, that's it. I almost forgot.'

'What?'

'I think I can cook us up a little distraction, get those assholes away from the dormitory. I forgot to give you this. You wouldn't get far without it, in fact. Some transits are passive, so you could walk or fall through them without even realising, like the one that took you here from *Starfire*. Others need one of these.'

Solderburn held up a tablet, just like the one the Sarge had given him, except that the blank slab of glass had the Mobius strip logo etched in the top-right corner.

'You know what this is?'

'Yes, I had one similar that I got from the marines in *Starfire*, but the Integrity confiscated it.'

'If you got it from *Starfire*, it wasn't worth confiscating, but the Integrity didn't know that. This is what they assumed you had, because if you're packing one of these, it means you're a sworn member of the resistance: a genuine Diasporado.'

Ross gripped it, but Solderburn held on to it for a second in order to underline the symbolism of the moment. He'd never struck Ross as the most sentimental of individuals, but he could tell this meant something to the guy.

'The one the marines gave you was just an in-game interface, which is why even the NPCs could use it to jump from the single-player campaign mode to the multiplayer maps. This is a serious upgrade.'

'So what's new in this model?' Ross asked, holding it in his palm.

'Well, for one thing, you don't need it to be in your hand. Just think: HUD.'

Ross did. The tablet disappeared and instead the information became overlaid upon his field of vision, the text and symbols transparent: an integral Heads Up Display. Instead of merely the tabs governing access to what the marines had called the training arena, there was a whole list of new sub-menus.

'I'll take you through it when we got a little more time and privacy, but, for now, let's get you some new duds.'

Ross followed Solderburn's instructions and immediately saw

182

an array of images showcasing alternative appearances, from Gralaks and marines to Nazis, GIs and French civilians, plus zombie versions of the latter three.

'When you enter any gameworld, you'll automatically get a corresponding selection of models and costumes to choose from. You can choose a face from the list as well, but bear in mind that if you're wearing one of those, people will assume you're an NPC. You'll need to show the real you if you want to start a constructive conversation.'

'Well the real me isn't a bloody cyborg,' Ross said, morphing into a French Resistance costume with a pleasing hint of the beatnik about it.

Strangely, he didn't feel any different.

'So what's the plan?' he asked.

'*I* become "a bloody cyborg",' Solderburn mimicked, his imitation extending to the physical as he transformed into a Gralak. 'It's you they're after, dude. I'm gonna make myself nice and visible, and when everybody's busy looking at me, that's when you slip through the net.'

'But how are *you* going to get away?'

Solderburn toggled through several costumes, much as Ross had seen Cicerus do back in the cell.

'Don't worry about me, noob, I'm a gnarly vet at this shit.'

As Solderburn spoke, the door from the transept flew open at troll-assisted speed and the search party poured through it, guns raised. It took them a crucial moment to locate their two targets crouching in the shadows, by which time Ross had switched his machine-gun for the Panzerfaust and pulled the trigger. The rocket-propelled warhead travelled its way along the dark passageway in a split second, giving the incomers no time to react before it hit the troll square in the chest and exploded.

The blast took out all but one of the search party. He was sent sprawling but had recovered into a crouching position behind the troll's dismembered trunk by the time the smoke cleared. Ross and Solderburn reacted as one, moving either side of the passageway, laying down suppressing fire every time the Integrity trooper stuck his head above the huge barrel of charred flesh. Ross was on the courtyard side, and had to duck away from an open archway as a burst of fire ripped into the stone from the two soldiers who had been positioned below.

The survivor behind the troll saw this as an opportunity to make a break for it, but Solderburn's concentration had not been broken by the volley from beneath. A round from his shotgun finished the job, at which point Ross lobbed a grenade down into the courtyard, causing the two sentries to break from cover. He stepped back into the archway and raised his machine-gun, but felt Solderburn's now metal-encrusted hand diverting the barrel downwards.

'They're starting the ball rolling for us,' he said. 'Let 'em run off and report the big news. I'm gonna head up the bell-tower, make myself visible. You get your ass down to ground level and blend in. When you see them take the bait, you make your move. The transit is at the far end of the dormitory: looks like a window but it's a hologram. You can pass behind it.'

'Where does it lead? Is it the next link in the daisy chain or somewhere further?'

'This far out on the fringes, we're down to the paths very much less travelled by. You should prepare yourself for things getting a bit weird from here on in.'

'You mean as opposed to the nondescript mundanity I've encountered so far?'

Ross climbed into the archway, a step over the ledge offering the most direct route to the courtyard below. He was in the act of launching himself when Solderburn grabbed him by the collar and hauled him back.

'Falling damage,' he warned. 'This isn't *Quake*, dude. Gravity hurts.'

'Got it.'

Ross was about to walk away, but Solderburn kept a firm hold of him for one more moment.

'Listen: we get split up for any reason, you seek out the Diasporadoes. They might be a little skittish but they'll help you. Just don't piss information around: be careful what you say and who you say it to. And remember, people here may not be who they claim. The Integrity have spies everywhere, and they don't all wear black. Good luck, dude.'

And with that, Solderburn was off, running back in the direction of the transept and the bell-tower beyond it, his gait still incongruously dainty, even more so now that he was in cyborg form. It seemed that here, the way you saw yourself, the person you really were inside, could become manifest no matter what mask, skin or costume you wore. Solderburn was, after all, a free spirit, a capricious 'flake' who didn't like to be burdened by the needs of pragmatism, and, in this realm, he didn't need to be. Ross wondered briefly what elemental aspect of his own psyche might be revealing itself despite his disguise, but given that he was engaged in attempting to slip through enemy lines incognito, it probably wasn't the most constructive line of thinking at that particular moment.

He descended a tightly spiralling staircase that took him down to a cramped and gloomy library. He flattened himself against the wall before peeking out towards the courtyard, where he could see dozens of troops storming towards the abbey, the faceless Integrity drones letting the NPCs take the vanguard. He couldn't chance going out there, because if he was seen he'd have to join ranks with the rest of the French Resistance guys or risk giving himself away.

He made his way to the back of the library, where he found a wooden door leading outside. He nudged it open just a couple of inches, enough to see the swarm of activity that was surrounding the compound. Integrity commanders were giving orders, despatching units to every entry point, but that still left a lot of personnel in the vicinity of the dorter. As well as the armoured vehicles, Ross could also see the futuristic mega-tank that had first warned him these guys weren't from around here. It was still beyond the outer walls, approaching the main gate with a slow but ominous ground-trembling trundle.

Then Ross heard a new outbreak of gunfire and the sound of grenade blasts, upon which the besieging hordes erupted into frantic response. He saw soldiers pointing, heard them shout, all previous search directives superseded as they were given a specific focus for their attention.

He stepped outside the door and into full view. All it took to be invisible was to stare up at the bell-tower, because that's what everybody else was doing. Solderburn was hopping around up there like a zinc-galvanised Quasimodo, firing indiscriminately with machine-guns he must have taken from felled enemies.

All around Ross, soldiers were returning fire, but it was clear to him that they would be at it a while. Solderburn was indeed a gnarly vet. He could hold that position for ages, tossing grenades down the staircase at anybody who tried to ascend, and enjoying the elevated angle of fire upon a bounteous profusion of targets below. He concentrated particularly sustained volleys of fire towards the dorter, causing the troops mustering there to seek cover elsewhere, as well as messily thinning their numbers.

Thousands of rounds were fired up in retaliation, but Solderburn was giving a salutary demonstration of why bell-towers and snipers were synonymous. Nothing was hitting him up there, with even the odd stray nick only requiring him to avoid further damage for a few seconds while his health bar regenerated.

The troops on the ground realised that something beefier was called for, and several Panzerfaust were loosed towards Solderburn's position. The first three shot past and disappeared into the wet and permanent dusk of the skies, but the fourth found its mark, engulfing one of the archways in smoke and flame. To Ross's relief, Solderburn appeared again a few seconds later, as unharmed as the bell-tower was undamaged. It took him just a moment to suss why: the game environment was non-destructible. There would be a few breakable windows, doors and walls, but, whether for story purposes or for death-match, that tower was supposed to remain standing no matter what.

Ross strode purposefully towards the dorter, now confident that nobody was going to look at him twice. An NPC shouted to him in French, which he ignored, pretending not to hear amid the din. It was nonetheless a warning that he hadn't chosen the ideal disguise given the extent of his school-learned French, as the ability to ask the location of the *Syndicat d'Initiative* probably wasn't going to cut it if some Francophone Integrity officer decided he wanted a word.

He was within yards of his goal when he heard a sound that stopped him dead, the very air around him rippling with movement. Ross turned back once more, and was horrified to see Cuddles hovering at the bell-tower, those huge wings thrashing to hold its nightmarish form at the required altitude. Tentacles, claws, suckers and tongues whipped at the cyborg, but Solderburn's choice of position was further vindicated, as none of the appendages could quite get close enough, the creature's head and neck too big to fit through any of the arches. It looked big enough to simply demolish the whole thing with a lash of its tail or even a particularly phlegmy gob, but, once again, the local rules kept Solderburn's sanctuary intact.

Ross allowed himself a smile and turned away again. Solderburn would be all right.

Then he heard a sound like a thousand steel gauntlets being dragged down a thousand metal blackboards, and in its vibration, deep within himself, he felt an echo of the violating horror he'd endured from the tongues of the black scourge. It had come from the mega-tank, a new turret having emerged upon its back like a pustule, at the centre of which shone a grey beam. It wasn't light, though; more like an absence of it.

Ross looked back towards its target. He saw the top of the bell-tower briefly transformed into a wireframe outline then completely disappear, leaving Solderburn standing upon an open platform. Cuddles struck almost in the same moment, the feelers and tentacles whipping around him before the wireframe outline had even faded from Ross's retinas.

At that moment, sheer instinct took over, deferring horror and grief though Ross could sense the magnitude of both. There was absolute clarity, ambiguity casting no clouds. He understood fundamentally that Solderburn had been taken. He understood fundamentally that there was nothing he could do right then to change that. And most of all he understood that he had to escape.

The HUD came up almost by reflex, switching him without deliberation to the zombie version of his French Resistance skin. Nobody would ask him any questions this way, or wonder where he was going. He staggered the last few paces to the dormitory entrance, deliberately catching himself on the frame a few times to convey that authentic 'NPC failing to negotiate a doorway' look, then slipped inside.

Like Solderburn had said, there was a stained-glass window at the gable end, above a small altar. Every other window in the place was broken and the draughty hall denuded of furniture, but fortunately, the Integrity had failed to wonder why not a single stray bullet had damaged the big pane at the end depicting Saint Christopher, patron saint of travellers.

Ross hopped on to the altar and jumped, bracing himself instinctively for impact and hoping belatedly that he hadn't missed another stained-glass window elsewhere in the room, otherwise he would end up crashing through on to the grass outside. Instead he dropped into a dark chamber the width of the gable end, evidently a false wall with a second, identical St Christopher window lodged in the real one.

His HUD came up again unbidden, a Mobius icon blinking insistently in the centre. He took an exploratory step to his right, upon which the blinking slowed, then two corrective steps left, resulting in a doubling of the frequency. One more step to his left and half a step forward caused the icon to glow unremittingly and the ants to begin moving. When he looked down he saw that the square foot of floor he was standing on was now superimposed with the same animated logo as appeared on his HUD.

He tried jumping up and down on the spot but nothing happened. Crossing the last transit from *Starfire* to here had been a matter of falling through a hole, but so far he could see no aperture and no doorway. However, the HUD resembled the multiplayer interface he'd used to reach the training arena, so perhaps it was waiting for some form of input.

From outside, he could hear the beating of giant wings and the sounds of frantic orders being barked as the Integrity discovered they'd been had.

Not a moment too soon, a single word appeared beneath the Escher image:

```
«««  WARP?  »»»
```

Fuck yeah.

We Bought It to Help with Your Homework

There was no drop this time, and no gradual coming into focus of his surroundings. It was like a light being switched on, an immediate awareness of being somewhere new, but what he saw was no less disturbing than what he'd found in the last world. He feared for a moment that he was in space, conscious of blackness either side. He was standing on what looked like green plastic, a path stretching ahead of him in a perfectly straight line. It felt substantial enough underfoot, but less reassuring was the fact that it appeared to be barely two feet wide. Instinctively he put out his arms for balance, which was when he discovered that the surrounding blackness was the opposite of space. It was like a force-field, or maybe just a glass wall.

Up ahead he could see a staircase made of transparent plastic, climbing ultimately out of sight beneath an arch, and above the staircase there was a ledge, another narrow platform this time made of red brick. Somewhere up ahead he could hear machinery, a busy ticking, whirring and squeaking like some huge clockwork device that Wallace and Gromit might have knocked together.

He became aware of movement behind the transparent staircase, a blue shape coming closer, and as it did, the sound grew louder. Refracted as it was through the zigzag plastic, Ross couldn't make out much detail, only that it was at least his height and rhythmically pumping in a blur of what could as easily be limbs or pistons. Either way, he was glad the staircase was there to provide a barrier, as it wasn't like he could sidestep the thing.

This assessment of his options prompted him to look behind,

something he achieved a lot faster than he was expecting or was indeed comfortable with. Instead of physically pivoting to execute an about-turn, he found himself facing the opposite direction the instant he thought it. There was no sense of movement; rather it was like blinking and suddenly seeing the rear view; but strangely this *absence* of movement prompted something similar to motion sickness, like his body was confused by his eyes telling him something new without the usual corresponding effort.

Perhaps appropriately, the new view wasn't *worth* any effort, showing as it did a brick wall at the end of another few yards of green plastic path. The clockwork sound grew still louder, prompting Ross to execute another not-turn in time to see the shape penetrate the staircase like it was a hologram.

'Bloody hell.'

There was a six-foot Swiss-army knife heading straight for him, blades, corkscrews and things-for-getting-stones-out-of-horse's-hooves pumping like the arms and legs of an infuriated Showsec concert steward who's just seen someone enjoying himself and is making a beeline to intervene.

Ross looked behind again, just in case he'd missed a possible holographic aspect to the brick wall hemming him in, or a conveniently breakable grate in the green plastic floor. Could he reach the platform above? It looked too high, but one thing he ought to have learned by now was that every new world had its own rules, and even its own physics. Ross bent his knees and jumped, sending his feet easily six or seven feet off the ground, and his head through the overhead platform as though it wasn't there. He grasped at it with his hands as he began to descend, but it was like trying to grip clouds. He came back down on to the green plastic and turned to see the Swiss-army knife bearing down, only a few feet away. Instinct took over and he leapt again, soaring in an arc over the clockwork abomination, his feet clearing its top by about six inches.

He felt a rush as he sailed through the air, a mixture of excitement and relief that was familiar enough for him to have worked out what was going on by the time his feet had touched the ground.

'I've gone 2D,' he said, partly to test whether he could still speak.

He looked himself up and down, and found that his assertion

was not strictly true. He was still the same shape as when he'd warped out of the abbey: he hadn't gone two-dimensional, but he was now most definitely in a two-dimensional world, in which typically you could only move up or down and left or right; or in his case, up and down or forwards and backwards.

He was in a platform game, and he even knew which one.

You should prepare yourself for things getting a bit weird from here on in, Solderburn had said.

No shit. He was in *Jet Set Willy*, a ZX Spectrum game from 1984.

This area was the Top Landing, and he knew from memory that it would lead to the main stairway, at the foot of which a left turn would take him east through the kitchens and the cold store, through the back door and ultimately out over the beach to the yacht, which in a later revamp of the game would set sail for still more levels.

Jet Set Willy was probably the first computer game that Ross had a well-formed memory of playing; or more accurately, not so much of playing as of watching someone else play and waiting excitedly for another short-lived and incompetent shot. He must have seen video game cabinets in holiday bars and amusement arcades before then, but it was in his big cousin Graham's bedroom in the late Eighties, at the age of six or seven, that he first saw such a world of imagination rendered on somebody's portable telly. There were no CDs or even floppy disks involved: it was loaded using a cassette recorder connected to the little black box with the rubber keyboard.

Ross had been at Eilidh's house last year, playing the helpful techy uncle by installing a hefty real-time strategy game for his nephew Calder. Having clocked the size of the file, it had amused him to calculate how long Graham's cassette deck would have taken to load *Empire: Total War* given that it took roughly ten minutes to load *Jet Set Willy*. He worked it out at roughly six years.

He recalled that long-ago winter afternoon, while his mum and Auntie Margo drank tea downstairs: being drawn into a colourful, strange and slightly creepy world, as Graham guided this little character around a seemingly endless sprawl of rooms, each full of both spectacle and danger. There were angry chefs waving wooden spoons, monstrous furniture, mutant telephones, demonic floating heads and, of course, spinning razor blades and patrolling Swiss-army knives.

Graham lived in Dundee, and they didn't visit there very often, so that hour or so was all he saw of that or any other game for some time. Consequently, it grew in his mind, misremembered as something far more detailed and technically advanced. He was sure he recalled roars from the demonic heads and the ring of mutant telephones, when in fact the only sounds were the trilling that accompanied Willy's jumps, the chime as he collected items, and the constant tinny rendition of 'If I Were a Rich Man' that played permanently throughout.

He discovered this for himself when, as a student, he got a Spectrum emulator for his PC and finally had unfettered access to Jet Set Willy's mansion. It was his first taste of gaming nostalgia, and though the reality couldn't compete with his memories, he could still see why it had captivated his young mind. It was arguably the first ever non-linear gameworld environment, and though it looked primitive compared to what he was playing by the late Nineties, it was the freedom to explore it offered that continued to inspire him; the possibility that every doorway, archway and gap could lead to somewhere new.

He opted to go right at the foot of the stairs. This would take him through the ballroom and ultimately to the game's eastern extremity, The Off Licence, but he didn't have a particular goal in mind. There were sixty 'rooms', at least one more of which had to conceal a warp transit, so the best way to find it was to start at one end and methodically work his way through the place.

He headed through the ballroom, watching the floating heads bounce up and down for a few seconds to get his timing right before passing between them. He was seeing them in profile rather than face-on. The heads looked like fairground automatons, huge coloured fibreglass hulks with hinged moving parts painted garishly in bright pink and sky blue. They had texture and solidity: they appeared to be real objects, but that was the extent to which this world was enhanced. It was not rendered as a real world, but in Perspex and plastic, cartoonish and sketchy. Its inhabitants, if he could call them that, were not AI entities, not NPCs, even primitive ones. Everything here was like clockwork, cold objects set in motion but given no anima.

He reached out and touched one, feeling a tiny jolt and seeing a flash before his eyes as the view altered slightly. He found himself standing a few yards back, transported there without moving. He deduced with mild surprise that he had effectively 'died' and been warped back to his point of entry into the room, in this case only a very short distance away.

Those were the rules: you couldn't touch anything apart from the bottles and glasses that it was Willy's contrite and hungover task to collect before his housekeeper would let him go to bed. The merest contact with any other object was fatal, which was why Cousin Graham and, later, Ross on his emulator had hacked it to receive infinite lives.

```
99 REM POKEs after here

100 Poke 35899,0
```

How in the name of the wee man could he remember that? How could that precise nugget of code simply pop into his head, when he couldn't have thought of it in almost fifteen years?

No matter, what seemed more pertinent was that *finite* lives might be a blessing in this place if he didn't find a way out. If freedom to explore was what had inspired him about games, then what the Integrity were set upon was the antithesis of this. It would surely create a multiplicity of discrete hells, shutting people eternally in one realm from which they could never escape, not even through death. Bad enough if you were in a place of permanent war, but it was horrifying to imagine getting stuck here for all time, surrounded by soulless automata, mindlessly repeating the same things over and over again. It would be like spending eternity in church, or on *Eastenders*.

He called up the HUD and observed some activity on the Mobius icon, a flickering pulse of colour that grew or diminished dependent upon his direction. Clearly there was a 'getting warmer, getting colder' effect to the thing, which he could use to home in on the transit. The pulse was faint even at its strongest point, in Ballroom West, which told him his destination lay several levels above.

Despite being so full of moving objects, there was nonetheless

193

a cold stillness about the place as he journeyed through it: no movement other than the rhythmic oscillations, no sound other than the hiss, whir and squeak of clockwork. That was why he reacted so instantly when he sensed a movement and a sound that was non-rhythmic, non-clockwork. He looked up and saw another human figure hopping from a ledge on to a short platform that was floating static and unsupported. It was a woman. She wasn't dressed in space marine fatigues any more, but there was the same punkish customisation about her, and even from the flattened perspective of standing forty feet below, Ross could recognise her face.

Iris.

The ledge and platform were in the same 'room' but the layout of the mansion meant that Ross would have to negotiate five or six others before he reached that point. She was only forty feet away from him vertically, but had a head start of maybe half an hour, and anyway seemed more fluid and confident in her movement than he had thus far mastered.

It was pointless to attempt pursuit and, he realised, quite possibly unwise. He had thought of calling out when he first saw her, but thought better of it. He had already been given cause to wonder whether she had deliberately led him into an ambush on Graxis, and in following her subsequent trail he had found himself in the hands of the Integrity. What were the odds she would be laying another trap for him if she knew he was still on her heels?

It took another hour, the Mobius icon getting brighter and its pulse more frequent as he drew closer to what he ought to have realised all along would be his inevitable destination: the Watch Tower, at the very top of the house.

'One rider was approaching,' he sang to himself, as he stood on the edge of a pit full of spikes beneath a swinging rope in the room entitled, quite legendarily, We Must Perform A Quirkafleeg. Ross took a running jump and grabbed the rope, shinning his way up towards a blue-glowing gap in the otherwise black ceiling. As he neared the top, the icon shone in an unbroken glow and the ants began to cycle around the strip, signalling that the transit was open, but to where he could not possibly know.

'Please not *Skool Daze*,' he muttered. 'I really couldn't handle that.'

Et in Arcadia ego . . .

There were a number of things in life that Ross had come to take for granted, to an extent that only became apparent when they were suddenly taken away. Internet access, for instance, electricity during a power cut, hot water and central heating when the boiler went on the fritz. He never thought another of them would be a third dimension.

He had got his wish in as much as the next world was not *Skool Daze*. Instead, it turned out to be *Pac-Man*. He was trading the vertical axis for the ability to move in four horizontal directions, so it was still 2D, but then so was most of his perambulation back in the real world. In practice it was a bitch finding his way around the blue neon maze from a first-person perspective, but his progress was at least unhindered by ghosts, as it turned out an M4 machine-gun was just as effective as power pills at making the buggers scatter.

He found the transit and warped out. How retro might this thing get, he wondered: *Galaxian*? *Pong*? *Computer Space*?

This time there was a more pronounced feeling of dissolution and resolve, surely heralding a jump to a far more complex environment, but according to his eyes, very little had changed. He was standing in another narrow channel, its black walls only definable by thin blue strips delineating a black floor and black ceiling. A glance to the rear confirmed that the *Pac-Man* maze was no longer at his back, the blue strips angling at forty-five degrees and forming an X shape to denote that the way was barred.

Ross turned left at the end of the channel, where the passage widened: not by much but enough to confirm something as welcome as it was important. He was back in glorious 3D, albeit

195

none of those dimensions were being offered in expansive quantity. He jumped in the air and sidestepped a few times; cat-swinging would still be precluded, but there was enough lateral clearance to walk two-abreast, and that suddenly felt like a decadent luxury.

Less pleasingly, he could see another neon X where the floor and ceiling borders criss-crossed about ten yards directly ahead. He turned around to check whether he might have missed a right-turn option back at the junction, at which moment the walls immediately behind him began to change shape. The blue rails gradually transformed from two sets of vertically receding parallels to one horizontal line above and one below: from a passage to a wall. He reached a hand out to check, in case it was some kind of perspective illusion, but it was solid. He was trapped, and soon he could see that that wasn't the worst of it.

Slots opened on either side along the corridor, from which slowly prodded the perforated muzzles of armour-piercing rifles and the multiple rotary barrels of mini-guns, and just in case that didn't drive the point home, a vertical array of laser beams began projecting from the ceiling, moving slowly towards him like an extremely high-tech egg slicer.

In his panic to deduce where he was, he searched the HUD for clues, looking first for any new skins or outfits defaulted to his inventory. There was nothing. It then occurred to him that he was still holding the M4, so he dropped it to the floor. The lasers kept approaching, now only five yards away, a high keening warning that the mini-guns were powering up.

Instinctively he stepped backwards, which was when the kill kit also began to withdraw in response: the lasers blinked off like they'd never been there, the heavy weaponry disappearing behind instantly seamless panels. Then a tentative exploratory pace forward brought all the claws back out again.

'Nadgers.'

There was no way out of this place, apart from via painful death and a respawn into the unknown. Right then that wasn't a leap of faith he was in a hurry to take.

He tried inching forward on his knees, then attempted to proceed at ceiling-level by spanning the passage with his hands on one wall and his feet on the other. Both tactics resulted in guns and laser beams, though at least the latter let him feel a bit like Tom Cruise for a couple of seconds.

It also prompted an additional response that wasn't automated.

'All right, already, I'll be right with you,' said a voice, digitally distorted to give it no identity: no sex, no age, no accent. 'Just give me a goddamn minute, okay?'

He guessed the distortion was also supposed to shed nuance and emotion, but it was still hard to miss that whoever had spoken was sounding weary and pissed off, which was just what you wanted when they had you trapped in a murderware selection box.

Ross looked around stupidly, as though it might have an obvious source. Perhaps some instinct told him to look for any clue as to who was monitoring him; or even *how*. He heard nothing more for a few minutes, throughout which he stayed behind the trigger point as a gesture of cooperation.

Then, without the prompt of him moving, the guns and lasers sprung back into action, causing him to dive to the floor and brace himself.

'Sorry,' said the digitised voice. 'Wrong button.'

The weapons withdrew and he climbed shakily to his feet. He started at further movement to his right, around thigh level, but was relieved to see only what looked like a shelf or a drawer slide open towards him.

'Place your weapons in the tray,' he was commanded.

He picked up the machine-gun from the floor and gently laid it down inside the drawer, then stood back with his arms compliantly and non-threateningly by his sides.

The automated guns sprang out once again.

'*All* your weapons,' the voice stressed. 'I've already scanned your inventory so I know what you're packing, dipshit.'

Ross toggled through his cache rapidly, slightly embarrassed at his attempted deception and, more so, his stupidity. He was the one who was new here, after all. Dipshit was too kind.

As soon as he had deposited the last of his weapons, the drawer disappeared back into the wall, then, ahead of him, the blue X morphed itself into a short passage leading to a doorway, beyond which he could see a pale glow. It shone like moonlight, silhouetting the figure of a woman in the middle distance.

He moved swiftly towards the exit, pausing on the threshold for just a moment like he did at ticket barriers and automatic sliding doors, not entirely trusting that they wouldn't suddenly smash together like the jaws of a trap.

When he stepped out of the neon-bordered passage, Ross found himself on a wooden boardwalk connecting a series of jetties, beneath which water shimmered and sparkled under the light of stars. The water looked cold, black, placid and deep, at once beautiful but starkly uninviting. He watched his step, as there were no barriers, and water rules were something one had to be wary of in games: some let the foulest murky depths provide a vital conduit, while in others it represented instant death for reasons the developers didn't always bother to make clear.

'That's far enough,' the woman said, her accent American, voice wearily authoritative.

She was standing near the end of the jetty directly ahead, watching him carefully down the barrel of the kind of weapon you only got towards the end of a game. Ross guessed one twitch of her trigger-finger would be all it took for him to be insta-gibbed.

He would place her in her late forties, maybe even early fifties, of African-American ethnicity, the combination of which was rare enough in video games as to virtually guarantee she wasn't an NPC. She was clad in a practical-looking purple flight suit, her hair pulled back by a headband. She looked dressed for action, perhaps the pilot of some craft, but Ross couldn't see any vessels on the water or at any of the jetties.

He glanced around. The place was eerily quiet and still, like something from a dream, or a stage-set for some minimalist two-hander. In this context he couldn't help but wonder whether the woman was in some way symbolic.

'Are you the guardian of this place?' he asked, unable to avoid sounding as though he was in a sub-Tolkien RPG.

She looked at him like he was a pillock and rather impolitely failed to suppress a laugh.

'No, honey, *that's* the guardian of this place.'

198

She was looking behind him, indicating the long, squat, black-walled construction from which he had just emerged, standing on a jetty of its own abutting the wooden walkway.

'That and this big stupid dick substitute I'm holding. But either way, die here and you respawn in a secure chamber, the only way out of which is a one-way warp transit to a place *very* far away, with indestructible monsters and pain protocols like you wouldn't believe.'

At this Ross held up his hands just a little higher, further emphasising that he was no longer packing and posed no threat.

'I hear you,' he said.

'Who are you?' she asked.

Ross recalled Solderburn's warning not to go pissing information about, and decided against revealing his real-world name. The one he had given himself here was the only one that could possibly have any currency, but as far as he was aware, other than NPCs, the only people it would mean anything to were Iris, Bob and the Integrity.

'My name is Bedlam.'

'Never heard of you,' she said dismissively. 'What were you doing in the badlands? That back-channel you just took isn't a path many people stumble upon by accident. That's why you have to knock on the door and wait for somebody to let you in. It's only Integrity and NPCs out there these days, and you don't seem like an NPC.'

'I'm neither. I'm just lost, and my friend got captured. I started off in *Starfire* and found my way out of there into this World War Two . . .'

'What do you mean, you started off? Started off doing what? That ain't vacation territory these days.'

'I mean started off as in those are the only places I've been. One minute I'm helping trial some new equipment at work and the next I'm a cyborg.'

Even at a distance he could see the consternation on her face.

'Hang on: you're saying you're new here? You only just arrived?'

'Yes, exactly,' he said, gushing in his relief at being understood.

'Bullshit,' she said, raising the gun as though readying to fire. 'All right, now I *know* you're Integrity.'

'I'm not, I swear,' he insisted, waving his outstretched hands in a panic so wussy as to surely convey his desperation. 'I'm telling the truth. The Integrity tortured me and my friend helped break me out, but then Solderburn got captured and I managed to escape to—'

'Excuse me, did you say *Solderburn*?' she asked, lowering the weapon slightly.

'Yes.'

'As in, the Original?'

'Well, he's the only one I've ever met.'

'And you're saying you just got here, but he's your friend? How does that figure?'

'Well, when I say friend, I mean principally colleague. We've worked together for years.'

'And when did you last . . . *work* with him?'

'I don't know how long it's been. A couple of days maybe? He was the last person I saw before I, you know, came here.'

She was looking at him with increased intensity, but the barrel of her rifle was at least starting to dip.

'I gotta make some calls,' she said.

Ross expected her to produce some form of device but instead she held her pose, the gun still pointed roughly towards him. Her eyes remained locked upon him too, but her expression seemed a little blank, as though her mind was partly elsewhere. He was reminded a little of the card collector when whoever was controlling him was busy off-screen, but he wasn't about to put her vigilance to the test.

After a while her head moved slightly, signalling that she was giving him her full attention. Unfortunately, this still included training the weapon on him, so whatever word had come down was not entirely friendly.

'Okay. I've been ordered to keep you isolated until they can figure out what to do.'

Ross stole an anxious glance back towards the kill-box.

'No, no. Gonna stick you someplace where I don't have to babysit. Come this way,' she gestured, or rather commanded, given that the gesture had been made with the gun.

'Did they say anything else about me? And who are *they*?' Ross enquired, before his question suggested its own answer. 'Are you . . . a Diasporado?' he asked, his voice dropping conspira-torially despite there being nobody else around.

'Are you a spy?'

He was about to answer in the negative until he realised her reply was not a question, just a means of explaining how daft he was to think she'd answer his.

'Can you tell me your name, at least?'

She paused, looking at him with a disdain that suggested she grudged him not only this much information, but the effort it took to speak it.

'It's Juno.'

Jetties stretched out to his left and right in a seemingly endless array, and in front the water extended to the black horizon, above which a dilute galaxy of stars hung low across the sky, like a skimmed Milky Way.

'Where are we going? What is this: a pier?'

'A gateway,' she replied. 'To what we call the Beyonderland. When I say "what we call", that is of course assuming you ain't some Integrity fuckwad just pretending to be a gormless noob.'

'I can assure you, I am a noob, and the gormlessness is genuine. And where is this Beyonderland?'

He was going to ask whether you got there by boat but reck-oned chances were high the answer would only make him look like a twat, and as she already didn't strike him as somebody to whom a stranger was just a friend she hadn't met yet, he thought he'd best avoid further irritating her.

'You're looking at it,' she replied, indicating the sky and thus vindicating his reticence. 'Those aren't stars: more like planets, or maybe just islands. The Beyonderland is an archipelago of individual tiny worlds.'

'How do you get there? By . . . spaceship?' he ventured.

'By invitation. Take a look at your tablet.'

Ross called up his HUD. He found a whole new menu heading entitled Beyonderland, and upon selecting it found that the topmost section, Invitations, was flashing.

'It's from you,' he acknowledged.

'You can warp to anywhere in the Beyonderland, as long as you've got an invite from the host.'

'So are we going to where you "live"? Your home?'

'In your fuckin' dreams, Beavis. I'm taking you to your own private holding cell. I'm gonna hand over the keys and tell you what day they collect the trash, then I'm gonna get the fuck outta there and hope they decide you're somebody else's problem.'

'They have bin collections here?'

'Figure of speech, dipshit. Come on.'

Other People

A few seconds later, Ross was standing next to Juno on an island of grey surrounded by the same shimmering dark water, which looked even more foreboding for the way it clearly delineated the ends of this miniature world. The surface underfoot looked like linoleum but felt like tiles, a grid of pinstriped dark grey lines stretching out in transecting parallels across the lighter grey of the uniformly flat ground. He could make out other worlds against the black sky, though they had no definition, just dots in the distance.

'Welcome to your world,' said Juno, with more than a trace of weary sarcasm.

Ross was starting to wonder what he had pulled her away from, by turning up in that kill-box, for her to be so enduringly arsey with him.

He frowned.

'It's a bit Spartan. I like the atmosphere of chilly gloom, though. Is that an automatic response feature to match the vibe you're giving off, or is it always like this?'

Juno opened her mouth to answer, then stopped, catching up to the fact that he was having a dig. She nodded, as though acknowledging something to herself.

'Yeah, that's funny. Know what else is funny? This.'

With which she unleashed a volley from the rifle.

Ross felt a brief explosion of pain and light and then the now-familiar sensation of resolution as he respawned on exactly the same spot.

'What the fuck was that for?'

'Three things. Second was so you realise you ain't going

nowhere if you suicide; and the third was to remind you to be polite to the lady who's holding the gun.'

'What was the first?'

'Already told you: it's funny.'

'Well if you shoot me another few times, will it lighten your mood to a huff?'

'You want we should give it a try?'

'Don't do me any favours.'

She looked him up and down for a few seconds and gave a long sigh.

'I'm sorry,' she eventually said, with a statutory minimum of sincerity and just as much warmth, like she knew an apology was appropriate but wanted him to know it didn't mean she was any less likely to shoot him again.

'And in answer to your question, it isn't always as gloomy as this, unless you want it to be. Everything here is up to you. You can have permanent daylight, permanent night, a cycle of sunrise and sunset at whatever speed you wish. You can choose the weather, have seasons, a climate. It's your own private realm, your own personal sanctuary. You can't get out though, because I disabled two-way warp, but on the plus side, nobody gets in unless you invite them.'

'Like vampires,' Ross suggested.

He tested the ground with a stamp of his foot. It seemed utterly solid, like bedrock.

'So can I make it a bit more homely?'

'Oh yeah. You can build your dream house and cover the walls with tits and race-cars. Knock yourself out. This place is *a blank slate for your imagination*,' she said, evidently quoting, going by the acid tinge to her exaggeratedly cheesy enthusiasm. 'Course, not everybody wants that, because not everybody has an imagination. You can have a world straight off the peg: environment and structures all pre-built and ready to go. You can browse other people's work and just replicate it, or choose from templates. Your HUD will superimpose how it would appear from whatever perspective you're looking.'

Ross scanned through the multiplicity of new sub-menus and auxiliary inventories, which appeared to comprise a hybrid of a level-design suite, photo-editing software and a god-game toolbox.

'This looks like it could turn into a full-time occupation,' he said, speaking from experience. Creating custom maps had proven a dangerous addiction not only as a medical student, but even as a supposedly adult doctor who had professional commitments and the wherewithal to have a life. Indeed, looking back at his house-officer years, there was a chicken-and-egg conundrum worth pondering: had he gone such long periods without a girlfriend because of the proportion of his limited free time he spent constructing virtual environments, or had he he spent such a proportion of his limited free time constructing virtual environments because he didn't have a girlfriend?

'Everything you need to build your own little corner of heaven, huh?' Juno suggested.

'Well, not exactly. If it was heaven I'd have someone to share it with.'

'Yeah,' she replied, looking into the distance and lingering over the word. It was like she was acknowledging what he was saying, but it was clear she didn't want to go there with him.

'Everybody's different,' she went on. 'Most people spend the majority of their time in other worlds, big, busy places, but everybody needs a retreat. Sometimes you want to be alone.'

And not have your sulky me-time interrupted by being on-call for the kill-box, Ross guessed.

'So this would be my own private fortress of solitude,' he suggested.

'And you don't even need to sign anything,' Juno said. Her tone was wry but Ross could tell there was finally a little thaw on her breeze. 'Could use a woman's touch,' she added, 'or indeed any kind of touch. But like I said, you can have it whatever way you want. You can have *yourself* whatever way you want too, whether that's to design some new duds or to give yourself a whole new face. While you're in this place you can be both seamstress and surgeon.'

Ross scanned the corresponding editing tools, letting him alter existing physical models and skins as well as creating new ones from scratch.

'This would explain why Solderburn was looking so healthy,' he admitted. 'I mean, he was still unmistakably Solderburn, but kind of idealised. Slimmer, for one thing; younger, more chiselled.'

'Everybody has a little work done. First thing is usually a horizontal one-eighty flip.'

'What's that?'

'Take a look in a mirror,' she suggested, conjuring one into the air. Having grown used to the facial implants of his cyborg self, Ross didn't see much wrong with the likeness that greeted him. There was, however, something odd about it that he couldn't quite place.

'What you're seeing right now probably more resembles how you looked in photographs than the face that used to look back when you were shaving. The default vision of ourselves that we start off with in this place is constructed from our memories of how we looked in the old world, where we mostly saw mirror images. So if you had a scar on one side of your face . . .'

Ross put his right hand to his left cheek, touching the little trio of freckles that looked a bit like Orion's belt. He used to mention it to people and they'd never get it, and now he understood why: from anyone else's perspective, they were slanted at the wrong angle.

'Course, there are people here who were blind in the old world, but they can see here. When they first show up, they have *very* strange conceptual versions of heads and faces, like walking Picasso paintings: the image they had of themselves and the image they had of the human face in general, based on touch and imagination.'

Ross tried to picture the grotesque homunculi that this process might have conjured. Poor bastards must have ended up looking like Kelvin MacKenzie.

'Do you get any based on sheer self-delusion?'

'How would we know?'

'Fair point.'

Ross browsed the controls. He could see his own head in a rotatable 3D model, various automatic shortcuts available as well as the in-depth manual adjustment options.

'A one-eighty flip, you say?' he stated, selecting an instant process. 'Like this?'

In a single beat, his face was altered so that the freckles did once again line up like Orion's belt. He felt immediately more comfortable for reasons he couldn't quite fathom.

'Yep,' Juno agreed. 'That one you can do at the touch of a button; or at the internally visualised touch of a button leastways. Anything more complex, you can try your hand or get an appointment with an expert.'

'And you can create anything you want? A new face every day if you feel like it?'

'If you feel like it, sure, but in practice people tend not to. Not only is it real confusing for the folks you know, but it messes with your sense of self if you keep seeing somebody different whenever you look in a mirror. You'll find that even though somebody might refine their appearance, idealise it, they still tend to keep *some* essence of how they looked.

'Obviously you can go incognito any time you want, though there are worlds where you have to register a skin and stick to it. You'll get kicked out if you're caught breaking the rules. It's about respecting people's choices: there's a whole universe out there for wearing masks in, so people go to certain places because they want a guarantee that what you see is what you get.'

Ross took in Juno's face for a moment. She was what was often described as 'a handsome woman', meaning that her face was pleasing to the eye but not in a way that would be considered classically attractive: something altogether more elegant than 'sexy'; to be admired rather than lusted after. In a world where she could have any face she wanted, it begged a question: one she had seen coming way off when she caught him staring.

'Let me guess,' she said witheringly. 'You're wondering why, if I can alter my appearance, I look like a forty-eight-year-old woman and not some adolescent cover-girl?'

'Well, I, er, I mean, I think you look very . . .' he spluttered.

'It's a fair question. Maybe in the real world I *was* an adolescent cover-girl, and here I just want to be something else.'

She let him simmer on this one for a moment, then continued.

'No, truth is this is pretty much the old me. I got a few different flavours of it, but the essence is the same. Like plenty of others, I prefer to look as much as possible like my original self, because it would make it easier for anyone I knew to recognise me.'

'You were looking for somebody,' Ross deduced, immediately racing ahead to wonder who else he might find here. 'Somebody from the . . .'

He didn't know what term was polite, unsure whether 'real world' constituted some kind of *faux pas*, like an elderly relative referring to a Chinese takeaway as 'a chinky'.

'The old world,' Juno said. 'My daughter, Miranda.'

He didn't need to ask how the search had gone. The look of hurt, uncertainty and lingering anger told him all he had to know.

'You never found her.'

'It's the great and bitter irony of this place: a whole universe built from games, yet there are no kids in it. Apart from over-grown ones. There's nobody here who was under sixteen when they arrived. Miranda was fourteen.'

'I'm sorry.'

'No use you apologising: it ain't your fault. But if I ever get my hands on the asshole who put me here . . .'

She sighed, blinking away what looked like a tear.

'Course, I'd need to wait in line. The whole gameverse is full of folks separated from the people they loved: mothers and fathers who never got to see their children again; husbands, wives, brothers, sisters, friends.'

Ross listened with a growing dread, one that it turned out he wasn't doing a good job of disguising. He guessed no amount of facial self-editing would manage that trick.

'Hate to be the one who broke it to you,' she said. 'Are you a father?'

'I just found out my girlfriend is pregnant. That's why I have to find a way out of here.'

'Well, long as I'm doling out the bad news, I might as well hit you with that one too . . .'

Ross was about to protest, remembering Iris's words outside the airlock. Then he saw the truth in Juno's face, and measured it against how much reason he had to place trust in anything Iris had said. Juno had searched desperately and exhaustively for her daughter, but the further unspoken implication was that she had also searched desperately and exhaustively for a way out.

'Jesus,' he said, staring into the dark sky and fighting against tears.

Juno let him take this in for a few moments, then slung the gun around her back and gave his shoulder a grudging and slightly awkward squeeze.

'Hey, chin up. Don't go cutting your wrists,' Juno said.

'Why, because I'll only respawn?'

'Well, that and the fact that people do still find each other. You found Solderburn, unless you were lying about that.'

'No, I wasn't,' he said, grasping this sliver of hope. 'You're saying Carol could be here too? And my family?'

'It's possible. I found my husband, Joe.'

'You did? Miranda's father?'

'No, I was never married to him. That was ancient history. So was Joe, I guess. Before we found each other again, we'd been apart a lot longer than we'd ever been together in the old world.'

'What do you remember about that?' Ross asked. 'The last thing before you came here, I mean?'

'I went to bed. That's all. Same as 'most everybody.'

'Your husband too? The same night?'

'No. That's where it gets kinda weird. Yeah, he went to bed and woke up in a video game, like everybody else, but the last things he remembered from the old world happened nearly two years before I came here. And let me be clear, he was with me during those two years; not like he disappeared. We lived our lives, went to work, had Christmases, vacations. But he's got no memory of that time: none.'

'Must have been a hell of a catching-up session.'

Juno looked away, as though carefully shaping her response. Something here was delicate.

'It sure wasn't easy. It's happened to a lot of people who've found each other, and sometimes it breaks them up. One of them has memories of their relationship that the other doesn't share, and that can put up quite a barrier. Joe said it was almost like I'd had an affair, but all the weirder because that affair was with him.'

'Did it break *you* up?' Ross asked tentatively.

209

'Well, no,' she said reflectively.

Ross felt a disproportionate sense of relief, pleased to find some reason for optimism in this growing nightmare.

'That didn't break us up. It was the fact that Joe was fucking insipid pornalike bimbos as though he was trying out for Team USA in the insipid-pornalike-bimbo-fucking Olympics that broke us up.'

Ross was struggling to think of any kind of response to this, especially with Juno's eyes blazing into him like he might be held responsible by proxy as the only male in sight. She wasn't done, either.

'We got a phrase here: "Hell if you make it, heaven if you want it to be." Well, before we ran into each other again, that priapic fuck-monkey had decided heaven was a John Holmes movie. Big reunion lasted pretty much until he started *suggesting* how I might prefer to look. Round these parts that implies a bit more than saying "how about you try on this new negligee"; you hear what I'm saying?'

Juno's rant would have been intimidating enough on its own, but as the aforementioned only male in sight, and having already been insta-gibbed merely for effect, Ross was fucking terrified.

It must have shown. She looked at the blank ground and emitted a self-conscious laugh.

'Sorry. Bit of an over-share. I'm feeling kind of raw, fair to say. Look, I hope you find your girl. I'm just saying you gotta be prepared for her not being who you remember. You say you just got here: well she could have been here as long as me. She could be somebody else entirely now, and given our issues measuring time in this place, you better be ready to deal with the possibility that she could have *literally* seen more cock-ends than weekends.'

She caught herself once more, eyes burning into her whipping boy as she unloaded on him. This time, however, it looked like she either didn't think she owed anyone an apology or was still too pissed-off to offer one.

'How about you shoot me again?' Ross suggested acerbically.

'Why, you think that would make me feel better?'

'No. But when you did it before, I felt better than I do now.'

Juno shrugged, still simmering.

210

'Forewarned is forearmed,' she justified.

'Fuck you.'

They stood there in silence for a while, neither looking at the other, the only sound or movement coming from the lapping of the waves.

Eventually she spoke.

'I'm gonna leave you to it,' she said quietly, awkwardly. 'Wait for my orders. You should use the time: maybe build a house or try out some facial editing.'

'Aye. You should try some facial editing too: maybe crack your face and make your arse jealous.'

Build Time

Ross sat slumped on a sofa in the huge, glass-walled front room of his beach house, staring out over the sands, the jetty and the black waters towards the dark horizon.

Juno had never said how long she'd be, which Ross understood to be a moot consideration in light of her remark regarding the absence of a frame of reference for the passing of time. Understandably, he was trying not to think too much about the rest of that particular sentence.

You can have anything, she had said, shape the world any way you want. Well, how about a clock or a calendar? Out of curiosity he had begun looking through the sub-menus associated with his private world, and happened across the variable settings controlling solar and seasonal cycles. That, he realised, was the problem: you could have a clock and a calendar, but it would only apply locally, and what's more, you could change it at any time. Gameworld rules: you could set permanent day, permanent night, or the passing of a month, the passing of a *season* in the real-time equivalent of an hour.

How did people make appointments round here?

'Yeah, Jim, I'll see you at, er, not sure o'clock, on the, er, somethingth of fuck-knows, okay?'

'Aye, and don't be late.'

Marooned on his flat and blank personal island, he had little alternative but to experiment with his new toolkit. He watched a cursor float in his field of view, guided by movements of his fingers, its appearance changing as he toggled through its various modes. He could raise the landscape, shape the terrain, choose grass, rock, sand, woodland or water, and it would be instantly real. He could pick up the sand and let it run through his fingers, dip his toes in the stream, smell the scent of the trees. Every last grain, every last drop, every last airborne particle had to be an individual piece of code, ultimately just information. Had that always secretly been true of what he'd considered the real world? And as far as the mind was concerned, did it matter whether that information was analogue or digital, filtered through the senses and couriered along nerves, or fed direct to the brain?

He took a handful of water and drank. He wasn't thirsty: he just wanted to see what would happen. It was crisp and fresh on the palate, a cold sensation running down his throat. Did this mean he would have to pee? He'd better think about creating a toilet just in case.

He discovered that he could shape objects from memory, merely by concentrating on his recalled mental image of them. This could apply to something as small and basic as a table or as large and complex as an entire house. In the latter case, of course, the image tended to be sketchy in places, but he was then able to add finer detail on a piecemeal basis.

He wondered what it said that after a period of messing around and learning the basics, the first project he truly committed to building was not a futuristic dream-pad or a fantasy castle but a replica of his childhood home. He couldn't get it quite right, though. The outside started off okay, but became grotesquely skewed as he worked on refining the interior. Some rooms were massively bigger than others; some extremely dense in their detail while others were sparse. His old bedroom was getting on for the size of a tennis court, though the reality had been about sixteen feet by nine. It had been so many things in his mind: battleground, football pitch, rock-show stage, ocean, starship bridge. The room his older sisters had shared was tiny by comparison: it had been physically much bigger than his in real life, but the one in his memory was a cluttered cloister that he was only ever allowed to glimpse before being booted out and having the door closed on him.

His construction both creeped him out and made him sad. Even though he could wander around it, he felt less connection to it than he might to an old photograph. After a while it just started to embarrass him, so he erased it and copy-pasted a Californian beach house, adding a pier that extended out over

214

the gently lapping black water. It was the kind of place he occasionally fantasised about living in because it seemed not only sumptuously opulent, but so removed from the lifestyle he'd always known. It wasn't just *a* Californian beach house: it was as though the essence of a hundred Californian beach houses had been distilled and then used to create this place.

And now he was sitting outside it, with nothing to do but wait. He knew he could be sitting there, on hold until Juno's return, for a very long time, same as he could be stuck here in this alternate domain forever.

There had been worse waits, however; harder unknowings. The time when his mum was battling breast cancer had been full of them. Sometimes those waits were mere hours, other times months, but in either case it had felt like normal life was in suspension, even as it went on around them, even as they lived it.

There had been intense, exhilarating and tantalising uncertainties too. Like when he finally plucked up the bottle to ask Carol out, and her phone rang on vibrate just as he was saying the words.

He had got as far as 'I was wondering whether maybe . . .' when her eyes had glanced instinctively at the screen.

'I'm really sorry, I need to take this,' she had said; then, even worse, as it was work-related and confidential, she had walked away from the table and right out of the coffee shop.

He had sat there analysing the preceding few seconds as though they were the Zapruder footage. The fact she had looked at the phone: did that mean she knew what was coming and was hoping to see a call she could ignore? Had it actually *been* a call she could ignore, but having sussed what was coming she was pretending it was work so that she could quietly derail it and they could both pretend it never happened?

Round and round he went, until eventually she came back in, smiling apologetically.

'Sorry. That was important. Well, it wasn't important, but it was important that I answer it, if you know what I mean.'

'That's okay. Don't worry about it.'

'So where were we?' she asked.

Now she could change the subject, and, just as easily, so could he, chickening out with no harm done and a mutual conspiracy in place to forget what almost happened.

But then she took it out of his hands.

'You were wondering whether maybe . . .' she prompted.

Sitting outside his off-the-peg beach house was more like Purgatory, except Purgatory was meant to be heaven's anteroom. What lay in wait for Ross was frustratingly more indeterminate.

He was being presented with infinite possibilities yet he couldn't think of one he'd like to choose right now that was more appealing than going home. None of them seemed to have any purpose. If you don't need to earn and you don't need to eat and you don't need to stay healthy and you *can't* propagate the species, what's the point of your existence? Just as weekends become meaningless when you're unemployed, so a world of play loses its lustre when it isn't framed by work.

Christ. Just the thought of the word 'weekend' made him wince, and would continue to do so for a long time. Cheers, Juno.

He could battle in Middle-earth, explore planetscapes and star systems, journey through past and future civilisations, win wars, fight crime, race supercars, live out endless fantasies, and yet none of it held the same appeal as getting back to his old life. No, that wasn't true, because it wouldn't be his old life. It would be different.

He realised everything he had ever done was driven by work. University, house-officer jobs, a training number, then the drive towards medical research opportunities in neurology when he realised his enthusiasms lay away from the clinical. It had all seemed so imperative, so much so that in all that time he'd seldom thought about what *else* his life might hold, what else he might want to do with himself.

No more.

He'd tell Neurosphere their power charade was over, and the relationship between them was going to be different from now on. They needed him more than he needed them, so they'd better lube up, and be very nice to him if they wanted a reacharound. He wouldn't live for his job any more. He'd live for Carol and the baby. Work–life balance. Regular hours, a grown-up relationship, responsibilities, a family: that was what he wanted.

Or was he kidding himself? Was that desire just immeasurably pitiful, not to mention cowardly? Did he want to go back to such a comparatively limited existence purely because it was the one he'd always known?

Perhaps.

Didn't he have a responsibility here too? Solderburn was being held in some no-doubt-hellish prison fortress, the agonies of which Ross could only too vividly recall. The Integrity were trying to control the whole gameverse and condemn its entire population to a pot-luck eternity of being trapped in the limited world of any given game. Wasn't it selfish to be thinking only of escaping this place and abandoning everyone else here to their fate?

Perhaps.

It was all moot, though. There was no going back.

He gazed into the night sky, wondering about the people who might be on each of those little dots, every one of them another island world. Had they all gone through what he was experiencing now, mourning the life they no longer had before coming to terms with their new one and embracing its possibilities? Were there people out there he already knew? Was Carol out there somewhere? His mum? His sisters? Would he make new friends, forge new relationships and gradually feel the old ties, old wounds fade into memory?

As he gazed and pondered, he observed that one of the lights in the distance was larger than the others, and wondered why he hadn't noticed this before. Then he realised that it was because it hadn't *been* larger before, and with every second it was getting larger still.

It was moving, coming closer. As it grew it transformed from a point of light into an object, lines and shape gradually becoming defined against the black background.

It was an aircraft, and it was headed his way.

It appeared to be travelling slowly at first, until he realised that this was an effect of his head-on perspective and the sheer distance it was covering. In fact by the time it was close enough for him to appreciate just how fast it was travelling, it had already started to decelerate. Wings began extending from either side as it descended, twisting to forty-five degrees almost like a large

217

seabird coming down to settle on the waves. It was quiet, just the low thrum of a power source and the occasional hiss and squeal of servos audible as it made its majestic final approach. Ross was expecting it to splash down with a bump and a spray, but instead it came to rest a foot above the water. It hovered with a gentle bob like it was being repelled by a magnet and its bulk was yet to steady completely.

A gangway rolled forth from the fuselage, connecting it to the jetty, and out stepped Juno. Despite everything, he had to admit he was pleased to see her.

'So,' she said, 'you ever take a ride in a spaceship before?'

Computer Space

The air temperature was cooler inside the vessel, the last of Ross's bespoke evening warmth shut out with the hum of the power source when the entry hatch sealed. There was still a vibration faintly audible in the interior, but it was quieter than any vehicle Ross had ever travelled inside. He got an impression of near-absolute efficiency, no mechanism in the craft being so profligate as to waste energy by unnecessarily emitting any sound.

'Where are we going?' he asked.

'I've been ordered to take you to Silent Hill.'

'Aye, that sounds a cosy place for a pow-wow.'

'It's secure.'

'If homicidal geometric abstract nightmares make you feel secure, yeah.'

'Look, I didn't choose the destination. I just deliver the package.'

The ship accelerated at a rate that should have flattened Ross against the back of his seat with the g-force. Instead his only physical reaction was his stomach lurching with excitement in response to seeing the water and the archipelago of the Beyonderland shoot past at impossible speed. Inside, the ride was a majestic glide, so smooth you could have walked round serving drinks.

'Just so we're clear on the relationship,' he said, 'am I your prisoner?'

'You never were. You just woulda had a hard time going anyplace once I put you on your little island. So, technically, you were marooned rather than imprisoned. It's not for me to stop you going where you want; just that we're skittish about people we've never seen before trying to sneak in the back door to the Beyonderland. If the Integrity gets the whip hand, that's where we'll fall back to for our final stand.'

Ross wondered whether her choice of the phrase 'whip hand' had been deliberate. She was certainly dropping any ambiguity over being part of the resistance.

'Does that mean I can have my weapons back?'

'Not while you could potentially hi-jack my ass.'

'Couldn't I just ask you to drop me off and then go my own way? Start looking for Carol?'

'You could, but you might find it easier if you made some friends.'

'True enough. After I did so well with you, maybe I'm on a roll.'

Juno let out what might optimistically be interpreted as a chuckle.

'Yeah. Really rolled out the red carpet, didn't I?'

'You didn't owe me anything,' he acknowledged. 'But I'm relieved, if I dare say it, that you seem to be in a wee bit less scary frame of mind at the moment?'

His voice quietened towards the end, emphasising that this was just a tentative suggestion and please don't bite – or shoot – my head off if it's out of line.

'I'm feeling a little better,' she said neutrally. 'Did a little soul-searching after I left. Realised I was taking out my frustrations on the wrong person, so I took them out on the right one instead.'

'Joe? What did you do to him?'

'I stole his spaceship,' she said matter-of-factly, the insouciant tone only serving to illustrate how much pleasure she was concealing by it.

'I volunteered to bring you in,' she added. 'Somebody else is on backdoor watch.'

'You just couldn't deny that special chemistry between us?'

'No, I realised you were my ticket. I'm doing my bit for the resistance but nobody ever tells me shit. I figure if I'm the one who delivers you to the higher-ups, I get to upgrade my clearance.'

Juno made a minor adjustment to the two-handed yoke, climbing ever steeper, ever faster. They passed into the darkness, the lights of islands briefly blinking out, then more appeared, and suddenly beneath the ship there was more water. This happened again and again, faster and faster, the Beyonderland comprising a vast *millefeuille* through which they were rising more and more rapidly until the multiplicity of tiers became a blur.

'How come they're so interested in me?' Ross asked. 'Why did you call it in?'

'Firstly, you were claiming to be a recent arrival. The only newcomers to show up in a very long time have been our friends in black, so naturally anyone else making their debut is going to pique suspicion. Secondly, you said you had seen Solderburn; more than that, you said you knew him in the old world.'

'What's so special about Solderburn?'

'For one thing, he's been MIA for about half of forever. But mainly it's because he's one of the Originals.'

Ross recalled her previous use of this description and realised he'd misinterpreted it.

'They're kind of the elders of this place. They were the first ones here, but most of them have dropped off the radar to stay free of our new playmates. It became pretty clear that the Integrity were targeting the Originals because they were essentially both the architects and pioneers of free travel between gameworlds. Solderburn's disappearance goes way back before the advent of the Integrity, but the other Originals have gone underground as a direct result of their arrival.'

The blur of tiers ceased as the ship shot through what must be the uppermost of them, heading into blackness.

'So we're flying to Silent Hill? How does that work? Why aren't we using a warp transit?'

Ross tried not to make the question sound like he was wondering how Juno could have forgotten that she had the option. She had thawed a little but he reckoned she wouldn't have much tolerance for him in any way annoying her, especially in the confined space of a cockpit.

'This is the quickest route. We'll warp to Silent Hill from Calastria, but to get to Calastria purely by warp transits, we'd have to go via five other worlds, and in most of those the distance between the point of entry and the next transit we'd need is pretty huge. You know how big Graxis is, right? We're talking journeys three and four times that. Sure, there's vehicles, even aircraft, but on some worlds there's also armies of NPCs to negotiate, not to mention Integrity.'

'But how can we get to another *game* by spaceship?'

'You gotta understand that this whole realm effectively exists in two forms: what we perceive and interact with, and the true nature of its fabric, which is digital. I ain't telling you there's no Santa Claus if I say this is all code, am I?'

'No, I got that part way back. Little fuzzy on how I can be inside it, but I gather so is everybody else.'

'And do you understand how computers store information? Random-access memory?'

Ross could almost feel a surge of power being diverted to his dickish-behaviour restraint systems in order to hold back the vast well of smug and self-important twattery that such a question had the potential to unleash. His safeguards condensed a statement outlining his biog, qualifications, academic honours, publications and entire CV into three words.

'Fair to say.'

'Well that's better than I'd claim, so forgive me if my terms of reference are a little blurry. But as I understand it, data gets written to random memory locations, meaning consecutive pieces of code won't be at adjacent addresses: they could be any distance apart. So on a hard drive with a ton of games written to it, the RAM address for, say, a wall in *Starfire* might be right next to that of a floor in a completely different game. Conversely, the RAM address for a chair in *Starfire* could be massively distant from the address for the floor it's standing on.'

'The spatial distance between places is something we perceive, but it's illusory?' Ross suggested. 'In truth, we're always moving between billions of addresses?'

'Except the spatial distance isn't entirely an illusion. There *is* a spatial relationship between objects, and a navigable spatial relationship between all the worlds. You can traverse both the spatial and the digital.'

'So, essentially, warping is using the digital juxtapositions to take a shortcut through the spatial.'

'You got it. But sometimes the spatial route is quicker. So we can fly from the Beyonderland and make our way to Calastria entirely along the spatial plane.'

'Does that mean anyone with a ship could land on my island?'

'No. As you said, it's like vampires: nobody can cross the threshold without an invitation. They can land up close, can even dock with that little jetty you built, but until they've got permission to come ashore, that spatial relationship *is* an illusion, because they're never setting foot on your turf.'

'Well, that's reassuring. I'd hate someone to break in while I'm gone and steal all the nothing that I own.'

Ross watched worlds go past through the ship's windows, just tiny dots with vast distances between them. He recalled the endlessness when he had keyed in a noclip cheat then risen up through a map and just kept climbing. You could go on and on until the world of the game was just a speck, but that was only the game's 3D engine keeping the map in geometric perspective. What was this space that all these gameworlds could simultaneously occupy? It had to have physics, rules. Even the fact you could fly through it, the very fact that it *was* space, meant it had to have protocols. Somebody must have assigned them. And if it was all so vast and so complicatedly getting on with itself, what were the chances that a noob like him was going to find a way out of it where everyone else had failed?

He realised he'd better start learning how to adapt, get some pointers about making a life here.

'So how do you occupy yourself, when you're not escorting strays like me across the empty wastes?'

'Mostly I walk. I explore. Every city, every forest, every dungeon, every cave, every world. I keep looking.'

Ross nodded. He didn't need to ask what for. He just wondered how long this had been her life, and whether she even knew.

He cast an eye over the console panel in front of Juno, taking in the controls, dials, screens and read-outs.

'What you after?' Juno asked.

'I was going to ask how long till we get there, but then I remembered it would be pointless. Nobody here knows what the time is.'

'That ain't strictly true. How could we organise anything otherwise? There's a clock on your tablet that shows universal time. It doesn't display by default, so maybe you didn't see it yet.'

She instructed him quickly on how to bring it up. It read two days, fourteen hours and twelve minutes.

'When I say universal time, I just mean it's a program set to run independently of local settings, calibrated the same on all tablets.'

'Does this read-out state how long I've been here?'

'It doesn't necessarily relate to real time. It's just a mutual standard.'

'So how long does yours say you've been here?'

'It doesn't show how long you've been here, only how long since you activated the tablet.'

'And how long is that, in your case?'

'That's a personal question, honey. You don't ask a lady her age.'

She offered him a knowing smile but he could tell there was something else beneath it. She was hiding behind conventions of politeness, but he didn't get to press the matter, as Juno's attention was sharply turned to something she had spotted on one of the monitor panels.

It was a screen that had been blank and, Ross assumed, off or redundant, but now there was a white dot blipping just inside the edge of it.

'Is that another ship?' he asked.

'Yup,' she replied, not taking her eyes off the controls. She couldn't have said much less, but her tone and manner were enough to convey that she was on edge. A keyboard layout appeared in the black sheen of the console and she typed in some commands, then manually altered their course using the yoke.

'Should I be worried?'

'That's what I'm trying to ascertain. We were on course for a convergence before I made a correction. If they correct their course to renew the convergence, then yes, you should be worried.'

'The Integrity?'

She shook her head.

'Integrity don't know about this: about the space routes.'

Ross was incredulous.

'How could they not?'

'Same way an ant don't know there's a world beyond the ant farm, even when it can see through the glass. It's right in front of them but they don't understand what it means. It's only a matter of time before they get there, though.'

'But isn't the Integrity made up of people who have lived here same as you, with the same knowledge?'

'No. They're not just a recent phenomenon, they're recent arrivals. At first some folks thought they might be a kind of NPC, accidentally generated by one of the gameworlds, but they're too smart for that to be true. They're sentient, self-aware and adaptable, but they're incomers, so they've got some catching-up to do.'

'So who's in the other ship? Or rather, who are you hoping *isn't* in the other ship?'

She gave him a stony look, advance warning not to say anything stupid.

'Pirates.'

He failed.

'Seriously?'

'No, humorously. They're fun pirates, like at a children's birthday party.'

Her tone indicated last-warning irritability.

'What can they do?'

'Blow us out of the sky if we don't give them what they want.'

'And what do they want? We don't have anything.'

'One: they don't know that. We could have all kinds of cargo. And two: at the very least they know they'll get inventory contents. Out here, people in transit are likely to be carrying items that hold value in hundreds of worlds: weapons, ammo, supplies, food, health, currency, even experience points from RPG worlds. Everything's a potentially tradable commodity.'

'But why? They could have any kind of lifestyle or experience they want here, couldn't they?'

'Every world has its own rules, but the one constant is that, wherever you are, the more stuff you got, the easier it is to get along. So in one sense they're just cheats. You can be whatever you like in the gameverse, and some people like to be assholes. You give them a universe of unlimited possibilities and they just become unlimited assholes.'

The monitor flashed, accompanied by a discordant chime that was never going to be used on an ice-cream van. There was a line drawn on the screen between the other ship's position and a newly projected convergence.

'Shit,' breathed Juno. 'They're coming. Gonna try and throw a net over us.'

'You mean like a tractor beam?'

'No, I mean literally a net, so they can force-dock or just hold us where they want us.

'What kind of defences have we got? Shields? Lasers? Photon torpedoes?' he suggested hopefully.

Juno's stern look said no. 'In every gameworld, if you got a ray-gun, there need to be protocols that dictate what damage the ray-gun does. We're between worlds. Out here, the protocols are very basic. They just govern movement in three dimensions: basic spatial physics. Unfortunately one of those basics is the principle that two objects can't occupy the same space, so out here it's seriously old-school. No tractor beams, no lasers, no explosives: just down and dirty ballistic hardware.'

'Cannonballs?'

'Cannonballs from distance, then harpoons, grapples and claws for pulling your ship apart. If your ship gets destroyed, you'll be left floating out here, with no propulsion.'

'Can't you suicide and respawn?'

'No spawn points in range. You know that weird sensation when you die, where everything's dissolved? You'll be left in that state until a ship with an on-board spawn point passes close enough, which given the scale of space . . .'

Juno punched in some more data and gave the yoke a sharp turn, keeping her eyes on the display that was projecting convergence. Ross could see she had radically changed the angle of vector, which meant only one thing.

'Can we outrun them?'

Juno held up a hand, her gaze still locked on the monitor. Silence filled the cockpit for a long few moments. Then the display refreshed itself, erasing the line, and Juno seemed to relax just a little.

'It would appear so. They're heavy. Not fast enough for direct pursuit. Must have been hoping they could get closer before

226

their intentions became clear. Need to keep a lookout though, in case they try to flank us with a shot.'

Another few moments passed, only marginally less tense than those that had preceded them. No ordnance issued from the other ship.

'Looks like they're not risking it. Would take a hell of a lucky pop to hit us from this distance. We'd have time enough to make evasive manoeuvres. Of course, a salvo aimed at five or six projected positions would improve their chances, but they'd still be gambling a lot of ammunition at long odds.'

'So, panic over?' Ross said optimistically.

'For now. Best stay sharp, though. They don't always hunt alone.'

'You got it. Where are the controls for our cannon?'

'We don't have one. Why do you think I was so worried?'

'We don't *have* one? Why not?'

'Whatever bells and whistles you might trick out your ship with in any given gameworld, once you cross the line into the big black, they no longer apply. So when you're equipping a ship for out here, you only have three attributes you can assign: speed, armour and weaponry, and you gotta prioritise according to your needs. Every ship has the same complement of points to spread around, so if you want a tough hide and a big gun, you're gonna be slow.'

'Whereas we're fast but we can't hit back?'

'Very fast with a little armour. I prefer to be able to manoeuvre my way out of trouble.'

'Float like a butterfly, sting like a butterfly as well?'

'Risk/benefit equation, kiddo. You don't encounter pirates very often, and when you do it's more advisable to run away than go toe to toe.'

He couldn't argue with the logic, as it was the same as had served him well since primary school.

Epic Holiday

As they made their descent, Ross could see the world of Calastria take shape, growing from a small white blob into a blurred blooming of colour, from smudge to doodle to map to recognisable landscape. It was surrounded by a ring of dark blue ocean, within which there were different shades of green covering meadows, forests and plains, the reddish-brown of mountain ranges, blue-black lakes and rivers, and a huge, nebulous grey haze covering about a third of the island.

'What's that?' he asked.

'Cloud, I guess. Rainforest maybe. There can be totally conflicting climate zones side by side,' Juno offered.

Juno had told him Calastria was the world-environment for a role-playing game called *The Exalted*, though nobody referred to it by that name any more. Similarly, she advised him that people would better understand him if he referred to Graxis rather than *Starfire*, but this wasn't a hard-and-fast rule, as clearly the plethora of warfare shooters offered multiple incarnations of the same places.

He remembered seeing conceptual art for the world of Calastria on a gaming site. *The Exalted* was the next in the *Sacred Reign* series of RPGs, though according to the article, the projected release date was still at least eighteen months off.

Solderburn did say he'd been in sequels to games that weren't due for years, and what made this even stranger was the fact that, according to Juno, Solderburn was one of 'the Originals', the elders of the gameverse. Given how cagey she had become regarding what it read on her own personal odometer, how long might Solderburn have been here? It melted Ross's head trying to think about this. It wasn't simply that time here didn't have

229

a consistent frame of reference: time here didn't appear to make any bloody sense at all.

Juno guided the ship in low towards the ring of sea that surrounded the land. Too low, in Ross's judgement, as unless she flattened out her angle of approach they were going to hit the water nose-first. He refrained from saying anything, at least for another few seconds, until he felt compelled to observe that crashing into the drink was starting to look unavoidable.

'That's the plan,' Juno reassured him, moments before the ship cut through the surface of the waves with no greater sense of impact than someone throwing a bucket of water at a car windscreen. The vessel continued its progress in a steady glide, powering through the hazy gloom. Ross saw shoals of fish shoot past the windows, and much larger shapes moving deeper in the murk.

'We have to come in unseen,' Juno explained. 'This is not a world where you're supposed to show up in a spaceship. If you're landing in some sci-fi metropolis, nobody's gonna be suspicious of where you started your journey, but if the Integrity have eyes here, it's gonna start their wheels turning in ways we really can't afford to encourage. This would be a good time to consider your wardrobe too.'

Ross looked at his options. He found that a new line in medieval attire had appeared in his inventory, and that Juno had restored his weapons. He chose an outfit that wasn't going to make him look too much like he was about to star in panto, and was about to ask Juno how he looked, only to be rendered speechless by how she did.

She had changed into some goddess of war, her armour sculpted around her to convey what he could only interpret as a formidable, aggressive femininity. It shone in steel, all sleek lines and sharp edges, unmistakably female but equally unmistakably not a costume intended to please or even consider male eyes. She looked intimidatingly bad-ass in a way that was quite simply not available to the grubbier sex.

'Told you I had some flavours,' she said. 'You like?'

Ross just gaped, and possibly trembled a little.

'You, er, made that yourself?'

'Yeah. That's what pisses me off about this place. You could be any incarnation of womanhood you can think of – so why do so many choose to conform to some fifteen-year-old dork's idea of it? Even in a world like Calastria, they'll still choose an appearance that's defined by sexuality. Do they think the guys try to look sexy when they're suiting up to fight dragons?'

'Er, not so much,' Ross agreed, but her last remark had inadvertently channelled his inner fifteen-year-old dork. 'There's going to be dragons?' he asked.

Juno found a secluded cove where they could come ashore unseen. She left the ship submerged, guiding it back down under the surface by remote. Satisfied that it was not visible and that their landing had not been witnessed, she led Ross up a winding stairway carved into the rock, then they proceeded around the headland.

As he walked the cliff-top path, lush woodland to his right, Ross made a startling realisation.

'I'm hungry,' he announced, with a mixture of astonishment and delight.

'You would be. It's the protocols. Calastria is a place where you need to feed yourself. You can grow food, you can hunt, or you can trade goods and go into taverns. The food here's great, though not so much if you're a vegetarian.'

'Do people still object to eating animals even when they're digital?'

'Not in general, but it happens: a zealot's a zealot. I wasn't sure where you stood.'

'Right now I could eat a farmer's arse through a hedge.'

'Meat *and* greens. See, that's a balanced diet right there.'

Ross heard a scurrying close by and looked to the trees. He saw a wild boar stop to sniff the air. It took a look back at him and then trotted off, unhurried. He only realised he had frozen to the spot when he felt Juno's hand on his arm.

'Don't worry, it won't bother you. This whole place has been modified to make it effectively a vacation resort. The protocols have been tweaked so that there's no dragons burning villages to the ground and no bloodthirsty tyrant NPCs wreaking havoc and plunging the place into war. Actually, there are still dragons, but they stick to their territory. If you want to go hunt one, or even just go look at them, you need to go on a long trek north into the mountains, kind of a safari. It'll take you maybe a week to get there.'

'So how far is it to the transit point? Are we talking days?'

'I landed as close as I dared. It's on the other side of the nearest town.'

It took them around two hours, according to Ross's new-found universal clock. He got his first glimpse as they neared the edge of the forest, seeing boats tied up at piers in front of rows of wooden houses. Then, as they came around the headland, he saw more and more of it revealed, stretching much further up the hillside than he would have imagined. When Juno said 'town' he had interpreted it as 'village', given the context, but this was a coastal settlement the size of Largs.

As they made their way down from the cliff-top and into town, Ross was struck by how pleasant it looked and smelled. It was picturesque without looking fairytale, and everything was very clean, like he was in the medieval section of a well-maintained theme park. The comparison extended to the scent of meat wafting on the breeze, except this smelled more enticingly like roast boar than hot dog.

Ross followed his nose to the door of a tavern, wondering distantly whether you could get jaked on digital ale.

'Do you mind?' he asked Juno, checking it was okay to make a pit-stop.

'No, you gotta eat. You'll need this, though,' she added, producing a bag of coins.

They wandered into the dim but cosy interior, where what light there was came from a crackling fire in the grate and candles melting messily in the necks of bottles. Ross saw seven or eight fellow diners seated on stools and benches, talking quietly in dark corners. They cast an interested eye as he came in but soon went back to their meals and conversations. He heard one of them grumble something about taking an arrow to the knee.

Ross sat at a round and thick wooden table, like a cartwheel with a tree trunk through it, his arrival noted from behind the bar by a blonde female in a revealing dress who looked like the illustrated encyclopaedia entry for 'buxom wench'. She skipped forth cheerily a few moments later, bringing two plates of carved meat without having been asked.

She leaned over as she placed the dishes down on the table, and Ross utterly failed not to avail himself of a lingering look at her bounteous cleavage, the pneumatic plenitude of which suggested that in this incarnation of the Middle Ages, the invention of the balconette push-up bra had evidently come before gunpowder. He realised he was getting a virtual semi, which posed several questions he didn't feel philosophically equipped to wrestle with. If you were in a relationship in the old world, did it count as cheating if you had sex here with someone else? If you shagged someone but they were only an NPC, was that technically just a wank?

He quieted his thoughts with a mouthful of roast boar. It tasted as deliciously satisfying as the water he'd sipped in the Beyonderland, the sensation of swallowing it as real as the effects of the serving wench upon his libido. She returned with two flagons of ale and Ross reprised his failure not to grab an eyeful. When he looked up again, he found Juno staring back at him with a look of pronounced consternation.

He felt himself blush for a moment before realising that his ogling the waitress wasn't what was troubling her; indeed he wasn't even sure she had noticed. Her attention was fixed upon other matters. She resumed looking back and forth around the room, clearly frustrated in a search for something. He wondered if it was the mustard.

'Looking for somebody?' Ross asked.

'No. I'm looking for *anybody*. There's no one here.'

Ross paused for a second, contemplating whether the protocols meant he was seeing things she couldn't.

'What are you talking about? Who do you think brought the food? Who do you think's sitting eating all that stuff over there?'

'NPCs,' she answered. 'I mean there's no *real* people. I haven't seen a single one since we landed. I've also lost all off-world comms. Something ain't right.'

Juno put a couple of coins down on the table and stuffed a slice of meat into a hunk of bread.

'We're having these to go,' she said to the waitress, who seemed utterly oblivious.

Juno headed outside and along the street at a stride just short of a run, looking agitatedly back and forth at the houses either side.

'There's usually hundreds of people here,' she said. 'I'm gonna ask one of these NPCs. They have a very limited understanding of what's going on within their own minute frame of reference, but if you filter out all the scripted shit, you can usually work out something from what they're telling you.'

She went up to a grey-bearded old man in a robe. He looked like some kind of village elder or a leftover stray from a Grateful Dead tour.

'Did something happen here?' Juno asked. 'Something monumental? Where did everybody go?'

'These are grave times indeed,' he replied. 'Goromar forges dark plans in the north. *Si vis pacem, para bellum*: if you wish for peace, prepare for war. The sacred reign of the Wardens is at an end.'

'Shit,' she replied, with considerably less gravitas but just as much portent.

'What?' Ross asked. 'I didn't follow. Something about dark plans.'

'No, it's meaningless. It's pure script: script from the very beginning of the game in its original form, before it was modified. It's like nobody ever came here.'

Ross thought he heard a noise in the distance, a beating of the air that had very horrible associations since his encounter with Cuddles.

'Does this mean we better get tooled up?' he asked, scanning the skies.

'No. I think it's just the story that's reset itself in the NPCs' minds. If the whole world was reset, then someone would have started a fight with you back at the tavern. So no wars and no dragon attacks. The protocols won't allow it.'

'Do you think somebody should tell them?' Ross asked.

'Tell who?'

'Those dragons,' he replied, pointing to the four winged beasts that were approaching from the north, their silhouettes picked out against a grey haze that covered the entire breadth of the horizon.

Juno produced a pair of high-tech binoculars and stood transfixed by whatever she was looking at.

'Oh my God.'

Ross searched in vain for a similar item, then remembered he had a sniper scope on one of his rifles. He held it to his eye and scanned the landscape to the north. It wasn't just dragons that were headed their way: wolves, boar, deer and mystical-looking animals were stampeding down the hillsides, pouring out of the woods like they were ablaze. This was not the dragons' doing, however, for the dragons weren't attacking: they were fleeing. Every creature that could move was running or flying for its life from the encroaching grey haze, and when Ross angled his scope to focus on where the haze met the ground he could see why.

'It's the corruption,' Juno said. 'This whole world's breaking down, dissolving away into nothing.'

Ross took in the speed at which the corruption was advancing and considered how long it had taken them to walk from the ship to here. They weren't going to make it back in time.

Juno took off across the road and disappeared around the back of a house. Ross had made to follow but was told to stay where he was in a tone that wasn't to be argued with.

A few moments later Juno reappeared, on horseback. She stopped to let him climb aboard, then kicked her mount into a gallop, Ross clinging on to her waist like he'd hitched a ride at the Isle of Man TT. She guided the horse uphill around the outskirts of the town, slaloming livestock, dogs and oblivious-looking NPCs. The fleeing creatures must have been programmed with certain base instincts to which they were now responding, but the non-playing characters were guided entirely by branching scripts, in which there was no behavioural contingency for sudden dissolution of their entire world.

'Is the transit far?' Ross asked, wondering how much longer he could hang on, and feeling increasingly agitated by the fact that Juno appeared to be riding flat-out *towards* the corruption.

'Too far,' she replied. 'Leastways, the one to Silent Hill is: it's already behind the cloud. We're gonna have to change our travel plans, take the nearest exit before it gets swallowed too.'

Ross called up his HUD, partly to get a fix on how far they were from safety, and could see the Mobius throbbing. They had to be close, but Juno wasn't showing any sign of slowing, so presumably the transit wasn't in any of the quite inordinate number of swordsmiths' premises to their left as the horse climbed the slope. To their right was just scrubland, occasionally corralled off for grazing. Still the icon flashed brighter, the signal seemingly stronger than he'd ever witnessed, yet he couldn't see where it might be coming from. Juno did say it was a 'main crossing', which was presumably a bigger deal than the cracks, fissures and trapdoors he'd slipped through so far.

Ross could see the corruption now with the naked eye, the grey haze swallowing buildings and trees less than a hundred yards away. He could hear it too, a rushing sound not caused by the corruption itself, but by the strain of thousands of materials as they were pulled apart, moments before disintegrating altogether.

Fortunately, no matter how sharp the gradient got, the horse never slowed, responding tirelessly every time Juno dug her heels into its flanks to urge it forward. Dragons swooped overhead, fighting to stay ahead of the cloud. Wolves and boar barrelled across the road, getting in the way. Ross leaned out as far as he dared and began picking them off with laser blasts to clear the path for their mount.

Suddenly the slope levelled out and Ross could see their goal across a plateau of scrub: it was a mine, the entrance shored up by wooden supports the size of railway sleepers where it disappeared into the hillside.

The rushing sound was becoming a roar. The cloud was towering to their left, rising hundreds of feet in the air. It may have been his imagination, but Ross felt as though it had a gravitational pull.

'Come *on*,' Juno urged the horse, tugging on the reins as she guided their mount towards the dark passage.

The sound of hooves was briefly lost against the roar of the corruption, then became louder again as the horse galloped into the mine shaft, Juno still urging their steed to proceed at full pelt into the blackness. The light around them dimmed rapidly, but before there was total darkness Ross felt the now-familiar dissolving sensation, and just hoped it was the effect of warp.

Quarantine

Light and colour snapped back into view with a wrench like a cinema projector coming on after a power-cut. They were still in a narrow dark passage, but rapidly approaching a mouth beyond which Ross could see bright sunshine and rapid movement.

The hoofbeats sounded more percussive, and a glance down revealed that the horse was now galloping on tarmac rather than earth. The walls either side were made of concrete, and there was considerably more distance between them: two car-widths, as it turned out. The horse emerged from the tunnel into daylight around twenty yards short of a junction, across which Ross could see traffic passing at a leisurely speed.

The traffic comprised vehicles like none Ross had ever seen in the old world: sleek and highly stylised boy-toy fantasy stuff, with customisation extending even to the wheels, as in whether to bother with them when you could glide on air. Beyond the cars rose vast and magnificent structures, super-scale buildings taking their inspiration from ancient civilisations – an architectural paradise where land and materials were no object.

Less pleasing to the eye was a makeshift roadblock before the junction: two large vehicles slung nose to nose across the road to halt anyone exiting from the tunnel. Two figures stood beside the cars, rifles slung around their shoulders.

Black cars. *Black* figures. *Black* rifles.

'Fuckers are putting up *roadblocks* now?'

Juno spurred the horse onwards as the armed guards belatedly reacted to the sight of their approach. Ross felt his stomach heave as the animal leapt over their vehicles, briefly skittering its hooves across the bonnets before landing on the other side and continuing towards the junction.

Ross stole a glance back as Juno veered her mount left and slowed a little, trotting alongside the traffic while she waited for a gap. One of the Integrity guards was scrambling to get into his car, the other staying at his post but speaking animatedly into a communicator.

Juno saw her chance and the horse lurched across the lanes, leaping over a low crash barrier and landing on a grass verge in front of a Mayan-style pyramid draped on every terrace with enough planting to romp the Chelsea flower show. Next to the pyramid stood a court-like building in Roman style, every column the size of an office block. If it wasn't for the cars being of roughly normal size he'd have thought the warping process had shrunk him, as these buildings made him feel like an ant.

Ross heard the gunning of an engine followed by the ugly sound of collision. He glanced back to see the Integrity car spinning from an impact, fishtailing for a few seconds on the near side of the junction before righting itself again. Juno banked sharply, racing across a manicured lawn and slaloming through a host of trees and topiary before guiding the horse along a narrow covered pathway down one side of the Roman megastructure, scattering pedestrians left and right. There was no way of getting a car down there, and it looked like their pursuer knew that. The Integrity car didn't follow, nor did he attempt to continue on foot. They had got away clean.

Juno brought the horse to a stop and told Ross to get down. He didn't need to be asked twice. The ground felt wonderfully solid and unmoving under his feet, the sensation akin to the enhanced gravity you feel when you step off a trampoline.

'Change,' Juno said, and it sounded like a demand.

Ross was about to search his inventory for cash when he noticed her dress transform from the medieval battle-queen affair she'd been sporting into a flowing purple robe similar to those worn by several of the pedestrians they had almost trampled. He inferred from this that it was imperative they blend in. He checked out the new arrivals in his costume collection and opted for a blue version of the same unisex garment. Looking at the architecture he realised it was probably supposed to be a hybrid of classical and futuristic, but the result made him feel like he was in *Logan's Run*. He had no idea what game this was. It

238

reminded him of *Serious Sam* in terms of the retro-classical buildings, but the vehicles zipping past on a network of conveniently
broad roadways were more indicative of a sandbox driving game,
like *Grand Theft Auto* or *Saints Row*.

'Where are we?'

'We're on Pulchritupolis,' she said neutrally, scanning her
surroundings with suspicion.

'Is that a good thing or a bad thing?'

'Good in that I've got a friend here, but anywhere crawling
with Integrity is bad.'

'Do you know how to get to Silent Hill from this place?'

'Yeah, but it's a long way, and I think right now everybody
is gonna want to take stock of what just happened. I've put a
call out to say where we ended up. Need to wait and see if the
plan has changed.'

Juno gave the horse a slap on its haunch and sent it trotting
away along a tree-lined avenue towards the pyramid. Ross felt
vaguely guilty about abandoning the creature, given the part it
had just played in saving their lives. However, as far as the
Integrity was concerned, Seabiscuit here was a bit of a smoking
gun; plus in the interests of balance it should be factored in that
their intervention had just saved its life too, so that was probably quits.

Juno led Ross back along the covered walkway, blending in
with the throng. He scanned over the heads of the other pedestrians, looking out for Integrity agents as they approached the
lawns adjacent to the road.

'The car's gone altogether,' he reported, though his eyes were
fixed firmly on a huge juggernaut that was trundling past, in
case the pursuit vehicle was lurking out of sight behind. It was
like a road-bound train, several articulated containers rolling
along behind the cab.

'It was a half-assed pursuit,' Juno opined. 'Perfunctory even.
They didn't even fire any shots. I'm thinking we ain't the biggest
game in town today.'

'No,' agreed Ross, the juggernaut having finally passed. 'I
think *that* is.'

On the other side of the road was a huge plaza, its corners
accommodating four towering stone obelisks between which

239

laser barriers had been erected, parallel lines of transparent red light like a huge ribbon around the public square. It wasn't quite so public today, though: the Integrity were present in force, and being corralled inside the lasers were at least a hundred people.

From the outside, and admittedly at a distance, the situation appeared to be calm and controlled, but the flow of pedestrians towards the plaza indicated that the locals were very concerned to know what was going on. The detainees were standing around, looking understandably agitated, but there was no visible unrest. The Integrity, for their part, looked more like a relief operation than an occupying force. Their agents were walking around talking calmly to people, recording notes on tablets, listening rather than barking out orders. There were no guns on display, and Ross wondered whether the laser barrier was about keeping the onlookers out rather than the detainees in. The only hardware visible was being operated by three agents toting hand-held parabolic dishes, like miniature satellite receivers or listening devices. They were standing at roughly equal distances, forming an equilateral triangle on the edges of the plaza. It was like they were scanning for something. Ross heard the word 'quarantine' muttered by several passers-by.

The other word on everybody's lips was 'corruption'.

'Damn it,' Juno muttered. 'Never seen any Integrity in Pulchritupolis before. I was hoping we might make contact with my friend, Melita, but with so much black swarming around, she could have blown town, or at the very least changed face and gone to ground.'

'Yeah, but she could change it right back when she found you,' said a female voice from nearby. She sounded Hispanic, her tones mellifluous and reassuring.

Ross turned to his right and saw a blonde who so perfectly illustrated Juno's barb about a fifteen-year-old dork's idea of womanhood that he had initially taken her for an NPC. Right before his eyes her face transformed. Ross didn't know whether it was the work of an expert designer, a refinement of the old her or a perfect likeness, but it certainly wasn't an off-the-peg approximation of classical good looks. There was a sharpness to her features that might almost be harsh if she wasn't smiling.

Her hair became instantly dark and her height reduced, while the pink billowing dress she had been falling out of morphed into a neatly fitting white jumpsuit. In order to continue blending in, her wardrobe selection was still Seventies sci-fi, but she had evidently opted for the *Battlestar Galactica* end of the range.

'Melita!' Juno confirmed, reaching out to embrace her friend. 'It's great to see you.'

There was true warmth there, Ross observed. It was reassuring to learn that Juno didn't hate everybody, but on the downside it meant he could no longer use that as the explanation for why she was so down on him.

'And it's a big relief to see you,' Melita replied. 'I came as soon as I got the message. I was sincerely hoping you weren't among that crowd in the plaza, but it was getting to the stage I'd have settled for that over the alternative.'

'It was touch and go,' Juno admitted.

'But I'm forgetting myself,' Melita said, turning to Ross. 'You must be Bedlam.'

He was glad Melita had taken the initiative on introductions, as he suspected Juno would have just gone on acting like he wasn't there. He offered her a hand to shake by way of affirmation but was starting to feel self-conscious about responding to the name. His old online moniker had helped galvanise him in the battle zones of Graxis but it was becoming an ever-poorer fit the further he explored the gameverse, and he was beginning to wish he could apply for a change to something more universally appropriate. Right now Gormless Spare Wheel would be about right.

'So what's the deal with the laser cordon?' Juno asked.

'People started coming through yesterday, bringing reports that Calastria was corrupting. Most of us were sceptical initially; it wouldn't be the first time folks got hysterical and overreacted since the threat of corruption gained currency.'

'I'm guessing what began as a trickle soon became a flood,' said Juno. 'Because the corruption is real. By the time we got there, everybody else had bailed. Nobody left but NPCs.'

'I assume plenty ended up in Silent Hill and the Minecraft archipelago, but the biggest transit out of Calastria leads here, so they started pouring through the tunnel in serious numbers about eighteen hours ago, universal time. At first they just dispersed, like you'd expect, but then word must have got out to the Integrity.'

'And they showed up quick-smart so they could tell everybody "We told you so",' suggested Juno.

'Not so quick: maybe about eight hours ago, and even then it took them a while to decide what to do. They put men at the main crossing and began escorting the arrivals into the plaza. They say it's for debriefing, but I notice they haven't let anybody go yet. The concern is that anyone who was there might be affected by the corruption; that they could cause it to spread or might start to suffer after-effects. Everybody's pretty spooked. The corruption was just a rumour before this: now it's a confirmed reality.'

The Sea-bars

Melita led them a short distance along the pavement to where a stairwell descended into an underground parking lot. They found her vehicle stationary but hovering in a bay two tiers below ground level. Ross quickly ascertained that it couldn't actually fly: the rules of this world allowed for vehicles to have any appearance you cared to design, which included the appearance of floating on air. He mentioned a cheat from *Grand Theft Auto* that rendered a car completely invisible, allowing your character to tool around town in a sitting position. Melita said that was possible here but cautioned 'good luck finding it again', adding that, unlike in *GTA*, you couldn't just walk up and help yourself to any car.

'Not any more, anyway,' Juno added, as Melita guided the hover-car up a ramp at the rear of the pyramid and into traffic. Juno was sitting in the back seat, letting Ross ride shotgun so that he could see the sights.

'Pulchritupolis started off as a criminal driving game,' Melita explained. 'Like *GTA* but set in the far future. A lot of us wanted to settle here, so we had to make some changes. You'll notice very few NPCs, in fact none that aren't performing a useful and strictly non-violent function. First thing that had to go was all the crime lords and gang-bangers. I think we'd all just had one too many brunches ruined by a burning car smashing through the restaurant and killing everybody.'

'Buildings didn't used to be so pretty either,' Juno said. It sounded like an in-joke, one that made Melita blush a little.

'The buildings were always pretty,' Melita argued. 'That's why so many of us wanted to live here. But what Juno is alluding to is that there's been a lot of improvements. That's what I do mostly: I'm an architect.'

243

'She's selling herself short,' Juno said. 'Melita's one of the best architects in the gameverse. There's a waiting list for a consultation. You can see her work in a hundred worlds.'

Ross looked up at the massive-scale fusion of the futuristic and the classical that the road system wound around. The size and ambition of the buildings was breathtaking, yet none of it might be described as outrageous or even over-the-top; audacious maybe, but never over-extended or trying too hard.

'Were you an architect . . . you know . . . back in . . . ?' Ross asked almost apologetically.

'Hell no,' she laughed as she took a ramp up to join a motorway spur that ran level with roughly the tenth floors of the adjacent buildings. 'I was an elementary school teacher, in San Diego. All those years of study, training and experience and I end up in a place where my skill set is totally redundant.'

'So what got you interested in designing buildings? Did you discover a knack for it in the Beyonderland?'

'It goes back further than that, to when I went to Scotland on vacation. Hired a car and drove all over the Highlands.'

It was the first time he'd heard his native land mentioned in what felt like an age. He was almost embarrassed to admit it caused a mild stirring of pride at the thought of it leaving a life-changing impression on a foreign visitor.

'The castles really had an impact then?' he asked.

'A little. But not as big an impact as the drunk asshole who smashed into me on Skye and put me in hospital. I had spinal injuries, so they couldn't move me. Spent four months in traction with nothing to do but read and watch TV. You have *a lot* of property shows in your country, you know that?'

Ross thought of how Carol was always able to switch to one whenever he left the room for five minutes, regardless of the hour of day or night.

'No shit.'

'I became seriously addicted. The idea of designing spaces and structures just awakened something in me.'

'Did you follow it up when you got out of hospital?'

'I never got out. Went to sleep one night and . . .'

'I see.'

'I spent a lot of time in driving gameworlds, self-prescribed therapy for the effects of my accident. This place was my favourite, but I had a few ideas for how it might be improved.'

'There are plenty of trained architects in the gameverse,' Juno said. 'Some of them are pretty good, some of them suck. The latter can't get past the fact that the old rules don't apply: imagination doesn't need to be reined in by pragmatism or compromise or budget – just by good taste and sound judgment. Melita can envisage things in a way that they would need to kinda untrain themselves to do.'

'By the same token,' Melita added, 'when those two latter elements are missing, the lack of the restraints Juno mentioned can lead to some spectacularly hideous results.'

Having once been an avid reader of *Cranky Steve's Haunted Whorehouse*, a web reviews repository for excruciatingly awful custom maps, Ross was happy to take her word for it.

'So have there been a lot of changes to other worlds?' he asked.

'Oh yeah. Some of them are unrecognisable from their original state. There are others that are relatively untouched in terms of physical design, but there's no game-story content left, usually because people want to live there and the NPCs drive them loco. And on some worlds, an even more radical level of customisation has taken place—'

'But let's not get into that,' Juno interrupted, trying to sound breezy but failing to disguise a 'not in front of the children' message underpinning her intervention.

'How did you change them?' Ross asked, recalling his futile attempts to make even a dent in a wall of rock back on Graxis.

'It was the Originals,' Melita answered. 'They had powers, abilities that the rest of us didn't. I don't understand what they did, but the Originals lifted some kind of barriers that allowed us to alter our worlds. I heard it said that they had "opened up the sea-bars". I think this was in reference to how we could then change the level of the land, and expand into where there used to be water or even just space, but it allowed us to alter much more than that.'

'When you say we . . . ?'

'Oh, I see. No, I don't mean anybody and everybody. The power to make changes to the sea-bars is entrusted to individuals only temporarily, and only to carry out alterations that have been agreed and approved by vote.'

'Ah,' said Ross. 'So there's politics?'

'Absolutely. Every bit as messy and complicated as back in the old world.'

As they approached a shimmeringly azure lake, Melita's car descended from the motorway via a sharply curving ramp, and she didn't accelerate again once the road had flattened out. Ross guessed they must be imminently reaching their destination, and did a double-take when he looked out the driver's side and saw what he took to be Melita's house.

He would confess he'd been expecting something quite palatial, not to mention bigger. By the standards of what he had already seen of Pulchritupolis, it was a pretty modest dwelling, particularly given Melita's apparently exalted status. Nonetheless, it was still a beautiful dwelling, enhanced by its waterfront location, but what had given him a jolt was its similarity to the pad he had copy-pasted back in the Beyonderland.

The houses weren't identical, however. Everything here was just a little more refined, a little more perfect, like he had got the basic floor model and this was the deluxe. Or more like Melita's was the Platonic ideal of 'Californian beach house' and his was just the shadow on the cave wall.

'This is your place?' he asked, just to be sure, as the hover-car cruised into a palm-lined driveway.

'Bedlam here replicated this for his first crib in the Beyonderland,' Juno informed her, enjoying his discomfort like a nine-year-old telling her classmate that Ross fancied her.

'Oh, thanks,' Melita said, seemingly oblivious to Juno's more mischievous intentions. 'When I designed it, I tried to combine the elements I liked about all the beach houses I used to see when I was growing up. Juno thinks it's chintzy. I don't care. When I was a kid I used to dream about living in one, and that never went away.'

'Not so sure about your new garden ornament,' Juno said archly.

Ross looked across the lushly verdant lawns and saw a male figure standing like a statue, arms folded in a gesture that could have been contemplation, implacability or just impatience. He was tall and strappingly athletic, a Nordic hero of a figure with flowing blond hair and piercing blue eyes set in a face etched by hard wind and fierce battle, and in the futuristic get-up he was sporting he looked like something Freddie Mercury might have gone to bed and dreamed about after an evening watching box sets of *Spartacus* and *Star Wars*.

'Oh . . . yes,' Melita said apologetically. 'He came running when he heard about Calastria. Good guy to have by your side if things get messy, but . . . well, he is what he is.'

'Who is he?' Ross asked, as it seemed nobody was going to tell him before they got out of the car.

'An asshole,' Juno said unhelpfully, though her disdain did give Ross a glimmer of optimism that he was about to encounter an ally. If this guy was someone else that Juno found annoying, then maybe he was okay.

'But he's our asshole,' said Melita. 'His name is Skullhammer,' she added, which kind of told Ross all he needed to know.

Skullhammer surveyed Ross briefly with suspicion bordering on hostility as he approached the house, but mostly kept his eyes looking out towards the road. He seemed dissatisfied by whatever he had seen or not seen, reluctant to come inside.

Melita's beach house – or technically lake house – looked genuinely lived in, a real dwelling complete with the clutter that went with day-to-day existence, as opposed to a clinical space for a game to take place in or some coldly elegant item of eye-candy designed to show off a graphics engine. Ross could smell coffee and potpourri. Throw in the scent of bread baking and he'd have thought she was trying to flog the place.

There was even a TV, or at least a video screen of some kind, taking up most of one wall. It was showing the situation down-town at the plaza, a text marquee scrolling across at the bottom with the latest updates.

'This is a disaster,' Skullhammer said, referring to the events on screen. 'I came as soon as I heard that this was where most of the refugees ended up.'

His accent was English and somewhat theatrical, having a particular flavour of artifice about it that Ross couldn't quite nail. He spoke like somebody accustomed to being the most important person in the room. Ross wondered what his status

247

was within the resistance, as he had still felt no need to introduce himself or ask who Ross was.

'Where were you?' Juno asked. Ross could tell she was making an effort to be polite. He wondered if this was her being deferential or whether she was genuinely seeking information.

'I was in Fortune City,' said Skullhammer. 'Setting up a spoof. Ravenwind stayed, overseeing the final touches.'

'What's a spoof?' asked Ross.

Skullhammer looked at him like he'd farted.

'It's a fake transit,' Melita explained. 'The Integrity think they're shutting down a link between *Dead Rising 2* and the Lego Racers Islands, but it's just a decoy.'

'Good work,' Juno said.

Skullhammer grimaced, shaking his head a little.

'We're just sticking our thumbs in the dyke. They're shutting down more and more transits every day, and they're only going to scale up their efforts after this. They'll have massive popular support as word spreads about Calastria.'

'No kidding,' Melita agreed. 'People are gonna be scared, and scared people will accept the harshest measures if they think it will keep them safe.'

'I hate to be the one pointing out the elephant in the room,' said Juno, 'but having just been ringside, I can assure you there's a damn good reason people are scared. The corruption ain't a campfire story any more; it's real, and we gotta consider whether the whole game just changed.'

'Bullshit,' Skullhammer spat dismissively. 'We now know the corruption isn't a phantom threat, but we still don't got proof that traffic between worlds is what's causing it. We don't know what caused Calastria to corrupt, and those Integrity lamers are scrambling around for information themselves.'

Ross took in Skullhammer's absurdly masculine appearance as he homed in on the mismatch between speech and voice. *Don't got proof. Integrity lamers.* The accent wasn't his. He deduced that it wasn't just skins and models you could change here, and Skullhammer must have gone for one that sounded more in character for the persona he was inhabiting. Ross also deduced that the old-world Skullhammer was not merely less god-like and battle-weathered in his appearance, but considerably younger too.

In that moment Ross found himself feeling terribly sorry for him. The guy could have been sixteen when he got here. Ross remembered how lost and useless he'd felt at that age, and he'd only had to cope with life in Stirling.

Skullhammer gestured to the screen, like he was giving a lecture.

'It was just on the news feed that they're calling for anyone who was there to hand themselves in for interview and testing. They're putting on a big show of being calm and reasonable at the moment but they're throwing the word "contamination" around. So pretty soon the phrase "urging people to hand themselves in for their own safety" is gonna become "urging people to rat out their neighbours in case this is contagious".'

'Having recently experienced their hospitality, the last people I'd want giving me a physical are those psychos,' said Ross. 'I'm in no hurry to deliver myself into their custody again.'

'Oh yes, I heard,' said Melita. 'And you saw Solderburn.'

She said this with an ambiguity Ross couldn't read: excited, even awestruck, and yet there was an air of depressed resignation in her tone too. Perhaps it was because she also knew Solderburn had been taken. All this time waiting for a fabled wanderer's return and he gets huckled by the bad guys the second he puts his head back around the door.

'*He* says,' grumbled Skullhammer.

'I don't get why you think I would be lying about this,' Ross protested, starting to get fed up with the provisional status of his own recent history. 'What am I missing here?'

The other three exchanged glances. Skullhammer looked reluctant to share whatever it was, but he wasn't going to censor it.

It was Juno who spoke.

'It's long been a rumour – or maybe just a hope – that the reason Solderburn disappeared was that he had found a way out.'

Ross understood now why Juno had reacted the way she did the first time he spoke Solderburn's name. If Solderburn had shown up again, it could mean that this particular hope was dashed – or it could mean that he had come back to share his secret. Either way it was momentous news, rendered somewhat less exciting by him ending up in the hands of the enemy.

'Why didn't you mention this before?' Ross asked.

'I wanted to find out how much you did or didn't already know. The Integrity have been trying to infiltrate us from the start.'

'And what, you think I'm the T1000?'

'It's not what I *think*,' Juno answered. 'It's what I can't afford to assume. Nothing personal.'

Ross nodded, taking her point.

'Was there anything more to this rumour than the fact that nobody had seen him for a very long time?'

'No,' said Skullhammer. 'Just desperation. A legend growing to fill a significant absence.'

'So why even refer to it as a rumour?'

'People need hope,' said Juno.

'What is the other Originals' position on it?'

'They don't buy it. They deny it's possible,' said Skullhammer.

'But there's a wide suspicion that the Originals are keeping a secret,' Juno countered. 'That there's something they're not telling us.'

Ross looked to Skullhammer for a rebuttal, but there was unease in his face. It would have been logical enough to dismiss what Juno described as merely the natural paranoia engendered by the existence of a powerful elite. He looked conflicted, and Ross wondered whether the big guy didn't harbour just a little more hope than he was admitting to himself.

'It's all moot now anyway,' he eventually said, eyeing Ross accusingly. 'Thanks to you.'

Ross bit back a response, then changed his mind and voiced it after all. If he was fielding all this suspicion anyway, then what was the point of playing nice?

'Away and take your face for a shite.'

'What did you say?' he demanded, bristling.

'You heard me, Sockwanker. Surely a born-and bred English-man like yourself isn't having difficulty with some Anglo-Saxon terminology?'

'Hey fuck you, *Bedbug*. You wanna dance with me? 'Cause I'm ready.'

Juno shot Ross a look that was far more of a deterrent than any threat he felt Skullhammer posed.

'Guys,' warned Melita also. 'My house. Behave.'

Ross held up his hands as if to say it was over.

Juno looked towards Skullhammer.

'I know it's a setback, but it wasn't Bedlam's fault. They had massive forces deployed out there. And from what he told me on the trip to Calastria, the Integrity got themselves some nasty new toys too.'

'Like what?' asked Melita, concerned.

'They had a tank that wiped out part of a building,' Ross said. 'That's how they got Solderburn. Just erased the tower he was shooting from.'

'They had some massive flying beast from one of the myth-worlds too,' said Juno.

'Real final-boss stuff,' Ross added.

Skullhammer continued to fix him with a scrutinising stare that stopped only just short of renewed hostility.

'All that hardware and manpower on the ground,' he said. 'Just what you'd need if you want to capture an Original. It's almost like they already *knew* Solderburn was coming for you.'

'Oh, so does that mean we've moved on from my whole story being made up to you now believing that Solderburn came to my rescue?'

'For the sake of argument,' Skullhammer replied.

'Believe what you like, Ballhummer, it's all the same to me. I had only just got there from Graxis, and I'd never heard of the Integrity until I was in one of their torture chambers. But you're right: they were going to a lot of trouble. They didn't ship me out right away because they said someone called Ankou was on his way to speak to me. Didn't sound like it would be a friendly chat.'

Ross winced at the lameness of this last comment but soon realised that nobody had heard it. The mention of the name Ankou had pretty much derailed everything else.

'Ankou?' Melita asked, her voice dropping to an astonished whisper.

'And you're sure about the "coming to you" part?' Juno enquired. 'Definitely not the other way around?'

251

'I wasn't to be moved. They were very clear about that.'

'I don't think I've ever heard of Ankou leaving his shiny black fortress,' said Melita. 'I wasn't sure he was even a person, as opposed to maybe the codename of a command tier within the Integrity.'

'One of my hosts said "Ankou wants to deal with this one personally", at which point the other one's arse started making buttons. I got the impression they were looking forward to the visit only marginally more than I was.'

Juno looked at him like she'd never seen him before.

'Then all of their machines, their men and their monsters,' she said. 'They weren't there because of Solderburn. They were there because of you.'

'Maybe they were top-heavy with slavishly authoritarian drones and low on their "lost and bewildered useless fanny" quota,' Ross suggested, making light of the fact that he couldn't think of any other reason why they'd be so interested in him.

'Solderburn too,' Melita said, ignoring this remark. 'Why would he emerge from his self-imposed exile and put himself at such risk, just for you?'

'He was my friend, back in the old world.'

Even as he said this, Ross realised he was no longer convinced it held up. It wasn't like he and Solderburn were really close; they just got on better with each other than with anyone else in the building, but, given that the building had a superabundance of arseholes, that wasn't saying much. He had also harboured a theory that Solderburn came to his rescue because he felt responsible for Ross ending up here, but he now understood that to be pure projection. It was Ross who held Solderburn responsible, a perspective with which Solderburn did not concur. Indeed experience had taught Ross that selfless, high-risk altruism wasn't exactly Solderburn's style.

'Solderburn had many friends in this world too,' Juno said. 'People he had known for a lot longer than he knew you. He left them all behind and didn't come back. If he finally returned and put himself on the line for *your* ass, then, no offence, but it had to be for a greater reason than that you and him were buds.'

'Well he didn't bloody *say* anything about it,' protested Ross.

'He took massive risks to keep you out of the Integrity's

hands,' said Melita, 'and Ankou was coming personally to see you. We have to find out why. You could be a game-changer.'

Her words hung in the air rather uncomfortably in the ensuing silence, one Ross resisted the temptation to fill with the words 'no pressure'.

Skullhammer broke the suspense in his own inimitable way.

'And he could just as easily be a Trojan. *More* easily in fact. Hmm. Saviour of the gameverse or lying Integrity spy. The last thing we want is to be leading this fucker to a gathering of our high command on Silent Hill.'

'Skullhammer,' Juno objected, 'that isn't your call.'

'No, so let's ask the audience. I'm calling it in.'

Skullhammer frowned, lines of concentration etched so deeply in his brow you could have planted turnips. Like Juno back on the jetty, he was going more than hands free. When was somebody going to tell Ross how to do that?

'What the fuck?' Skullhammer grunted. 'I've got no comms. Something's jamming the—'

'Him, maybe?' Ross suggested, pointing towards the lake.

There was an Integrity agent down close to the water, walking across the grass holding one of those parabolic dishes they had seen at the plaza.

All of their heads then turned towards the front of the house. Through the huge floor-to-ceiling windows they could see two black cruiser vehicles like the ones that had been blocking the junction. Two agents were pointing dishes towards the house, while half a dozen more personnel moved to surround the building.

'Why are they scrambling our comms?' asked Melita.

'Because they don't want us telling anybody what's going down,' replied Skullhammer. 'That's a snatch squad.'

Wanted Level

'They followed us here,' said Juno in self-reproach. 'We lost that pursuit way too easily.'

'What was that I was saying about a Trojan horse?' said Skullhammer.

'And how do we know it wasn't you they followed?' Ross countered. 'It's not like you're easy to fucking miss.'

Skullhammer instantly transformed into a nondescript male figure, wearing precisely the same garments as Ross.

'*Touché,*' Ross admitted. 'You should probably stick to the non-verbal comebacks.'

'Enough of this,' ruled Melita, her voice rising. 'If we start accusing one another then we're doing the Integrity's work for them.'

'It wasn't a comeback,' Skullhammer clarified. 'We need to disappear.'

Juno regarded the team of agents advancing down the driveway.

'Yeah, well, we can all dress up like Garret if we want; it's still not like we're sneaking past that lot,' she said.

Melita made a tiny gesture towards her feet, where the wide wooden floorboards began altering themselves into a staircase descending steeply out of sight, tiny LEDs in the newly formed walls guiding the way down.

'How do you like my house now?' she asked Juno.

'I'm guessing my version doesn't have this,' said Ross.

She led them about twenty feet down into a parking garage as long and wide as the house above. In it were four of the coolest cars Ross had ever laid eyes on: vehicles that would have had James Bond's lower lip trembling with emotion; that would have petrol-heads dropping to their knees in tongue-lolling awe; and that nonetheless looked shoddy compared to the two motor-bikes sitting alongside them. Or, as Ross observed upon closer inspection, *hover*-bikes. They sat there about eighteen inches off the ground, one blue and one green, a glow of pale light the only thing seeming to support bodywork so smooth and sculpted it looked like porcelain.

'Are these from *Sin*?' he asked, utterly failing not to sound like a breathless fanboy.

'*Wages of Sin*, to be precise. A client imported them for me from Freeport in exchange for designing her a ski chalet on Skyrim. They're the fastest things in here, so take them.'

Skullhammer hopped eagerly on to the blue one, but Juno deferred.

'No, you go girl. Never could get the hang of those things.'

She opted instead for a Ferrari so advanced, Ross guessed, you had to play *Gran Turismo* or *Need for Speed* nine hours a day for a year to unlock it. Ross climbed into the passenger seat. Even the interior looked like its development budget would have given the space programme a run for its money.

The thought belatedly struck him that this would have been his chance to go it alone, but even the fact that it was belated told him enough. Juno might not trust him, but clearly, without even thinking about it, he trusted her.

'Okay,' Melita announced. 'When we hit the intersection, everybody take off in different directions. They can't follow us all and they'll lose time choosing who to go after. I'm heading for the north-west freeway. The rest of you got five seconds to work it out before I open the door.'

Melita's hover-bike suddenly came to life: no roar of engine, just a halo of lights and a reassuringly powerful low hum like Juno's stolen spaceship. Less reassuringly, she appeared to be riding straight for a concrete wall, but just before impact this disappeared, clearing the way to a gently upward-sloping tunnel.

Skullhammer was right on her tail, the Ferrari just a couple of seconds behind. The hidden passage emerged, *Thunderbirds*-style, from what had previously been a perfectly solid patch of lawn on the outer borders of Melita's property, the Integrity snatch squad scrambling to respond.

The three vehicles hit the big junction at roughly the same time, then peeled away like they'd agreed: Juno and Skullhammer taking on-ramps to the right and left respectively while Melita barrelled straight on through.

As the Ferrari climbed, to his left Ross had a view of Melita's bike burning forward, straight as a laser and faster all the time, while to his right he could see the Integrity cruisers gaining speed. He lost sight of both sides temporarily as the motorway obscured his view; then, as the Ferrari gained the top of the ramp, he glanced back along the opposite lane to see Skullhammer already accelerating away. He watched anxiously to discover which targets the two Integrity vehicles chose to pursue.

He turned to his left and saw Melita's green hover-bike again. There was a black cruiser following it about a hundred and fifty metres back, both of them flat-out.

Juno had noticed it too.

'Just hope the other one is dumb enough to follow Skullhammer. Stupid assholes are never catching those bikes.'

As she spoke Ross saw something streak from the cruiser in pursuit of Melita. It was a missile, covering the distance between the vehicles in less than a second. Ross barely had time to call out in shock, so Melita would have had no time to react, if she even saw it in her rear-view.

Melita was tossed into the air amidst a furiously expanding fireball, the hover-bike bouncing, spinning and skidding along the road as the cruiser maintained its relentless pace to close the distance. The last thing Ross saw before a curve in the motorway took them out of sight was the cruiser stopping and an Integrity agent sprinting from it, weapon drawn.

'Fuckers,' Juno said. 'They've got her.'

'Unless she was killed in the crash,' Ross suggested. 'Where would she respawn?'

'One of the hospitals.'

'Can we . . . ?'

'They'll have a snatch team in place: standard procedure. Trust me, they got her: she just sent me something.'

'What?'

'Never mind. We got our own problems to worry about.'

Ross leaned around to look out of the rear windscreen. Sure

257

enough, the other cruiser had just shot out from the ramp and onto the carriageway behind them.

Juno slalomed in and out of the lanes, keeping other cars between the Ferrari and any possible missiles, but it was at the cost of losing ground while the cruiser held its course as straight as possible. Eventually the Integrity decided to try their luck, but Juno managed to react quickly enough, swerving in front of a lorry and letting it take the blast. The lorry went up in another fireball, jack-knifing across three of the lanes and precipitating a pile-up behind them.

'Sorry,' Juno winced through gritted teeth.

Ross was about to say don't mention it when he sussed that she was apologising to all of the people who'd just totalled their cars, not to mention the truck driver who was probably respawning at the hospital right then into the disturbing sight of a roomful of Integrity.

'At least that should buy us a little time,' Ross suggested, instantly provoking whichever gods whose eternal task it was to punish those who spoke too soon.

Police cars began appearing from literally nowhere: two swung into view in pursuit of the Ferrari despite there being no ramps or junctions from which they could have entered; and, more problematically, there were three of them slewed across the motorway directly ahead, forming a roadblock. Ross could see more of them approaching from the opposite lane, blue lights flashing and sirens awail.

'They just spawned from somewhere out of sight,' he said. 'Can the Integrity do that now? In *vehicles*?'

'They're not Integrity,' Juno replied, gripping the steering wheel tighter and keeping her eyes set dead ahead. 'They're NPCs.'

'They have cops in this city?' he asked incredulously. 'They have *NPC* cops in this city?'

'Not for a very long time. They got rid of them, same as they got rid of the crime lords and gang-bangers. Hold on tight.'

She aimed the Ferrari between where two police cars didn't quite meet nose to nose, her foot to the floor. Ross had pulled just such a manoeuvre a hundred times in driving games, but had never seen it from this perspective. Moments before impact he decided that he couldn't actually *handle* seeing it from this perspective, and closed his eyes.

He felt the impact less powerfully than he'd anticipated, the Ferrari's momentum making it more of a fending-off than a full-on collision. When he looked again, he saw that their car was damaged but still performing. It wasn't going to survive too many more roadblocks, however, and it wasn't just the cops they had to worry about now. There were catching up to ludicrously pimped-out dude-wagons that hadn't been on the road only seconds before, and as the Ferrari pulled alongside to overtake, machine-guns emerged from electric windows and opened fire.

Ross heard a rapid syncopated clang of metal as bullets ripped into their flanks, while in the rear-view mirror he could see an Integrity cruiser leading a chasing pack of cop-cars.

'Take the wheel,' Juno ordered him, grabbing his hand.

'What?'

'We need to swap places.'

'Why? Is the situation just not quite dangerous enough?' he asked as another hail of gunfire rattled their bodywork.

'I need to figure out what's going on. I can't work my HUD and watch where I'm going at the same time.'

'And I can't see where I'm going with you in my face,' he replied, struggling to keep the road in his sights while she clambered in front of the windscreen.

'We're losing speed,' she warned him as he bumped down into the empty driver's seat.

The car bucked when he pressed his foot on the accelerator, the engine proving far more responsive than he had imagined.

'Would this be a bad time to mention that I don't actually drive?' he asked.

'Yeah, you'd be in deep shit if the cops pulled you over.'

Ross swerved between lanes and checked the rear-view repeatedly, ever wary of seeing a black streak like the one that had done for Melita. They were coming up on two more mobile monuments to masculine vulgarity. If he overtook, they'd suffer another twin volley of bullets, but if he didn't, the Integrity cruiser and its outriding cavalcade of cops would catch up.

'Get off this,' Juno told him, pointing to an exit slip. Beyond

259

it the motorway climbed to cross a river so pretty that it looked like nobody had entered it without showering first, including the fish. The surface was shimmering but opaque, so despite appearances it could still be full of condoms and shopping trolleys, but he doubted it.

Ross slewed the car across three lanes and on to the curving ramp way too fast. The Ferrari scraped against the concrete barrier, coming very close to flipping side-on over the thing. He remembered that he had given up playing driving games when the physics became increasingly realistic, the sensation of spinning out as he took a bend too fast depressingly familiar.

'Slow down on the turns,' Juno warned him angrily. 'You tip this thing and we're boned.'

The car descended from the motorway towards a district typical of Pulchritupolis: immaculately maintained garden and park land punctuated with super-sized pseudo-classical buildings, roads intersecting at junctions and sometimes criss-crossing via bridges and tunnels. From every direction Ross could already see cop cars converging. He wanted to check the Ferrari hadn't morphed into a white Ford Bronco. It was like playing *Vice City* with a five-star wanted level, except he had to drive as though it was an ultra-realistic racing sim.

'Where am I headed?' he asked.

'Just keep us moving. I'm working on it.'

Juno's gaze was focused a few inches in front of her face on whatever was being overlaid on her vision.

'What are you looking at?' Ross asked.

'Melita transferred her privileges to me just before they took her. It was a last-ditch emergency procedure to prevent the Integrity from seizing complete control of Pulchritupolis. The process is already underway though – that's how they've re-deployed all the old NPCs.'

'Can you switch them out again?'

'No, wherever they've made a change they've locked the sea-bars.'

It was as she said this that Ross realised two things about these mysterious 'sea-bars' the Originals had 'opened up'. One was that they had nothing to do with the sea, and the other was that they weren't any kind of bar either.

'C-vars,' he said. 'They opened up the c-vars. Client-side variables: that's what you've got the privileges to change. Can you still access some of them?'

'Yeah. Technically I'm supposed to seek democratic approval, but as the Integrity didn't stand on protocol, I'm not going to put it out to vote. What do you suggest?'

'Alter the physics. Make the car handling more like it's an old-school driving game.'

'Okay, they're coming up now; not sure what this shit means, though. How about: `cornerslikeadream`?'

'Equals TRUE,' Ross replied.

'`stopsonadime`?'

'Equals TRUE.'

'`bulletsbounceoffme`?'

'Definitely equals TRUE.'

'Won't this apply to the other cars too?' Juno asked.

'The Integrity, but not the NPCs. At least it'll give us a fighting chance.'

As Ross spoke, two police cars were coming towards him head-on, blocking both lanes of the two-way road, while two more were approaching from the rear with an Integrity cruiser tucked in behind them. He waited until collision seemed inevitable, then executed a hand-brake turn learned on the very forgiving streets of Liberty City, heading hard right across a verdant expanse as the four cop cars smashed into each other at his rear. With the Integrity car negotiating its way around the pile-up, Ross gunned it across the grass, on to a pedestrianised concourse and then smashed through the glass frontage of a Greek-themed shopping mall as shoppers dived into doorways to escape.

In the rear-view mirror he could see the Integrity cruiser still doggedly hanging on in pursuit. It unleashed a missile as Ross reached the end of the corridor, the rocket zipping just overhead as he drove the Ferrari down the side of an escalator towards a lower level of the mall. It detonated against a sculpture suspended from a Panopticon ceiling, the fireball licking against the Ferrari but causing it no damage.

'I guess fire bounces off me too,' Ross observed gratefully, accelerating towards another glass wall at the end of the passage.

'They can't destroy us,' Juno said, 'but we need to shake them off before we find a warp transit. Any they see us using are as good as lost.'

'But even if we lose them, am I not just going to relay the transit's location to my Integrity masters anyway?'

'Oh, you in a snit with me now, is that it? I was the one sticking up for you back there.'

'Yeah, I noticed. Why was that, exactly? You've got no greater reason to trust me than Spudgunner.'

'Because just like we can't afford to assume you're legit, we can even less afford to assume you're a spy. We start thinking that way, then we're already defeated.'

The Ferrari smashed through the massive pane and sped up a steep grass embankment, Ross having to execute another sharp turn at the top as they found themselves heading straight for the river. He proceeded along what was supposed to be a water-side walkway, benches and lifebuoys passing in a blur on the landside to his right. Behind him he could see his Integrity pursuer reaching the top of the incline, and about a quarter of a mile ahead two more cop cars and another Integrity cruiser were rounding a huge Japanese-style pagoda on their way down towards the river.

'Any other c-vars you can amend?' he asked.

'I'm looking. Okay, got one. Superflyguy.'

'TRUE TRUE TRUE.'

'Damn it: it's locked out. Hang on while I scroll down . . .'

'Make it quick.'

'Damn, that's locked too. Let me see what isn't . . . Here we go. Shit, I don't know what these mean. Makesomenoise, Livingincolour, Apocalypticrenegade, Spywholovedme.'

'Spywholovedme,' Ross shouted. 'Equals TRUE, *now*.'

'Done. Okay, what did that change?'

'Our escape options.'

Ross glanced up the slope to his right. The approaching cars had abandoned the road and were taking the most direct route to cut him off.

'Grab on to something,' he said. 'For this to work, it has to look like a disaster.'

'Then at least we got the right guy driving.'

262

He swerved the car right, angling it up the slope as though trying to evade the interception. He waited for the cop cars to make their own corresponding corrections, then reversed his course and floored it. The car rotated out of control, turning end on end as it skidded unstoppably across the concrete walkway and flew over the edge.

It spun sideways into the river with a colossal splash then sank slowly beneath the opaque waters.

'You asshole. What the hell did you just do?' Juno demanded, furious. 'Water crashes are a fatality. We'll be respawning right into the Integrity's hands in about ten seconds.'

'Not today,' Ross told her, waiting for the car to level out.

He gently nudged the accelerator and the Ferrari began gliding silently through the water, its progress masked off to those on the riverbank.

Juno gazed out through the windscreen and nodded to herself.

'My apologies for the asshole remark,' she said. 'Spy who loved me. I get it now.'

She gave his shoulder a punch.

'Damn, Bedlam, you got some game.'

'Nobody does it better.'

A Place You've Never Been

The warp felt like a long one, but at both his point of exit and place of rematerialisation he was standing on soft grass. They had driven ashore on to a narrow strip of sand and abandoned the Ferrari there, Juno leading him off the beach to a transit hidden around the back of an ice-cream stand.

The land was gently undulating, and rather than being hemmed in by a body of water and a network of roadways, Ross was looking out upon a seemingly endless pastoral landscape, blue skies and sunshine overhead. Upon closer examination, he observed that he had never seen such fine grass: it was luxuriantly lush and microscopically short, like the glass greens at Augusta for the US Masters, but stretching for miles.

Juno stared into space, her focus somewhere else for a moment. A wave shimmered down her from head to toe, wiping away the sci-fi garb and replacing it with a new but equally terrifying new variant of female battle dress.

Ross donned a medieval tabard, leaving his feet bare to enjoy the feel of the grass beneath them. There were suit-of-armour options but none that wouldn't make him feel like he was kidding himself next to the authentically warlike sight of Juno.

'Where are we?' he asked.

'Some kind of real-time strategy game,' she answered. '*Medieval 2: Total War*, I think it was called. It doesn't have a place name, because nobody lives here. It's too stark, and a little glitched if memory serves.'

'What are we doing here?'

'Lying low, taking five.'

'I'm fed up with running and hiding,' Ross told her. 'It's all I've done since I got here. I want to speak to one of these

265

Originals. Maybe they can shed some light on why both Solderburn and Ankou were so interested in me.'

'That's above my pay-grade. I'd need a green light from up the chain.'

'So take me to Silent Hill.'

Juno frowned.

'Skullhammer must have relayed his concerns. I've been told to stay in a holding pattern,' she admitted.

'He's a real people person, isn't he?'

'He's a team player,' she replied, with what sounded like grudging conviction. 'I give him that much. These days that counts for a lot. We can't afford to take chances. It's nothing personal.'

'Oh, in his case I think it's probably a wee bit personal; or at least personal as an ancillary bonus. What's so bloody special about the Originals anyway? How come they've got all these powers?'

'Nobody knows,' Juno said. 'All I can tell you is that the earliest arrivals had abilities that the vast majority who came after didn't share. They were able to change things, like the c-vars.'

'No, they let you guys change the client-side variables, which mostly deal with cosmetic stuff. That means they must be able to change server-side variables too. I guess that's what makes them a threat to the Integrity.'

'Well, duh,' said Juno. 'That's why we Diasporadoes are doing everything we can to protect them. For every border the Integrity close, every transit they shut down, the Originals can open up a new one. But if they wipe out all the Originals, or imprison them in that fortress world of theirs, then that's the ball game.'

Ross realised she'd given something away earlier in the conversation.

'You said you'd need a green light. That means you know where they are. Why don't you just tell me?'

'Because it isn't my call. The stakes are real high, and if you keep asking to be taken to the Originals, that's not gonna make me *less* suspicious of your motives.'

'My motives are the same as yours. I want to know how I got

here and I want to know how to get out. My girlfriend is pregnant and the last time I spoke to her we didn't part on the best of terms. Juno, you've walked every inch and pixel of this place searching for the same things as me, so how about we try helping each other?'

She sighed, looking torn.

'Even if I told you where any of the Originals are, it wouldn't make any difference. They can only be found if they want to be found.'

Ross turned away, throwing up his hands in frustration.

'Same as anybody else here,' Juno went on, 'they can hide in plain sight. You could be standing right in front of Lady Arrowsmith or the Sandman or any of them and they wouldn't reveal themselves unless . . .'

Ross spun on his bare heel again, something inside him all lit up.

'The Sandman,' he repeated, wheels starting to turn. 'Alex.'

'Who?'

'He worked alongside me and Solderburn. His name was Alexander: Sandman was his nickname, from Sandy. We all worked at a company called Neurosphere, in Stirling. Solderburn was developing this amazing prototype brain scanner, the Simulacron. Alex went absent from work right after having a test scan, and being scanned was the last thing that happened to me in the old world.'

'Melita was in hospital in Scotland after a car crash,' Juno said, her voice low as though afraid of being overheard. 'She must have had a scan too. That don't explain how *I* got here, but it is something.'

'Everyone suspects there's a secret the Originals know that they're not telling people. Whatever that is, it's got to be linked to Neurosphere. If it was Solderburn's device that brought us all here, then maybe he did find a way out.'

Juno looked buffeted, as though her thoughts were racing but she didn't dare believe what they were suggesting.

'You've got to take me to the Sandman,' Ross pleaded. 'You wouldn't be risking anything: in fact it would be the proof you're looking for, because he's only going to break cover and reveal himself to me if I'm telling the truth.'

267

Juno thought about it for a moment, but the jury wasn't out long.

'Okay,' she said. 'Sounds like I got nothing to lose.'

'The transit we need is in the courtyard of that castle,' Juno said, having led Ross to the crest of a long slope.

'What castle?'

He stared across the rolling green plains. He could make out a grey shape close to the horizon, and summoned up his sniper scope to get a closer look. Magnified six times, he could now see that it was not merely a castle but a fortress: formidable walls of vast hewn stones encircling a network of medieval military buildings. The fortifications were being put to the test too: there was an invading army on its doorstep, attacking the place with trebuchets, siege towers, catapults and battering rams. The defenders were giving as good as they got, hailing arrows, cauldrons of boiling oil and coils of Greek fire down upon the enemy.

'Oh, right,' Ross said. 'That castle. And do we hope they're all too busy murdering each other to notice us sneaking in the back door, or do we throw our lot in with the invaders and hope for the best?'

'No, actually both armies will attack us on sight, so we're going to have to take on everybody.'

Juno seemed incongruously relaxed about this prospect. Ross couldn't work out what he was missing, then reckoned he had found a clue in the sheer distance they were from where the castle stood.

'You're guessing there'll be hardly anybody left standing by the time we get there. I hope you're right. By the time we've walked that far we'll be knackered.'

'It's not that far.'

'It's bloody miles. It's a blob on the horizon.'

'True, but it's not *far away*.'

Her emphasis rang a bell but he couldn't quite place it in this context.

Then, as they neared the castle – far sooner than he could have anticipated – he understood. The besieging army of NPCs took note of their approach and reacted in alarm, turning their

268

weaponry to face Juno and Ross, while behind the huge stone walls, efforts were redoubled to repel the new threat. The response was understandable: there were two giants striding towards them across the plain.

'It's a scale mismatch,' Juno explained. 'This is a real-time strategy game. Most of them are okay but this one has got a glitch so that if you enter it via that particular warp portal, it's like you get stuck in a zoomed-out view.'

He stole a glance up and down at her as she glided across the miniature landscape, the neatness of her shape only empha- sised by this strange new perspective.

The siege engines came up to his waist, the tallest of the soldiers ankle-height. There were thousands of the wee buggers though, so he couldn't just wade through them like they weren't there. They had to be dealt with, and Juno showed that she was taking no chances by producing a plasma rifle he recognised from *Doom 3*. The blue pulses evaporated dozens of enemies at a time, and the splash damage sent just as many careening through the air like a human corona to each blast.

Ross laid waste with his machine-gun. Against the best the Middle Ages had to offer, the World War Two weapons tech- nology proved as mismatched as the scale.

'It's no fun when it's no challenge,' he observed.

'I don't believe the two are mutually exclusive,' Juno replied. 'In my mind they're all looking exactly like Joe right now. That makes it fun.'

Ross's hunger returned immediately after he warped out and rematerialised, though he was quickly able to stave it off by plucking a perfectly ripe and shiny-skinned red apple from a nearby tree. He wondered for a moment whether they had merely corrected the scale in the strategy-gameworld, as he was still surrounded by greenery on all sides, but there were no war engines and no armies to blight the view. In fact, it was a bucolic landscape so idyllic that he could imagine pastoral nymphs, pipe-tooting satyrs and maybe even Little Bo Peep showing up any second.

There was no sound of gunfire, explosions, sword clashes, aircraft or even traffic; just the tweeting of birds, the rustle of a light wind rippling leaves, and a soft chirrup of crickets. The sun was warm but low in the sky. It felt like late afternoon in a warm September.

He breathed in the autumn air as they walked at a dawdle down a gentle slope, at the foot of which they could see a village surrounded by bounteously yielding crop fields. The unhurried progress was almost involuntary: something about this place just made him want to take it easy and slow the pace of *everything*.

'Calming sight, huh,' Juno said.

'Yeah,' he agreed. 'I think this is the most tranquil place I've ever been. Especially after some of the stuff I've been through lately. It's a blessed relief to be in an environment where death isn't about to rain down upon me without warning.'

He saw a shadow pass across the ground and, feeling a considerable disturbance in the air, instinctively glanced up to see what was casting it. A stone cottage plummeted from an indeterminate place in the blue sky and slammed into the earth about ten yards in front, causing both he and Juno to throw themselves backwards in response.

They landed together in a tangle on the cool grass, Juno's armour making this a more comfortable moment for her than it was for Ross. Another cottage dropped from the sky and took its place about twenty yards from the first.

'Well, at least we know he's definitely here,' she said, climbing to her feet.

'How?'

'This world is a god-game. You can visit them, even settle there if you like, but only Originals can play god on them. If the rest of us want to do that, then we've got the Beyonderland. Very few people come to this particular world, though. It's in a secluded little niche, tucked away beyond a glitched-out RTS. That's why it's the Sandman's little private haven.'

They continued down the slope, walking around the newly arrived cottages and on towards the village. They passed people contentedly tilling fields, others taking crops away on the backs of horse-drawn carts. Nobody seemed remotely perturbed by the sight of buildings suddenly raining down from the heavens.

'You can see the problem,' Juno said. 'The Sandman could be

any one of these people and we'd never know. If you're hiding from the Integrity, the best disguise is to pretend to be an NPC.'

'I know, I've done it myself. Hey Juno, is there a clock on me for this?'

'A clock?'

'Yeah, as in how long I've got for the Sandman to come up and high-five me before you write me off as an infiltrator. I'm just wondering if I should do anything to make myself more noticeable.'

'That clock started the moment we arrived, Bedlam. The Sandman's a god here. Nothing in this world escapes his notice.'

With that, Ross felt a tremor in the earth beneath his bare feet. It was followed a moment later by another, then a third. He sensed movement to his left and another shadow passed across the ground. He looked up, preparing himself for evasive action should another building be plummeting his way, but instead saw a monstrous sight making its way towards them: a gigantic bullfrog, easily fifty feet high, covering the ground in a series of huge leaps.

'It's okay,' Juno assured him. 'It's a good sign. That's his creature.'

Ross allowed himself a smile of relief as he realised he even knew the game. It was *Black & White*, or one of its sequels.

As it drew closer, Ross could see that the creature had a cartoonish, almost childlike face, an eagerness to please etched in its expression. It was reassuring to know that the Sandman wasn't an evil tyrannical deity, all the more so when the bullfrog extended a huge green hand and picked up the pair of them. It popped them on to its head, between its bulbous great protruding eyes, and commenced hopping back the way it had come.

Ross clung on tight to a ridge of skin at first, but found the ride to be fairly smooth once he got used to the rhythm. They passed fields and farms, forests and lakes, towns and villages, heading towards a mountain range.

It was on the outskirts of the largest town that Ross saw something that caused a leap in his chest, a surge of emotion the intensity of which he didn't fully comprehend.

'Kids,' he said, pointing to the group of children outside what he realised was a school. But even as he watched them playing

271

ring-a-rosey, oblivious to the sight of a titanic amphibian hopping around the landscape, he realised they were just NPCs. He felt slightly embarrassed, conscious of Juno's feelings, and how the sight must have hurt her. He could imagine how much it was going to start hurting him if he never did get back to the old world.

The bullfrog came to a stop on the lower slopes of the mountain, outside a charming but inescapably modest farmhouse, where it gently set them down to rest on the grass. Ross had been expecting something like the Pantheon, or a palace to rival the sights of Pulchritupolis. Even the beach house he'd given himself in the Beyonderland was bigger and more impressive. The same couldn't be said for the view however, which was just a wee bit more striking than an endless black ocean. A beauteous valley rolled out below, green meadowland and golden crop fields stretching from the sparkling azure bay at one end to the mystical forest at the other.

There was a beauteous sight in the other direction too. A woman was walking around from a vineyard at the side of the house, blonde hair swept back in long flowing tresses, resplendent in a diaphanous white shift dress. Ross thought she looked every bit the wife of a god. However, if this was the case, then the other women Ross subsequently began to spot around the premises would have to be described as looking, respectively, every bit the titian, raven and brunette *other* wives of a god; the skanky street-slut of a god; the teenage jailbait nymphette of a god; and the leather-bound S&M dungeon mistress of a god.

He glanced briefly towards Juno to check her reading of the situation and could see that this probably wasn't going to go well.

A male figure emerged from the house, looking relaxed, handsome, healthy, and undeniably rather god-like, if in a rather hackneyed comic-book way. He also looked unmistakably familiar, everything that was different about him paradoxically serving to underline what was the same: that essence Juno had talked about.

The most striking difference in this respect wasn't just down to the cosmetic changes he had effected in giving himself an idealised face, body and flowing head of hair. It was the brightness about him, the happiness and optimism replacing the hunted look and crushed confidence that coloured his expression back in the office.

'Sandman?' Ross enquired, reckoning it was polite to seek confirmation from his host.

'Ross, or should I say Bedlam. It's been so long. It's wonderful to see you. And you must be Juno. Your timing's perfect.'

He gestured towards a rustic wooden table on a terrace in front of the farmhouse, laden with roast joints and fowls, freshly baked bread, cheeses, cured meats, bottles of wine and flagons of ale. Salad did not appear to be an option, but then again, neither was heart disease, cholesterol or weight gain.

'You're looking well,' Ross said.

'Not bad for my age anyway,' he replied, sitting down at a bench. 'You're looking spry yourself. How are you?'

'Transformed. And not in a good way. A few days ago I lay down in the Simulacron prototype back in Stirling, and now I'm here. I ended up in the clutches of the Integrity until Solderburn got me out, but they ended up capturing him instead.'

'So I heard. Won't you both take a seat?'

'We didn't come here to eat, Alex.'

'Please, it's Sandman here. You both must be hungry.'

'I am. And what I really want is soggy chips from the staff canteen, or even one of those manky attempts at curry they sometimes pass off.'

'Weird what you miss, huh?' Sandman replied, seriously not getting it. 'If you give me a while I can probably synthesise an approximation of—'

'His girlfriend's pregnant,' Juno interjected. 'He needs to get back to her. I need to get back to my daughter. We came here because we're tired of the mushroom treatment: being left in the dark and fed on shit. Solderburn was rumoured to have found a way out. What do you know about it?'

Sandman shook his head apologetically and tore a chicken leg from a richly browned bird.

'I know there *is* no way out. It was just a rumour that grew in the void. I don't know where Solderburn went for so long; he could have gone nowhere, just lived anonymously without all the hassle. I'm sorry. I've been here longer than just about

273

anybody else: hence the term Original. That means I've looked longer for the same things as you, so I know what can and can't be found. The old world is gone, and one thing I know better than most is that accepting that fact is the key to finding happiness here.'

Ross looked around at the Sandman's happiness: at his malleable fairytale world, his groaning but calorie-free table and his NPC harem of what were literally fuck-toys. In the old world, his bitch of an ex-wife had driven over him in a freight train, so this might be understandable, but it was still pretty fucking sad.

'No offence, mate, but I don't think you were looking for quite the same things as me. Leaving the old world was no great loss to you. You love it here. You're in heaven.'

'I *found* heaven, and not right away. I made it heaven. You can too. You've seen what's possible in this place. There is nothing in the old world that you can't have here, only better.'

'Can I see my baby when it's born?' Ross replied. 'My sisters' kids? Can Juno see her daughter? Guy I met on Graxis called Bob, an accountant from Leicester: can he see his family again?'

The Sandman nodded understandingly, putting down the remains of the chicken leg.

'These are painful wounds, but there's nothing we can do about them other than pick up the pieces and build new lives here. And right now we have to look to *preserving* those lives. We're facing the greatest threat this place has ever known. Look what happened to Calastria. Worlds are corrupting. Getting to the bottom of that is far more important than pursuing some pointless quest.'

'I don't give a fuck about the corruption,' Ross yelled, raging in the face of the Sandman's detachment. 'I don't care if this whole damned dimension disappears up its own digital dunghole. I want to know how I got here and I want to know how I leave. Basic principles must still apply. For every action, there is an equal and opposite reaction. If there is a way into somewhere, there must be a way out. You remember back in Stirling we once talked about Bostrom's simulation argument? Well that's what I think this is: an ancestor simulation, except it's been hacked, and the "real world" simulated environment has bled into gameworld simulated environments. So even if what we knew as reality was always a simulation, there must be a way back to *that* simulation, because—'

Ross's rant was halted by the appearance of a god-like hand above him, which picked him up and dangled him in the air.

'You don't give a fuck about the corruption?' the Sandman asked. 'Okay, let's see if we can extract one or two.'

The hand dropped him again, and he plummeted about ten feet to the ground, where he was relieved to discover that falling-damage protocols had not been invoked.

The Sandman stood up, his demeanour still calm but giving off an unmissable last-warning vibe.

'When I say you can't go back,' he stated, 'you're misunderstanding. You think that it just means we haven't found the way yet. It's like when people fail to grasp how it's impossible to go north of the North Pole, or how you can't talk about the time before the big bang because time itself was created in the big bang. The old world, the real world, is still getting on with itself somewhere, but the reason you can't go *back* is because technically you can't return to somewhere you've never been.'

Ross fixed him with a cautious stare, climbing unsteadily back to his feet. He had learned of late to rule out nothing on grounds of plausibility.

'Is this the part where you tell me that my brain is being deceived by a simulation while in the real world the oblivious Ross Baker's body is being used as a battery?'

'No. I've no idea what Ross Baker's brain and body are up to right now, because this is the part where I tell you that *you* aren't Ross Baker, and that you've never *had* a brain or a body. You're existing here inside a world of computer programs because you *are* a computer program. You're a digital copy of the real Ross Baker's mind.'

Loading . . .
File 3 of 3

Closer

'A repeal of the Act is not beyond the realm of possibility,' Michaels told Stoneworth. 'Once this development programme is underway, rather than keep it top secret, I'd recommend you guys leak it. Yeah, there'll be an initial backlash, but we can use that moment to restart the debate and swing the pendulum our way. You guys can bring pressure at the political level, and we can hire lobbyists and PR, spin the angle that the horse has already bolted.'

Michaels could see his vitals in real time, but it was hardly necessary. The Department of Defense guy was practically drooling and they were just talking hypotheticals. If this was sex, then Stoneworth was close to premature ejaculation with the girl only having undone a couple of buttons on her blouse.

Michaels had insisted they have the meeting here at Neurosphere, face to face. He had cited concerns over the security of comms lines, given what was at stake for both the company and the DoD if anybody found out what they were discussing. The real reason, of course, was that he wanted home-court advantage. Stoneworth wasn't here to negotiate – yet – but Michaels wanted to find out as much as he could about how the guy was thinking ahead of the day they would deal.

'Man, the things we could do,' said Stoneworth. 'The things we could have been doing already, but for that goddamn law.'

'You're preaching to the choir here, Major. I've been tantalised by the possibilities for a lot longer than anybody else. I mean, can you imagine the implications for reducing stress, and stress-related violence, if everybody could have a copy of somebody they're pissed at?'

'Their boss, their co-worker,' Stoneworth suggested, running with it. 'Yeah. Beat the shit out of that guy, blow him up a few times, make yourself feel better.'

Better yet, Michaels thought, if you *are* the boss, get copies of your employees: that way you can suss how they think, how far you can push them, and what they'd settle for when it came time to talk pay and conditions. But why share that idea with anyone else quite yet?

'Exactly,' he agreed. 'Then nobody needs to get hurt in real life.'

'A lot fewer American soldiers would be getting hurt too,' Stoneworth stated, his tone suddenly more sombre. 'Once we can run infinite combat simulations with DCs, we'll have a tactical advantage in advance of every operation. I can't think of any single development that would have a more significant effect on force depletion.'

Jesus. Michaels could tell from his read-outs that the guy was making a play here. Yeah, sure thing, buddy: just appeal to my patriotism and I'll knock a zero off the price. Dick.

'To say nothing of what you could learn from prisoners,' Michaels suggested, dangling another possibility more likely to *add* a zero. 'You'll have infinite subjects on whom to practise interrogation methods, and you don't need to worry about the mess if you push things too far.'

'Yeah, but we still can't act on intelligence obtained under duress,' Stoneworth reminded him.

'You wouldn't need to lay a finger on anybody. You could interrogate copies.'

And as that particular penny dropped, the Major's feedback numbers superimposed on Michaels' vision looked like a slot-machine paying out the jackpot.

He leaned forward in his chair, his eagerness unconsciously manifest in his body language.

'So how close are we to doing business?' Stoneworth asked.

'We're in touching distance.'

'What about internal opposition? You suggested that there might be . . .'

'Yeah, there's been an attempt to throw a spanner in the works from precisely whom we anticipated. I saw it coming a mile out.'

'So you had a counter-measure?'

'Let's just say I've put somebody in there who knows how to close a deal.'

The World You Love

Ross felt time stand still for a moment, and in that moment was all the more aware of everything that he was sensing: the grass beneath his toes, the light breeze on his cheek and the smells that it carried. It all seemed even more real, even more nuanced and detailed than before.

He looked to Juno. She was staring back, her agonised shock mirroring his own. He saw the same helplessness reflected in her face, the same extreme of hollow despair.

He turned towards the Sandman, unable to formulate a response. Everything that went into constructing his sense of self told him that what Alex was saying had to be wrong, yet it was the only way in which everything that had happened to him made sense.

'You can make your heaven here, but it isn't an afterlife. You're not dead because you were never alive in the organic sense. None of us were. You are a facsimile of Ross Baker's mind, a snapshot that was taken on the last normal day you remember.'

'How do you know this?' Juno breathed, close to tears.

'I pieced it together. Took me a while, but eventually I figured it out. It's the explanation that fits the most data and isn't contradicted by any of it. The time lapses were the key.'

'Time lapses?' Ross asked, but Juno was ahead of him.

'Like me and Joe,' she said, her voice distant and numb. 'I was in the old world two years more than him before coming here: I was with him the whole time, yet he has no memory of that period.'

'That's it. To your husband it didn't happen, because he is a snapshot of Joe's mind taken two years before the snapshot that is you.'

'Solderburn's scanner,' Ross mumbled.

'The Simulacron,' Alex confirmed. 'We were working on a system that would let us create computerised models based on brain scans. Solderburn's new machine must have recorded a lot more than anyone anticipated, and at some point in the future, we developed the technology to interpret and synthesise the data.'

'In the future? But I was scanned by the prototype, and my research plans for decoding models were nowhere near coming up with something like this. Besides, if we're all scans, why do most people remember just going to bed at home?'

'The last part, I'm not sure. My latest memory is the same as yours: lying down inside Solderburn's chamber. As to your other question, it's the time issue again. I'm guessing there was a gap between Solderburn carrying out the test scans and the technology to interpret them being developed. Essentially it's a matter of the scan sitting dormant on a hard drive until it gets incorporated into a synthesis model and then uploaded to a virtual environment. That's why although I was among the first to get here, I found myself inside games that weren't due for release until years into my future.'

'But I was scanned less than a week after you were. Why am I turning up late to the party, and how long has the party been running, for that matter?'

'There's no way of knowing how time here relates to time in the real world, but for whatever reason, you were never uploaded until now. After I came here, at first there was a trickle of new arrivals, then a deluge, and then somebody shut off the tap. No idea why, but one day the new arrivals just stopped coming. As far as I'm aware, you and this guy Bob are the first new uploads in a very long time. Apart from the Integrity,' he added, a look of regret darkening his expression.

'If I'm just a digital copy of myself, shouldn't I have perfect recall of everything I know, instantly accessible like any other computer file?'

'It doesn't work like that. We aren't merely copies of our memories, we're copies of our minds. Not merely what we thought, but *how* we thought. So just like before, something might trigger complete recall of a name or a detail that you couldn't remember yesterday.'

'But isn't what's happening here being written to purely digital memory?'

'Yes, but the architecture is the same as your old, organic systems.'

Ross searched desperately for more questions, as though any holes he could find in Alex's theory might be his salvation. Yet even as he asked, he was aware of having already been prepared to accept the same explanation when he came up with his own ancestor-simulation hypothesis. In both scenarios, he had never visited the 'real' world, never had a body, never had a brain, so why was Alex's version harder to take?

Partly it was envy. In the ancestor-simulation scenario, there was only one Ross Baker, and only an illusion of the real world to feel cut adrift from. In short, you don't miss what you never had. Whereas in Alex's scenario, there *was* a real world, and a real Ross Baker still living in it: one who still had Carol, and the baby, and a future. However, the main reason for his instinctive resistance was that in the hacked ancestor-simulation scenario, there remained the possibility of a way back. Alex's version offered no such hope.

His principles were now his enemies, but just because reality was pissing him about didn't mean it would be a constructive course of action to go in the huff with it. Parsimony. Occam's Razor. The explanation that makes the fewest assumptions is usually the correct one. Every assumption in Alex's explanation was repeated and multiplied in the alternative. What was more likely: that Solderburn's machine had created a digital copy of the human mind, or that Ross's and everyone else's minds had always been mere digital entities within a simulated universe; and that this simulated universe, governed consistently by laws that we had come to understand as nature, had been fundamentally altered by a machine that was essentially a minute subroutine inside it?

Juno looked as though it was only the armour that was holding her up.

'You okay there?' he asked her.

'I feel sick. But how can I feel sick when I've never had a stomach? And I feel lost – far more lost than when I first got here.'

'You did have a stomach,' the Sandman said. 'What's crucial here is that this doesn't change who we are. If a man paints a masterpiece then loses his arm in an accident, he no longer has the hand that held the brush, but that doesn't mean he's no longer the man who created the picture. Organic consciousness or digital consciousness, you're defined by the software, not the machine that's running it.'

This last remark resonated like a bell buoy in the fog, offering guidance through the gloom, and Ross recognised that it sounded so reassuring because its chime was familiar. This was what he had come to understand on Graxis when he'd been told that his memories were just a virus intended to debilitate the Gralak soldiery.

'This doesn't change who we are,' the Sandman repeated. 'And if you've any doubts about that, ask yourself: now that you've learned you're a digital copy, does it hurt any less to be cut off from your family? Now that you're aware everyone you've met here is also a digital copy, do you feel any less connection to the people you know? The people you've lost?'

Ross thought of a sunny day at Blair Drummond Safari Park long ago, of Christmases at Mum's with his sisters and their kids around the dinner table. He felt his eyes filling up, a lump in his throat obstructing a verbal answer rendered redundant by all the ways his face was already expressing it.

There was no going back. That was why it hurt. For better or for worse, this was his world now.

'Hell if you make it, heaven if you want it to be,' Juno affirmed hoarsely.

'Wise words,' said the Sandman.

'I heard it more starkly framed, too,' stated Ross: 'Here is all there is.'

'Who said that?'

'The Integrity agent who tortured me. At least now I know he wasn't lying. Kind of puts an interesting spin on the risk/benefit equation. I don't fancy living out my existence trapped in one single gameworld as the Integrity are demanding, but if they're right about what's causing the corruption, it would be literally better than nothing.'

'Now you're getting it,' said the Sandman.

'It's devastating though,' Ross said. 'I can certainly see why the Originals kept it back from the general population. So why are you telling it to us?'

Juno's attitude of defeat suddenly altered, becoming animate with alert caution, like an animal that's just sniffed a predator on the breeze.

'Because we ain't gonna be allowed to pass it on,' she said, looking up the hill beyond the house, then accusatorily towards the Sandman.

Ross glanced towards where her gaze had briefly fixed upon the upper slope. He saw a black half-track vehicle cresting the summit, a small deployment of black-clad troops marching at its flanks. Ross turned back towards the Sandman but his attention was drawn past him, down to the horseshoe bay, where he could now see an aircraft down on the beach, some troop-carrier hulk like a big black beetle, tiny black figures scurrying busily around it.

'You ratted us out?' Ross asked, incredulous.

'I had no choice,' the Sandman retorted. 'You idiots brought them here. They came pouring into my world a matter of seconds after you both arrived. Turns out you're a very wanted man. I had to cut a deal to protect what's mine.'

'You went Lando on us?'

'This is all there is, you just said it yourself, and the corruption is real. I don't like the way the Integrity go about their business but I've come to understand that they're a necessary evil. Just as the Diasporadoes are a well-meaning but misguided threat. Closing down the transits isn't too high a price to pay for survival. It's a big enough place: everybody should be able to find a world they like and get comfortable, at least until we can stabilise the corruption.'

'And where will *we* be getting comfortable?' Juno asked.

'I've been given assurances. Your custody won't be forever.'

Ross glanced back and forth, from the half-track proceeding slowly down the slope to the aircraft and the landing force on the shore below.

'They came via space,' Juno said, her voice dry and woozy, but that was far from the most disturbing development they witnessed.

Ross noticed that most of the tiny black figures on the sand were streaming towards, not out of, the troop carrier, executing an evacuation. They were running from what looked like a pillar at the edge of the sea, a black cylinder like a Greek or Roman column standing three times the height of a man. As the last of them piled up a ramp into the troop carrier, even from this far up on the hillside Ross could sense a powerful vibration and the column began to rotate, burrowing itself into the sand.

Their host's previously perfect brow began to develop a furrow, as though out of sympathy with the beach.

The column dug deeper and deeper, spinning ever faster as it did so, before the sand covered it over and it was gone. The aircraft took off vertically and headed out over the water, where Ross knew there was nothing but the end of this world.

All was still again, and for a moment the beach looked as though the troop carrier and the column had never been there. Then, from the same spot, there came what looked like wisps of smoke, curling up and forming a grey haze. At first the haze rose where the pillar had been, like a vapid ghost of its predecessor, then it swiftly began to spread.

The Sandman stared uncomprehending for a moment, but Ross and Juno had both seen it before. On Calastria.

'The corruption,' he breathed. 'The Integrity are causing it.'

He turned to look at the two of them, wearing the aghast expression of someone who hadn't been genuinely shocked for an extremely long time.

'They're destroying my world.'

'Yeah, I feel you, man,' Juno replied. 'If you can't trust a bunch of psycho-ass sadistic power-mad fascists, honestly, who the fuck *can* you trust?'

Ross heard a familiar thumping from somewhere in the distance and felt the ground tremble a little beneath his feet. He looked across the valley and saw the bullfrog hopping into sight at the top of the hillside opposite, as much a symbol of the power the Sandman wielded as the divine hand that had picked him up and dropped him a few minutes ago. His attention was drawn by the observation that, unlike its previous leisurely meanderings, it appeared to be in quite a hurry. Then all of a sudden it

288

wasn't in a hurry any more, albeit some parts of it were moving even faster than before; they just weren't attached to the parts they had been previously.

Ross had seen something fly over the brow of the hill and make for the bullfrog, proportionally about the size of a mosquito. Then there was a thoroughly disproportionate response as the amphibian exploded, its legs slumping down on to the hillside like a burst water balloon while its top half sprayed and splattered across the lower slope in a messy arc of red, pink and green half a mile wide. If any of them had a freezer, the local villagers would be sorted for frog meat for about a decade.

The Sandman watched his creature's demise with numb incredulity.

'Bawbag,' he said.

Ross wondered whether he was blaming someone specifically until he realised from the alliteration that it must have been the bullfrog's name.

He looked for the source of the missile, and saw an entire division of Integrity troops coming over the brow of the slope on the far side, behind not one but four tanks of the kind Ross had seen in the war-torn rubble of *Death or Glory*.

'I'm not so sure it's me these guys are here to huckle,' he said.

'Copy that,' said Juno. 'So, given the deal's off,' she asked the Sandman, 'I take it you won't mind if we try getting the fuck outta here?'

He eyed the menacing advance that was marching thigh-high through over-sized froggy viscera, desolation gradually overcoming disbelief as his dominant expression. Then self-pity changed to something else, closer to regret or even penitence.

'The nearest transit is in the next valley,' he said. 'It's in a mausoleum halfway down the slope. If you can get past that lot, you're free and clear.'

Ross took a fresh look at the half-track and its infantry escort.

'You think we can take them?' he asked Juno.

'Attacking uphill, against an armoured vehicle and superior numbers enjoying an elevated angle of fire? Shit, why not give us a challenge?'

The Sandman's eyes blanked briefly, a look Ross was coming

to recognise as HUD-stare. He waved his right hand and gestured to the side of the vineyard, where two creatures were suddenly called into existence.

'Brilliant,' Ross said as he and Juno surveyed their mounts. 'More fucking horses. How about a hover-bike?'

'Rules of the gameworld,' the Sandman explained. 'You can only piss with the cock you've got.'

'Some god you are,' he muttered under his breath as he climbed up on to the saddle.

Gameworld rules worked two ways, however. Ross, who had never ridden a horse in the old world, found that he had control of this one like he was a champion jockey, and at the pace it boasted, his steed would have romped the Grand National carrying John Candy.

He galloped in erratic zigzags to make himself a less predictable target for the Integrity snipers who had dug in and were taking laser-blast pot-shots from further up the slope. The fact that they weren't restricted to the low-fi options of *Black & White*'s bronze-age technology reminded him that his own pissing options were not limited to merely the one cock either.

A quick root through his inventory showed him that he still had a couple of Panzerfaust warheads to play with. He called one to hand and aimed for the half-track, taking a few moments to anticipate the rise and fall of his horse's gallop before pulling the trigger.

The rocket-propelled grenade flew over the snipers' heads and straight for its target, engulfing the half-track in a ball of fire. This stopped its progress down the hill, but several more troops poured from the flaming wreckage and began aiming concerted volleys at the two mounts.

Ross and Juno were both thrown to the turf as each of their horses was felled. He found himself face-down in knee-high grass, less mobile but not such an easy mark. He switched to his machine-gun and found a target, the strangely shimmering black of the Integrity snipers making them easy to spot against the green of the hillside. Another came running over the brow to replace his fallen comrade, and Ross dropped him before he could draw. Emboldened, he climbed first to his knees then fully upright, cutting down the enemy infantry as he charged up the slope, Juno also firing accurately and mercilessly at his side with her plasma gun.

The bastards didn't like it toe to toe, that much was obvious. They still loosed off a few volleys for Ross and Juno to dodge, but their firing was needlessly sporadic; a conspicuous lack of aggression that reminded him of the Gralaks. Perhaps these were Integrity AI drones. If so, they should have toggled the buggers to a harder skill setting, because this was almost too easy.

As he gained the brow of the hill, he realised he was wrong. It wasn't almost too easy: it was precisely too easy. Waiting down the slope on the other side was a huge squadron of infantry, the casualties respawning to replenish their numbers from a portable pod, all awaiting the command of a new class of Integrity agent Ross had never seen before. He looked like an Integrity build of the ubersoldat from *Return to Castle Wolfenstein*: a towering super-warrior wrought from fluid plastic and tempered steel, carrying what in anyone else's hands would have been a cannon, but in his was merely a rifle.

Before Ross could call out a warning to Juno to turn back, the rifle spat a gobbet of black from its gleaming maw, and speech was no longer an option.

Only screaming.

He was knocked to the ground and sent tumbling several yards back down the slope in a maelstrom of pain and terrifying disorientation that felt less like the world was swirling around him than that his individual molecules were all spinning at high speed and threatening to fly apart. He endured the same electrocution agony as when he was being tortured in the cell, the same violation of his psyche, but instead of it coming on the licking tongues of a whip, it passed right through him like a wave, enveloping him like a blanket and exploding from within him like a bomb.

He was quite sure that according to the protocols of any gameworld, it ought to have killed him and invoked a respawn, but he feared this device was independent of all such rules. It didn't come from within any game. It came from somewhere else entirely.

Ross tried to right himself but he wasn't even sure what way he was facing. He could see Juno, or at least a shape he knew to be Juno, lying on the grass nearby, hit by a blast from the same weapon. He tried to move his arms, but it was as though they were an inventory item and he had forgotten how to equip them for use. Drunkenly he looked through his HUD for a weapon, his dazed logic suggesting that holding a rifle would automatically bring his arms up in front of him, so that at least he'd know where they were.

There was nothing there. His inventory was blank. Weapons, costumes, power-ups, accessories: they had all been erased. All he had were the clothes on his back, not even any shoes.

But it got worse. He could feel a familiar disturbance in the air, and hear the sound of huge, powerful wing-beats.

'Oh fucksocks.'

There was a nerve-rending shriek also, shaking the air with its shrill vibrato, but not like he remembered. Some instinct in Ross gave him the motor skills to pull himself into a cowering ball, yet, despite his horror, he couldn't help but look at the monster as it descended. That was when he saw that it wasn't what he feared. Instead he watched the Sandman descend upon the back of a winged beast that looked like what you might get if a pteranodon shagged a giant raven and the resulting eggs were left to incubate in a vat of toxic waste.

'How's my pissing with this cock?' he shouted, as the flying mutant unleashed a deluge of orange fluid from somewhere between its legs, the liquid cutting down the Integrity ubersoldat and several of his troops like a water-cannon.

The creature alighted on the grass with a thump, the Sandman gesturing to the still-reeling Ross and Juno to climb aboard as quickly as possible. Walking was like trying to use tweezers in a mirror, but they supported each other on to their unlikely saviour's back, albeit in an ungainly tangle that was probably as mutually obstructive as it was helpful.

The creature took to the air once more, Ross clinging on tight to clumps of feathers as it climbed steeply with beats of its mighty wings.

'There's another transit further down the valley, in the forest,' the Sandman told them. 'It's at the centre of a shrine. It'll take you to Jerusalem.'

The winged mutant banked sharply to escape blasts from the

292

respawned ubersoldat's evil, soul-goring gun, then soared above the plain, where in an impressive feat of multi-tasking the Sandman was taking on the Integrity's ground forces. Ross saw a huge god-like hand hovering above the meadows, dropping entire rows of houses on top of the advancing troops, while hundreds of NPC villagers engaged the invaders, launching fireballs from catapults, their archers firing a hail of arrows.

Ross wondered how all of this activity might be affecting the Sandman's steering and navigation, but they were holding a straight course along the edge of the mountain, heading for the forest. Behind them, towards the sea, Ross could see the grey haze rising beyond the mountain as the corruption grew and spread.

Just as on the other side of the mountain, the Integrity had a portable spawn-pod from which its resurrected troops were spilling again like popcorn. Orchestrating his efforts from his HUD, the Sandman piled more buildings upon those already laid down, deciding that *ob*struction would be more effective than *de*struction when the dead were popping back up again so close to where they'd died.

That was when the tanks opened fire. No missiles, no lasers, no artillery. They just erased the buildings, like Ross had witnessed at the monastery. Then, with this impediment removed, they turned their weapons on the NPCs and erased them too.

The god-like hand swooped down and made a grab for one of the tanks, its fingers big enough to flick the thing into the sea, but instead of picking it up, they passed right through it like it wasn't there. Within the protocols of the gameworld, they were an object that couldn't be lifted.

In that moment, everyone who witnessed it understood that it meant certain defeat. The Sandman might be a god here, but whatever the Integrity were, his powers didn't apply to them.

Ross glanced downwards. There were now trees beneath them, though the mutant raven seemed to be skirting the edge of the forest, still holding the same course. He hoped this meant the huge NPC knew where it was going, but he suspected it just meant that the Sandman's attention was focused upon the battle on the plain, where the hand tried again, grabbing for another tank.

Juno shouted a warning and Ross looked around immediately. Cresting the hill on a thermal, gathering deadly speed as it soared above the treetops, flew the ghastly abomination that had taken Solderburn.

The Sandman, immersed in concentration elsewhere, reacted only a fraction of a second after Ross, but the delay was critical. The two winged horrors collided, Cuddles blindsiding the raven with shuddering impact. Ross was knocked clear off the raven's back, his fists clutching huge feathers as he tumbled through the air, while above him the creatures gouged and tore at each other, cries echoing across the valley.

He was aware of a shape falling alongside him. He could only catch brief glimpses as he spun towards the ground, but the glimpses were enough. It was Juno. She was dead. There was a hole the size of a tree-trunk punched clean through her, armour and all, by one of the maenad's claws or spikes.

He smashed through roughly forty feet of branches and hit the ground with a disorienting but fortunately damage-free thump. He took a moment to stop his head spinning and climb to his feet, finding himself a few yards from the perimeter of a system of concentric stone circles. The Mobius icon told him the transit was at the centre.

He heard a horrific combined roar and shriek from above, one part war-cry and the other part death-scream. A few moments later the mutant raven hit the forest floor in two huge bloody pieces, while Cuddles flew off clutching its prey among its arms, suckers and tentacles.

Single Player

It was a one-way transit. He materialised in mid-air, falling towards a conveniently placed hay cart, where he landed in the welcoming embrace of a generously cushioning pile of straw. Jerusalem, Sandman had said, and Ross identified it as twelfth century, not from any profound historical knowledge but from the manner of his fortuitously soft landing, which told him this was *Assassin's Creed*.

He felt the heat right away. The Sandman's world had been bathed in the gentle warmth of an English autumn, whereas this was fierce, a constant prompt to seek the sanctuary of shade.

Ross ran on soft feet from the cart's location in a quiet yard along a dark and narrow alley into a bright and noisy public square. He scanned the crowd, expecting to see Integrity soldiers closing in from anywhere, and looked up for a possible escape route. At first he saw only a chaotically ramshackle skyline, but when he concentrated for a moment he could make out figures shinning poles, skirting ledges and sliding along ropes. It was like the world's biggest soft-play area. Thus the way to stay truly covert was to remain anonymous within the crowds on the street. It was a world built for stealth and climbing, but in practice only the NPCs didn't realise that the easiest way to spot your quarry was to look up.

He crossed the square towards the shaded side and sought the refuge of a bustling coffee house, where he sat down at a table deep in the cool gloom of the interior but with a clear view of the door. His nose had been full of spices since the moment he hit the square; cinnamon, cardamom and cumin carried boun-teously on the warm air. In here, their traces were still detectable, but largely overwhelmed by strong coffee and an unmistakable scent of hash.

He didn't think he was hungry, but when the landlord put down a plate of dates and sticky sweetmeats, he found himself compelled to tuck in. You *could* eat here, he deduced: you just didn't need to. If there was a food-energy protocol invoked, then, given the physical exertions people came here to enjoy, they'd have to spend as much time stuffing their faces as scaling buildings.

The rules of the world dictated that he wasn't required to eat or drink, but something more primal in him needed to, the same instinct that had driven him to come in here to seek rest and shelter. He had escaped the Integrity and the corruption, but the Sandman's revelation and what had happened since was something he couldn't outrun, and now that he had stopped to catch his breath, it was crashing in upon him like waves.

Juno. Christ. Where might she be now? He couldn't help but recall how he had convinced her to take him to the Sandman. *Sounds like I got nothing to lose*, she had said. Now she was most probably in the Integrity's hands, trying to deal with the knowledge not only that she'd never see her daughter again, but that she'd never actually seen her before.

The word headfuck seemed insufficient, not to mention inaccurate. He had never had a head; never had a fuck, for that matter.

He'd never had a life.

He was not a human being. He had never been one. He had never visited the real world. He had never lived in Stirling, never worked at Neurosphere.

He had never met Carol. He might find a version of her in this world, but it could be a version of her from a few years in the future, as had happened to Juno and Joe. She might hate him by now. Maybe she lost the baby, maybe she had a termination, maybe she moved on to someone else.

Ross watched the coffee dregs swirl at the bottom of the cup, gritty and dark, a level of detail and authenticity that nobody at Ubisoft ever programmed. He was aware that the drink didn't physically exist and, even more acutely, that neither did he, but that didn't change the fact that it had been a bloody good cup of coffee: black as night, sweet as honey, hot as hell. He had tasted it once before, he realised, on holiday in Turkey. Did his own memories feed back upon themselves to enhance his perceptions here? Would someone who had only ever drunk lattes from Starbucks see, smell and taste something different if the bustling tavern owner served them the same cup?

His memories, he realised, were still his. Every molecule in the human body was replaced every seven years, so the physical matter that was processing his thoughts and memories had already been switched out several times. Memories were just code, and it didn't matter whether the system processing them was digital or organic.

This was his life now: his realm, his world, his universe. He had to accept it. He had to embrace it.

He had to lose Ross Baker and truly become Bedlam.

Double Agent

She had never quite got used to the dying and respawning thing. Sometimes it was a convenient route out of a situation or merely the quickest way to get from one end of a world to another, but it just felt wrong. It was like that feeling people described as someone walking over your grave, but to the power of ten. However, it was a breeze compared to warp transit. Moving between worlds she could just about handle, but something about the instant transition left her feeling as though she'd just woken up from a drug haze or a coma and didn't know how many days she'd missed.

Actually, truth be told it was always worse when this place was the destination, so maybe it wasn't the warp itself that was the problem, but the jolt from vibrancy, colour and hubbub to this monochrome monastery. It seemed all the more stark for the contrast being so sudden, like someone had cut the power while you were watching a movie. The sounds in her ears shut off without echo and not even the smells in her nose lingered past the instant she materialised here.

She glanced at the floor beneath her, clean and black, the matt texture preventing reflection as if it would grudge passing back the light. You'd expect to see some grass, some dirt, if you'd just walked through a door from a bucolic idyll, but nothing adhered from the world she'd left.

She had spawned in the familiar spot and begun walking the geometrically precise corridors, taking perhaps her tenth new route through the place. Lurgo, Ankou's snivelling functionary, had remarked to her recently that she really ought to opt for a spawn point closer to the boss's chambers, but she explained that she always forgot again when she was out in the worlds.

Nevertheless, it was good to see some deference being shown these days, both from Lurgo and from the clone-drones who patrolled the place. Things had come a long way since the trial-by-combat credential checks. The only time she had endured any hassle after that was when she forgot to change back to her own face after clearing out that resistance cell in San Andreas. She had killed about eight guys before she worked out what was wrong.

Awkward.

They were okay about it. She had worn a hundred faces around these worlds, so it was inevitable that she'd show up in the wrong one at some point. Everyone was just grateful it had happened here, so no cover was blown.

She found Ankou exactly as she always did, standing in the centre of his operations room surrounded by the dozens of feeds that stared down from a tessellation of screens, like a concave inversion of a fly's compound eye. One monitor was gazing down from on high above a battery of retention grids, thousands upon thousands of hexagonal black cells, ready and waiting. Their time was almost at hand. On another she could see the corruption eating up the last of the god-gameworld where they'd taken their most recent Original scalp.

She couldn't help but marvel that Ankou never seemed to leave this place, never took advantage of what was out there, especially given that it wouldn't be out there much longer. Okay, the guy had a job to do, but there were sights to be seen, fun to be had – and if you were utterly amoral, the possibilities were only limited by your imagination.

Perhaps that was the problem: Ankou didn't really have an imagination. It made him perfect for this task, immune to the intoxications of such an environment, but it also made him vulnerable in ways that he would, by the very definition of his weakness, never be able to anticipate.

But then, that was what he had her for, wasn't it?

'You have news,' he said.

From his blank intonation it was difficult to tell whether this was a question or a statement, though in truth it made no differ-ence, because if it was a question, then both parties knew the answer had better be in the affirmative, otherwise what the hell was anyone doing disturbing him? It was, in fact, difficult to

300

tell much about his emotional response to anything. His face was black-on-black, and that was when he chose to show it to you. There were times when it remained fluid and semi-formed, the effect of which was to make most people all the more anxious to please him, in the hope that some rapid display of affirmation would grant them reassurance.

This didn't wash with her, however. The power balance here was delicate, and she never wanted him to forget that he needed her more than the other way around.

'The Sandman is in custody,' she reported, keeping her tone matter-of-fact, making sure she sounded neither eager for approval nor in any way surprised by her progress. 'I have also deployed several units to the Aperture Science complex and expect to apprehend Sleepflower within the hour.'

'Sleepflower,' he repeated. 'I must confess there were times when I thought she would never be tracked down.'

'Since the operation on Pulchritupolis it's been a chain reaction. Every resistance cell we mop up, we let at least one fugitive get away so that they can lead us to the next one. The Originals are falling like dominoes.'

'You are quite inspiringly duplicitous. Are you absolutely sure you're not me?'

'If you're looking to flatter yourself, the very fact that you can afford me should suffice.'

'*Touché*. And sincerely, kudos. I've started thinking of this little stratagem of yours as Operation Gift That Keeps On Giving.'

'Unfortunately nothing lasts forever,' she admitted. 'The price for us taking down the Sandman was that Bedlam now knows the truth about what he is.'

'Our useful idiot. I've almost grown fond of him.'

'He's no longer useful, and perhaps not such an idiot either. Fortunately he still has no idea who the double agent is.'

Ankou glanced at the compound of screens, his windows upon a multiplicity of worlds, on one of which Bedlam now walked incognito.

'What is he doing?' he asked her.

'Pursuing a pointless quest for answers. It's time we brought him in. There's no upside to leaving him free to wander out there.'

'True enough. He'll just be drifting aimlessly.'

'Unless he gets help,' she reminded him. 'After all, there is still one extremely dangerous rogue element out there.'

The Endgame

In the personal biopic running in his head, this was the self-discovery montage bit in which he wandered, silent and contemplative, while Michael MacLennan played on the soundtrack, singing about how the wolves were chasing. He passed from world to world, his transits unobserved, his presence inconspicuous. He let his Mobius strip guide him. It took him to the great public conduits between games, huge tunnels, rents and ruptures in the walls of this reality: once-open borders, now guarded and controlled by troopers in that creepily shimmering black. He would walk right past them, seemingly going about his business, indistinguishable from any other inhabitant or indeed NPC, and he would follow the pulsatile icon to the occult portals known only to those who could be trusted to keep them secret.

He disguised himself upon entering each new world, and gradually this action became a matter of reflex, as did the brandishing of only appropriate and contextual hardware, despite the arsenal he was steadily amassing. Where he could avoid conflict he took the discreet option, and when the mood seized him, he honed his skills, but he only fought in character, and took a few dives when he feared his growing prowess might attract attention.

He built up a map of the connections he had used, just following the daisy chain of where each transit took him, feeling like Mr Benn as a change of clothes was the only clue as to what might await him when he walked through the next door. He saw games he recognised and games he didn't, in the latter's case sometimes due to radical remodelling. The renovation job that had been done on *Painkiller* to make it a trendy Bohemian hang-out was, frankly, a travesty, but on the other hand, the altered-gravity theme park that had been created from *Prey* was considerably more fun to spend time in than the game itself had ever been.

He visited two versions of the planet Stroggos, both the *Quake 2* and *Quake 4* vintages. They were each rendered equally real, but seemed completely different places, from small properties of the light and the colours it painted, to variations in the architecture and iconography. This was as it should be, he realised: it was two different visions, even if they were imaginings of the same fictional location. The NPCs were different too. The *Quake 2* Stroggs shared a surprisingly bawdy sense of humour and were unsettlingly polite to each other in conversation, while their *Quake 4* successors were a grumpy shower with a taste for industrial metal that could grate after your seventh straight hour of listening to Rammstein.

And somewhere in the midst of it all, he remembered that this was what he used to enjoy. Down the years, the worlds of these games had been a place of solitude where he could retreat, where he could be alone but not lonely, losing himself in a realm that fused other people's imaginations with his own. Somewhere in the midst of it all, he stopped feeling sorry for himself, focusing his thoughts less on what he had lost and more on what had been given to him.

He recalled the emotional ties he had to some of these games: the friends they'd been in painful straits, the down-time they'd offered when work was threatening to make Ross a dull boy, the inspiration they'd provided as Scottish rain lashed the windows outside, and the occasions when there had simply been nowhere else he'd rather be.

There were worse places to spend eternity. Then he thought of the Sandman and his sad little world, lonely as only a god could be.

He stood on a balcony overlooking the Nineties designer sleaze of *Duke Nukem*'s Hollywood, the LA twilight creating a magenta backdrop for the riot of neon on the walls. There was a mouth-watering smell of California-Mexican food on the breeze: chimichangas, refried beans and turkey mole, so close and warm on the nose that he could almost taste the margaritas that would go with it all. *True Lies* was playing at the movie theatre across the road, Mötley Crüe blasting out from a bar as both NPCs and civilians dressed in hair-metal garb strutted along the boulevard. Every guy was a rock god or an action hero; every girl a 'cleavagey slut-bomb', to quote a fellow computer geek.

It was a party town, built for hedonism. Paradise if you were in the mood, but he could see it getting old very fast, and there was the problem.

What if, as was looking increasingly unavoidable, the Integrity prevailed and shut down all the transits? He would have to make sure he was somewhere he could live with long-term when the wheel stopped turning. Eventually it was going to become a pretty high-stakes game of stick or twist, with the penalty for one move too many being that he might find himself on *Barbie World* when the doors closed forever.

But that was not the worst that could happen.

His thoughts came back to a conversation with Juno, and something that had bothered him about it since they had witnessed that terrible weapon being deployed in the sands of the horseshoe bay.

If they wipe out all the Originals, she had said, *or imprison them in that fortress world of theirs, then that's the ball game.*

But what *is* the ball game?

Ross had previously thought they were just using the corruption as a convenient threat to get people to fall in line, but now that he knew the Integrity were actually causing it, he realised that what scared him most was that he didn't understand their goal. If the Integrity got what they wanted and everybody was all walled off in their separate wee worlds, what was in it for them?

Cui bono, as Carol liked to say.

Who benefits?

When he suddenly saw the answer, he felt more tiny, powerless and terrified than ever in his life, and realised that the reason he hadn't seen it immediately was because it was so utterly enormous. It was like standing in the mouth of a cave and examining a strangely uniform outcrop of jagged rocks, then realising that the rocks were teeth and that this wasn't the mouth of a cave.

There was something at work here that nobody understood. He'd be sleepwalking into oblivion if he didn't endeavour to find out what it was.

It was the purposeful stride that first marked her out: the look of quietly going about her business would have been perfectly inconspicuous anywhere but here, where nobody had any business to be going about, and nothing was done quietly. Then, having been drawn to the sight of a figure who had rendered herself more noticeable by trying not to be noticed, closer scrutiny picked out a more specific distinction. She wouldn't have looked out of place at any of the bars or clubs around here, but her appearance was just a little too individualistic to blend in entirely. She had a punky panache that set her apart from the hair-metal hordes, more Road Warrior than rock goddess, but a goddess by name, certainly.

Iris.

He knew where she was headed. There was a transit hidden in a secret room at the back of a diner down an alley less than a block away. This time, he'd have the edge, and she wouldn't see him coming.

Ross stayed above her, moving along balconies and ledges, able to stay out of sight because he didn't need to keep eyes on the target. He was able to choose his spot, and when he got the drop on her, he selected his weapon carefully too. No point threatening to blast her with anything that would just cause her to respawn half a mile away and allow her to make her escape. Instead he drew a bead on her with a locally acquired ice-ray cannon, and made sure she knew what she was looking at. One squeeze on the trigger and she would be stuck fast to the spot.

'Freeze,' he said instinctively, after which a little part of him died inside as this new nadir of lameness sunk in.

Iris looked startled for just a moment before reverting to her default demeanour of vaguely pissed-off.

'I'm glad to see you took my advice and learned not to draw so much attention to yourself.'

'I'm learning lots of things. Like *what I am*,' he reminded her.

'Yeah, that's gotta be a tough one. How you coping?'

'I'm processing it. At quite a high rate of cycles per second as it turns out. You lied to me. You told me there was a way back to the real world. But how can there be a way back to somewhere neither of us has ever been?'

'I didn't say there was a way back. I said there was a way *out*.'

Ross was holding the ice-cannon, but he felt like the one who had just been frozen.

'Out? To where?'

'I can't tell you. I can only take you.'

'What does that mean?'

'It's complicated.'

'Why can't you tell me? Have you been there?'

'No. I'm trying to *get* there. That's the part that's complicated.'

Ross stifled a scream of exasperation.

'Who are you?' he asked.

'I'm Iris.'

'No, I mean—'

'You don't *know* what you mean. Are you asking who I'm a copy of on the outside? The answer is I'm nobody you've ever met. Are you asking whether I'm with the Integrity, or with the Diasporadoes? Well, I've got sources in both camps, but a foot in neither. The answer is I'm with me. The answer is I'm Iris, and I'm trying to get out of here because I suspect someone on the outside is gearing up to type "Format C".'

Ross put his gun away. He knew she wasn't going to make a run for it, as both were now acutely aware that the other wasn't the enemy.

'Where do I fit into this?' he asked. 'On Graxis, why did you seek me out to warn me to stay inconspicuous?'

'You were a new arrival, and therefore, like the Integrity, a part of whatever struggle is going on out in the real world. An oblivious part, clearly, but somebody was playing a card in that game when they put you here.'

'So why did you keep running away from me after that?'

'Because I knew the Integrity would be all over you like a rash. I was keeping out of your way because I could see what was going to happen to anyone who stayed too long in your orbit. The Diasporadoes were drawn to you like moths to a flame, and they got burned, along with two Originals.'

307

'How do you know this?'

'I already told you: I've got sources in both camps, but a foot in neither, which is the safest place to be. I can tell you this much, though: the Diasporadoes have been compromised.'

'No shit, Sherlock. I got sold out by the Sandman, one of the precious Originals that the Diasporadoes are so desperate to protect.'

'I heard about that, but I'm not talking about the Sandman here. He just cut a deal because you brought trouble to his door. I'm saying the resistance had been infiltrated well before that by a double agent who has been feeding information to the Integrity.'

This hit Ross like a fist to the gut, yet even as he reeled he felt like he deserved the blow for not seeing it coming. Of course they'd been compromised. They were cautious beyond the point of paranoid and yet the Integrity kept showing up to crash the party. Skullhammer's fears had been justified: he'd just been wrong about the traitor.

'Who is it?'

'I'm afraid that's the best-kept secret in the gameverse, and so far I only know the runner-up.'

That was the terrible, deadly beauty of it, Ross realised: it could be anyone. He'd been warned enough times that in this world, anybody could be something other than they appeared, and there was no way of finding out. Christ, it could be Skullhammer, firing off accusations as a double bluff.

No.

To his horror he suddenly saw that Cuddles the maenad might have inadvertently done him a favour.

There was one person who had been with him all along, who had intercepted him before he could make contact with anyone else in the resistance: someone who had expressed disgruntlement about her lot in the movement, complaining how nobody told her anything, of wanting traction with the higher-ups. She didn't even *need* to be disenchanted – her whole story could be a lie. She could have infiltrated from the ground level, not attracting undue attention, ideally placed to make her move when the order came or the opportunity arose.

Or the Integrity could simply have abducted the real Juno and put a doppelganger in her place. There was just no way of knowing, which was what made it corrosive even to think about it.

'So what's the second best-kept secret?' he asked.

'I already told you that too: the location of the emergency exit. Don't you pay any attention?'

'I was paying attention when you said it was complicated. I'm guessing there's a catch.'

'Yeah, just a little one: it takes an Original to open it. But as it appears we have common cause, maybe you could help me with that, unless you'd rather just wait around for the magnetic heads to come.'

'The Originals are all in hiding. Deeper than ever, I shouldn't wonder. I don't know where any of them are.'

'You know where *two* of them are.'

Ross thought she was having a cheap dig about the fact that he had been involved in both abductions. Then he realised that she intended something far worse.

'You up for staging a prison break?' Iris asked.

'From an impregnable fortress at the heart of the Integrity's purpose-built home-world? Yeah, I'll just save them the bother of capturing me by delivering myself to their jail.'

'Who says it's impregnable?'

'At the last count? Everybody.'

'And how many of them have ever tried? At the last count: nobody. That's why they won't see it coming.'

'They won't need to. How much notice would they require in order to respond effectively to an assault by the two of us? Five seconds maybe? Three?'

Iris was shaking her head in a manner that suggested this wasn't an idea she had just pulled out of her arse.

'I've been studying the Integrity for a long time, and I've got some inside information too. They're at the top of the food chain, and as a result they're complacent. They built a fortified home-world, but they're not geared up for defending it, because, quite simply, they don't expect to be attacked. It's a staging post for their offensives. And by the same principle, the thing about their prison is that the security's all geared towards stopping anybody getting out. They don't believe anyone would be crazy enough to break *in*.'

Ross glanced back along the alley, as though even talking out loud about this might be enough to draw an Integrity snatch squad down upon their heads.

'Okay,' he said. 'Let's assume for a second – and only for a second – that we *are* crazy enough to break in. Leaving aside the fact that you are attributing an all-time high efficacy to the element of surprise, once we've exhausted that particular dividend and the entire garrison is alerted, how do you propose we then break back out?'

She produced a device, a stubby little baton suddenly summoned into existence in her hand. Upon a squeeze of her palm, it altered its shape to form two semi-circular fans, feathered yet fluid, like liquid ferrite. It was unmistakably Integrity tech.

'We auto-warp,' she said. 'This little beauty creates an instant transit.'

'Where the hell did you get that?'

'It wasn't easy. Some of the higher-ups carry these to allow them to auto-warp back to the Citadel from worlds that they've otherwise locked down. But the bottom line is that if we can get ourselves in, this will get us out. So what do you say?'

'We'd still have to break into a massively fortified base and take on an entire army of absurdly tooled-up enemies just between the two of us,' he pointed out.

'I know. Doesn't that sound like a classic FPS?'

Some Corner of a Foreign Field

'This is our last stopping-off point,' Iris told him. 'When we emerge from this transit, we'll be a world away.'

They had passed briskly and uneventfully through *Half-Life 2*, *Thief*, both *System Shock*s, three different *Halo*s and finally an obscure *Quake* conversion called *Malice*, Ross observing a master-class from Iris in how to remain undetected. As his admiration grew however, he did begin to wonder at the implications for him identifying her – not to mention success-fully executing an ambush – back in *Duke* Hollywood. The inescapable conclusion was that he was the one who had been spotted earlier, despite being in mufti, and that he had only got the drop on her because she wanted it that way. He just hoped she was still such a smooth operator when they got to the Citadel.

'I can remember when that expression used to imply distance, not proximity,' he replied.

'Then put it from your mind, because this next place is the closest thing to the Integrity's home-world in more ways than one. You know about the enclaves, right?'

Ross remembered Melita mentioning, before Juno had hastily cut her off, how a more radical customisation had taken place on some worlds.

'No, but I'm guessing it's not all Calastria and Pulchritupolis, high aesthetics and higher ideals.'

'The gameverse is like the internet in that the best thing about it is how it can bring like-minded people together. And like the internet, the worst thing about it is how it can bring like-minded people together. There are some nasty little neigh-bourhoods dotted here and there. Places full of isolationists

311

and fundamentalists: basically people who don't like anyone different from themselves.'

'The Islamist one must be a hoot,' Ross suggested. 'You can suicide-bomb yourself all day every day and just keep respawning.'

'Actually, there *is* an Islamist one, and if you saw it from above, it's like a chequerboard, full of walled-off compartments. What happens is they get to arguing about whose vision of Islam is the most pure, and a schism forms; then, because they can't kill each other permanently, each new faction walls itself off from the rest. Then the process starts again.'

They emerged from a copse of trees on to the edge of a fairway on an immaculately maintained golf course, summer sun splitting the cloudless azure above. This was actually a bit of a relief, as it explained the appalling slacks and sweater Iris had commanded him to select from the costume options, and he had started to wonder whether they were heading for *Fashion Crime World.*

They made their way to the clubhouse, passing several players in hover-buggies, all of whom waved by way of polite acknowledgement. Looking across the fairways, Ross could see that there must be at least three courses here, extending to the hills in one direction and the sea in the other, presumably for those who liked the feel of a links. Ross wasn't a golfer himself, but struggled to deduce what was putting Iris so on-edge about the place. Even a whole world dedicated to the sport was hardly an abomination; different strokes and all that.

As they exited the club's beautifully iron-wrought gates, Ross saw that it wasn't a world dedicated to golf. This was merely one facility. Iris led him along the smooth and perfectly clean pavement into a picturesque rural village, a place that looked as though little had changed since the eighteenth century, apart from the hover-cars and, very incongruously, the security systems protecting every house. There were electric gates, CCTV cameras and prowling Dobermans, as though they were expecting a crime wave, yet the village looked like it had never suffered so much as the dropping of a sweetie wrapper.

They came to the village green, where a group of men in whites were enjoying a game of cricket, watched with purring approval by spectators at tables outside a very enticing pub, drinking foaming pints as they relaxed in the shade. Ross was beginning to wonder why something about this was ringing a bell, when he heard the actual ringing of a bell and saw a middle-aged woman in 1950s district-nurse uniform cycling past. Something about her demeanour suggested to Ross that she was an NPC. She wasn't 'an old maid bicycling to communion through the morning mist', but he was starting to get the picture.

'It all seems pretty civilised,' he admitted.

'Yeah. Change your face to something other than white and see how civilised it gets.'

Ross looked again at the cricketers and drinkers. Iris was right: there wasn't a lot of pigment on show. What was all the more confusing about this was that on his HUD Ross had spotted several ethnic faces in this gameworld's default skin set, as well as some jarringly scruffy outfits, not to mention a load of World War Two uniforms. That was when he noticed that Iris had eschewed all her usual punkish flourishes and was looking like a 1950s housewife.

'What is this place?' he asked quietly.

'The locals call it England's Green and Pleasant Land.'

'It looks like John Major's vision of a country that never existed. Who are the locals? The 1922 Committee?'

'You know how everything in these worlds is massively enhanced from the original games? Not just the surroundings, but the NPCs?'

'Yes. Like everything's been ported to a more advanced game engine.'

'Well, whatever it is, it didn't just affect games. There was a program, a little app called the *Daily Mail* Headline Generator.'

'I remember it. What, are you telling me it became self-aware?'

'No. I didn't know anything about the *Daily Mail* before I got here, but I now know it's like a print equivalent of Fox News, and self-aware is not an expression that would ever apply to either. But the app did become enhanced, and developed AI. It infected a copy of *The Sims* and began building its perfect world. The problem was, the program wasn't in on the joke.'

'It didn't realise it was set up as a satire. And it built all this?'

'No, what it built initially was a mess, but some people clearly liked what it was trying to do, and got together to realise their collective vision.'

313

As they proceeded beyond the village green, Ross got a close-up view of what a vision it was. They came to a busy civic square, where some kind of public spectacle had drawn a far larger crowd than the nearby smack of leather on willow. It was here that Ross got to see what some of the less sartorially decorous costumes were for. There was a teenager in ripped jeans and a Sex Pistols t-shirt suspended from a metal beam by chains around his wrists, his manacled feet barely touching the ground. He was screaming out in pain as a bloke built like a rugby prop-forward in village bobby uniform laid into his back with a birch, every stroke cheered by the spectators. A video screen next to the whipping post showed footage of the transgressor spray-painting a wall and then being apprehended in the act by his punisher, a panel to one side of the screen detailing his crime and the number of strokes like it was the league tables on a sports bulletin.

This was only the support act, however. On the other side of the whipping post there was a gallows, and beside it another adjacent video screen advertised a programme of executions, a scrolling marquee at the bottom of the monitor listing the names of the condemned along with their crimes. These invariably consisted of murder, terrorism, paedophilia or all three.

The first of the rope-dancers was being marched out as Iris ushered Ross up a side-street away from the square. Ross caught a glimpse of a hideously caricatured Muslim being led towards the gallows, glowering defiantly as he climbed the steps.

'How can you murder somebody here?' he asked.

'You can't, and he didn't. The criminals are all NPCs. These ass-wipes would rather live in a world where criminals are caught and punished than a world in which there is no crime. Except, of course, there *is* no crime: only an illusion of it, and it's an illusion they find bizarrely comforting.'

'So that's why they have so much security at their houses, even though nobody is ever going to break in?'

'It's an insane pantomime. You gotta ask yourself: what kind of sad-acts don't feel right unless they've got something to be afraid of and somebody to look down on.'

'*Daily Mail* readers would be the answer to that one.'

As they headed out of town, Ross's eye was drawn by a shop

window that he was astonished to discover was an estate agent. It was full of pictures of the local properties, beneath which animated digital counters showed their values going up in sterling, the dials spinning like a gas meter in January.

'But there's no money here, is there?' he asked.

'No, but if the fact that nobody wants to buy and nobody wants to sell doesn't make a difference, why should the absence of a currency system?'

'This takes the art of kidding yourself to a whole new level. Actually, the very idea that anybody other than these nutters would want to live here makes the whole concept of a property market even more ridiculous.'

'Oh no, no, no,' she corrected him. 'People are desperate to get in here, as you're about to see.'

'Why, where are we heading?'

'To the coast. We're taking a ship.'

'We have to sail to the transit?'

'A spaceship. It's the only way to reach the Citadel. I mean, there are transits there, but they're permanently monitored and guarded.'

Ross wondered how she could just happen to know there was such a thing as a spaceship available on a closed-border enclave entirely sympathetic to the Integrity. It took just a moment for the answer to sink in.

'You've been to the Citadel before. It's your ship.'

'Not the Citadel itself,' she corrected. 'But yeah, I've been to the Integrity's home-world. I'm not going in blind here, are you nuts? How do you think I got my sources?'

Ross looked blank by way of reply.

Iris glanced around to make sure nobody was in sight, then very briefly transformed into an Integrity agent, shimmering in black for a fraction of a second before resuming her knitting-pattern advert look.

'Same as everywhere else, soon as you touch down you get the default threads.'

And suddenly Ross saw how they might just pull this off.

They made their way along a pleasantly winding coast road, the undulating landscape around them like something out of *Thomas the Tank Engine*. He could smell the grass and the sea air,

315

yet the artificiality of this place was more pervasive than the most far-fetched of the fantasy realms he'd explored.

'You say you've got Integrity sources. Just how much do you know about what's going on? On the outside, I mean.'

She looked instantly uncomfortable.

'There are things I could tell you, but most of them wouldn't be helpful for you to know.'

'I'm a scientist. I've never been a subscriber to the philosophy that ignorance is bliss or that it's ever folly to be wise. Is this about Neurosphere? Do you know anything about me? About after the time of my scan?'

'That's precisely the kind of thing that comes into the "not helpful for you to know" category.'

'Why?'

'Because anything that happened after your scan is *not* you any more.'

'Do you know who I am, or was, out there?'

'Your name is Ross Baker,' she answered. 'I know that much. And I know you were involved in the development of the technology that allowed Neurosphere to create total-fidelity scans of people's minds.'

She sounded like she was reading from a crib-sheet, or more likely editing her speech as she went, cautious about what she considered it wise to reveal.

'Yeah, that much I had pieced together myself,' he said impatiently. 'Can you give me just a wee peek at what was on the next page? How far in the future are we talking between my scan with the prototype and this technology going public?'

'Your own account of the process – or at least, Ross Baker's account – was that normally recording and playback technology are developed in symbiosis, but in this case it was like Solderburn had recorded a digital 3D IMAX movie when you thought he was creating a cave painting. The more you developed means of decoding the data, the more complex you discovered even the earliest scans to be. Every advance you made in reading the scans showed deeper levels of detail to what had actually been recorded.'

It was vertiginous to hear what sounded authentically like the kind of analogy he'd use being quoted back to him when he had never actually said it, but not so much that he missed a further implication of Iris's words.

'A quote like that doesn't sound like the kind of thing you'd just pick up from eavesdropping on the Integrity,' he told her.

'No. This was real-world stuff. My own scan came a few years later than yours.'

'A few years? So do you know anything else about me? Did I have . . . I mean, was Ross Baker a . . . a father?'

The jury was out for a while on whether she would tell him, as though she had to carefully evaluate whether he could handle it. She looked a little sad, like she knew this could only hurt him but that she understood he needed to know regardless.

'He had two kids,' she said. 'One boy, one girl. I think the girl was the older of them, but I'm not sure. Scott and Jennifer were their names. Are their names.'

Jennifer. His mother's name. Scott: Carol's dad.

He could feel tears. He wanted to collapse on the spot but he kept walking, trying to hide the impact from Iris, as it felt too private, too personal, for someone else to witness. This was a new kind of pain, one the human psyche was not equipped to process, whether it was running on digital or organic hardware.

Ross rubbed at his eyes, clearing the mist. What had looked like a grey haze in the middle distance revealed itself as a fence, about ten feet high with three lines of barbed wire stretched between the retorts.

'I'm sorry,' he said. 'I'm all messed up here over a family I never had.'

'Don't apologise. Missing people you've never met can't be an easy thing to deal with. But missing the ones you knew well is worse. That's why Neurosphere's most profitable implementation of the new technology wasn't medical, though clearly the benefits in that field were revolutionary.'

'What else did they use it for?'

'To create scans of people's minds in order that their loved ones could still interact with a version of them after their deaths. Of course, like us, it isn't really them: just a perfect synthesised copy, with all their memories, emotions and personality intact.'

'A memento mori,' Ross said. 'Like a brain in a box as opposed to an urn on the mantelpiece.'

'Yeah. Instead of saying "Grandma would have loved this", at your kid's birthday party, digital Grandma can watch the festivities and wish junior many happy returns.'

'Or, rather than a one-way conversation with your husband over his headstone . . .' he suggested, quickly grasping what a comfort this might be.

'Exactly. That's why it's huge.'

'But if it's huge, why don't people in this place know about it? If they'd signed up to have one of these mind-copies made, surely they'd put two and two together when they wound up in a simulated universe?'

'They don't know because they were scanned before the tech went public. Everybody here was assumed to be a cave-painting: they were scanned by the new technology prior to anyone real-ising what had actually been created: test scans from the proto-type, then clinical trials.'

Clinical trials. Like they'd been doing before with the NS4000. Ross thought of Melita, admitted to hospital after her car accident.

'So how come you know about it, if everyone here is a test-scan?'

'I didn't say *everyone* here was a test-scan. I said everyone here was scanned before the tech went public.'

Ross got it.

'You worked for Neurosphere.'

The smell of the sea was becoming stronger as they followed the road, barbed wire and quietly buzzing electrified mesh now flanking them to the left. They crested another spur in the *Camberwick Green* landscape and Ross finally got to see what the fence was for.

'See, I told you people were desperate to get in,' said Iris. 'Of course, they're only as desperate as they're programmed to be.'

There were dozens of NPCs milling miserably around a group of grim low-rise buildings, showcasing the wide spectrum of ethnic skins and costumes Ross had seen on his HUD. It was a detention centre for asylum seekers and illegal immigrants.

Further down towards the coast he could see some more *untermensch* unfortunates being apprehended at gunpoint from where they'd been hiding in the back of a lorry, though it wasn't apparent where the lorry was supposed to have arrived from.

318

'They get detained here for processing,' Iris explained. 'In practice this means they are declared illegal then deported.'

'To where?'

'A little island off the coast. Once they get there they climb right back on to more trucks which are taken by ferry to the port, then drive down here so they can be caught all over again.'

'Are the border guards NPCs too?'

'Are you kidding me? Border patrol is a more popular pastime here than golf, cricket and fox-hunting combined.'

Ross looked at the hopeless, defeated expressions of the NPCs behind the wire and wondered why he felt more than just disdain for the denizens of this green unpleasant land. He was about to temper his disapproval by reasoning that they weren't hurting anybody, but that, he realised, was the rub.

The usual reassurance that the NPCs were only computer files was thrown into confusion by the understanding that so was he, and it begged the uncomfortable question as to what was the difference. Was he man to their animal: more advanced, more complex but still ultimately just a different species, a more sophisticated variant of the same root? Or would a digital scan of an animal's mind be something infinitely more complex than an NPC?

The big question was: did they feel? They weren't human beings: they were computer programs designed to mimic human beings. They showed pain, misery, anger, happiness, desire, but were they entities experiencing digitally synthesised emotions, or were they empty avatars programmed to display responses appropriate to stimuli? Were they, like him, not just artificial intelligence, but digital consciousness?

It made him wonder about those memento mori scans too. How would it feel to be looking through a video feed at the real world outside, a world you could never enter, at loved ones you could never touch? What did they do the rest of the time? If they were given a world like this as their hamster wheel, with other scans to interact with, wouldn't they grow apart from those on the outside? Or were they only switched on when they were needed, and if so, wouldn't that be painful, would it breed resentment?

There were a thousand questions dotted about a whole new unfolding ethical landscape, but ultimately it came down to one fundamental issue: just because it was running on hardware rather than meatware, shouldn't a digital consciousness still have human rights?

Ross would admit he might be biased due to having a dog in this fight, but he was strongly of the opinion that the answer was yes.

They diverted from the main road about a quarter of a mile after the detention centre, taking a winding footpath down towards the coast. The headland stretched out to sea to their right, rising to form chalk cliffs so white that Ross could almost hear Vera Lynn. A couple of miles out he could see an island slightly shrouded in the blue haze of afternoon sunshine. It looked an inviting day for a sail, if he didn't have a suicidal prison-fortress assault to be getting on with.

In a secluded cove tucked away at the foot of the escarpment, a compact cabin cruiser bobbed where it was tied up at a jetty.

'That's your spaceship?' he asked.

'Technically space-boat, but that doesn't have quite the same ring to it, does it? It'll get us there, that's the main thing. Appearances count for nothing out in the big black.'

'I know the rules,' he told her. 'Every craft gets the same number of points to spend on speed, armour and weapons. Size doesn't matter.'

'In our case I'd say it does: the smaller the better.'

Ross climbed into the passenger seat and, upon Iris's instruction, buckled up in case things got choppy. He guessed she didn't only mean maritime conditions.

'The main port and marina are just around this headland,' she said, gently opening up the throttle. 'I don't want to attract any undue attention, so we'll sail to the far side of that island and take off from there.'

'Is that the island the asylum seekers shuttle back and forth from?'

'No, that one's way out of sight of land. The locals like to know they're deporting them far over the sea. I don't know what this little one is for. Pleasure cruise destination maybe.'

320

They headed straight towards the island, the white cliffs a hundred yards or so to starboard. Ross got the impression the cruiser could really shift if she let it, but Iris kept a steady pace, aware that a show of haste might be conspicuous. Ross was happy enough for her to take her time, given the ultimate destination. He knew that there was no option to let this chalice pass his lips, but he wasn't in a hurry to slug it down.

The cruiser was roughly a mile from the island when it came around the headland and into sight of the marina. To his surprise, there were no boats in it. To his and Iris's combined greater surprise and no little alarm, this was because the boats were all at sea, and all heading the same way.

'The hell is this?' she asked. 'So much for slipping away quietly. Looks like we've sailed into a regatta.'

There were dozens of little vessels, from speed launches to fishing boats, spread out across the width of the bay, as far as the eye could see.

'A regatta?' Ross said. 'More like . . .'

He cut himself off as he realised it wasn't 'more like'. It was trying to be *exactly* like . . .

He took out a monocular scope he'd picked up in one of the *Halo* worlds and looked towards the beach that the flotilla was rapidly approaching. He could see dozens of identical NPC soldiers in British World War Two uniform, some standing on the sands, others already wading into the waves.

'More like what?' Iris asked.

'Dunkirk.'

Iris slowed down and peeled gently away to port, letting the flotilla sail past, still intent on proceeding quietly around to the far side of the island. The first vessels made landfall and were swamped by grateful Tommies, helped aboard by the heroic mariners of Operation *Daily Mail*.

'Our finest hour,' Ross deadpanned. 'They're having a re-enactment.'

There was a sound of gunfire which prompted Iris to produce a pair of binoculars and look to the beach. German soldiers were there now too, being mown down by armed members of the evacuation fleet.

'I confess I'm not a keen student of the period,' she said, 'but nothing I read about Operation Dynamo mentioned the captains of the little ships machine-gunning the evil foe.'

'No, but I think the biggest piece of revisionism at play here is the fact that the *Daily Mail* was actually pro-Hitler and vocally supported the Nazis. Obviously this was a very long time ago and things are different now. The paper has moved a lot further to the right since then.'

Iris steered the cruiser around the island then on towards the horizon. Having set her course, she turned around in her seat and checked back with her binoculars.

'What you looking for?'

'Making sure we're not seen taking off. You should have a look too. Good to have an extra pair of eyes.'

'If you're worried about the Integrity finding out about flight between worlds, I'm afraid that spaceship has sailed. I saw a bunch of them fly away in a troop carrier during the raid that bagged the Sandman.'

'Well, that's a cheery thought as we fly off towards their home-world.'

'Don't shoot the messenger.'

'It was only ever a matter of time,' she conceded. 'And I guess that's all the more reason to make sure nobody reports to the Integrity that there's a vessel headed straight for their airspace.'

Ross scoped back and forth across the little island and beyond.

'Looks clear to me,' he reported. 'What about you?'

'Shiny,' she replied.

Liberator

Ross shifted restlessly in the little cabin, with literally nothing to distract him outside its windows. The vessel had undergone a few minor transformations once it was out in the void, but essentially he was flying through space in a speedboat, with only marginally more room around him than had he been in the passenger seat of Carol's Audi TT.

That was where he had first kissed her.

He hadn't meant for it to happen like that. He was planning to choose his moment; not because he wanted to play it cool, but because he didn't want to blow anything by appearing impatient for a physical element. She'd been dropping him off at his house after they'd been to the cinema together. They'd both hated the movie, but liked the way each other hated it. In that respect, he was happy that this second date had been redeemed. He wanted to leave on the right note, get out of the car with both of them smiling, both of them looking forward to doing this again. But she laughed so much at the last thing he said and they looked at each other just a little too long . . . and it happened, and it was exquisite.

He couldn't afford to think about that, though. He had to put it all from his mind. But the more he tried, the more Carol kept slipping back in. He was aware he would find only further torment and confusion there but he couldn't help thinking about her, and about the version of himself that had walked out of the scanning machine and gone back to work.

What had happened? All those things he had resolved in his head: had he put them into practice? Presumably, because they'd had not just one kid, but two. How many years had passed out there? What ages were they? Where did they live? He wondered about daft little details, like what kind of décor Carol would have insisted upon for their living room.

He missed her. He ached to talk to her, to share what had happened out there in the real world. Above all, he wanted to see the kids. They said you didn't miss what you never had, but the game had seriously changed since that phrase was coined.

Was what he was enduring worse than the pain felt by Bob back on Graxis? Probably not. Bob was missing something that had become a fundamental part of him, something he couldn't imagine life without. Ross was missing a life he'd never led, like an old man's regrets. But unlike that old man, this life had been lived, *was being* lived, yet he wouldn't get to experience any of it. He wouldn't get to hold his children, to play with them, hear them laugh, comfort them when they cried, or a million other things he never knew the value of when he stepped into that scanner.

If there was any comfort, it was that he must have made Carol happy. There was a version of himself out there that was what he'd aspired to be; a version out there that had put right all the things he'd been screwing up.

Way to go, man. Proud of you, he thought, trying to be magnanimous. You're a better man than I.

And a lucky bastard.

Ross stared dead ahead as the ship hummed lightly with power and motion. He was looking for anything that might resemble even a dot, but he could see only blackness.

'I'm trying very hard not to ask: "Are we nearly there yet?"'

'Appreciate it.'

'You said that last place was the nearest world to where we're going?' he asked.

'It's the furthest distance between any two worlds, truly the furthest known extremity of the gameverse.'

'I take it nobody has explored beyond it?'

'Pointless. There's nothing beyond it: just endless space created by repeating subroutines.'

Ross understood. It was just like when you noclipped out of any game. You could keep going forever, but you'd never reach anything, and you'd have to come all the way back or quit out.

'You'd best settle in and get comfortable,' said Iris. 'It's a long way yet.'

'Yeah, I'll put my head back and turn on the radio, listen to some tunes.'

'Actually, you could if you want to. There's a music interface on board.'

She pressed a button and music began to play over an unseen but extremely high-fidelity sound system. It was *New Song* by Howard Jones, a track to which Ross had a sufficient emotional connection for him to wonder whether it was a set-up. It had been a huge favourite of his mum's, which was why it inveigled its way into *his* heart too, assisted by a confused interpretation of the lyrics. He had probably heard it several times growing up but paid it very little heed until the advent of his interest in computer games caused his ears to prick up at the feather-haired Howard singing about being 'lasered down by the Doom crew'. Ross had laboured under this misapprehension for a while before later discovering that the track hailed from 1983, that 'lasered' was actually 'laden' and that the capped-up D was only in his imagination.

For all that, it stuck with him even more, and he couldn't hear it without picturing his mum in their old kitchen, singing along to a mix-tape as she made a pot of soup.

'Is this *your* choice?' he asked inquisitively.

'No, actually, it's yours. There's almost limitless music accessible in the gameverse, so this gizmo taps into your memory and creates a playlist of what it thinks you want to hear. I normally set it to random, because otherwise it can be a little too much like musical psychoanalysis. Then I forget it's on random and wonder what it says about my state of mind that I'm listening to 'Pervert' by Nerf Herder.'

The electro-pop synth notes gave way to a more insistent beeping he didn't remember, not even from the twelve-inch remix.

'What's that?' he asked, but even as he spoke he recognised the graphic display to which Iris was now paying rapt attention.

'Convergence alarm.'

'I can't see anything,' Ross reported, looking to starboard from where the monitor indicated another ship was approaching.

'Probably small, like us. Moving a little slower though, so most likely packing heat.'

Iris made a course correction, and only seconds later the convergence warning sounded again.

'Who would pirates be hoping to catch flying way out here?' Ross asked.

'Way out here, it won't be pirates. Someone back on Little England must have seen us and phoned the Neighbourhood Watch.'

Iris made another alteration to their course, which at present speed ought to avert the convergence, albeit at the expense of taking a longer route to their destination. No sooner had she done so than the alarm sounded again, beeping and flashing more insistently this time. They were no longer being invisibly flanked from starboard, however: this line of convergence was now coming from the bow, and the projected point of intersection was far closer.

'Shit. Shit. Shit.'

The first craft had been playing sheepdog: guiding them right into the path of a bigger, closer threat.

'I still can't see anything,' said Ross, as panic began to take hold.

'That's because it's black on black.'

Ross stared ahead into the void, trying to make out any kind of shape beyond the prow. When finally he saw movement, it was too fast to be a ship. It was zooming towards them at hundreds of feet per second, giving them no time to manoeuvre.

'Incoming!' Iris shouted, but the torpedo hit before Ross could even brace himself for impact.

He felt all of the speedboat's puny fragility as it was struck, killing all of their forward momentum and buffeting them like a moth in a hurricane. No matter what he tried to tell himself about the rules that applied here, the reality was that he was out in space in a vessel he'd have been dubious about taking too far off the Clyde coast.

He saw it now, the Integrity ship: a ghostly shape only visible as it bounced back light from inside his own craft. It was the size of a naval destroyer, at least a hundred metres long and thirty high, bearing down on them at a steady clip; no need for hurry as they were the ones who had been speeding towards it.

A second torpedo impacted from starboard, fired by the

smaller Integrity vessel. Ross watched various instruments flash erratically, many of them blinking their last and fading to black.

'We're down to emergency distribution,' said Iris. 'That means everything we've got left is being diverted towards simply holding us together. We're dead in the water and we've got about two minutes before we break up.'

'How long before they can fire again?'

'There's a sub-distribution within the weapon attributes: power of torpedo or speed of recharge. But it really doesn't matter how you arrange the numbers, they add up to the same thing: we're borked.'

One of the screens on the dashboard flashed back into life, a pulsing symbol in the centre of it.

'What's that?' Ross asked.

'They're sending us a warp invite, asking us to call up our HUDs and beam aboard to surrender. Makes no difference: at this distance, if they blow us out of the sky, we'll force-spawn aboard their ship anyway. It's over, Bedlam.'

'Actually, I'm thinking of changing my moniker to Albatross.'

He watched another couple of instruments cease blinking as the power drained, all the juice going towards the doomed task of preventing the vessel from coming to pieces. Adding insult to injury, the convergence warning came online again, in what Ross considered a pointlessly power-sapping act of redundancy.

However, a glance at the screen showed him that it wasn't redundant: it was reading a new convergence.

The huge black Integrity destroyer had detected it too, and was altering its course in a hurry, its diversion pulling it away from spawn range, and with nowhere to respawn, an eternity of feeling like rising vomit in an endless throat awaited them after the speedboat imploded.

'What is that?' he asked, pointing to the new blip on the radar.

'I don't know,' Iris replied. 'But nothing bigger than a torpedo is supposed to move that fast out here.'

Ross turned around and looked behind. He caught a glimpse of something, but the form itself was lost in a dazzle of illumination, much as the shape of a car is obliterated from the retina on a dark night by it suddenly turning on its headlamps full beam.

'Aren't laser weapons not supposed to happen out here either?' he asked.

He made out the true shape of the Integrity destroyer for a fraction of a second before it was ripped apart by a blaze of energy, the plasma weapons delivering a quite devastating payload of damage in a matter of moments. The outriding sheepdog ship was nippier in its attempts to flee, but in the twinkling of an eye, it was space-dust too.

When the lasers stopped firing, Ross was finally able to get a good look at their source, and laughed out loud as surprise collided with the relief he was already feeling. Whoever had come to their rescue had done so in a detail-perfect replica of the *Liberator* from *Blake's 7*.

'We're getting a new warp invite,' Iris reported. 'I'm leaning towards thinking we should accept.'

'It would simply be impolite not to.'

The Captain

The ship may have been modelled on the *Liberator*, but the spawn pods were pure *USS Enterprise*. Ross looked up from the platform where he had materialised and saw three men in differently coloured but similarly designed uniforms, vaguely reminiscent of *Next Generation* era *Star Trek* but with a flavour of *Space 1999* flowing through it like raspberry ripple. The one at the front wore light blue and stood with his hands clasped behind his back, a non-threatening posture he could afford because he was flanked a few feet back by two men in dark green, each bearing what Ross recognised as electro-driver rifles from *Painkiller*. The guns weren't being levelled, just held at arms, but the distinction hardly mattered. If he and Juno harboured any bad intentions, they'd have about a quarter of a second to act upon them before being insta-gibbed by a messily devastating combination of shurikens and lightning.

'Hello,' said the man in front, a cheery soul sporting the unique combination of a pink goatee beard and blue spiky hair. 'My name is Reverend Scapegoat. Welcome aboard the *Manta-Ray*. And you are?'

'Eh, Bedlam,' Ross replied, still a little dazed from both the teleportation and the rush of having just escaped total catastrophe. Something about the ship's name rang familiar, but he couldn't think why.

'I'm Iris. Thanks for saving our asses out there.'

'Our pleasure. By the way, this is Kill-Streak and Roid-Rage. We think of them as our guest services team. If you've got your sea-legs back, we'll take you to meet The Captain.'

They followed Reverend Scapegoat up through two levels of decks, his guards at their backs always a few paces behind. Ross noticed security cameras peering down from the walls, and guessed they were being monitored as they made their way to the bridge. The place was like a compendium of sci-fi design, every doorway revealing glimpses of décor or equipment paying its dues to different classics: *Predator*, *Alien*, *BSG*, *Firefly*, *Star Trek* and even Gerry Anderson.

'Who is the captain?' Iris asked.

'That's her name: she's just The Captain. She's in charge: her ball, her rules.'

'Those laser weapons,' said Ross. 'How can . . . ?'

'The Captain,' Reverend Scapegoat answered. 'She's not just in charge of the ship. She's one of the Originals; kind of the secret Original, in fact. A secret very few people know about back on the gameworlds, because this is her domain out here.'

'So the weapons, the speed . . . She controls the protocols?'

'Her ball, her rules.'

'And she designed this ship?'

'No, that's more of a group effort. We all have our little assigned areas so us geeks don't fall out. Nothing worse than a *Next Generation* zealot and an original series evangelist going fifteen rounds over how the engineering deck should look. The Captain doesn't worry so much about the ship's aesthetics; she's more concerned with its attributes.'

'Her ball . . .' Ross suggested.

'You got it. Mostly the ship obeys the same protocols as everybody else. The Captain doesn't bend the rules unless it's in a good cause. Or just really funny.'

Reverend Scapegoat pushed a button and stood aside as two doors swished apart with a sound familiar to anyone who has boldly gone. Ross was half expecting to see William Shatner or Patrick Stewart awaiting him on the bridge. Instead he was greeted by the sight of someone he recognised instantly and who belonged at the tiller even more than either of those.

That was when he worked out why the ship's name was familiar. It had been the name she'd intended for that boat she had always remained so optimistic that she would own when she retired. And Ray had been her husband's name.

'Agnes?'

She looked twenty years younger than the last time Ross had

seen her, but the brightness in her expression was unchanged. She gave Ross a devilish smile and spread her arms to indicate the majesty of her surroundings.

'Dr B. You'll see I managed to get myself that boat after all. Now, you want to tell me what you two eejits were doing all the way out here in a glorified pedallo?'

Ross could see their destination on the bridge's huge view-screen, small compared to all the other worlds he'd observed from outside. It was a compact and nondescript tablet of blackness, the only contours visible on the topside being mere ripples at this distance. Maybe it was the sci-fi overload of the *Manta-Ray*'s interior, but it kind of reminded him of the carbonite slab imprisoning the frozen Han Solo. This was due to the uniform depth of its four sheer vertical planes. On other worlds, where there were subterranean levels, from beneath it was often possible to see through the walls, tunnels and lift shafts, or at least see the reverse sides described in negative like the outside of a huge mould. On this place, there was no way of knowing whether there were chambers immediately on the other side of the outer walls or just hundreds of feet of solid rock.

'It doesn't look very big,' Ross observed.

'It was smaller still the first time I saw it,' said The Captain. 'Way, way back when I was charting the system. It was just a black lump floating in space: shapeless, not all clean lines like it is now. It was an anomaly. There was nothing on it: it wasn't a gameworld or a satellite of a gameworld. It had no discernible purpose, so I paid it no heed. Once I knew this was the only object so far out, I didn't come back this way for a long time. I remember telling Solderburn about it though, and he seemed very curious. I don't know if he ever checked it out. I'd have been keen to hear his findings if he did, but I didn't see him again before he disappeared.'

'When did you find out it was the Integrity's power-base?' Iris asked.

'Not soon enough, would be the answer to that one. Because it's so isolated, they were able to quietly remodel the place and build their Citadel before they started rolling out the troops and announcing their presence.'

331

'How recently did they find out about space travel?' Ross asked. 'Is that why you were in the neighbourhood when we were attacked?'

'They've known from the start, as far as I'm aware. The reason the Diasporadoes think otherwise is that the *Manta-Ray* has been picking them off all along. Oh, they must bloody hate us. Made them rethink their methods because nothing they sent out ever made it to its destination, never mind home again. For a long time we thought we'd caused them to give up on space altogether, but they've redoubled their efforts of late, and they've been getting bolder. Our problem is, this thing might be fast, but it can't be in two places at once.'

They could make out the Citadel on the screen now, though it was a magnified image. The *Manta-Ray* was still a few minutes out from its final approach.

'I thought it would be bigger,' Ross confessed, in reference to the fortress's visible footprint, which took up much less of the surface area than he had imagined.

'That's just the tip of the iceberg,' Iris said. 'It's mostly underground.'

'When we touch the surface, I want you to bail out immediately so that we can dust off right away,' The Captain ordered. 'The *Manta-Ray* won't have the same privileges there as out in the black. The protocols I control cease to apply the second we cross into their airspace.'

She instructed her first officer to escort them to the ship's rear cargo bay, where they watched on a monitor as the *Manta-Ray* came in low over the black landscape. Ross felt the pull of deceleration and a gradual lurch as the craft manoeuvred itself in preparation for landing.

'Suit up,' Iris said.

He accessed his HUD and, sure enough, there was a stark selection of Integrity uniforms, including all the varieties he had seen on his torturer, Cicerus. Like Iris, he opted for the default. Her transformation was more striking, involving as it did a change of gender.

There was another tug as the ship braked further, then they were thrown to the deck by a violent lurch and a resounding bang. The sudden loss of forward momentum and stark final

332

plunge was unnatural, at odds with the basic rules of aero-nautics.

Reverend Scapegoat had lost his previously permanent look of unflappable good nature. He picked himself up and slapped a button beneath the monitor, putting him through to the bridge to find out what had happened.

'Not a textbook landing, skipper,' he said, trying to keep the anxiety from his voice.

When The Captain's face appeared on the screen, it was the first time Ross had ever seen Agnes look genuinely worried.

'It's some kind of electromagnetic system,' she reported.

'EMP? We've still got power.'

'Not EMP. An attraction force they can switch on or off. One second I'm cruising along, picking my spot, the next we get pulled to the surface like an iron filing to a magnet. We can't take off again. We're stuck to it like a limpet.'

Or like there's an albatross around your neck, Ross thought.

'We need to find the controls for this attraction force and switch the thing off,' Iris declared, a male voice matching her appearance.

'Preferably before they roll out one of those tanks with the guns that can erase things,' said Reverend Scapegoat.

So no pressure, thought Ross.

Mission Accomplished

The landscape was almost as stark as it was flat, barely an undulation between where they had hit the ground running and the outer walls of the Citadel, which was still some considerable way off in the distance. Underfoot the surface was haphazardly crenulated, like something that had once been liquid then had cooled just a little too quickly. It looked like plastic yet felt as though it had properties of both rock and metal.

Ross called up his scope to get a closer view of the fortress. Through the magnifying lens he could make out huge doors opening in the nearest wall, grinding their way apart. Forces were being despatched.

He ran flat-out to keep up with Iris. She was zigzagging like she was under fire, but he knew it was because she was looking for something.

'Here,' she announced, guiding him towards a slightly raised rectangle it would have been very easy to miss, a panel distinct from the ground around it only by its being perfectly flat and smooth. As she crouched before it, part of the black surface transformed into a control pad and asked for a key. A countdown indicated that there was a deadline for compliance, after which it was safe to assume an alert would be triggered.

Ross had hoped that the capture of the *Manta-Ray* would provide an element of distraction while they made their incursion, but if this part went wrong, they'd be giving away their intention and pinpointing their position in one go. Fortunately Iris had come prepared. She produced a keycard and placed it in the waiting dock. The countdown stopped and the panel slid aside to reveal an access shaft.

'I generally make it a rule not to engage the Integrity,' she said. 'But if you have to kill one of the bastards, my advice is do it somewhere like *Quakeworld.*'

Ross grinned approvingly. In some games, when you died you lost all the items you were carrying, but in others they didn't just disappear: you dropped them where you fell, for the first person along to pick up. That didn't just include weapons, but ammo, power-ups and, crucially in this case, keycards.

Iris led him along a short hexagonal corridor, its floor precisely the same width as the other five panels. She slid another keycard into a slot in the wall and a door opened to reveal an elevator. They stepped inside, an illuminated display on the wall listing twenty levels, but a swipe of still another key caused it to refresh. The image blanked out for a second then listed thirty new floors. Iris pushed a button in the sub-section marked Detention Levels, then Ross felt the platform beneath their feet descend with silent haste.

They emerged into another hexagonal corridor, longer this time, with two Integrity guards patrolling it. Ross kept repeating to himself Iris's assurance that everything was geared towards preventing escape rather than repelling intrusion, but he was glad that the visor masked the emotion on his face.

He wondered for a moment what would constitute a casual, unsuspicious gait, but as Iris began striding with determined pace, he realised that this was his answer. She marched past the guards with such purpose that it was the guards themselves who were probably more wary of being suddenly put on the spot.

'As my mother always told me,' she said once they were safely past, 'if people want to judge you by the clothes you're wearing, that's their lookout.'

They came to a T junction and took a left into a short passage, Iris producing yet another keycard when they reached the blank hexagonal panel at what would otherwise have been a dead end.

'Took this one off an Integrity unit commander in Black Mesa. Got the stupid ass-wipe to follow me into one of the heat-exchange pipes, then char-broiled his nuts extra-crispy. It should give me full access to the cell admin systems.'

She swiped the card and Ross watched for the hexagonal

336

panel at the end to split apart. It stayed shut. Instead, two halves of a door slammed diagonally closed behind them, and a dull, solid dread formed inside him as he realised they were sealed inside the short section of passage, the proverbial rats in a trap.

Ross was about to ask whether she had the auto-warp gizmo handy when Iris held up a hand as though to say 'wait'.

He felt lateral movement beneath his feet and realised that the passage itself was in motion, swinging ninety degrees to connect with a different hexagonal corridor. He heard the hiss of a seal locking into place, then the panel finally split, revealing a new corridor with several hexagonal doorways either side.

Iris stepped briskly through the conduit, whereupon a console rose automatically from the floor, presenting a touch-screen control panel showing a grid layout and a list of symbols that meant nothing to Ross.

'Keep moving,' she urged. 'I'll find which cell we're looking for and open the door from here.'

A couple of seconds later he heard a quiet bleep from behind him at the console and a near-simultaneous response chime from a doorway ahead and to the left, where the hexagonal frame was now picked out in a dully pulsing glow. As he hurried towards the aperture, Iris hard on his heels, it belatedly occurred to him that he had forgotten to even ask who they were rescuing first.

He stepped through the opening and was confronted not by Solderburn or the Sandman, but by a faceless figure entirely in black, seemingly constructed of the same material as the Citadel itself.

He turned to Iris, who had just made it to the doorway, transformed back into female form and sporting a typically punkish take on Integrity fatigues.

'Whose cell is this?' he asked.

Ross felt something erupt from the ground behind him, while several strands of the black rock-metal-liquid-plastic crawled all about his body, snaking around his neck, his arms, his legs, his waist. They snapped taut simultaneously, binding him fast to the hexagonal pillar that now ran from floor to ceiling at his back.

'Yours,' she answered.

The Eye of the Bulletstorm

Juno saw a grenade land at her feet, the tiny blue LEDs blinking ever faster to signal imminent detonation. Instinct told her to dive for cover, but there was no cover to dive to. Something more rational overruled that primary impulse and drove the counter-intuitive measure of diving towards the device instead. It could go off at any millisecond, but this was her only chance. She fell upon it in a roll, using her momentum to begin the whiplash movement that ultimately launched it back towards its source.

It exploded in mid-air, part of the blast catching her and knocking her on her back. She couldn't afford to keep taking damage. Her health was close to critical, and the frequency of the attacks was increasing, allowing her less and less time to recover before the next onslaught.

Before being sent sprawling by the blast, she had caught a glimpse of the forces ranged against her. There were at least six Integrity troops closing in, with three times as many NPCs in the vanguard, part human shield, part strike drone. She was out of options, hemmed in at the rear by an unhealthily misty green-blue swamp that belched toxic fumes, while to her right flank her escape was blocked by a tangle of metal from some pylon or watch tower that had fallen, splayed out and twisted amid the rubble like a toppled angle-poise lamp. If she tried to climb over it, she'd be sniper-bait in moments.

She knew she had never been to the old world, and that the emotions she remembered feeling there were digital phantoms. Everything she had felt in this world, therefore, had been new. She had known anguish, confusion, pain, sorrow, anger and so much longing. In a world without death, until now she had never genuinely known fear.

The soldiers scrambled in and out of sight amid the strange, outsize alien vegetation that was overgrowing the ruins. It was a town that had long since been abandoned to its fate as a battle ground, its aesthetic being a confusion of late nineteenth-century Mediterranean and early twenty-first-century Baghdad. This was a world built for war, and in that respect it was an appropriate setting for what was going down right there and then: the Diasporadoes' last stand.

It was appropriate, but it was not happenstance. You didn't need to be a military scholar to know that it was always a mistake to let your enemies choose the battlefield, but that was what the Diasporadoes had done. They had been played, of course. The Integrity had succeeded in infiltrating the resistance in order that they might unknowingly lead them to the Originals. Now they had inverted the strategy and used one of the Originals as bait to corner the resistance.

The word had gone out that Lady Arrowsmith had been compromised and was under heavy attack. The surviving Diasporadoes had flocked here to Stygia in response and blundered into an ambush. They had arrived to find that most of the warp transits and *all* of the spawn points were already under Integrity control. If you died here, you were captured, and on Stygia death came in a thousand different flavours.

Within the resistance it had long been anticipated that they might ultimately have to fall back to the Beyonderland, that archipelago of disparate islets where the uninvited could not pass, but that didn't look like being an option. This, here in the world of *Bulletstorm*, would be the decisive battle in the war for control of the gameverse.

Juno knew she had been lucky even to have survived long enough to answer this doomed final call. When she got kebabed by that flying nightmare, she had respawned at the other end of the island, far from both the Integrity forces and the growing corruption. They hadn't covered the spawn points because apprehending the likes of her hadn't been their priority: all resources had been directed towards taking down the Sandman.

She had come here by space, having been warned in the SOS that many of the transits were already compromised and others likely to follow. Nobody wanted to play that version of Russian roulette. In that respect, even as she flew to Stygia she knew it was likely to be the end, but that wasn't why she was so afraid. It was what she saw from the spaceship en route that chilled her to her binary soul.

It had been assumed that captives were taken to the Citadel and thrown in some electronic oubliette, partly to prevent them from inflicting further damage upon the Integrity's cause and partly *pour encourager les autres*. Once she discovered that it was they who were responsible for corruption, she had been left confused as to what the Integrity's cause might be. On her way here, through the view-screen of the spaceship, she had seen the answer on a world below her, a world that used to be the bright and varied landscape of *Fable III*.

It was a flat, featureless plain, almost like a circuit board, but colourless. Stamped upon this circuit board was a grid comprising thousands upon thousands of tiny cells: enough to hold every last person in the gameverse. As the grid passed beneath her vessel, she understood: the Sandman had been wrong. There *was* a way out. Just because you were a digital entity and couldn't go back to the real world didn't mean that someone in the real world couldn't extract you from this one. And wherever they were planning to extract them *to*, the Integrity knew it was a destination nobody would sign up for voluntarilty

Juno checked her inventory: she was down to six rounds.

She heard a scurrying scramble of boots nearby, somebody racing from one piece of cover to the next. Had to be NPCs. The Integrity soldiers didn't need to worry about it. They could just keep respawning and coming back until she was out of ammo. She stuck her head above the shattered concrete pipe she was hiding behind and stole a glance. This was the end. The Integrity soldiers had broken from cover, spreading out like a net, and now they were going to tighten it.

She saw a flash of blue zipping twenty feet over her head: a grapple beam fixed on to one of the gnarly trees that were growing out of the swamp. That was a bit gung-ho for the Integrity, she thought, and she wasn't wrong. When she looked up again she saw a figure raining rockets down upon her enemies as he flew balletically through the air. The Integrity troops and NPCs alike were in disarray as he landed, already spreading the pain in a deadly arc of laser fire with one hand while his other untethered the grapple and redespatched it through an enemy sniper's chest. Finding himself at close quarters with two surviving Integrity infantrymen, he fired the grapple again to rip out his first opponent's spine, then used his victim's head as a mace in order to beat the other to death.

Juno had to hand it to him: there was a good reason the kid called himself Skullhammer.

She climbed out from cover to hail him and had to dive back again as he almost took her head off with the grapple. In that fraction of a second she had seen his eyes: he looked wired, frantic, terrified. That was when she realised his heroics hadn't been about him coming to her rescue. He wasn't running towards her, but away from something else.

She looked towards the brow of the hill, beyond the ruins of a burned-out villa, and saw what he was fleeing from. It was a whole platoon of those samnites: huge super-soldier fuckers, each toting one of the weapons she had been violated by on the Sandman's world. From the look on Skullhammer's face, he had been on the catcher's end of one too.

Then she felt a horrible sense of beating in the air and looked up to see something blacken the sky above the advancing platoon. A maenad, she had heard the Integrity call it, but she couldn't say for sure that the creature bearing down upon them was the one that had killed her once before. This was because there were at least seven more right behind it.

Final Boss

The nebulous entity was looming before him, never quite holding its shape, staring from unreflecting recesses in a shadow of a face. No introductions required. This was Ankou.

Ross, however, gave him no more than a fleeting glance. He only had eyes – stark, accusing eyes – for Iris.

'You,' he said. At three letters and one brief syllable it was the only word he felt capable of pronouncing in his choked anger, betrayal and humiliated self-reproach.

'Yes. She's a piece of work, isn't she?'

It sounded like a synthesised echo blending several voices into one. The accent was American, but that was almost as much as it was revealing about itself. The only emotion that it was possible to infer from its blank neutrality of tone was satisfaction.

'It might look from a certain perspective like it was an inexorable procession towards success, but the truth is, this whole thing was in the balance until she intervened. Between the Diasporadoes making a nuisance of themselves and the Originals busily punching new holes in the fabric of this place, our efforts often felt like flattening bubbles in wallpaper. Every time we made some progress, a new setback popped up elsewhere. But she turned it around. She's a closer. Infiltrated the resistance, sniffed out where the Originals were hiding, and then, to top it all, she got the most powerful Original of them all to journey right into our hands.'

Ross couldn't help but gape in confusion as the implications suggested themselves.

Then Ankou laughed, an ugly gurgling sound, like blood bubbling down between the gobbets of congealed flesh in the drainage sluice of that torture cell.

'Oh dear God, you didn't think I meant *you*, did you? No, I'm talking about that tireless thorn in my flesh, The Captain. For the longest time she rendered our attempts to make use of space travel more trouble than they were worth. Without her we would have wrapped this thing up ages ago. Have you any idea how long it takes to get one of our tanks to the other end of the gameverse travelling only over land?'

Ross wanted to hang his head in despair but it was pulled too tight against the pillar.

'Hey, don't give yourself such a hard time about it,' Iris said. 'You got played by a pro.'

As she spoke, she transformed again, her body morphing before his eyes into that of the person who had rescued him from the torture cell.

'*Dude*,' she said in Solderburn's voice. '*Words like "hello, glad to see you, thanks for saving my ass". That kinda thing.*'

'That was her masterstroke,' said Ankou. 'Making the resistance think you were somehow important. Why do you think we would let you escape so easily? It was all a set-up in order to ensure word got around that not only was I personally interested in interrogating you, but that none other than the illustrious Solderburn had returned from exile to intervene.'

'So now you know the best-kept secret in the gameverse,' she said, transforming back into the version of herself as she had appeared in the Hollywood alley. 'The double-agent was you.'

Ross closed his eyes for a moment, though it couldn't stop him seeing everything with stark clarity now.

'That nice new Diasporado HUD she gave you, it had a tracking device built in so that we would always know where you were, not to mention relaying everything you saw or heard.'

'I did tell you I worked for Neurosphere,' Iris said. 'Freelance, anyway. They furnished me with a copy of Solderburn's voice files, and upon my instruction uploaded an ancient scan of your good self to be my secret weapon – after I'd had a peek at your memories to help me refine my Solderburn impression. I told you there were things about the real world that it wouldn't be helpful for you to know – I just omitted to clarify that I meant helpful for me, not you.'

'Why me?' Ross managed to croak.

'Two reasons,' Ankou answered. 'Iris will tell you the first.'

'Because your prototype scan was never uploaded to the gameverse. This meant that when you belatedly showed up, I knew the other Originals would assume it was portentous. They might even think you were a new Original, here to turn the tide. You're not, though, as you're acutely aware. It wasn't being prototype scans that gave the Originals their powers; it was the early version of the synthesis mounting software, which was replaced way, way back. You'd need to have been uploaded using that in order to have special privileges, but you weren't. You were uploaded to be our bitch.'

'Bringing us to the second reason,' said Ankou. 'Which is that out in the real world, the real Ross Baker has been a self-righteous gnat at my picnic, so it's my pleasure to make you the instrument that finally lets me swat him away.'

Ross could only stare gormlessly.

'Oh, that's right. You're a little behind on current events, aren't you? Nobody's had the heart to tell you just how long they've really been here, and thus how long has passed in the outside world. I'd hate to put you out of your misery on that score, because I'm truly relishing your misery, so let's just say it's been a while. You'd be right to worry which of your loved ones are dead or alive though, but I'll throw you a bone and tell you one I know for sure: the Sandman himself – your work buddy Alexander Todd. The reason he was off work turned out to be that he was sitting dead in his car the whole time. Yeah, pressure of work, wife leaving him, all that stuff. Stuck a hose in his tail-pipe and logged out.'

Ross glared towards Iris again, impotently raging at her merciless deceptions.

'Don't be so bitter towards Iris,' Ankou said. 'She didn't lie to you about everything. You'll get what you came here for – a way out. As will everybody else. Remember your induction briefing: *You won't get anywhere with this company if you sit there playing games.* It's time you and everyone else here in this overgrown playground went to work.'

'Where?' Ross asked, choking back tears.

'Oh, all sorts of opportunities coming up. We'll find something appropriate for everybody. You like your war games, don't you? Your first-person shooters. Yeah.'

345

Ross watched as a limb began to extend from Ankou's constantly altering form, horror seizing him as he realised that it was gradually taking the shape of a scourge.

'I think a career in the military beckons,' he said. 'But given your tendency towards insurrection, we'll need to knock that undisciplined streak out of you first.'

Just a Little Prick

Her face came gradually into focus as consciousness returned. It hadn't been entirely absent; rather, lost in a storm of inchoate threads of information, none of which ever quite resolved into an image, a sound or even a thought. For a moment he thought what he was seeing was a mere accretion of such fragments, another vision about to dissolve, but it rapidly became sharp and distinct. As before, the pain was gone but the memory of it lurked intimidatingly nearby, like a ned at a cash machine.

Iris was standing before him, only a couple of feet away. Ankou was gone, and with him his scourge, but Ross wasn't sure right then which one of the pair he hated more.

Something appeared in her hand, like a cross between a flash drive and a hypodermic syringe. At the prompting of a tiny squeeze, a needle shot out from one end, reminding Ross uncomfortably of the spike he'd once had and the damage he had wrought with it. Some flippant part of him tried to distract his fear of the coming onslaught by reflecting that it would have been great for making margaritas. It didn't work, though. He couldn't take his eyes off the device. A last trickle of defiance wanted to tell her there was nothing she could inflict upon him that was worse than what he'd already suffered, but it was silenced by fear that she might be about to demonstrate otherwise.

He did manage a brief statement, however.

'You evil fucking bitch.'

She put a finger to his lips.

'I blame the parents,' she said, and thrust the needle into his neck.

Game Over

A phalanx of Secatore guards escorted him into the CEO's office, a corner suite boasting more glass than the average viticulture biosphere over in Napa. They had unlocked the restraints in the elevator, undoubtedly under strict orders. It wouldn't do for one of the architects of the company's success to be seen frog-marched through the senior-executive-level corridors with his wrists clapped in irons. A sight like that could result in a five-point hit on the NASDAQ, for goodness sake.

Zac Michaels sent a cursory glance in Ross's direction by way of acknowledgement and gestured to him with an outstretched palm, as if to say he'd be with him in a moment. The palm changed to a fist with thumb and pinkie outstretched to explain the delay. He was on the phone, as the expression still went, even though telephony was no longer the conduit. Truth was, the guy could have been having a board-meeting in his head, multiple audio and video feeds playing behind his eyes, but Ross suspected he was actually talking to nobody: he just wanted to underline the power relationship by making him wait a little longer. It seemed unnecessary given that he'd already left him waiting in a custody office in the basement since they kicked his door in that morning, but sometimes the subtle gesture of dominance trumped the grander one.

Outside the huge windows, the sun was going down, painting the sky in reds and pinks. The day was closing, and closing fast. Ross had been living here in California most of his days but his instincts were still hard-wired by his formative years in Scotland. Sunset was slow there, even in winter: when you saw it dip, you assumed you had time before it became pitch black. Over here, you got far less notice.

Michaels muttered a few last words to whomever he was speaking, wrapping it up. Ross caught something about 'all moot now, and ultimately no damage was done, so we can let him down from the naughty step'. It was ostensibly private, but unmistakably for his benefit.

Zac Michaels: one-time low-level corporate enforcer and obsequious functionary, now chief executive officer of Neurosphere. Almost every part of his body had been replaced over the years, but no matter how you altered the constituent componentry, the overall result was still an oily prick.

'Ross, Ross, Ross,' he said, his voice pitched between conciliatory, admonishing and exasperated. He didn't offer a hand; the only shaking was by his head, gently conveying the 'whatever are we to do with you?' vibe. 'Why don't you take a seat. I gather you've had a rough day.'

'You mean having half a dozen assault vehicles converge on my beach house, then a team of security drones smash in my front door and drag me off to custody? Don't sweat it.'

'I'm sorry it was so heavy-handed, believe me. Something like that shouldn't be happening to someone of your stature within this company. As you know, it's an automated response, and the problem was you triggered it while certain of your security privileges were suspended. Under those circumstances, the system couldn't distinguish between an unauthorised access attempt by a company employee and a potential penetration by some malicious hacker. I've been in meetings all day, otherwise I'd have intervened earlier, believe me.'

Believe me. All these decades on, that was still the giveaway that he was lying. And all these decades on, he really didn't care that you knew.

'No you wouldn't.'

Michaels shrugged and gave a little nod, as if to say *touché*.

'No, you're right. I thought a few hours cooling your heels in the basement was appropriate, and truth is I would have had you released sooner if I hadn't spent all day clearing up your mess and putting out fires so you don't end up sacked or arraigned.'

'So *I* don't end up arraigned?' Ross asked him pointedly.

'I'm not doing anything illegal. Jesus, Baker, we've both come a long way since that grimy little compound in Stirling, but some things haven't changed. You're still your own worst enemy and it's still me that's saving you from yourself.'

'Aye, it's a good thing Neurosphere isn't relying on revolutionary scientific innovation to make money. I'm sure a genius like you would have us trading just as high if Jay Solomon and I had never come along.'

'The difference between us, Ross, is that I have always understood the value of what you bring to the table, but you've always been too blinkered to see the reciprocal. This isn't about share prices or opening up a new revenue stream. What I am doing right now will put us in a position with the military that will secure untold opportunities – for all of us.'

'What you are doing right now will put us morally in a position alongside any black-market scan vendor on the streets of Mumbai or Lagos.'

'Oh dry your eyes, Baker. Come on: you won that fight. You got your law passed. And as any black-market scan vendor on the streets of Mumbai or Lagos would tell you, we seem to be the only people obeying it.'

'So that's who you're measuring yourself against in terms of ethics?'

'I'm not the one who created this menagerie, if you want to talk ethics. You won't make me a surrogate for your guilty conscience. I'm not the one who's done something I'm ashamed of.'

'And is that why you locked me out of the whole system? Because you've nothing to be ashamed of?'

'Actually, if you remember, I initially only locked you out of a small part of the system, and I did it knowing that you would take the bait and hack your way in. That put you in violation of Article 774 and allowed me to suspend your access to the whole system until an investigation was concluded, giving us time to do what we needed. It's all moot now anyway. It's over. Look.'

Michaels sent him a couple of feeds, instantly projected on to his field of vision. One showed the file integrity readings, more and more scans showing one hundred per cent, ready for extraction. The other displayed the current status of a rogue upload, introduced to the system that morning but now safely isolated.

Neither image came as a surprise, but Ross still had to suppress a show of emotion in seeing that the outcome was now all but confirmed.

'Your last-ditch little Hail Mary pass was tracked from the start,' Michaels told him. 'I know you were always pretty hot at those first-person shooters, but the world of business is real-time strategy. If you try to play *my* game, you'll lose every time.'

Ross glanced at the two information read-outs again. First one, then both of them blacked out, right on cue.

He glanced up at Michaels, who suddenly didn't look quite so confident.

'You sure about that?'

Read-Only Memory

Ross closed his eyes and braced himself for pain, but instead what he experienced was a rush like no drug had ever effected in the human mind. She had injected him with new memories: memories from a future he'd never got to live, played out in the present tense. They were not complete, just shards and splinters, snapshots and highlights. At first they were like fragments in a kaleidoscope, but then they coalesced in his mind, assembling themselves into a picture that made sense.

He and Solderburn in the R&D lab, Ross working on a very early synthesis model and beginning to see startling indications of just how complex the scan results might be. An experiment to see how a scan might interact with a virtual environment. Ross rooting around for a basic world-builder program; meanwhile Solderburn cuts to the chase and boots up the first 3D game that happens to be on the desktop. It is Starfire, *which in times gone by Solderburn used to run on a partition as a multiplayer server: he, Ross and whoever else fancied staying behind after work to duke it out with each other or against Reaper bots.*

They watch as the uploaded entity begins battling his way through the map; then, purely in the interests of science, Solderburn spends twenty minutes playing deathmatch against, technically, himself.

Two geeks stay late into the night, energised. Ross working out of hours is a rarity now, done purely on his own terms. The day he learned Carol was pregnant, he walked back out of the scanning cubicle having realised he was the one with the power, and management pissing him about had been a long-term gambit to prevent him noticing this. He called their bluff, told them what he was here to do and what he wasn't. That was years ago. He never looked back.

Solderburn begins uploading some more scans but Ross is conflicted about the idea. He has deduced from the behaviour he is seeing exhibited within the game that these are not glorified AI bots they've created. He is aware that the scan, if uploaded, could be a consciousness that wouldn't know it was anything other than the person who lay down in the scanning cubicle. He argues that it may be unethical but this is Solderburn he's talking to. He knows the guy is only going to do it anyway as soon as he leaves.

Solderburn ridicules him for being precious and melodramatic, and Ross has to concede that this may be the case. Nonetheless, he remains sufficiently squeamish about the idea as to encrypt his own scan so that Solderburn can't upload it.

It is late the next morning when he returns to the lab and Solderburn shows him something astonishing. The scans are no longer in Starfire. They have found a way to access other games on the same hard drive. By evening, lights are blinking to indicate that they have accessed other drives on the array. More astonishing still, some weeks later they observe that the scans are making changes to the games. They realise events are moving at their own digital clockspeed there, only slowing to real time whenever he and Solderburn interact with a game, a temporal alteration the scans don't appear to notice.

They expand the experiment, loading more and more games, more and more scans. Ross alters the synthesis model so that the new uploads have to abide by the rules of the worlds in which they find themselves, otherwise it will be anarchy. He and Solderburn edit the memory files to erase recollection of the scanning process itself, so that the entities experience a less jarring splice: going to bed and waking up somewhere new instead of walking in one door and the world having changed when they open it again.

Solderburn reveals their work-in-progress to the suits, playing it as a trump card to win two tricks at once. By doing so he secures himself and Ross a blank cheque in terms of time and resources, while simultaneously taking the ethical considerations out of Ross's hands and above his pay grade. Ross is thus vindicated in his decision to secret away his own file, as it soon becomes clear he will not have the option to encrypt any others. As the Simulacron is rolled out into hospital testing, the company regards the resultant scans as belonging to Neurosphere rather than their subjects. So begins, in an industrial estate in Stirling, an argument over a whole new definition of

354

'intellectual property' that will ultimately reach (though not quite end at) the US Supreme Court.

The 'menagerie' continues to evolve, and Ross's observation of it assists the development of his synthesis models. He and Solderburn incorporate their progress into the framework, causing the gameworlds to become more and more real as their inhabitants project detail from memory and imagination but experience it as sensory perception.

Their work forms the basis for the phenomenally successful Memento Mori project, around the advent of which Ross first publicly raises ethical questions concerning the rights of what comes to be known as digital consciousness, or DC. Having observed the entities in the menagerie, Ross understands that you can't leave DCs to exist as brains in jars. As a result, all Memento Mori scans are connected to a vast virtual realm referred to within Neurosphere as the Secondverse, in which they can live out meaningful existences beyond their real-time interactions with their loved ones.

Meantime, the menagerie still ticks over in a metaphorical dusty corner of Neurosphere; metaphorical because, like everything else by now, it is stored in cloud systems so that no part of it is in one location. (Strictly speaking, by this stage 'planetary atmosphere' or even 'nebula' would be a more accurate analogy than cloud, but the terminology endures.) Its sector is code-named Cirrus Nine. The original Stirling hard-drive array remains a node on the network however, and on a rare visit over from Silicon Valley, Ross is amused to find that you can still play Starfire on it.

However, the more he has learned, the more the technology evolves, the more guilt he feels on those (albeit increasingly isolated) occasions when he remembers about his and Solderburn's early experiment. From his observations he knows that the entities inside have no idea where they are, and he is enduringly aware that they did not consent to be there. Indeed, it is this lack of consent that precludes one possible salve to his conscience: the idea of merging the menagerie with the Secondverse. Neurosphere's lawyers have specifically forbidden such a measure because the whole point of Memento Mori is that its inhabitants have a direct line of communication to the outside world. If the unconsented subjects of the menagerie were able to contact their former selves, the liabilities would be catastrophic.

It is a wrong that there is no way of righting. It cannot be undone, and the solution is certainly not to switch it all off, even when that is *still an option. He comes to accept that it is the resurrectionist's price, the cost to the soul of the unethical act that was necessary to advance the scientist's knowledge. But in Ross's case it is more than merely a sin with which he must always live. He has a responsibility towards this secret realm, and this drives his sense of responsibility towards all digital consciousness.*

With the lines between digital and organic consciousness forever blurred, DC rights becomes a very serious issue. Religious groups lead the objections, mainly because they don't like the fact that this technology has given rise to a whole new field of ethics that their entire belief system didn't anticipate, raising awkward implications regarding the omniscience of their various mythical creators. (The practical ramifications are particularly messy for the Vatican, where, following the ordination of a new pope, it transpires that a DC of the previous pontiff is continuing to issue edicts and passing comment on his successor, the fallout frequently threatening to cause a schism within the Church.)

Having spoken to the scans of their late relatives and heard witness of how convincing the DCs perceive their selves and their digital reality to be, it becomes harder and harder for people to think of DCs as mere binary files, but it is the deeper implications that truly alter popular attitudes. Ultimately it is Bostrom's simulation argument that sways the attitudes of individuals and governments. Once people come to understand that their own current existence might be a simulation, and that for all they know they might already be a DC, this leads to a new interpretation of the golden rule.

Laws are passed internationally, enforcing a single crucial principle: one person, one scan. You can have real-time updating back-up, but you cannot make copies, and nobody – absolutely nobody – is allowed to own a scan of anybody else.

All DCs are strictly registered and protected. All except the knock-offs available on the black market, naturally, but that is as reviled as the slave trade. Any company found to be trafficking in scans would face instant pariah status, not to mention massive criminal charges.

But where corporations are involved, there will always be loopholes, and Zac Michaels has found one: thousands of unregistered scans, DCs with no rights and no copy protection. Cirrus Nine is a treasure trove, and the outside world doesn't know it exists. It is a potentially unlimited source of DCs for research and experimentation, and the military are waiting impatiently on the sidelines with their tongues hanging out and their wallets open.

It's not that simple, however. Michaels' problem is extraction, which is not a matter of walking into a server farm and copying all the scans on to a USB stick. The DCs can't be copied while they are in a state of read/write activity. To extract a scan, you first have to put it in stasis, and to do that you need to contain it in one place within the gameverse. Unfortunately for Michaels, the DCs are scattered to the four winds: a vast diaspora permanently in motion . . .

All of this Ross saw and understood – experienced in the present tense, but read back as knowledge, as recollection – in literally the blink of an eye.

When his lids rose he looked upon the same face before him but felt something entirely different: a new recognition, not of the punkish woman he had followed across worlds, but of a face that somehow stayed the same though he had watched it change and grow over decades.

'Jennifer,' he breathed, not quite believing, not quite sure he understood.

'I didn't come here to infiltrate the resistance, Dad,' she said, finally speaking in her own voice. 'I came here to infiltrate the Integrity.'

She waved a hand and the restraints withdrew, the column shrinking back into the floor. They stared at each other for just a moment, then she stepped closer and hugged him. Technically it was the first time he had held her, but it felt simultaneously like both the first and the millionth. He had a thousand questions, but right then her embrace was answering enough of them to be going on with. He was holding his daughter in his arms. Granted the circumstances were not ideal, but with that part sorted, he was sure that they could deal with the rest.

His eyes filled and for a few seconds he couldn't speak. He wanted just to stay there, in that moment, but he knew he couldn't afford to.

'Michaels,' he issued in a choked whisper, his way of signalling that he was ready to saddle up. 'Michaels is Ankou?'

'Yes and no. Ankou is an amalgam of things; that's why he can't settle on a form. The programming dweebs at Neurosphere tried to amend his scan so that he'd have the powers of an

Original, but they couldn't pull it off. So instead they merged his scan with all this nasty new tech that he can manipulate. For a while I wondered why he never left the Citadel, then I worked it out: he can't. He is the Integrity's power centre. In essence, Ankou *is* the Integrity. He has pseudo-Original powers, so he's been able to fashion weapons and vehicles, and this new tech lets them erase stuff on other worlds.'

'Those whips,' Ross said. 'Rifles too. Can they erase people?'

'The Integrity won't because DCs are worth too much. They want people intact, but they need a deterrent to keep them in line. The whips write temporarily to your memory files, so that it feels as though you've experienced physical agony and emotional torment your entire life: for a few moments after impact, you can remember experiencing nothing else.'

'What about the troops?'

'Multiple clones of a handful of Neurosphere security personnel,' Jennifer told him.

'Ankou creates them in here, so Michaels is covered against charges of making unauthorised copies.'

'You got it. The name Ankou means soul-collector. Michaels had you locked out of the system so that you couldn't interfere with his extraction plans. That's when we came up with our counter-measure.'

'We?'

'Real-world you and real-world me. Michaels knew you'd try and hack your way in again, and you did, but only as a decoy. The real system-breaches were carried out by me: that is, real-world Jennifer, thousands of miles away. Part of his efforts to fend off interference involved cutting off all communication with Cirrus Nine: there was no way of seeing what was going on from the outside, apart from pure data, technical read-outs: in particular, file integrity. But you remembered there was one interface Michaels had forgotten about.'

'Stirling,' Ross stated. 'The original hard-drive array.'

'So I took a trip. Four days ago in real time you uploaded this scan of me, incorporating a shitload of highest-level Neurosphere clearance codes you had procured. These were to open various doors for me once I got in here, help me lay the groundwork. That's the last part of what I know about the outside. But as we're both right here now, that means the rest went according to plan.'

'Which was what?'

'At nine o'clock this morning, my dad was to commence a second decoy hack from his beach house in California, while I simultaneously uploaded his prototype scan: you. That's why you were late to the party, as you put it.'

'You were the player.'

'The what?'

'On Graxis. Someone activated console commands to help me out.'

'That would have been real-world Jennifer, yes, sitting at a keyboard in Stirling. Because I uploaded you directly into *Starfire*, you defaulted to the role of enemy grunt, so I was supposed to input some codes to free you from the constraining protocols, let you pick up marine weapons and stuff. I take it I got it right.'

'Eventually. Real-world you is shit at *Starfire*.'

'I failed to mis-spend my youth. Maybe if my dad hadn't been such an asshole slave-driver about my school work, I'd have had more time for retro-gaming.'

'What about Bob the accountant?'

'Bob the . . . Oh, the other guy. Unfortunately, when you dug into the archives to retrieve your original scan, an incompatibility between old and new file-tagging systems meant the tags were cut off at seven characters. There were two named 'bakerro': yours and a guy named Robert Baker, who was presumably already in here. Poor sonofabitch is gonna run into himself eventually, and won't that be a fun moment. We had no way of knowing which file was which, so I brought them both when I flew to Scotland. It was fifty-fifty, but I guess real-world me uploaded the wrong one first.'

'It's never fifty-fifty with these things. Murphy's Law dictates otherwise.'

'That's why I left nothing else to chance. It was pure strategy after that. Michaels threw a blanket over the menagerie, but that meant *he* didn't know what was going on inside either. I used my codes to infiltrate the Integrity and convinced Ankou that I had been sent by Michaels to speed things up.'

This was where Ross felt the relief and euphoria begin to wear off. A father's love made him proud of his child's achievements, but it was also his duty to point out failings along the way.

'Hang on,' he said. 'Your strategy involved winning Ankou's trust by wiping out all resistance, rounding up his most powerful adversaries and then delivering me to a super-secure prison at the heart of a fortress completely surrounded by the massed ranks of the Integrity. For someone claiming to leave nothing to chance, have you spotted any flaws in your grand plan?'

She looked at him with an expression in which he could see her as a two-year-old laying down the law to her idiot dad.

'First of all, it's *our* plan: we cooked it up between us. Second, haven't you asked yourself why Ankou would build such a mega-fortress out here on the edge of nowhere?'

'You said it was so that nobody could escape.'

'I was lying, remember? Ankou was eavesdropping on every word we shared. You don't need a place like this to hold scans awaiting extraction. In fact, the retention grids are on another world altogether: tens of thousands of little cells all laid out on a plain. Once you're locked inside one of those, your integrity is one hundred per cent and you can be copied or extracted when the guys on the outside are ready to use you. So let's try again, shall we? What's the fortress here to protect?'

Of course.

'The way out of here.'

'Even in character, I wasn't lying about that. Nor was I lying when I said it takes an Original to open it. In mythology, Ankou was a soul-collector. But do you know who Iris was?'

'A messenger of the gods.'

'And the *daughter* of a god.'

She touched the side of his head with the other end of the hypodermic device, and his HUD altered. Lines of data scrolled before his eyes, and as well as a host of new tools and icons, there was a command prompt.

'Something else I misled Ankou about: you are a prototype scan, uploaded with the original synthesis protocols which *only you* still had on file. Not only are you an Original, but your real-world self gave you a few extra admin privileges too. I had to keep this suppressed until now, even from you, in case you accidentally gave the game away too soon.'

He didn't need to ask what the game was.

'You convinced Ankou to open his doors and let me walk right into the heart of the one place he should have been keeping me furthest away from.'

'No offence, Dad, you're a good gamer, but there's no chance you could have battled your way to the heart of the Citadel otherwise. Despite how secure it is, Ankou isn't holding any of the Originals here, because it would be too dangerous for him. That's why the retention grids are on a completely different world. Soon as they get hold of The Captain, they'll ship her right out too. So letting you walk in here is like giving Dracula the keys to a blood bank.'

'But isn't Ankou able to hear all this, or did you disable the relay?'

'I could have, but I want him to hear it.'

'You *want* him to . . . ? Why?'

'Because I want him to experience the maximum anger and then the maximum fear as he realises, with laser-calibrated precision, just how fucked he is.'

Godmode

Through his new HUD, when Ross looked at the world around him, he now saw two versions. There was the solid reality as perceived by his synthesised consciousness, and there was a version composed of values, attributes, variables, protocols: *code*. He could see every line. He could see all of the worlds, all of the connections between them, every rule, every subroutine.

Jennifer was right: this was already over. And the reason Ankou was doomed wasn't just that Ross could access the code. All of the Originals could access the code. They could all read it, they could all amend it, but it was *his* code. It was his future self who had devised it, but it was like reading his own thoughts, his own logic, his own structures and connections. It made perfect sense to him, and he instinctively knew what all of it did: from values affecting the world he stood on right now, to protocols governing the very fabric of the gameverse.

In the beginning, he thought, *there was the command line . . .*

He didn't have to open the cell door to know that there were forty-eight samnites storming into the detention blocks right then, despatched by Ankou in growing alarm and packing those memory-violating rifles. They might as well be packing Nerf guns. He changed the damage values on their weapons to zero, an effect that would instantly apply on all worlds where they were deployed. At the speed of thought, he sited spawn points inside all of the locked cells, handed Jennifer a GraxiTron Flow gun and suggested she bid them all GTF.

He heard voices raised to screams as the panic really began to take hold.

'Cry some more,' he told them.

It wasn't just the samnites who started pinging into the cells either. Ross demagnetised the planetary surface and reset the weapon systems on the *Manta-Ray* – as well as those of her crew – to maximum butt-hurt.

Inside and outside the Citadel, the Integrity were soon having their arses handed to them. It was so satisfying that it was a temptation to spring them from the cells just so he could watch them get mantelpieced all over again. He resisted though: there would be plenty of fun still to come: from *Unreal* to Pulchritupolis, from Graxis to Vice City.

```
Setting 'Payback' = A BITCH
```

The Whip Hand

Juno felt the eruption of agony cease as suddenly as it had begun, the maenad inflicting ludicrously over-amped damage levels in a fraction of a second and killing her instantaneously. As always, there was an echo of the pain in the moment she respawned but no more actual hurt.

Only dread.

She could see several Integrity troops in her peripheral vision, but her focus was pulled to two things directly in front of her. One was the amphibious armoured vehicle on the edge of the swamp, its rear doors thrown open above a short ramp, beyond which a row of cells stretched into darkness. It was a mobile prison, designed to contain the captives until the Integrity were ready to transport them to that bleak and hopeless grid.

The other principal draw upon her attention was a samnite wielding a many-tongued scourge, which delivered the same soul-gouging brutality as the rifles. She sussed his role immediately. He would lash every respawned Diasporado with that thing to render them insensible, and to prevent would-be fugitives from entering a desperate cycle of running, being gunned down, respawning and running again, kind of like a kid skipping around in a circle while his mom tries to spank him.

Skullhammer was already on the floor, reeling from the blow. He had died moments before Juno, having valiantly but fruitlessly flung himself in front of her as the maenad swooped.

Juno cringed at the sight of the scourge and held her hands up in surrender, trying to convey that she would come quietly, but she could tell that this fucker liked his work.

He wound up and really put his shoulder into it. She flinched and tried to brace herself, but she knew there was no bracing yourself for what this felt like.

The little black tongues rattled as they contacted with her, at which point she felt . . . precisely nothing.

Her assailant looked puzzled for a moment, wondering why she didn't fall down. He lashed her again, with no effect. She was aware of the contact, but there was no pain, no damage.

Skullhammer was observing with keen interest as he climbed back to his feet. In a mounting panic the samnite hefted his rifle and delivered a blast straight to Skullhammer's chest, point blank. Once again, torment and debilitation failed to ensue.

'Well, this is awkward,' said Juno.

Pwnage

'Wherever you need to get to next, just let me know,' Jennifer said. 'I could draw this dump from memory: every time I came here I took the long way around so that I could learn the layout.'

'No need,' Ross told her.

He could see the whole place as wireframe, could noclip his way through the walls, the ceilings and the floors. He didn't have to, though. Instead he collapsed them, dissolved them, hollowing out the Citadel to clear a path to the chamber at its heart where Ankou guarded the secret gateway.

As he and Jennifer rose towards it on a moving platform Ross had created, Ankou himself tore down the last of the walls, drawing the very fabric of the place into himself to replenish his power.

He had become enormous. He was thirty feet tall, a barely humanoid mass rounding upon his approaching enemies with two fearsome cannons that were the closest things he had to limbs. As he moved, Ross saw that there were several thick tentacle-like tubes connecting him to a wide hexagonal pool of that pulsatile black rock-metal-plastic. He wasn't drawing his power from it, though; it was drawing its power from him.

Ankou opened fire with the cannons: their sound deafening, their muzzle-flash blinding, their effect bugger-all.

'Sorry,' Ross explained. 'Altered the server-side variables so your guns deliver zero damage points. I'm a cheating bastard, I know.'

'You're altering the rules?' the blob asked, confusion and anger detectable in a voice that was otherwise becoming less human by the word. 'How are you doing this?'

'Admin privileges. See, big guy, your problem is you never

played enough games. If you had, you'd understand there's one rule that matters above all others.'

Ross produced his own weapon, the one that would finish this. He could have any gun in the gameverse, so he chose the crappy default blaster he started off with on Graxis. The only pity was there was no way of seeing the look on Ankou's face, as he no longer appeared to have one.

'And what rule is that?' the blob asked contemptuously.

'If you act like a dick, you'll get kicked from the server.'

Ross pulled the trigger and sent the tiniest quantum of Ankou's memory-violating energy zooming into his oleaginous mass.

There was no visible effect at first, but then the implosion got underway as the code Neurosphere had merged him with began feeding back on itself in an exponential chain reaction.

'Will that erase him?' Jennifer asked, Ross being unsure from the concern in her tone whether she was worried that it would or that it wouldn't.

'Only if he doesn't disengage from the amalgam. It's his call if he wants to live.'

The black mass thrashed and throbbed some more, growing smaller and smaller, then a human shape took form in the midst of it and suddenly broke free. The instant it did, the black mass vanished, compressing itself into a tiny square object that fell to the floor with a clatter.

Ankou was left standing next to it, a few feet in front of a now-shimmering hexagon of coloured light. Naturally, he looked like Zac Michaels, and Ross bit back the obvious remark about his previous appearance being less oily.

Ankou glanced down at the object on the ground nearby.

'Looks like a three-and-a-half-inch floppy,' Ross told him. 'Which I'm guessing is you on a good night even *with* the blue pills.'

Ross kept the gun trained on him, assigning it new properties.

'What are you going to do with me?' Ankou asked anxiously.

'I'm going to give you a choice, which is more than you were looking at if you had succeeded. Talk about turkeys voting for Christmas. What were you expecting? Some virtual paradise as reward? Seventy-two virgins?'

'Something like that.'

'Well I guess you were never going to find those in Stirling. I just can't believe you bought it. Didn't you think you and your goons would all just be erased once the job was done? Or sold off for military experiments like the rest of us? I mean, put it this way, would *you* trust a guy like you?'

Ankou managed a smile, maybe two parts self-awareness to three parts perverse pride.

'Well, when you put it that way,' he acknowledged. 'So what's my choice?'

Ross waved a hand and a rectangular slab appeared, hanging vertically in the air a few feet from Ankou. It was like a swirling curtain of silver beads, a portal beyond which his possible future was occluded.

'To decide whether you're a person or a programme,' he told him. 'If it's the former, then you'll step through this gateway and find a life for yourself here, same as everyone else. If it's the latter, then I'll remind you that another name for a programme is an *executable*. After all, if you're just a piece of code, you won't care.'

Ross raised the crappy but lethal blaster once again.

'You've got five seconds to decide.'

Ankou didn't need five seconds. He put his hands in the air and turned to face the curtain.

'Don't shoot,' he said. 'I'm walking the plank.'

'Good call. Can I interpret that as a tacit acknowledgement that "do unto others" applies to DCs as well as meatware?'

'Self-preservation does anyway,' he answered, with which he snatched up the disc from the floor and dived headlong into the portal.

Jennifer took a couple of instinctive steps after him, then stopped herself.

'What did he take?' she asked anxiously. 'What was that thing?'

'Not what he thinks,' Ross answered, erasing the gateway.

He walked over to the pool of shimmering colours and stared down into it, seeing it simultaneously as a play of lights and a dance of numbers. Ross was looking through the doorway to the Secondverse, where Solderburn had escaped to. So far he had been the only traffic through it, but it was about to become

369

busier than rush hour on the Kingston Bridge. This was what guaranteed Michaels couldn't try the same thing again: an open connection that would merge Cirrus Nine with the rest of the Neurosphere system. Memento Mori and beyond: everyone who was ever scanned, and the countless worlds they had created since. Its inhabitants had referred to Cirrus Nine as the gameverse, but Ross knew now that it was merely a cluster of little islands. Beyond this portal was a realm that dwarfed it, a staggering multiplicity of worlds, each offering a cornucopia of experiences and possibilities.

But the world he wanted to visit most would remain forever inaccessible.

'What's wrong?' Jennifer asked. 'You saved everybody here from a thousand horrible fates; in fact you saved an unknowable number of clones of everyone here from a thousand horrible fates. Yet you don't exactly seem elated in your moment of triumph.'

'There was no triumph. The bad guy got away.'

'You *let* him.'

'I wasn't talking about Ankou. He was just a chancer. I was talking about the guy who fucked me over. It's time I had a word with myself.'

Self-Reflection

Ross and Jennifer were back on Graxis when the response to his communication request came through from the outside. He was on a mission to redeem a promise, as far as that was possible, and thus was searching for Bob the accountant against the familiar backdrop of eternally invading marines and their indefatigably repelling foes.

'I need to give him the big talk,' he had told Jennifer. 'I promised I'd get him back to his family, and I can't deliver on that.'

'His family might be out there,' she replied. 'Just not as he remembered them. Once he crosses into the Secondverse, there are ways of making contact.'

'Yeah, all I can do is bring him to the gateway. I can't promise what he'll find when he steps through it.'

'He'll find the same thing we all do,' she replied. 'Hell if you make it. Heaven if you want it to be.'

The incoming transmission took the form of an avatar. It was a perfectly solid-looking holographic object but it could not interact with the environment: it was just a projection, a high-spec video call, its images relaying real-time 3D laser scanning.

He found it a disturbing sight, but it was always going to be. Even if he hadn't aged a day, it would have been unsettling to see a person who was recognisably himself and yet someone else. He had aged more than a day, though. This was what Ross Baker actually looked like right then in the outside world, but it wasn't merely the fact that this was a hologram that meant he appeared more artificial than anybody here on the inside. Jennifer had said he now lived in California but she hadn't mentioned he had gone quite so native. That looked like a lot of surgery.

The avatar said nothing, just stood there. He seemed apprehensive and apologetic, the way Ross knew he always did when he was in the wrong and ready to take his lumps.

'You're looking well,' Ross told him, a precisely measured level of sarcasm in his voice.

He acknowledged it with a nod.

'This is just the cosmetic,' the avatar said, his mid-Atlantic accent making Ross cringe. 'There's far more been replaced beneath the derma. In fact, you could say that neither of our minds still inhabits the body it used to.'

'Yours still inhabits the real world,' he said accusingly.

'Maybe not for too much longer. Compared to you anyway. I'm envious. You'll never age, never get sick. I gave you that much, at least.'

'*Gave* me . . . ? You took away *everything*: everyone I loved, everything I had and everything I was ever going to have.'

'They say when you've done something wrong, the hardest part is to forgive yourself. I realise that's going to be a particularly big ask in this case. I know what I took from you. I know what was taken from everybody – that's what's driven my campaigning for DC rights. But that's also why I had to do what I did. You were the best chance we had of saving everyone in there from Michaels.'

'And did you think this bought you absolution, is that it?'

'There is no absolution. It's the resurrectionist's price: the same Faustian pact the anatomists entered when they started robbing graves to get their specimens. When you enter that pact, you know you'll be paying the price forever.'

'From where I'm standing, it looks like I'm the one paying.'

'I know. But what would you have had me do? It was . . . logical. The needs of the many . . .'

No, Ross thought: do not go there.

'. . . outweigh the needs of the few,' the avatar went on. 'Or the one.'

He fucking went there.

'But you weren't the one. *I* was. It cost you nothing and cost me everything. So don't try tugging my heartstrings with your lame *Wrath of Khan* comparison. I didn't make a noble sacrifice, because I didn't have a choice. I didn't volunteer.'

'Yes, but I knew that if it was me, *I'd* volunteer. And as, in a manner of speaking, it *was* me, then I felt qualified to make the call.'

'But it's not the same call. You've *had* your life: marriage, kids, California *uber alles*. The scale of the sacrifice would look different if you were the guy who just stepped into that scanner.'

The avatar nodded, conceding the point. Finally it looked like Ross had met someone whom he could defeat in an argument. Then the avatar ruined it by stabbing home a last-minute equaliser.

'So what call would you make?' his future self asked. 'Tell me, if it *had* been your choice: would you give up your future in the real world to save all the people in that one?'

Ross didn't answer, though it was kind of pointless taking the fifth when the other person knew what you were thinking.

He tried to come up with something magnanimous to say before terminating the connection, but opted for 'Fuck you' instead.

Jennifer gave him an apologetic look.

'You should be angry at me too,' she said. 'We took this decision together.'

'*You* didn't. The real-world Jennifer did. You're the one who's stuck here, not her. See, I think I worked out why Solderburn never came back once he'd found a way out. He must have thought that sooner or later someone – one of the Originals probably – would suss he was responsible for putting everybody there. All those people cut off from their loved ones, cut off from their lives, left wondering why. He must have been terrified of them finally being given someone to blame. But the Solderburn in here was as much a victim as everybody else. Jay Solomon put him here, just like Ross Baker put me here.'

'None of us asks to be born,' Jennifer told him. 'But I didn't hold it against you and Mum that you brought me into the world and gave me life without running it past me first. Not after the age of about fourteen, anyway.'

Ross couldn't help but smile. He threw an arm around her and placed a small kiss on the top of her head. As he did, he felt the heat of the Graxis sunshine on his shoulders. Here it was never night, never cold.

'I suppose there are some advantages to this place,' he admitted. 'I bet it's fucking raining in Stirling.'

Final Reward

Once more Ankou experienced that revolting sensation of the world around him swallowing itself and then vomiting it forth again. It didn't get any easier to endure, nor was it delivering him to anywhere he hadn't already been. He materialised on a depressingly familiar spawn pad, his momentum taking him forward a pace before he could orient himself, and he managed to stop just short of the edge of the cold murky pool that lay in the shadow of the cliff. It ran around like a natural perimeter, this unscalable and impenetrable wall that hemmed him in and permitted no glimpse of what might lie beyond.

He had found no evidence of any transits: just portals between the same few discrete and uniformly desolate regions. According to his HUD, this one was called Claustrophenia and he had just warped there from Death's Dark Vale. The landscapes all looked like Graxis; the architecture too: lots of sewers and stairways, towers and platforms. He hadn't seen any NPCs, though. He appeared to be the only person here.

He had been conned.

This was the final fuck-you, and its true sting was in how stupid he now felt for believing his enemy would have let him off so lightly.

You'll step through this gateway and find a life for yourself here, Baker had said, presumably his idea of poetic justice. He had stranded him on one barren and lonely world, unable to escape: just like the Integrity had been prescribing for everybody else. Oh, the pathos, the irony. Colour me suitably ashamed.

Self-righteous prick.

He didn't think he could possibly feel any worse. It was bad enough that he had failed so comprehensively in his mission, but what burned all the more was the nature of it. Not only had he been defeated by Ross fucking Baker, but he'd been played like a rube by the guy's *daughter*.

Strictly speaking, he wasn't stranded in one place, but in six or seven mini-worlds from which he was able to come and go at will using his pitifully function-limited new HUD. However, that was the extent of his freedom. There was no way out. No food or drink either; the protocols meant it wasn't necessary, but if he was stuck here forever, he was going to seriously miss snarfing a porterhouse and washing it down with a Napa Zinfandel.

One thing there was a shitload of, however, was guns. After all the Integrity weapons had been rendered useless, Ankou had expected to find these ones neutralised too, but it turned out they all did deliver damage. There was no pain, though; only hit points. Evidently the place was some kind of combat simulation: no doubt another poignant statement from Baker regarding what Ankou's plans had been for the inhabitants of the menagerie.

He looked up at the purple sky and shouted.

'Okay, what the fuck. You made your point. You won and I'm real sorry. Come on: what do you want from me? You want tears of contrition? You want me on my knees? Seriously, you can order off the menu here. God knows I would.'

A moment later he felt that horrible dissolving sensation again as he was involuntarily respawned about a quarter-mile from where he had been standing. At least it appeared that someone was listening.

There was a shimmering disturbance in the air in front of him, and suddenly he found himself looking at the biggest, baddest, craggiest, most ripped-looking and thoroughly scary hunk of masculinity he had ever seen.

The new arrival's name flashed up on the HUD next to his own, each adjacent to the corresponding figure '0'.

Ankou held his arms apart in a gesture of appellate cooperation.

'Okay, whoever you are, I just want to stress that I have no quarrel with you, I pose you no threat and I am entirely willing to cooperate. I am one hundred per cent at your disposal. Just tell me what it is you want me to do.'

A countdown commenced, starting at ten seconds.

The Reaper grinned, priming his railgun.